D0094610

REGARDING DUCKS AND UNIVERSES

NEVE MASLAKOVIC

PUBLISHED BY

amazon encore

The characters and events portrayed in this book are fictitious. Any similarity to real persons, living or dead, is coincidental and not intended by the author.

Text copyright ©2010 Neve Maslakovic
All rights reserved
Printed in the United States of America

No part of this book may be reproduced, or stored in a retrieval system, or transmitted in any form or by any means, electronic, mechanical, photocopying, recording, or otherwise, without express written permission of the publisher.

Published by AmazonEncore
P.O. Box 400818
Las Vegas, NV 89140

ISBN-13: 9781935597346
ISBN-10: 1935597345

For my father

THE
DEPARTMENT OF INFORMATION MANAGEMENT'S
REGULATION LIST

Regulation 1:   News & Media

Regulation 2:   Places (maps, atlases,
                  town & street names)

Regulation 3:   Citizen Privacy

Regulation 4:   Inter-universe Travel

Regulation 5:   Intra-universe Travel

Regulation 6:   Documents & Historical Records

Regulation 7:   Alters

Regulation 8:   Pet Ownership

Regulation 9:   Identicard & Money Matters

Regulation 10:   Office/Corporate

Regulation 11:   Legislative

Regulation 12:   Courts/Judicial

Regulation 13:   Presidential Responsibility

Regulation 14:   Naval/Maritime

Regulation 15:   Technology

Regulation 16:   Sport/Hobby

Regulation 17:   Health & Medicine

Regulation 18:   School/Educational

Regulation 19:   Science & Research

Regulation 20:   Arts

THE LUNCH-PLACE RULE

The DIM official had just asked, "Reason for crossing to San Francisco B, citizen—business, family visit, pleasure?"

It was none of them.

What had me in front of the DIM official's booth, bag in hand, instead of at my desk at Wagner's Kitchen contemplating the virtues of rice cookers and vegetable peelers, was this: Felix B. I needed to find out if he was less of a procrastinator than I was. Or if *his* job, whatever it would turn out to be, kept him less busy. And whether he required only six hours of night sleep rather than my usual nine, giving him plenty of free time to do with as he pleased. That sort of thing.

"I'm—just a tourist. Wanted to see what Universe B is like," I said, nervously pushing my newly corrected identicard through the booth window.

The official reached up to take it, his avocado-green and turtlenecked uniform, standard issue for Department of Information Management employees, rising up in the back in the process. He glanced at the identicard but made no comment other than, "You look younger than thirty-five, Citizen Sayers. Just missed it, eh?"

"By a hair."

As I waited while he typed something into his computer, a nearby ad, one of many that dotted the crossing terminal, caught my eye. *Sourdough bread—Warm. Tangy. BETTER in B*, it said; virtual baguettes tumbled from the old Golden Gate Bridge onto an ocean liner entering San Francisco Bay. Well, really, I thought. I'd heard that their sourdough bread was good, but *BUTTER* in B would have been catchier—not to mention more tactful. (Not that we A-dwellers didn't have our share of ads bragging about pristine national parks, clean air, and the like, but none of them at Wagner's Kitchen; Wagner made sure of that.) The virtual baguettes threatened to overflow the ship like a too-small breadbasket; then the ad changed and their place was taken by premium quality almost-cat food now available in both universes—

"Citizen Sayers?"

I turned my attention back to the booth. "Yes?"

"Regulation 7."

"Right."

"It prohibits you from seeking any information about your alter."

"Right, right." Even those of us who had grown up thinking they were uniques knew about Regulation 7.

"And from contacting your alter unless expressly invited to do so by Citizen Sayers B himself."

"Right," I repeated, swinging my backpack up across both shoulders. How Felix would know that I was in his universe to expressly invite me over for dinner or whatnot, the DIM official didn't say, and I didn't care. I had no intention of actually running into him, with or without an invitation.

The DIM official lifted a hand stamp, thwacked my ticket, and pushed it along with my identicard back through the booth window. I proceeded into the crossing chamber. A circle of seats had a glass ceiling above it and a luggage rack in the center. I put my bag on the luggage rack, found a seat near the door, and took a second look around. The Friday afternoon San Francisco–to–San Francisco crossing had attracted a mix of travelers, business types in suits and tourists in shorts and sandals. The more closely cropped hair on A-dwellers and the unwieldier-looking omnis around the necks of B-dwellers hinted at who was from which universe—the thirty-five years that had passed since Y-day had yielded the strangest differences. I leaned forward to get a better look at the luggage stacked in the middle of the chamber. There they were. Suitcases with two little wheels on the bottom and an inverted-U handle on the top. Someone had told me that we in Universe A used to have them, but the wheels and handles not being recyclable, they were gone. I rubbed my shoulders, sore from standing in line with my beige, biodegradable backpack. It was well known they were more relaxed about these things in Universe B.

Nothing in the chamber suggested that it was a vessel capable of ferrying us from one universe to the other. I had imagined heavy machinery and wires and flashing lights, not a sparsely filled round room with metallic walls and a skylight. For a moment I thought I saw a shimmer above the luggage rack, like a bit of warm summer air dancing over hot pavement, but decided I was imagining things.

"*Excuse me,*" a testy voice overrode the low music emanating from the seat speakers, "are we expecting more passengers?" The A-dweller (or B-dweller—she was one traveler about whom I couldn't tell) seated on the other side of the luggage rack had lowered the magazine in her hands and addressed a crossing attendant walking by.

A wave of whispers swept through the chamber, like it was bad form to bother the attendants going in and out the narrow door. "We don't give out traveler information, citizen. Regulation 4 concerning crossing procedures and privacy Regulation 3." The attendant stepped out, then stuck his head back in. "And no calls in or out."

She frowned, a slim omni in hand. "My companion is late."

"It interferes with our equipment. Regulation 4."

She let the omni fall back down around her neck, picked up the magazine again, and irritably started turning its pages. A couple sitting near me was very obviously sneaking glances in her direction and I twisted my head to see better around the luggage rack. A formfitting dress as orange as a carrot—no, a midwinter tangerine—drew attention to trendy ice-white hair and perfect skin. As I sat there trying to guess whether she was from A or B—she didn't look old enough to have an alter, so it was possible she traveled freely and often enough to blur any distinctions—she looked up suddenly from the magazine, right at me. Something passed across her face. Caught staring, I quickly reached around my neck for something to read and she retreated behind the magazine again.

I had just began to browse mystery titles (nothing like a murder in a vicarage or a hound-haunted moor to keep one's mind off the stresses of inter-universe travel) when someone asked, "Is this seat taken?" Face rosy and sweaty above her T-shirt, knitted hat askew, a large travel bag on one shoulder, the twenty-something B-dweller sat down with a thump into the empty seat on my left. "Whew, made it." She pulled off the striped hat to reveal chestnut locks framing dark eyes and a round face.

I sat up a bit in my seat. After a moment or two while she settled in, I cleared my throat and said, "I'm looking forward to seeing what your universe is like."

It was, I felt, a very courteous statement on my part. She didn't hear me. She was looking up. I followed her glance but the only thing visible through the chamber skylight was the low-lying afternoon fog with a patch or two of blueness where the clouds had began to part. Feeling snubbed, I reached for the omni again, wiped a smudge off the screen, and went back to browsing the mystery section. As I scrolled down the list, I paused for a moment and imagined my name immediately below that of my namesake (no relation, this one) Dorothy Sayers, she of the eleven novels and twenty-some short stories starring the gentlemanly and monocled Lord Peter Wimsey. Or perhaps, I mused, switching to a different page, the mystery novel I'd write one day would be found in the New Arrivals section, where well-regarded and heavily advertised books usually began their journey into public awareness.

One is free to dream. Most likely anything I wrote would end up in the crowded Read for Free section.

"One hundred," came a slow whisper from my left. "Ninety-nine...ninety-eight...ninety-seven..."

I glanced over to find our late arrival studying me and talking to herself under her breath. She closed her mouth and hastily looked away and I dabbed at my nose just in case there was something hanging off of it.

"I hate the waiting part," she said after a moment. "So I try to distract myself with a countdown, like I'm in charge of the whole thing."

"Does it work?"

"Not really. I think I know too much."

"About—?"

"This." She waved her hand around the small chamber. "Luckily I only have to cross once or twice a year, for work. It's all we can afford."

"Money," I sighed. "Don't we all have that problem." I reached for the omni and the mystery list again, assuming that that was the end of the conversation; the Department of Information Management's Regulation 3 all but prohibited people from sharing personal details, like names, with strangers. She continued speaking.

"I know there's nothing to worry about. No one has been scrambled in a long time. Still...as I said, it's just that I know too much." Her stomach let out a low rumble. "Sorry. On my way to the crossing terminal I kept passing only restaurants that we have back home in Universe B. You know, the Lunch-Place Rule." She unbuckled the large bag and started to rummage in it. "There should be a box of pretzels in here somewhere...I'm sure of it..."

"I'm sorry, the what rule?" I raised an eyebrow at her. Across the room, the A-dweller (or B-dweller) in the tangerine dress loudly snapped a magazine page into place, something that's difficult to do on a product made of soft plastic, and sent another impatient look in the direction of the chamber door. Our eyes met again and this time there was no doubt—she seemed to know me.

"Did no one warn you about the Lunch-Place Rule?" A set of keys, a stick of gum, and a packet of tissues emerged from the bag, then disappeared back in. "About what would happen if walking around San Francisco B you came across your favorite lunch place—"

"Coconut Café," I supplied. "Something about the spices. I can taste the food."

"—that is, assuming your favorite lunch place exists and isn't a parking lot or somebody's lawn. So you go in and order whatever you like to eat—"

"Italian wedding soup. The Persian plate. The cheesecake of the day."

"Soup, then. You taste the Universe B soup and perhaps find that it's exactly the same as the soup in the Coconut Café of Universe A. Disappointing. After all, you've come all that way. Why can't I ever find anything in here?" She closed the bag and dropped it on the floor where it landed with a soft thud. "Or the Universe B soup *isn't* the same and you're sitting there wolfing down a bowl of mouthwatering broth, knowing full well that the soup back home will never measure up again. Or"— she wrinkled her nose—"you're sitting there horrified that your lovely lunch place has been replaced by a fast-food joint serving soup out of a can. There's no way to win." She glanced up again as the sun made a brief appearance, momentarily giving the metallic walls of the chamber a brighter sheen. "The Lunch-Place Rule applies to everything—buildings, waterfalls, even your favorite tree, if you have one."

"Avoid everything familiar. I'll keep that in mind. What's up there?" I pointed.

"Any minute now the lid will slide into place."

"The lid?"

"Same material as the walls."

"And then?"

"We get swapped. It's like this," she went on before I could ask, an odd experience for me since I'm usually the one trying to keep the conversation going when it comes to women I've just met. She leaned across the elbow rest and continued, "Molecules stay, information travels. When the lid glides into place, the Singh vortex will activate and suck the information out of everything in the chamber, us, the chairs, the bags, like taking apart a house to see how it was built, then sending the blueprints elsewhere for it to be rebuilt—and building a new house in its place from the heap of materials left. After all, the human body is just an object, a shape, and yours is"—she looked over at me—"a medium-sized one, with light brown hair on top—"

I'd never realized I looked so ordinary.

"Really, blueprinting you is just a math problem. I'd need a couple of digits to describe the exact shade of your hair— more brown than light—a moderately long sequence for the shape and arrangement of your freckles, a *really* long sequence for what's stored in your brain cells...It works something like that, only at the molecular level and in binary, zeros and ones. Your luggage gets turned into a sequence of its own. No chance of losing your bag."

"Too bad—I wouldn't mind returning home with one of those handy suitcases instead of my backpack," I said, reeling from all the math. I had a sudden image of a conga line of zeros and ones, like Sherlock Holmes's little dancing men, spiraling into the vortex that would hurl us into Universe B.

"At the other end—by the way, an equivalent amount of information has to get here, which is why crossings from A to B and B to A are synchronized—if they are a little short on one side they throw in the *Collected Works of Shakespeare* or a dictionary—where was I? Right. At the other end of the vortex you pop out in San Francisco B as you. Except, that is, for any interference errors, uncertainty principle ambiguities, or vortex anomalies."

"Hold on." I looked down at my body. "An approximation of me will arrive in San Francisco B? *And* I'm switching molecules with someone?" My voice had risen more than I'd meant it to. "When I head back, I'll return as an approximation of an approximation?"

"You won't notice any difference. Still, I always worry that a glitch will transpose a bit somewhere and I'll step out of the crossing chamber bald. I think that's why I always travel with a hat." She dropped the knitted hat onto the bag next to her feet. I was self-consciously running my fingers through my hair, thinking how nice it would be if the bit for hair thickness accidentally flipped in my favor, when something cold touched my knee, bare below my khaki shorts, startling me.

"Murph, c'mon, we're already late." The lanky A-dweller who had just burst into the crossing chamber had a suitcase in one hand and a leash attached to a dog (an unusually pink-eyed and chubby dog) in the other. "Let's put our suitcase on the rack. C'mon, Gabriella is waiting," he urged as he scanned the room, presumably looking for said Gabriella.

"What kind of a pet are you?" the math woman inquired, reaching over to gently rub the creature's head. Ignoring her as well as the tugging on its leash, the creature gave my knee another moist, scratchy lick.

"Sorry about that, citizen. Murphina's a—" The A-dweller glanced down for the first time and stopped. The same look that had materialized on the face of the tangerine-dress woman across the room appeared on his face.

Figures, I thought. I'd run into two people who know Felix B and I had yet to set foot in Universe B.

"She's an almost-dog?" the math woman prodded.

"That she is," he said, still looking at me. "What extra genes Murphina has—well, I don't know exactly. We met at the pound a few years ago and I never bothered to get her tested. She is who she is."

"Good for you," the math woman said, gently continuing to scratch Murphina's head. "Too many people are obsessed with nature and trying to get it back to its—well, its natural state."

"You know, I've always thought that myself," he concurred, letting Murphina's leash slacken and slicking his black hair back a couple of times.

A dog (even of the almost kind) has always been a time-honored way of meeting members of the opposite sex.

I got to my feet and asked the math woman, "Would you like a chocolate bar? New samples came in at work this morning."

"Thanks, that'd be nice." Her stomach rumbled again.

The lanky A-dweller accompanied me to the luggage rack, where he left his suitcase and I bent down and unzipped my backpack, shooing away an expectantly sniffing Murphina. The A-dweller led the pet away and I dug out a chocolate bar, briefly wondering if there was enough dog DNA in Murphina to render chocolate toxic to her system. The fluffy, rabbit-like tail that came into view as she waddled away perhaps explained the pink eyes, the perky ears, and the chubby white torso. Or not. Speculating what creatures contributed to a pet's DNA based on appearance only was a stab in the dark. You can't judge a book by its cover, as the old-fashioned saying went.

There was a sudden increase in activity. Murphina and her owner settled into a seat next to the woman in the tangerine dress, who gave Murphina a cold look, and I handed the chocolate bar to the math woman and took my seat again. The crossing attendant came back for a final check of the room, then left.

The chamber door closed behind him almost seamlessly and above us the lid moved into place, blocking off the skylight. Muted floor lights heightened the feeling of being packed in a metal crate.

"Any minute now," I said, trying to reassure myself as much as the math woman, who was looking a bit worried, "any minute now and we'll find ourselves in San Francisco B."

"Six."

"Six what?"

"Minutes. That's how long it takes to go through. Don't worry," she added, one of her cheeks round with chocolate, "time doesn't run within the vortex and we won't remember a thing. Um"—she swallowed the chocolate—"um, speaking of remembering, I was wondering if—"

The light music in the seat speakers ceased. "Citizens, we have commenced the crossing procedure. Enjoy your stay in San Francisco B and make sure not to miss any of our popular destinations. Shop at Pier 39 or go to Baker Beach to ride the largest Ferris wheel in both worlds—"

I exchanged a brief look with my neighbor acknowledging the impossibility of further conversation about impending damage to my persona, leaned back in my seat, and closed my eyes. This was it. There was no turning back now. Unraveled like a sweater, the pattern of my being sucked into the vortex, re-knitted elsewhere. I hoped every single one of what Hercule Poirot liked to call "my little gray cells" (or *grey* cells, in his case) would arrive in Universe B. I would need them all. Spying on Felix B without alerting him to my presence—*and maybe even my existence*—was going to be tricky. I had found out about *him* by chance and so was here risking loss of personal detail instead of finishing up the workweek at Wagner's Kitchen Appliances,

Gadgets, and Cutlery. I was pretty sure he didn't have a clue that I existed.

The seat speakers were still rambling on about tourist sites not to be missed and, across the room, Murphina's owner was having a heated discussion with the woman in the tangerine dress. I tried to concentrate on something trivial so as not to lose any important thoughts, like a mind-bogglingly clever idea for a mystery story, during the unraveling, but couldn't think of anything.

Next to me, I heard the whisper again. "Ninety-six... ninety-five...ninety-four..."

UNIVERSE
B

Shapes were in my mind. I was just a shape, and an ordinary one at that.

But that wasn't what nagged at me.

I thought of the first weeks after Y-day, all those years ago, when nobody knew yet about Professor Singh's experiment and universes A and B had just began to branch off and change *their* shapes: a car accident here, a mudslide there, different sperm fertilizing a different egg. When the news broke, everyone had to get used to two versions of everything existing now. It must have been something. And me—well, I was just six months old then.

That wasn't it, though.

It was a particular shape, a convex one, and I was worried about it for some reason. I wanted to lose it, but I also didn't want someone else to have it.

I catalogued what was in my mind: wheeled suitcases, metal crates, chestnut hair, pink-eyed chubby pets, little dancing men, chocolate bars, Regulation 7—hold, go back one. That was it. Food samples, the hazard of working at Wagner's Kitchen. Even my diminished taste buds sprang to life when a new cheese wheel or a stack of chocolate-pecan biscotti was brought in (cheese, chocolate, and nuts being foods I could always taste) and this was why my stomach seemed to have forgotten its flat state despite my daily bike commute.

Suppose it turned out that Felix B worked in an equally hazardous job and so had an equally convex stomach—would I be forced to dye my hair green or grow a goatee just to retain my sense of uniqueness?

I realized I was being ridiculous and opened my eyes to find that we had arrived.

🦆

Outside the Universe B terminal, personal vehicles—*cars*—filled the road. Bumper to bumper, their gleaming reds and greens and yellows making the street seem like a lively if noisy fruit basket, they moved not much faster than the pedestrians crowding the sidewalk around me. Buses puffed by, traffic lights alternated, a crammed cable car with passengers overflowing onto its platforms clanged closer. Above, a flier was descending on the crossing terminal roof to deposit passengers. The Friday afternoon rush hour. I'd heard about it.

There wasn't a bicycle in sight. No people movers either.

I glanced at the sign on a nearby streetlamp. Hyde Street, it said, but this was not the Hyde Street I knew so well and biked along five times a week (ten if you counted the return trip) from the people mover station to my office at Wagner's Kitchen. The day, however, was just as I had left it: cold, windy, and foggy, the norm for a San Francisco summer. I dug my jacket out of the backpack, in the process noticing that the few worn threads hanging off one of the backpack straps had been faithfully reproduced during the crossing. Pushing aside the unsettling thought that I was now sporting someone else's molecules,

I shook the wrinkles out of the jacket and spotted the math woman on the other side of the street. She had the striped hat back on and was standing at the curb looking around as if waiting for transportation.

Aware that a significant nook or cranny in my brain possibly *did* get wiped during the crossing, I decided to go and talk to her. Perhaps she would know where I could find a taxi, I reasoned as I headed for the crosswalk, sliding the jacket on—

"Are you prudent with your power, citizen?"

I swung around, one arm in sleeve. Popcorn-colored robes fluttered in the wind. The leader of the group was cradling a large potted sunflower in his arms. "Join us, citizen, and learn how to be prudent with your power," he urged as he conjured up a pamphlet from under the sunflower pot and tried to put it into my hands. "We're Passivists, citizen. We try not to disturb the universe."

"Really? No thank you in any case." I finished putting on my jacket and turned away. The crosswalk light was red. I decided I didn't want to risk my life by sprinting across the busy intersection.

"Careless choices create new worlds, citizen, thoughtless actions spawn new places, a misstep might be the seed to a new universe. We're universe makers all, yes—"

I chuckled to myself. Well, that was just ridiculous. Professor Z. Z. Singh was the universe maker, everyone knew that. He'd made a copy of the universe in his lab on Y-day and now we were stuck with connected worlds where an alter might throw a wrench into your best laid plans anytime.

"—a word hastily spoken may produce a new dawn—"

The rest of his group stood behind him and I suddenly realized what was odd about their stance. All of them, except for the fluttering robes, were standing very still. *Exceptionally* still, in fact.

"—our very breath can move cosmic mountains," the sun-flower-holder continued, his lips the only thing moving,"—our hands can erect new territory—

The light was taking an awfully long time.

"—but the power, it is dangerous, citizen, dangerous. It must be kept under control—"

A loud buzz came from around my neck. "I have to answer that," I said. The Passivists gave me a look of disappointment and moved on. Stepping behind a streetlamp to avoid the foot traffic, I flipped open the omni and peered into it, excited to try inter-universe communications.

"Ah, Felix," said my boss from his desk. "How's Universe B treating you?"

"Hello, Wagner."

"How was the crossing? Made it in one piece?"

"Seems so."

"Speak up, Felix, I can't hear you. What's that noise?"

"Traffic. And some group with wacky ideas."

"Listen, Felix, I don't want to bother you on your well-deserved vacation," Wagner said, clearly oblivious to the fact that he was, technically, already bothering me, "but there are a couple of *small* issues I wanted to take care of before the Pretzel Makers competition."

"What small issues?" I asked. My boss was quite comfort-able with his short stature—and got along well with everybody. Spending the weekend watching eager contestants compete in making the largest pretzel the fastest would not have been my cup of coffee. Wagner was going as a judge.

"The Spud Fryer—no one seems to know the whereabouts of the user guide. I talked to Egg, she says it should be here in my office—she and Rocky send their greetings from the Sierras, by the way—but I can't seem to find it. We need the user guide by the end of the day," he said, rubbing his chin, a gesture familiar to me from countless office meetings.

I looked up, giving Wagner a nice view of *my* chin, and took a moment. The last thing I'd done before leaving for the crossing terminal was to put the final touches on the user guide for the new Spud Fryer, a countertop potato-peeler-slicer-cooker model available in seven colors and two sizes, then sent messages about it to Wagner and to the company staff, Egg and Rocky. (Even from the Sierras, Eggie and Rocky were really in charge of running the day-to-day operations of the company.) "The user guide should be on your desk. I put it there this morning before I left," I said to Wagner.

He lifted a fruit juicer off his desk and checked underneath. "You were at work today?"

"Half a day."

"A customer came by wanting to talk to you, must have just missed you."

"Huh," I said. Customers rarely requested to meet with me, a lowly writer of user guides as well as the occasional ad.

Wagner had put the juicer down and was now rummaging through a box of discarded stuff. "Hmmm...don't see it...I wish we were allowed to make dozens of copies of these things. Sometimes I think we go overboard on security. What color is it?"

"Golden. And you know as well as I do that we're merely complying with Regulation 10."

"A fryer of potatoes hardly constitutes an item that needs to be kept under wraps. Golden, you say. Oh, for french fries, I see." Wagner's chest, or possibly his stomach, must have covered the omni as he searched, because all I could see was his shirt, peach-colored and probably an expensive Peruvian import. It occurred to me that Wagner must have an alter, unlike Egg and Rocky, my young and carefree coworkers (who, like many uniques, had nature names). For a second I thought about asking Wagner what his alter was like, then decided against it.

Wagner's face reappeared on the screen. "Found it." He waved the disk at me. "I'll take a look at the user guide and dispatch it with the fryer. Now go enjoy your vacation."

"Wait—what's the small issue number two?"

"Oh, that—I was thinking, while you're there, you could pick up some sourdough bread starter for the new bread maker. The good kind. Our sourdough bread here—"

"Is lousy, I know."

"I have a contact that might be willing to share for a price. When I know more, I'll be in touch with the details."

"Well, all right then."

I let the omni fall back around my neck, zipped up my jacket, and stepped out from behind the streetlamp. Wagner liked to keep his employees busy, even on vacation, but I wasn't too sure that I wanted to go out of my way to break Regulation 10 (workplace information), especially since I was already well on my way to running afoul of Regulation 7 (alter privacy).

Having made a mad dash across the intersection, which wasn't particularly pedestrian-friendly even with the walk light green, I ground to a stop next to the math woman, who was talking animatedly on her omni, a cumbersome, older-looking model.

"—Arni, I don't know—I didn't see him—the terminal was very crowded—"

I thought the polite thing to do would be to stand by while she finished her conversation.

"—yes, I know—no, I *didn't* find out—" She saw me and stopped in mid-sentence, mouth open. "Arni, I'll call you back." She flipped the clunky omni shut.

"I guess we survived the crossing after all," I said by way of a greeting. "Sorry to interrupt your call."

"Not at all." She grinned. "Was worried there for a second, didn't see you outside the crossing chamber."

"That would have made the news, wouldn't it? Traveler lost during the Friday afternoon San Francisco-to-San Francisco crossing. Scrambled into a hideous piece of luggage with no handles and no wheels. No, I was, uh...delayed. Had to use the restroom," I blurted out, unable to come up with a more socially acceptable excuse on the spur of the moment. In reality, I had been directed to a separate line for those with alters in town. I didn't want to admit it to her, however. Nothing wrong with having an alter. It was just that it made me seem—well, not young. Someone turning thirty-five was middle-aged, almost. The line had culminated in front of a morose DIM official who heard me say I was a tourist, added an *Alter in the Area* tag to my identicard, and warned, "Your entry permit expires Saturday afternoon. You have a week and a day. Don't try to make contact with Citizen Felix Sayers B. Regulation 7."

We made room for the Passivists to walk by—having crossed the street, they seemed determined not to break stride or veer from their straight path—and she murmured, "People make fun of Passivists, but they have the right idea, really, though *universe maker* is a misleading term. It implies intent." She pulled out a thin copper-colored shawl from her bag, absentmindedly plucked off a piece of paper stuck to it, then wrapped the shawl around her shoulders and tied a large knot in the front. "Cold today. Do you think they exist?"

"Who?"

"Many universes, like the Passivists claim." She checked the street again at the clang of an approaching cable car.

"I hope not. Two is enough for me."

"Why do cable cars always show up in the opposite direction of the one you want? I'm better off walking home to get my car and driving." She added, "To the Bihistory Institute. I'm carrying some Universe A data that needs to be inputted."

It was a little odd for her to be revealing workplace details to a perfect stranger, but I had noticed that uniques (of which I used to be one) tended to be less concerned about privacy. Though I had only a vague idea what bihistory was (documenting differences big and small between our two universes, that sort of thing), I said, "Bihistory? That sounds interesting."

"It is, on occasion. Speaking of which—"

We parted to allow a pair of avocado-uniformed DIM officials through. They were headed toward the Passivists, who had formed a circle around an unsuspecting tourist. One of the DIMs gave me a long stare as they passed, making me nervous that it was somehow obvious that I was here to ignore Regulation 7 and spy on my alter.

"You were saying?" I turned back in a show of nonchalance, but the math woman's gaze was focused over my shoulder. Behind me I could hear the Passivists attempting to give pamphlets to the DIM officials and regulations being quoted. She pulled her shawl closer around her body. "I'd better go."

"Oh, okay," I said.

"Thanks for the chocolate," she said and turned away.

"Wait, I don't think you mentioned your name—?"

I thought I heard her say, "Bean," as she hurried toward the intersection where the cable car tracks turned from Hyde Street onto an uphill lane. She rounded the corner and disappeared from view.

And that was that.

The DIM officials were escorting the Passivists, who were passively acquiescing, away from the terminal.

It was time to catch that taxi. There were none to be seen.

Why did I need a taxi anyway? I was a man in the prime of my life, just at the three-and-a-half decade mark, and perfectly capable of walking to my hotel. In fact, it was probably a good way to set about reducing the pesky convexness of my stomach. True, it was a little cold, but, it being San Francisco, there was a good chance the fog would clear up any minute. I adjusted the backpack more comfortably across my shoulders and set a course along Hyde Street in the direction of Broadway.

Before I had barely covered a block, a short honk rose above the street noise. A car, one of those with a top that opens up, as indeed it was open now, had slowed down to a crawl next to me. The almost-dog Murphina, her woolly white coat flattened by the westerly wind, sat comfortably ensconced in the front passenger seat of the cucumber-green vehicle. "Can we give you a lift?" Murphina's owner asked from behind the steering wheel. He gestured toward the only unoccupied seat in the car, next to the A-dweller (or B-dweller) who had attracted attention in the crossing chamber and who was sitting composedly in the back, the white scarf tied around her hair just touching the tangerine dress, her gray eyes fixed on me.

"Thanks," I said, "but I think I'll walk. I need the exercise."

The lanky A-dweller leaned across Murphina and handed me a business card. "We'll see you around, then."

I glanced at the card—*Past & Future,* it said and was otherwise blank—as they reentered the traffic stream and disappeared down the street.

[3]

A BIT OF GOOD NEWS

The following morning found me at the Queen Bee Inn, a three-story Victorian row house nestled between neighboring Victorians on a hill overlooking the bay. Behind the highly polished antique front desk sat Franny, a petite silver-haired woman with a square chin. "I hope you enjoyed your night in the Lilac Room, Citizen Sayers. There was a call for you early this morning, but Regulation 3 protects the personal information of our guests, so we did not disclose that you were here. But I *know* our guests don't mind if *we* get to know them better—"

Franny had already ascertained what my business on this world was ("just a tourist") and what I did in life and even that I was single.

"Someone was looking for me? That's strange," I said. "I don't know anyone in town."

"Seemed like a nice young man. Curly hair, prominent nose."

"Doesn't ring a bell. What was the name?"

"Didn't leave a name, Franny," a male voice called out from the back room.

"Of course he left a name, dear," Franny called back and reached for a message ledger. She opened it and started turning the pages. "Now where—"

My stomach tightened with late-morning hunger and, as I waited, I went through a quick mental list of restaurants that served nice, big breakfasts. It didn't seem right that I was forgoing Coconut Café (*Did* it exist here?) and its weekend pancake special because of some impractical rule about avoiding familiar places. Would it really do much harm to jump in a people mover—that is, hail a taxi—and take a little drive to see if Coconut Café was in its place on El Camino Real in the Redwood Grove neighborhood and if their menu included pecan pancakes?

Luckily I had chosen the Queen Bee Inn. Breakfast was included, already paid for, and set in a buffet in a cozy room to the right of the stairs.

Franny tapped the message ledger. "Here it is, two calls, one right after another. The first citizen, the one with the prominent nose, didn't leave a message. The second caller—voice only, that one—she said she was trying to get in touch with Citizen Sayers of Universe A because of a development of mutual interest. Didn't leave a name either."

A petite silver-haired man with a square chin came in from the back room carrying a cloth and what looked like furniture polish. "Didn't I tell you that, Franny?"

"You were right, dear."

He grunted in response and, nodding at me in passing, headed for the row of cubbies where antique keys hung under room names.

"Start with the Rose Room keys, Trevor, dear. We're expecting newlyweds today." Echoing my earlier breakfast worries, she added, "I wanted to make sure you'd been warned about the Lunch-Place Rule, Citizen Sayers, before heading out to see the city—"

I had approached the front desk looking for tour brochures.

"—because it's better not to compare things between our world and your world, that's for sure," she added.

Trevor grunted again in agreement without bothering to look up from the large key he had begun polishing.

"Though I have to admit I've always wondered what Franny A and Trevor A named *their* inn. The Queen Bee, the B is for the universe, you see. Used to be the Tipsy Sailor." She sighed. "What a year 1986 was—we were young and had just bought the inn and were struggling to keep it in business…and then to find out that Professor Singh had made a copy of the universe and everything in it! And we were still getting used to solid ground."

"I beg your pardon?"

"Trevor and I were born and raised on an ocean liner, the *Two Thousand Sails*, have you heard of it? We were educated by reading and by traveling the world. The day we married, we got off at the closest port and settled down for good. The port happened to be Oakland, just north of here. They raised the Golden Gate Bridge and we sailed into the bay."

"That," Trevor said, still polishing the same key, "was then."

"Quite right, dear. The ship wouldn't fit under the bridge nowadays."

"Why not?" I asked, curious. "The old Golden Gate Bridge is a drawbridge, isn't it?"

"The ocean level is too high, Citizen Sayers. The drawbridge leaves don't raise far enough."

"Speaking of the old bridge—"

"That's right, Citizen Sayers, you were asking about tours. I must say it's nice to see an A-dweller on vacation. So many seem to come only for business."

"People have to earn a living, don't they," grumbled Trevor, which might have been the longest sentence I'd heard him utter yet. He hung up the newly cleaned key and picked up another.

"Everyone needs a vacation, no matter what their job is, I say," Franny shot back, briefly sounding like Wagner, my boss, commanding one of his employees to take time off. "And you are a culinary writer, how nice," she added more mildly, nodding toward me from behind the front desk. "Do you write restaurant reviews?"

"No."

"Cookbooks, then?"

"I put together user guides for culinary products."

"Well, how nice. What kind of culinary products do you make user guides for?"

"All of them. I work for a kitchenware company," I said, shifting my weight from one foot to the other. Honestly, it was like the woman had never heard of DIM's Regulation 3 (citizen privacy).

"Oh, a kitchenware company?" She paused, inviting more details, but none were forthcoming. "Well, how nice. Let me get you the tour brochures. By far the best way to get to know the city. Our Universe A guests are always surprised how different everything is, forgetting that we didn't have the earthquake here, of course."

She went into the back room for the brochures and I switched my weight back to the other foot, the blisters on them being painful proof of Franny's words. The city *was* different, as I had found out while looking for the Queen Bee Inn. Having declined the ride from Murphina and her entourage, I'd headed away from the crossing terminal eager to see more of this town that bore the same name as the one I'd just crossed over from, the letter appended at the end seeming something of an afterthought. But not long passed before my step had slowed down to the hesitant gait of a tourist in a foreign land. Hyde Street was where it was supposed to be, and so was Broadway, but where was Memorial Park with its familiar macar trees and the arrow-shaped fountain pointing toward the ocean? Everything felt slightly *off*, like being served chocolate mousse on a paper plate or wine in a mug. I tried one street that I thought should lead toward the bay, then backtracked and tried another. It didn't help that the fog, instead of dissipating, had continued rolling in from the ocean, shrouding everything in a cool, smoky mist and making me wish I'd brought not sunglasses but gloves though it was mid-July.

San Francisco is a hilly town. As I trekked up one of the bigger hills to the faint distant sound of the foghorn, I came upon a row of Chinese restaurants and tourist shops. The restaurants had looked inviting, and the wise thing to do would have been to go in for an early dinner, then call a taxi. Wise, yes. Human nature, no. Reluctant to admit defeat, I pressed on. After all, my map had shown the inn to be only fifteen stadia from the crossing terminal, a distance which had looked perfectly manageable—and misleadingly flat—on my omni screen.

By the time I found the Queen Bee Inn a couple of steep blocks away from the bay, the sun was low in the sky, my hair was damp from the fog, and I had developed a deep hate of my backpack. I checked in, trudged up the stairs to the Lilac Room, which had a view of the parking lot and not the bay, kicked the sandals off my aching feet, and sat down on the bed determined not to move until morning. For dinner I ordered delivery from a local (and, as per the Lunch-Place Rule, unfamiliar) Chinese restaurant and spent the rest of the evening pleasantly enough, rereading *The Red-Headed League*. I ultimately drifted off to sleep with the thought that Holmes (had he been a real person) would have loathed having an alter—Holmes B, the ultimate adversary, even more so than a doubled Professor Moriarty, competing with Holmes A at every turn for the distinction of solving the next great case. It occurred to me that Hercule Poirot would have been none too pleased either, but Miss Marple would simply have invited the *other* Miss Marple over for afternoon tea, and Lord Peter Wimsey—well, the Lords Peter Wimsey would have studied each other across the room through their matching monocles—

"Citizen Sayers?" Franny had placed several tour brochures on the desk in front of me. "Our breakfast area, the Nautical Nook, is through the glass doors there."

"I'll bring these back when I'm done with them."

"You can keep the brochures, Citizen Sayers."

"Right." I was used to plastic, not the use-once-then-toss-out philosophy of paper products.

Speaking of paper—

It was the logical place to begin. Why had I not thought of it before?

"One more thing," I interrupted Franny, who had turned to help Trevor clean keys. "Is there a store nearby that sells tr— that sells paper books?"

"Oh, what kind of books do you read, Citizen Sayers?"

"Cookbooks and history of cooking for work, mystery classics for fun."

"How nice. There is a bookstore a few blocks up Starfish Lane. You could take a cable car, but it'll be faster to walk. Our Universe A guests often ask about bookstores—books made of paper are a waste of trees, they'll say to me—nothing easier than reaching for the omni around your neck to find a good read. I don't know about that. Never liked that weirdly shaped screen and all those pictures and whatnots marring the good old-fashioned written word. In any case, don't judge us too harshly, Citizen Sayers. This world might not be as good as yours when it comes to preserving nature, but we have our good points too."

"Of course," I said quickly, avoiding looking at the dozen paper brochures she had just given me. "As a matter of fact, I've recently finished putting together a user guide for a kitchen accessory invented by a B-dweller. A potato-peeler-slicer-fryer."

"That's kind of you to say, Citizen Sayers. It's the little things that often matter the most, isn't it? We all have to do our part."

Trevor dropped a set of keys with a clang and reached for more polish.

As I went through the glass doors into the Nautical Nook, I overheard Franny say, "Citizen Sayers seems like a nice young man."

&

A pleasant stroll along Starfish Lane, with its tiny flower shops, specialty shoe stores, and boutiques, brought me to the front of a large store that spanned almost half a block. The sign above the doors said, *The Bookworm*. I realized I had walked by it yesterday while looking for the inn without realizing what it was. A colorful display of maps, travel guides, and double globes in one of the windows caught my eye and I stopped for a moment before going in.

Summer is our slow season at work—too hot, Wagner likes to say, for customers to think about cooking. Every year, reasoning that his employees' kitchen-product-idea-generating and user-guide-writing skills could always benefit from new experiences, he signs us up for travel sites which clog our omnis with ads touting sandy beaches and ancient ruins. (I think Wagner overestimates how much he pays us.) I had been wavering between joining Egg and Rocky on their hiking holiday and taking a train tour of the wine country. Going to Universe B had never entered my mind. Too expensive. Egg and Rocky had left earlier in the week to hike the Sierras. As for me—well, I had found out that my official birth date was wrong, that I was older than I thought, *and that I had an alter.* I'd emptied my bank account, bought my ticket, made my reservations at the Queen Bee Inn, and packed my bag. Beyond that—

I was here now.

I went in.

🦆

It was a store with, well, books in it.

There were many: Books on tables. Books on bookshelves. Books of all sizes, colors and, presumably, subject matter, filling the available space from wall to wall.

Near the entrance I noticed a table labeled *Bestsellers* and picked up at random one of the books stacked on it. The book felt surprisingly light. The description on the back promised a riveting story of love and revenge in the Wild West, penned by an author whose grasp of historical accuracy, judging by the dirt-free and perfectly toothed intertwined duo on the front cover, seemed to be lacking. I took a peek inside the book—there were no further images, not even ads, just text—then put the bestseller back on the stack of identical books and proceeded deeper into the bookstore. It was quiet. Not a museum kind of quiet, more of an upscale-restaurant-that-serves-wine-no-soda kind. I was one of a handful of customers scattered throughout. A single clerk stood at a row of registers attending to a sale. Among the neatly packed shelves, in the very center of the store, a wide curving staircase led to an upper floor.

Tree books. I did not recall reading them, though I must have as a child, before the Great Recycling Push of the 1990s. It was then that luxury paper items had been collected and turned into paper products whose job could *not* be taken over by omnis. Toilet paper. Cardboard boxes. Egg cartons.

But that was in Universe A.

An angular face with a strong nose and an *s*-shaped pipe stared at me from a cover. (In the midst of reading the Sherlock Holmes stories, I had automatically gone to look for them.) I took the book off the shelf and opened it. This one had a few illustrations. I chose a page and read a bit, the paragraph being a letter to Holmes by *the* woman, Irene Alder, then flicked my fingers—and shook my head and advanced the page by hand, though with some trouble because the pages stuck together slightly—and read some more. The font was tiny, the lines too close together, and the page lacked color. Even so, the book had a charm of its own, like an old mortar and pestle sitting on a counter in a home kitchen.

The outer wrapper, in addition to the drawing of the Great Detective on the front, had a somewhat sensationalistic synopsis on the back. Genuine Morocco leather, it advertised. Red silk ribbon bookmark. I searched for the price, found it in the lower right corner, and let out a gasp. Four hundred dollars!

Everything was more expensive here—their runaway inflation had been faster—but that was still quite steep. Perhaps a smaller book, one of the ones with the flimsy covers, would be more in line with what a tourist from afar could afford, I thought, gingerly sliding the Holmes back in its place among fellow editions bearing Sir Conan Doyle's name.

I took a moment to run my hand along the spines of the C-to-D books in what was clearly the section of the bookstore devoted to novels of all kinds. Agatha Christie, with a long row of mysteries overflowing from one shelf to the one below it. (Eighty plus novels—where had she found the time?—took up a lot of space.) Below, I saw Dickens, Dostoevsky, Dumas, others. I tried to imagine my novel-to-be—once I got around to writing it—sitting on a shelf waiting to entice a customer into parting with a bit of hard-earned cash. I failed. The prospect of creating an object you could hold in your hand seemed fraught with more problems than creating an omni memory link nestled among countless others. What if, for instance, you made a typo and noticed it *after* the book got printed, when it was too late to correct it? And what did authors do when they needed images to convey settings and plot points too difficult to describe in words? And if readers didn't like a book, all they could do was to dispose of it in the thrash after having purchased it, there being no possibility of a free preview—a waste of money and resources. No way of obtaining feedback from readers, no comments section to fill up with praise or criticism of the book. Perhaps, all things considered, it was a good thing that I didn't live here in Universe B, given all their peculiarities.

Suddenly I remembered why I was here in the first place.

Quite calmly, I located section S several bookcases behind me. Bent down, looked. Double-checked—

And breathed again.

It wasn't there.

As my heart, beating as rapidly and insistently as Poe's tell-tale one, started to subside to its normal rhythm, I heard a light cough behind me.

"Can I help you find something?" It was a bookstore employee.

"No, thank you. I was just looking for—a book."

"Did you find it?"

"No, but—"

"Let's look, then." She pushed her horn-rimmed glasses up toward the top of her nose and looked at me expectantly. "What's the title?"

"Er—I'm not sure—that is, I have no idea whether it even exists—"

"Do you have the author's name, then?"

I had the name, all right. "Felix Sayers."

"Sayers." She squatted down by the bottom shelf, where the S-es began, as if I wouldn't have already looked there myself. "Let's see. Sayers, you say...Dorothy, of course...*Strong Poison*... that's a nice one...*Busman's Honeymoon* too...no, I don't see any others with that name." She stood back up, almost losing her glasses in the process. "I do believe these shelves get lower every year. Sometimes I think we should just have one *very* long shelf that circles the store at eye level. Much easier. No bending down or having to reach up or wondering if you are in the right section. Speaking of which—"

"Yes?" I said, trying not to reveal that a lack of (non-Dorothy) Sayers authors was good news.

"Your Felix Sayers is to be found among favorite authors of the past?"

"I beg your pardon?"

"You are in the classics section. Pre-twenty-first-century authors."

I looked around, deflated. "Classics—oh."

"To which section can I direct you instead?"

"Well—most likely, mystery, I suppose. Is there a mystery section?"

"Mystery is over in that corner, but let's check our list first." She turned to a nearby computer station and squinted at it. "Visiting A-dwellers, you see, often forget that what's on the shelves is only a fraction of what's available. Let's see, Sayers in mystery…first name begins with an f…don't see anything…"

"No Felix Sayers," she said after a minute or two. "It's not, by any chance, Flavio Sayer-Solomon?"

I shook my head.

"Sorry I couldn't find your book," she said, pushing her glasses up her nose again. "Anything else I can help you find? Dorothy Sayers, though that wasn't quite the name you wanted, has a nice collection of mystery novels—"

"Eleven of them. A reasonable number."

"—or may I suggest Daphne du Maurier's *Rebecca*—or her *The Birds*, which though not a mystery *per se* is quite a riveting read—"

🦆

The wide curving staircase led to an upper floor, more of a balcony really, where there was a counter with beverages and snacks. Though it was embarrassingly soon after breakfast, I ordered tea (they gave me a blank look when I asked for coffee) and a plate of almond thins. I found a free table by the railing and sat down.

A cooking competition, that was the brilliant idea that had stuck around in my head since I'd talked to Wagner, who was by now no doubt knee-deep in pretzel dough. Set somewhere rustic, say in the Sierra mountains where Egg and Rocky had gone on their hiking adventure, a cooking competition presented all sorts of interesting possibilities: motives (kitchen sabotage and contestants stealing each other's recipes); murder methods (hiking accidents in the summer, icicles as stabbing implements in the winter, and the more obvious chef's knives all year round); and clues (ingredients in killer cupcakes traceable to local markets frequented by the poisoner and so on). I would have to ask Wagner what went on behind the scenes at these things.

Of course, an idea, even a good one, is a long way from that short, satisfying phrase, "THE END." Even someone like me, who (culinary user guides aside) had been more of a reader thus far, knew that.

Squashing down the patently obvious problem that newly published books would appear on the shelves below as soon as tomorrow and that one of them might belong to Felix B, I let out a sigh of relief that for the moment at least the shelves had been devoid of any Felix B books.

"Astonishing, isn't it?"

The man had his hand on the back of the chair across from me. "Hope you don't mind. I can see you are a fellow A-dweller." He took the chair and set his tea on the table. "Astonishing, isn't it?"

"What is?"

He gestured down at the books with his thumb. "All those trees."

"I suppose so." I took a sip of my parsley tea and made a face. I'd never been much of a tea drinker. I tried an almond thin, which wasn't bad, and offered him one.

He accepted the almond thin and dipped it in his tea, spilling a couple of drops on the sleeve of his tweed jacket in the process. "You can't get a decent cup of coffee in the whole city, but they sell something called coffee-table books. And a whole rack of stand-alone dictionaries. Why bother? Dictionaries always need updating. Atlases too. I get it with the really *old* books, the ones written before we figured out how to do things better. Let's keep those around, but the new stuff? Why print on paper?" He bit into the almond thin.

"What, out of curiosity, do you read?" I asked with an inner shudder.

"True-life crime. And I tell you what, I wouldn't buy a tree book, even a true crime one. Forget the environment, it's just impractical. I wouldn't have anything to read"—munch, munch—"if I didn't have my trusty omni"—he tugged on the omni around his neck—"because it makes little sense to pack a bunch of heavy books and lug them along when you travel. But what gets me most of all is this. What if someone else has *just* purchased the book you want and the shelf sits empty?"

"I don't know what happens." I was watching a customer who'd come up the stairs carrying an armful of books. She set them down on the table next to us, then returned with a pastry. It didn't seem like the merchandise had been paid for, yet neither she nor anyone else seemed concerned about potential fruit smudges from her scone or tea spills or wrinkling of book pages. Wished I'd known about that policy, I thought. Could have brought up a book or two to browse. It would have made me look busy and kept any chatty co-dwellers away.

The chatty co-dweller took a final slurp of his tea and peered into the empty glass. "Not bad for tea. Something called *ooh-long*. I'm off to meet my alter. I've heard through a neutral party that he's filed paperwork giving me permission to visit him. He is a lawyer and I run a paper products conversion business—we turn old documents into cereal boxes. Good for privacy and Regulation 3, good for nature. Mind if I have another?"

He took the last of the almond thins and walked out of my life before I could make one or two additional points that had just occurred to me.

One, how curiously—well, *satisfying* it had been to touch a book. Solid, tangible, earthy.

Two, so what if there was no practical side to it? The Venus oil painting that had hung on my parents' living room wall and fascinated me as a teenage boy had required a canvas, something to paint on. On the other hand, I had to concede immediately, paper books far outnumbered oil paintings (how many reprintings of *Twelfth Night* to two *Starry Nights*?) so perhaps that wasn't a fair comparison after all.

My hand found its way to the omni hanging in its usual spot around my neck. It knew my preferred audio level (five) on days I felt like being read to and my usual font (Helvetica, size twelve) and background color (wheat) on days that I didn't. It kept a list of my favorite authors and notified me of upcoming releases and offered reading recommendations from friends, colleagues, perfect strangers, the Queen of Lichtenstein…And yet this place felt right too. I realized I had come prepared to dislike everything about Universe B, mostly because it wasn't mine but *his*. Franny of the Queen Bee Inn had been right to warn me not to be judgmental.

It suddenly occurred to me that I didn't really have any idea what materials got squandered in the making of an omni and its yearly batteries, or how that would compare to whatever percentage of a tree it took to make a paper book.

I picked up half an almond, all that remained of my almond thins, and considered whether that most famous scientist of all, Professor Z. Z. Singh, deserved all the blame heaped on his head. Creativity, the force behind all the books spread below me, applied to physics as well and had led him to make a copy of the universe in his laboratory just before noon on January 6, 1986, earning him the title universe maker. In fact, the only non-creative side to the whole incident was the name Professor Singh—by then two Professors Singh—had given the newly branching universes. Rumor had it that they'd tossed a coin, or whatever the physics equivalent was, and that there had been plans to produce additional universes further down the alphabet. Ridiculously, I had always felt rather proud to be from Universe A.

As I scanned the nearby posters of upcoming releases for my shared name and finished the last of the lukewarm parsley tea, I wished that Professor Singh hadn't been *quite* so creative, however.

🦆

Having given up on the idea of purchasing a book (there were so many I couldn't decide on one to buy) I walked out of the Bookworm empty-handed and set a course along quiet Starfish Lane toward busier Lombard Street and the tourist bus depot. As I stepped into the first intersection on the way, a car as sleekly black as—really, nothing in a kitchen except perhaps the inside of a nonstick pan—approached fast, like the driver behind the tinted windows was in an awful hurry, and would have splattered me if I hadn't jumped back onto the sidewalk at the last moment.

The car continued on its way without slowing down.

[4]

A BIT OF BAD NEWS

"**B**est do nothing, citizen."

"I beg your pardon?" I said.

"You look like you're trying to decide something. But you must be prudent with your power, citizen. Careless choices create new worlds, thoughtless actions spawn new places, a misstep might be the seed to a new universe—"

I shook my head at the Passivists, who moved on, and eyed the office building across the street from where I was, about to enter the renovated firehouse that served as a tourist bus depot. The office building was one of those rundown, depressing places with peeling paint and neon signs advertising moneylending and such—except for a discreet plaque near the front entrance, which simply read, *Noor & Brood, Investigative Services. Leave It to Us.*

The building had tall, narrow windows through which little could be seen. Several cars were parked on a rooftop parking lot.

There had been nothing bearing Felix B's name in the Bookworm and all its books, which was all well and good. But what if in his computer sat a finished first draft? Or second draft? Or the final version of his masterpiece, ready to be sent out at the touch of a button? It wasn't like I could knock on his neighbor's front door—that's if I managed to find out where my alter lived—and ask, "Is Felix Sayers B writing a cooking-themed mystery, do you happen to know?" Nor could I pretend to be Felix B and glean information by getting together for dinner with his close friends, whoever they were (here I thought of Murphina's owner and the tangerine-dress woman from the crossing, both of whom had seemed to recognize my face). It wouldn't have worked either way—I couldn't pose questions as a stranger because I looked an awful lot like him, nor could I get away with pretending to be Felix B because I probably didn't look *exactly* like him. Visions of fake mustaches, tinted contact lenses, and wigs flew through my brain, but I ruled them out, for the moment at least, as being undignified and impractical.

Hiring a private detective was something that had simply not occurred to me. Like mustachioed disguises or those other mystery staples, a message written in a strange cipher or a dead body in a locked room, it's not something that often comes up in real life, at least not in mine.

I watched as a man came out of the office building, glanced around furtively, pocketed an envelope, and hurried away. I hoped he had been there for the moneylending and not as a typical client of Noor & Brood.

The clang of the firehouse bell alerted me to get out of the way as a bus packed with sightseers exited the firehouse behind me and made a wide right turn into traffic. The bus headed down Lombard Street and I went to join the short line already forming at the back of the firehouse. As I waited to buy my ticket for the city tour, I toyed with the idea of hiring Detective Noor (or Detective Brood) to see what he could do for me. Would he take my money, tell me to come back in a few days, and then put his feet up on his desk and take a nap on my dime because there was no alter-surveillance he could do under the law? Or would he laugh me out of his office and call the neighborhood DIM bureau to report me? DIM took its job of protecting citizens' privacy very seriously, along with their other duties: raiding data black markets; overseeing the destruction of old phonebooks, maps, and other documents; inspecting scientific research centers; and so on.

The next tour wasn't scheduled to leave for forty minutes. I took it as a sign.

Besides, I reasoned as I headed across the street, what aspiring mystery writer would miss a chance to talk to a real-life detective? If nothing else, I could ask Detective Noor for tips on how to make my fictional sleuth, whose name I hadn't decided on yet, not come out looking completely amateurish. Tips on police procedure, or how someone stuck in the Sierra Mountains would go about analyzing various types of cigarette ash without having access to a well-stocked lab. That sort of thing.

🦆

The detective turned out to be an affable, stout B-dweller who exuded a connectedness to the city and everyone in it, rather like an urban Miss Marple (that is, if Miss Marple had been dark-complexioned, middle-aged, and ran a business in a town that dwarfed the fictional village of St. Mary Mead). I introduced myself and said, "And you are Citizen Noor...or Citizen Brood?"

"Call me Mrs. Noor or Detective Noor. I don't like all that citizen nonsense." She offered me a chair and refreshment from a small fridge squeezed under her desk. "This office is my center of operations. Pip, Ham, and Daisy—my two sons and my daughter—do most of the footwork."

"Lovely nature names," I said, accepting a glass of water and a cheese ball and taking the chair. Documents and news articles lay strewn across the detective's desk. Uneven stacks of papers rested against the back wall of the cramped office, and maps and photographs covered most of the available wall space. There was a rack with clothing on it (for disguises?) in one corner.

"And what can we do for you? A lost love, perhaps? A background check on your fiancée?"

"No, nothing like that. Er—"

Mrs. Noor waited a moment for me to speak, then pointed, without turning around, at a brass plaque mounted on the wall behind her. "Up there. Read it to me."

Feeling like a schoolchild, I read the two-word phrase out loud. "Hypothetically speaking."

"I'm sorry, I didn't quite catch that."

"Hypothetically speaking," I repeated more loudly.

"Now you can say whatever you like." She moved a few papers around on her desk and dug up a pen and a tiny plum-colored notebook. "It's perfectly legal to *say* anything as long as you are not planning on actually doing it. Not wise, perhaps, but legal. You could come in here and suggest that I follow your wife and report on her daily activities—which, if I did it, would be a clear violation of her privacy and Regulation 3. But I would not be obligated to report you for merely suggesting it. If you tried to *pay* me to do it, that's another matter. Another cheese ball?"

"I'm not married."

She partook of a cheese ball herself. "It was just an example. I can see that it's nothing that simple."

"I was born before Y-day."

"An alter." She wiped her hands, uncapped her pen, and opened her notebook to a fresh page. "Tell me."

Aware that the only person I had chosen to confide in thus far was a complete stranger who was probably out to con me, I told Mrs. Noor, who took notes as I spoke, about the call I had received early one morning about a month ago informing me that my Aunt Henrietta had passed away. From his office in Miami, as I lay in bed making sure my pajamas were buttoned, Aunt Henrietta's lawyer had said, "To you, her great-nephew, she left her collection of—let me see, here it is—one *half* of her collection of porcelain figurines. Dolphins. Your share is forty-two of them. You can expect them in the mail."

"How big are they?" I'd asked, a trifle concerned. I remembered Aunt Henrietta's Florida home as being a sort of museum for all the knickknacks she had acquired during her work abroad. Some of the knickknacks had been quite large.

"Each dolphin is about the size of an orange, I believe, and comes with its own individual stand. She left you something else," he added.

"Yes?" My hopes raised, I sat up, accidentally knocking the lamp off my bedside table.

"It's a photograph."

"A photo—oh."

"Henrietta generously gave the bulk of her money to charity while she was still alive," he said, his tone carefully devoid of anything but professionalism. "I'll send the photograph with the figurines."

A couple of days later on my doorstep there arrived a large wooden crate in which forty-two dolphin figurines sat carefully packed in bubble wrap. At the very bottom of the crate was a plain manila envelope. In the envelope was a photograph. In the faded photograph was my father, and in his arms was an infant. Me.

On Y-day, according to the date on the back of the photo. Ten days *before* the official birth date listed on the identicard that I'd carried all my life.

Which meant that I had an alter. Everyone born before Y-day did.

I don't know why, but the news had hit me like myriad bricks. It's the kind of thing you expect to find out as a small child from your parents who reassure you lovingly and often that in their eyes you *are* unique and that having an alter is like having a brother or sister, not the kind of thing a grown man expects to hear, along with the news that he is a bit older than he thought. Why my parents had bribed someone to change my birth date, I had no idea. Some digging around had revealed that the true date of my birth was not in January but July, a full six months earlier.

"It was all—a bit of a surprise," I said to Mrs. Noor. "Why Aunt Hen—my great-aunt, really—why she had a baby photo of me in the first place, I don't know. She was a relation through marriage, my Uncle Otto's second wife, and came into the family when I was already at the San Diego Four-Year. None of it makes much sense." I shook my head.

Mrs. Noor looked at me kindly. "Parents. We do try our best, you know. It's just that sometimes it's hard to know what's best. Take my daughter, Daisy—she likes her work here at Noor & Brood, enjoys the unpredictability of it all, the potpourri of people who walk in here every day. Pip too. But Ham, I'm not so sure. Sometimes I wonder if he's here only because we've kept it a family business. I can't come out and simply ask, that's what's so difficult."

I couldn't imagine Mrs. Noor being uncomfortable talking to anyone.

"Perhaps your parents simply wanted to shield you from the knowledge that you had an alter," she added. "You have to understand what it was like. All the uncertainty, the turmoil we were thrown into after we found out we were connected to another universe. I was a young girl then, just starting in life and in the detective business. And here I am thirty-five years later running my own agency, unlike my alter, who—well, that's neither here or there." She sighed and wagged a finger at me. "But your little difficulty, now we can do something about *that*. We'll begin, of course, by finding out where Felix B lives. That might take some time. *You* live in San Francisco A, but for all we know he might live in the Nevada desert or in an Alaska hunting lodge or in a Carolina greenhouse."

"The DIM official at the crossing terminal tagged my identicard with an *Alter in the Area* tag."

"That simplifies matters." She jotted that down in spidery, Miss-Marple-like handwriting. "And we have the parents' names, Klara and Patrick Sayers of Carmel, you said? Are your parents still living?"

I shook my head.

"Sorry. What happened, if I may ask?"

"Boating accident."

"And *his* parents, I wonder? A boating accident is unlikely to have happened in both universes, but you never know."

"That's why I'm here. I need you to find out these things for me, Mrs. Noor."

As she jotted down a few more things, my eyes went to the articles strewn across her desk. The range of topics was wide—I suppose everything is of interest to a detective—and the headlines were just like the ones that sold Universe A newspapers, only printed. There was a large, alarmist one warning that a new disease, something to do with pets, was close to making its way from Universe A into Universe B; a medium-sized one lamented the diminishing numbers of elephants and giraffes; and a small one (often the most useful) gave a positive review to a newly renovated downtown restaurant, the Organic Oven.

"You keep client information in notebooks?" I pointed out the obvious as Mrs. Noor put down her pen.

"My notepad? Entirely the best way. Nothing safer than taking notes in your own handwriting and keeping them in your own pocket."

"Do you often get clients seeking information about their alters, Mrs. Noor?"

"We get them occasionally."

"How will you find out more about Felix B? Without incurring the attention of DIM, I mean." I glanced around. The small, windowless office seemed to harbor many secrets of its own on its shelves and in its corners.

She opened a desk drawer, reached inside, and handed me a business card. "In case you need to contact me, Felix. As for DIM—the laws are here to protect us all, especially citizens whose unscrupulous alters might try to take over their lives, which, as you probably know, is not unheard of. That's not the case here, of course," she said, giving me a quick appraising glance. "We merely require some information about Citizen Sayers B, after which you'll go back to your own universe."

"You understand, Mrs. Noor, that I don't want him to know that I know about him?"

"Leave it to us. We will tread lightly."

🦆

Having paid a moderate advance to Noor & Brood, I hurried across the street to make the city tour. It being Saturday, the bus was full and the only seats left were in the back. I made my way down the length of the diesel-powered monstrosity, which long ago had been banned in my California, and took a seat by the window. A couple of minutes later a jovial-looking woman took the seat next to me as the doors closed and the tour guide tapped a microphone and spoke into it from his position near the front of the bus. "My dear guests, how many of you are B-dwellers?" A hand went up next to me, as did a few others. "And how many of you are visitors from Universe A?" I raised my hand, along with most of the passengers; not among them, I was glad to see, was the man who had disliked bookstores and eaten my almond thins.

"My name is Lard—that's right, Lard, like in pork." The guide tipped his cap, which had the logo *See B from a Bus* on it. "And it's my pleasure to welcome you all to San Francisco B."

"Thanks, Lard," came the cheerful response from the B-dweller in the seat next to me. (Every tour has a talker. They invariably seem to end up in my vicinity.)

As the engine shuddered to life and we headed out the fire-house doors and down Lombard Street in the direction of the Embarcadero, Lard expertly balanced himself in the aisle and spoke into his microphone. "My dear friends, let me tell you the story of the California Gold Rush and the fifty-fivers, the prospectors who in 1855 arrived seeking gold and baking their sourdough bread—"

Lard's words reminded me that Wagner hadn't called yet to say that he had secured a contact for authentic sourdough starter. Hoping that that meant he'd been unable to find any-one, I shaded my eyes from the sun with my hand and gazed out the window at Lombard Street—and immediately pulled back in a reflex action. A vehicle had zoomed by. The next car went by just as fast, and the next, each seeming like a near miss; there couldn't have been more than an arm's length separating us from the ten-thousand-libra machines thundering by in the opposite direction like stampeding, angry buffalo. A sudden swerve on the part of our driver—sneeze, heart attack, whatever—and we'd all morph from happy tourists to crushed tourists.

"Are you all right, honey?" the B-dweller in the seat next to me whispered.

I was unsuccessfully feeling around for a seatbelt. "The cars—from the sidewalk they look close when they pass each other—from in here they look *really* close."

"It takes some getting used to for A-dwellers, I've heard. You mostly have one-way streets?"

"And people movers. Crowded but reliably computerized."

She patted my hand, which was gripping the armrest between us. "My husband used to say, 'Danger makes life worth living.'"

"Did he?"

"Of course that was before the hang-glider malfunction, the poor dear."

The bus driver turned a corner in a wide arc, tilting us sideways and narrowly missing a pedestrian. I locked my gaze up, at the buildings and billboards. As minutes passed and nothing drastic happened, I loosened my grip on the armrest. The B-dweller next to me gave me a reassuring smile and went back to listening to Lard. I cracked the window open a bit and, wincing every so often at another close traffic call, settled back and let Lard's words wash over me and played the spot-the-differences game. As I had found out while searching for the Queen

Bee Inn, chance and man had done their bit in three-and-a-half decades.

Faded nineteenth-century building façades sat where I was used to seeing new construction that had followed our quake. Where the buildings looked the same, their occupants weren't. The familiar City Art Gallery had a drugstore and a shoe store in its place. Farther down the Embarcadero we entered Fisherman's Wharf, its piers as I remembered seeing them in old photographs, not a hint to be seen of the transit-boat marina that had taken their place in San Francisco A. Only Pier 39 looked the same with its tourist shops and restaurants.

When we stopped at a traffic light and the bus engine quieted for a moment, I could hear the seagulls thronging Pier 39, but missing from the cacophony of urban and sea-life sounds penetrating the open bus window was the *swoosh* of the people mover lines. In its place was the steady hum of car engines. But all the cars (if one ignored their inherent dangers) did make the town seem quite cheerful, the fruit-basket effect of the reds and greens and yellows boosted by the midday sun.

There were billboards on practically every building we passed, I noticed. Did we have quite so many?

And was there this much trash on the streets of *my* San Francisco?

The real question, I thought, leaning back and hastily removing my elbow from the armrest, having set it down on the arm of the friendly B-dweller in the adjoining seat, the real question was, would Mrs. Noor report cosmetic differences between Felix's life and mine—or *cosmic* differences? Did we part our hair on the opposite side and that was it, or was he a self-made trillionaire with a mansion with private beach access, two tennis courts, three saunas, and an orange tree grove?

He was *somewhere* nearby, according to the *Alter in the Area* tag on my identicard, going about his daily business. For all I knew, he could have been driving the eggplant-purple car that had carelessly changed lanes in front of the bus, making our driver slam on the brakes and jolting everyone forward. More likely, I thought, if he was anything like me, he'd be getting around on a bicycle, though now that I thought about it, where were all the bicycles? We had passed only a couple, nowhere near the number that thronged the streets of San Francisco A and kept us efficient, alert, and fit. The few bicyclists I did see sported tight-fitting clothing in bright colors, as if biking were an activity one needed to be specially dressed for, like going to the opera, and not a practical pursuit.

"My favorite actress," the B-dweller next to me elbowed me in the ribs and pointed.

We had stopped at a red traffic light under a billboard.

"You don't have them anymore, do you? Movie theaters."

"Nope," I said. Dashing in her khaki explorer's outfit and wide-brimmed hat, the movie star in the billboard ad swung jauntily on jungle vines from tree to tree, her long ice-white hair sailing behind her, a python loosely wrapped around her neck. With a start I recognized her as the traveler who had garnered attention in the crossing chamber, the one in the tangerine dress. So she was a B-dweller, after all, and a famous one at that.

"She's beautiful, isn't she? That's Gabriella Love. I've already seen *Jungle Nights* six—no, seven times back in New Jersey. I've never understood why movies went out of style in your Universe A. I thought you preferred group activities—more environmental and all. If you get a chance, honey, you should go see the movie while you're here."

The star of *Jungle Nights* was now on foot, trying to evade an energetic pack of angry monkeys. How curious it must be for people to recognize your face wherever you went, I thought. Even if an author achieved fame with his keystrokes, his visage remained hidden behind a curtain—

"Mint?"

Lard, having temporarily put down his microphone, was handing out treats. As I unwrapped the mint, my omni buzzed. I fumbled to answer it, got it tangled in its neck cord, and finally managed to flip it open. "Wagner," I hissed (thereby disproving anyone who claims a sibilant-free word can't be hissed), "Wagner, I thought you were at the Pretzel Makers competition."

"I am. The dough is rising and the judges are on a break. Listen to this. Baguette slicer. Four speed. Vertical cut, horizontal cut, lateral cut. What do you think?"

Wagner liked to try out new ideas on me. The focus this month at work was bread of all kinds, from buns to baguettes to brioches.

"What do New Appliances think?" I spoke more loudly than I meant to as I popped the mint into my mouth. The B-dweller next to me put a finger to her lips.

"Sorry. What do New Appliances think?" I repeated more quietly.

"They are looking into it. I asked them to design the slicer to look like a mock guillotine." He was standing in front of a door-sized pretzel (a fake one, I was almost sure) and had taken a Napoleonic stance, whether as a nod to his short stature or the French character of the baguette slicer, I couldn't tell.

"Not a bad idea," I whispered. "We wouldn't need to actually use any French in the user guide or the ads."

"Where are you anyway?" he asked as the bus went over a bump in the road and the omni and I flew up briefly.

"Sightseeing."

"You're aware of the Lunch-Place Rule, Felix, aren't you?"

"I'm nowhere near my apartment, the office, or Coconut Café. We're headed first to the old Golden Gate Bridge, then the Baker Beach Ferris wheel, then the zoo, Strawberry Hill, a peculiar part of Lombard Street that's crooked for some reason…" I remembered something. "I'll send along the Golden Gate Bridge write-up when I finish it."

"Good. I'm still working on arranging you-know-what." Just before Wagner disconnected, I caught a glimpse of a team of contestants hastily re-braiding the large pretzel behind him, which apparently was real and which had started to sag. I turned off the omni, mulling over that I still wasn't sure that I wanted anything to do with obtaining sourdough bread starter on the Universe B black market. The yeast strain responsible for the tangy bread enjoyed, as Lard had said, by the fifty-fivers of the California Gold Rush, as well as the builders of the bridge we were nearing, had been lost over the years in Universe A. The replacement was, everyone agreed, not that great. If we *were* able to get our hands on the starter for the Universe B sourdough, which I had yet to try, we'd probably have a hit on our hands with the new Bygone Times Sourdough Bread Maker. It was just that, Regulation 10 (workplace information) aside, I wasn't sure that it was right to underhandedly obtain a trade secret in order to produce our own version of it in Universe A. With any luck, I decided, Wagner would be unable to find anyone willing to sell the starter and the question would not come up at all. In the meantime it was probably safest to stay away from sourdough bread completely. No one could accuse me of wanting to bring a flavorful taste to the Universe A masses if I had never partaken of it myself.

"Folks, our first stop will be the old Golden Gate Bridge." Lard's microphone was back on. "The one and only, the original, the edifice that has lasted a hundred years. That is, if we ever get there in this traffic."

It was a relief when we finally reached the bridge. Navigating the steep San Francisco streets, awkwardly turning corners, the bus had rumbled and shook as if its tires were made of wood instead of rubber and I had gotten increasingly queasy. The driver took the bus across the bridge, an experience I would have otherwise enjoyed, maneuvered up a narrow, winding road, and pulled into the overlook parking lot and turned off the engine.

Lard offered a steadying hand and the words, "Please watch your step," to his passengers as we exited via three narrow steps to the ground. The bus driver already had his feet up and his omni tuned to a sports channel.

As I climbed the unpaved trail to the overlook, the gusty wind inflated my jacket like a life preserver, carrying with it the cool ocean air, and my nausea subsided by the time I reached the top. The overlook itself was sparsely populated. There was a lone macar tree, with its luxuriant insect-eating blossoms, and a couple of low bushes. A handful of tourists milled around taking photos and exploring Battery Spencer, a nineteenth-century gun battery standing guard over the Golden Gate, according to Lard. (The Golden Gate was the strait—the water entrance to the bay—but why golden, I'd never known. The bridge spanning the strait was built of cherry-red brick, the water was a deep blue, the city white, and the hills a dry brown.)

"Go to the bridge, Felix," Wagner had said before I'd left, "and write me some poetry." He didn't really mean poetry, of course, just some pretty words that we could incorporate into the ads, brochure and user guide for the Bygone Times Sourdough Bread Maker.

Nothing beats a first-person account of a place, Wagner had said.

He was right.

The cliff we were on rose above the bridge, the bay to the left, open ocean to our right, the city spread out beyond like a miniature of itself. Something was missing from the scene and it took me a moment to realize it was the transit ferryboats, which in Universe A crisscrossed the bay and connected the city to the surrounding suburbs and towns. Here only sailboats, clearly weekend diversions with their white sails swelling proudly in the wind, dotted the bay, along with a few tourist boats. On the open ocean side, the gated wall that protected the city from rising ocean levels peeked out of the water in a massive semicircle.

As to the bridge across which we had just rumbled—

The two turreted towers, with their famous red brick, soared up out of the water. A line of cars snaked across the drawbridge segment between the brick towers, to and from the cabled suspension side-spans. I could see tiny tourists ambling in and out of the towers and along the bridge sidewalks, which were lined with lampposts on both the bay and the open ocean side. A wide girder the same color as the cables—red, like the bricks—connected the upper levels of the two towers.

The last time I'd laid eyes on this scene, I had been about twelve. I realized I had been expecting the bridge to be smaller and less grand, like things remembered from childhood often are when you see them again as an adult.

I swatted a fly off my arm. *Their* Golden Gate Bridge was still here, and ours had been lost in the quake and not rebuilt right. For one thing, it wasn't a drawbridge at all—the new bridge curved in an elegant arc to accommodate ship traffic. It had exactly zero towers. People mover line number 88 crossed the bridge and allowed for an easy connection to the Marin Peninsula. It was a nice, practical bridge. There was not a thing wrong with it.

The fly came back and this time I smacked it flat.

A few strides brought me back to Lard's tour group, which stood gathered far closer to the edge of the cliff than seemed reasonable.

"—the brick towers were completed in fourteen months," Lard was saying. "Quite a feat." He had taken off his cap and was holding it in his hand. "The builders suspended a net under the bridge during the construction phase. Nineteen workers fell into the net and lived. Rumor has it they dubbed themselves members of the Halfway to Hell Club." He paused to let a loud seagull squawk away and I took a couple of photos to aid me in composing inspiring prose that would sell myriads of Bygone Times Sourdough Bread Makers. Lard went on, "The color of the cables and the girder, officially called international orange but which frankly looks more like rusty red to me, was chosen to match the tower bricks. Nowadays, my dear visitors, there's still plenty of work to be done to keep the bridge in shape. The rain, the fog, and the salty ocean air are constantly eroding the paint and crumbling the bricks."

"Can't you paint the cables with permanent paint? Make the bricks watertight?" an A-dweller in the group asked.

"That would be against our policy of historical authenticity. After all, there is only one of these bridges left." Lard gave a little sniff. "Caretakers who attend to the bridge are quite safe these days, of course. Best of all, we'll be able to view them at painting work, for a small fee."

A short murmur of dissatisfaction propagated through his audience, understandably, in my opinion. Having paid a solid price for the tour, I didn't see why additional fees should be snuck in; $350, the price of a nice book, had already been added to the tally on my identicard.

"Lard, honey, I don't think people want to pay any more money," said the sympathetic B-dweller from the bus.

"Yeah, can't we see the painters from the shore?" someone else said.

"I'll see what I can do," Lard consented.

"What about earthquakes? Has the bridge ever come close to falling down, like ours did?" It was an A-dweller in the group who had asked the question. (I was beginning to understand what the Lunch-Place Rule was about.)

"We do as much as we can to preserve the past," Lard said, straightening his tour-guide blazer with a two-handed tug, "but, yes, steel has been used to reinforce the frame to avoid an incident of the kind that befell the *other* bridge." He gave another sniff.

Well, really. He made it sound like it was our fault, the 8.1 earthquake that had crumbled the bricks of the Universe A bridge towers, as if we hadn't been careful enough. Not only unfair, but a downright insensitive thing to say to an audience of mostly A-dwellers. I wanted to retort, "Oh, yeah? What about Yosemite and Yellowstone? *We* haven't mucked up *our* national parks!" Ferris wheels at both parks, I'd heard, and at Yosemite motorized vehicles to take hikers up Half-Dome and a tourist-enticing elevator to the top of El Capitan with a death-defying drop *down*. "Now just a minute," I began, but Lard seemed not to hear. The tour group, as if of a single mind, was looking intently behind me.

I turned and beheld a silver flier silently bearing down on us. With a surprisingly gentle bump, given the windy conditions, it landed on a grassy ledge not too far away from where we were standing. One of the doors lifted up from the inside and two DIM officials in avocado-green uniforms jumped out one after the other. Briskly, single file, hands on hats to keep them from flying off in the wind, they strode toward our gathering point.

For a wild second I surmised they were here to take us to see the bridge painters at work.

"Is this the *See B on a Bus* tour, bus number five?" the one in front demanded.

"*See B* from *a Bus*," Lard corrected her, his mild tone belying his clear annoyance at this interruption of his tour. "And how can we help you?"

"Our records show you have a Citizen Felix Sayers in your party, is that correct?"

Lard thinned his lips. He looked around at his tour group. "Do we?"

"Uh—that's me," I volunteered. "I'm Citizen Sayers." My voice sounded odd, rather high in pitch.

The DIM officials took me by the elbow and led me to the flier.

[5]

CASE NUMBER 21

But I've done nothing wrong yet, I kept repeating to myself—there was no one to hear me in the small room where I found myself after being flown to a building south of the city, deposited onto the roof, and hurriedly led down a long staircase—hadn't broken Regulation 7 yet, hadn't contacted my alter or followed him or rifled through his trash—or even partaken in a single slice of sourdough bread as a prelude to breaking Regulation 10. Had Mrs. Noor called the nearest DIM bureau as soon as I'd left her office (very Miss Marple-*un*like behavior if true) to report my Regulation 7–breaking behavior? Client requesting information on alter under the pretense of being concerned that alter had already written *his* book, a lame sounding story indeed.

The DIM officials in the flier hadn't been very communicative. When, in an effort to draw them out, I asked if they were the ones who had tried to reach me at the Queen Bee Inn early this morning, the only reply was a brusque headshake. Somewhat reassuringly, I'd overheard one of them radio in, "Target acquired, on our way," and not "Suspect arrested," or anything of that sort.

I looked around the small room. White walls. An exam table in the middle, with accompanying instruments and paraphernalia. Also doctorly advice on several posters. All of the

furniture bore the label *Property of Palo Alto Citizen Health Center.*
I'd never heard of Palo Alto or their citizen health center, but
whoever they were, it was their chair I was sitting in.
After five long minutes, I heard a knock. Before I could
answer, the door opened and a B-dweller dressed all in white
came in. Without taking his eyes off the omni in his hand, he
walked over to the chair I was perched on. "My name is Chang.
I'm a nurse. It looks like there are twenty-two of you."

"No, only two," I said.

"Hmm?"

"Two."

He looked at me for the first time. "No, it definitely says here
there are twenty-two cases. You're Number 21. Citizen Felix
Sayers, just arrived from Universe A. Your health file should be
coming in any second—oh, here we go." His omni had beeped.
"By the way, sorry you had to come down to the health center
on such short notice."

"Notice? I was touring the city on a bus—"

"Right, I heard they had to send a flier to pick someone up.
Must have been disconcerting to have DIM officials swoop in
like that. Did you think you were on your way to a work camp?"

"I did, rather."

"Why don't you sit here," he smacked the padded exam
table, "and I'll measure your vitals. Dr. Gomez-Herrera should
be in at any moment."

"I think there's been a mistake—"

"You have nothing to worry about, Citizen Sayers. May I
call you Felix? You have nothing to worry about, Felix. This is
all just a precaution."

I hoisted myself up onto the table. I don't consider myself
short, or tall for that matter, of average height really, but my

legs swung over the edge without touching the floor. It was a tall table. Chang took my blood pressure, which must have been high, then my temperature, and finally, somewhat strangely, listened to my stomach. He tapped a few omni keys and left before I could get anything useful out of him.

I jumped off the table and went back to the chair.

Dr. Gomez-Herrera turned out to be an imposing B-dweller in her fifties who wore a grave expression that made me highly concerned for my well-being. She took a chair and a moment to glance over my health file, then said, "Sorry you had to come into the health center on such short notice, Citizen Sayers."

"They sent a flier to pick me up."

"Have you heard of the North American Pet Syndrome?"

"The—I'm sorry, the what?"

"The media refers to it as the pet bug, though that is a misleading term. It appeared in Universe A about a year ago."

I *had* heard of it. In fact, I seemed to recall seeing the headline on Mrs. Noor's desk. The malady, having started among Universe A pets living in the wild (giant squirrels and such), had found its way into human populations and was now on the verge of getting a foothold in Universe B. I was relieved, maybe even more so than when I realized I hadn't been brought to a work camp, that I wasn't Number 21 of some new, secret, universe-making experiment that had produced additional copies of me.

"A carrier crossed yesterday into B," Dr. Gomez-Herrera continued. "We have been trying to contact everyone who may have been exposed. Do you remember a—how did they describe it?—a dog-like creature in the chamber during your crossing? Overweight, white, pink eyes. An almost-dog."

"The animal touched my hand," I said, sitting up. "I wasn't trying to pet it or anything."

"I see."

"Does that mean I've caught the pet bug, Dr. Gomez-Herrera?"

She paused just enough for my panic to peak, then said, "It's not a bug. An insect is a bug. This is a virus. And to catch it you'd have to come into extended contact with the animal or its droppings. That doesn't seem to be the case here. Still—"

"The dog—pet—Murphina—didn't seem sick."

"An infected animal usually has only minor symptoms. An infected person, on the other hand, can experience heavy sneezing, loss of appetite, nausea, and intense facial itching." She leaned forward. "Have you noticed anything like that, Citizen Sayers?"

"No," I admitted.

Seeming almost disappointed, she sat back in her chair. "Some patients have also exhibited disorientation and abnormal behavior. But that's rare."

As I mulled over the phrase "abnormal behavior," which gave rise to images of patients frothing at the mouth being kept in locked rooms, Dr. Gomez-Herrera got to her feet.

"Wait," I stopped her on her way to the door. "So you'll test me for the pet bug just to be sure?"

"There are no tests, Citizen Sayers."

"None?"

"No. Medication, yes." She paused with one hand on the doorknob. "You understand—we do not have the North American Pet Syndrome here in Universe B. *Did* not. This almost-dog is the first case we've seen."

And that, finally, explained the flier and the urgency with which I had been whisked to the health center. I didn't think it had all been for my own good. Feeling the need to apologize for the unwelcome contribution from fellow A-dwellers, even if they were only viruses and pets, I said, "Sorry we brought the pet bug over."

"Not to worry, citizen. We'll sort out who is infected and who is not."

"How?"

"Quarantine."

[6]

THE QUARANTINE

t was afternoon by the time I found myself alone again.

After Dr. Gomez-Herrera had left me staring open-mouthed after her, Chang, the nurse, had returned with the pet bug medication, a thimbleful of purple paste that was almost as hard to swallow as the idea of a forty-eight-hour quarantine. Chang had promised to contact Franny and Trevor at the Queen Bee Inn to have my luggage sent over, then led me to a small wing on the top floor of the health center; whether the guard posted at the double doors was there to prevent people from going in or out, I had no idea. I followed Chang down the corridor, catching glimpses through half-open doors of rooms already occupied, presumably by the other twenty-one patients who'd come in contact with the pet Murphina. My room was at the far end. It looked like I was among the last to be found and brought in.

The next couple of hours, now dressed in a salmon-tinted patient gown, I spent lying in bed receiving far more attention than I've ever received at a medical establishment. I continued to feel fine, as I told Chang and other personnel who kept coming into the room to ask questions—"Does your face itch?"—"Have you been sneezing?"—"Are you feeling nauseous at all?"—and made sure to refrain from accidentally scratching any body part in their presence.

As the door swung shut behind Chang for the third time, I eyed my jacket, which was hanging on a door hook along with a bag containing the rest of my clothes; one of its pockets, I'd remembered, held a chocolate bar. There's something about being in a health center that makes you want to stuff your face: The starkness of the white walls. The utilitarian furniture. The unnatural cleanliness of the place. The aura of other people's sickness. Besides, no one had warned me about dietary restrictions or brought me a snack.

I got up to fetch the chocolate bar, then got back in bed. Lying next to me was the questionnaire Chang had left regarding my whereabouts since my arrival in Universe B. I ate most of the chocolate bar (no loss of appetite for me so far) and then looked the questionnaire over. Among other things, it posed some *very* personal questions regarding possible exchanges of bodily fluids. I must have been their easiest patient ever. Potentially full of contagious germs, loose on the streets of San Francisco B, free to do anything, what had I done really—fondled a few paper books and stared out a bus window.

Halfway through the questionnaire, I took a break to finish the chocolate bar. I tossed the empty wrapper in the direction of the bedside bin, missed, and had to get up and pick up the wrapper off the floor and drop it into the bin. A quarantine, of all things. I would be a guest at the Palo Alto Health Center until Monday—longer if I came down with facial itching and heavy sneezing—with nothing to do but wait until I got *out* of the Palo Alto Health Center to begin my sleuthing.

At least I had Noor & Brood working on the case.

I was absentmindedly rubbing my lip (where there was a chocolate smudge), when I realized that the action could be misconstrued as scratching and ceased immediately. In response to my new fear of itching, my face and scalp instantly developed thousands of prickly spots, like ants crawling all over my skin. I busied myself with the questionnaire.

🦆

By late afternoon, interest in me having somewhat dissipated and the chocolate bar having long been digested, I decided to venture out of my cramped, windowless room in search of dinner. I put on a pair of padded sock-slippers, made sure my gown was tied securely in the back, and went out into the hallway. The math B-dweller from the crossing was standing at the far end, by a door marked *Cafeteria*. She too was in a patient gown and padded socks, and was talking into her clunky omni. As I neared she gave me a nervous grin as she carried on her conversation. "—But Arni, isn't the direct approach the best?—No, I know we have to be careful...I can be subtle. What? Yes, I do know *how*, Arni—"

After a brief internal debate about the wisdom of eating in a room filled with quarantine patients, some of whom might actually *be* infected with the pet bug, hunger won and I went into the cafeteria. Set out on a long table covered with a plastic tablecloth was the usual warmed-over health center fare, but having essentially skipped lunch, I wasn't feeling particularly choosy. I picked up a tray and selected a turkey sandwich, rice chips, and a pudding, then looked around for a seat. Murphina's owner was sitting alone near the cafeteria windows, his willowy form bent forward as he ate his dinner. Like everyone in the room who wasn't serving food, he was wearing the salmon-tinted patient gown; the revealing and rather coarse garment made me wish I'd thought to pack a robe in my luggage, which had yet to arrive from the Queen Bee Inn.

He looked up as I approached. "Sorry about the quarantine," he said, making room for my tray across from his lasagna plate. I sat down. At the very least I wanted to find out why a grown man takes his pet along when visiting the other universe. "Felix Sayers," I said, keeping my hands firmly on the tray as a precaution against potential pet-bug-bearing handshakes. "I'm just a tourist."

"I'm Granola James. I'm here on business—"

"No *coffee?*"

I turned my head to see Gabriella Love, the movie star I had shared a crossing chamber with and seen on multiple billboards, expressing dissatisfaction to a cafeteria staff member. "You cannot be serious. No, I do *not* want tea." She grudgingly accepted something and strode over to a free table, clicking her high-heeled slippers, her satiny pink robe streaming behind her. (Apparently she *had* thought to pack a robe in her luggage.) For a moment I wondered how the famous actress had ended up here with the rest of us mortals, since she didn't seem the type that would have paused to pet a pet, but then I remembered that I had seen her in Granola James's car. She was certainly ignoring Citizen James now. She wasn't the only one. As I opened a mayonnaise packet and spread it on the thin white bread in an effort to make the dry-looking turkey sandwich more palatable, I couldn't help but feel the stares. At the neighboring table, a couple of kids were having a grand time while their parents looked grim and every so often sent a displeased look in our direction. Feeling sorry for the man, who was (like the almost-dog Murphina and her viruses) a fellow A-dweller, I asked Citizen James, "So where's Murphina?"

"At the vet, quarantined like we are, poor thing. I hope she likes the food."

I eyed my sandwich and removed a wilted lettuce leaf. "So what brings you two to Universe B?"

"Business in Carmel. As to Murphina, I take her everywhere. She's a useful and well-behaved animal. We'd planned to take a flier down to Carmel today, but when Murph woke me up this morning, I could tell she wasn't feeling well. I took her to the vet. Next thing I knew, I was being rushed here."

"How did she catch the pet bug anyway?"

Clearly having been asked that question many times, he answered in short, ready sentences, lightly tapping his fork against his lasagna plate. "We live in Napa Valley. There's a wooded area behind the house. Giant squirrels like the trees. Murph and I take a walk every day. Frankly, she needs the exercise." The hand with the fork hovered for a moment. "But when she comes across squirrel droppings in the woods, she has a tendency to, well, eat them. No one is perfect."

"This is silly," said the math woman, having apparently finished her conversation with Arni, whoever he was, and lowering herself into the free chair between us. She planted her tray on the round table, causing dishes to clatter. "Why don't we detect diseases *before* they spread from one universe to the other? Instead we get the same old questions when we cross, the purpose of the visit, what's our identicard balance, does the traveler have an alter in the area—as if it's humanly possible not to at least sneak a peek at your alter, if you have one—"

She stopped, as if she'd said something she hadn't meant to. I wondered if she thought one of us—James or I—looked old enough to have an alter. I glanced over at Citizen James, but his lean countenance and slick black hair made it impossible to pinpoint his age; he could have been thirty or fifty.

"Never mind that," she said and reached for a lemon packet from the bowl in the center of the table. She squeezed it into her glass of ice tea. "Pleased to meet you—"

"Granola James."

"Pleased to meet you, Citizen James."

"Call me James. Or Granola if you must."

They shook hands.

"I'm Bean. And Felix, we met yesterday of course—"

I shook her hand, pleased that she had taken the trouble to find out my name. Was there a chance she had been the one who'd called this morning at the Queen Bee Inn looking for me? If so, why didn't she leave her name? And who was the other mysterious caller, the curly-haired, prominent-nosed fellow described by Franny?

"At least our quarantine is only forty-some hours," Bean, examining her soup, was saying, "and not forty *days*, which is how they used to do it in the Middle Ages. Whole ships kept in isolation to ensure no one on board was carrying the plague. We should be able to do better nowadays, though. Detect diseases rather than have quarantines. It would be an interesting math problem."

James and I stared at her. "Math problem, did you say?" I said.

She took a tentative sip of her soup, then reached for the pepper shaker. "Every problem is a math problem at heart. Some are just trickier than others. Detecting the pet bug—not one of the trickier problems, I imagine—whatever contraption we'd build to do it, what will it measure? A quantity. Body temperature. The number of sneezes per hour, or viruses in a phlegm sample. It would then compare the measured number to a threshold—another number—and make a yes-no decision—a binary one—about whether you have the pet bug or not."

"Sounds quite doable when you put it that way, Bean," said James. "An excellent nature name, by the way. Much better than Granola in every way. So what are you? Coffee, vanilla, jelly, cocoa, green...?"

"No idea. My parents are Passivists."

"What do you mean?" I asked. I shifted my position in the chair as I reached for a rice chip, then had to pull the patient gown down to cover my knees.

"Passivists believe the branching between A and B was caused by a person."

"It was," I said. "By Professor Singh. He made a copy of the universe in his basement laboratory. Everyone learns that in first grade."

"No. I mean, yes, everyone does learn that in first grade." She dipped a piece of the thin bread in her soup, realized it was too soggy, and left it in the bowl. "Passivists don't subscribe to the idea that you can make a universe in a lab. According to them, people create universes when they do things without taking into account consequences, like making a careless remark or sleeping in late or running a stop sign."

I noticed that James's fork had paused on its way from his lasagna to his mouth.

"There were Passivists at the crossing terminal," I said. I remembered that she had seemed uncomfortable watching DIM officials ask the Passivists to leave the terminal area. "One of them was carrying a potted sunflower. But what does passivity have to do with names?"

"My parents chose my name by sticking a pin into a list of nature names—the ones for newborn uniques, though usually people go through and choose a name they like. The names are supposed to 'evoke the sights, scents, sounds, and savories of nature,'" she quoted, stumbling a little over the copious *s* sounds in the sentence. "I'm the savory. Thyme—my brother—is the scent, and my sister Cricket is the sound. There was no fourth child, but he or she would have been a sight. At least they are all easy to spell. Well, except for Thyme. It's spelled like the herb."

James put his fork down. "Listen—Professor Singh's work aside, I don't think it matters all that much. If there *are* other universes, then successfully avoiding the responsibility of choosing your child's name means that's merely the case in *this* universe. In some other universe your parents named you Jane and in another, Hildegard."

"Thanks." She pushed around the limp vegetables in her soup. "So what brings you gentlemen to Universe B?"

James apologized again for all the trouble he had caused, and I said, "Curiosity."

Someone in the room sneezed, and we all turned to look at the guilty culprit. A teenager with large mismatched earrings and spiky eyebrows looked aghast at the possibility that she might have to stay beyond the forty-eight hours of the quarantine.

Bean cleared her throat. "How do you like it here so far? Other than the quarantine, obviously."

I took a moment to consider the question, because, really, what could one say about a place where one has spent only a day or two, but James, clearly more forthcoming with his opinions, said, "I've got to admit—I like all the cars. Rented one myself. A green convertible. Fun to drive."

"You mean even though it's environmentally irresponsible? I have a car too, bought it secondhand. From a bubble-gum maker. But how would I get around without my Beetle?"

"The public transportation system in San Francisco A works quite efficiently." As soon as I said it, I realized that it wasn't a particularly diplomatic statement to make. Almost pompous, in fact. Hoping she wasn't offended, I said, "Well, you've seen it. No private vehicles allowed downtown, only people movers and bicycles. It's clean, safe, and efficient."

Bean gave up on her soup and picked up a donut from a plate on her tray. "But is it faster?"

"It is if the alternative is that you are stuck in crawling traffic."

"All right, I'll give you that."

"Though I did take a bus tour of the city this morning and discovered I disliked that particular mode of public transportation," I admitted, following her lead and pushing away the remnants of the turkey sandwich and reaching for the pudding instead. "Too bouncy. Seasickness inducing. I mean bus-sickness inducing."

"I recommend a boat tour of the bay. Oddly it's not too seasickness inducing. Speaking of which," she added, gently shaking the powdered sugar off the donut, "do either of you have any pet bug symptoms—sneezing and such?" She took a careful bite. "Remind me to avoid donuts while in here. Powdered sugar can be a major nasal irritant."

🦆

After the dishes had been cleared away, Dr. Gomez-Herrera and Chang returned with the evening dose of the medication. There was something somber about the procedure and, as I waited in line, I was keenly aware that this little, patient-gown-clad group of people may have brought with them a new disease to Universe B and changed the course of history. At least it was an inconvenient rather than an incurable disease. Bean, clearly struck by the same thought, commented in an undertone from behind me in line, "One of these days, I bet, there'll be a deadly epidemic. Not a good thing in itself, obviously, but it would lead to a race for the cure between Universe A and Universe B scientists, and that would have the effect of loosening DIM's hold on research."

"Even so, I'm glad Murph and I aren't responsible for anything like that," I heard James say.

I took two paper cups, one with the medication, one with water, and proceeded to drink them in turn. Bean was right. Surely not even DIM's Council for Science Safety, charged with enforcing Regulation 19 (science & research) could stop such a scenario. Not once people started dropping like flies. But there had to be a better way, I thought, barely managing to avoid gagging on the medication, which would have been embarrassing, a better way than waiting for a deadly epidemic to free up the sciences a bit. I crinkled the two empty paper cups together, threw them in the trash bin, then turned to hear Dr. Gomez-Herrera say, "Let me know if you experience any side effects," and realized I had tuned out part of her speech.

I stuck around the cafeteria for a while, listening to twenty-one citizens fervently discuss the day's events. Not surprisingly, everyone was highly dissatisfied with the unexpected detour from normal life, especially Gabriella Love, who declared, "This is *absolutely* unacceptable. I have a new *project* I'm working on." She spotted me and gave me a long look, probably because I was standing next to James, to whom she still hadn't spoken a word.

I exchanged a few words with Quarantine Case 11, the teenager with the spiky eyebrows, who was bewailing a party she was missing, and also with the more-mature Quarantine Case 3, who admitted to being an insurance salesman in town for a bi-universal convention but did not reveal further details about himself, as his alter was also in town for the same convention and they were not on speaking terms. Prodded, I introduced myself in a couple of terse sentences, one of which was, "I'm just a tourist," a phrase I was becoming tired of saying; but it would have been unthinkable (though it would have surely generated more interest in my audience) had I said, "I'm here to spy on my double. It's illegal, but a lot of things are."

Although nobody flung any direct accusations at him, it all must have been very uncomfortable for James. After a while he moved to the back of the room and stood there silently, arms crossed across his patient gown, meeting everyone's stares and winning my admiration. Me, I would have been a nervous wreck.

When Gabriella Love finally walked over to him, I overheard her say, "This proves that you should never take *pets* on a business trip, don't you think?" which struck me as outrageously rude even for a movie star.

He held his ground. "I have a feeling things will work out for the best."

"And what about the other?" I heard her say, but James's reply was lost as the teenager Quarantine Case 11 shrieked loudly, having put two and two together and realized that she would be missing Sunday night's party as well.

My backpack awaited me on the health center bed, along with a handwritten note from the Queen Bee Inn. Mostly it was the usual get-well-soon stuff, but Franny had added a P.S.: *I've enclosed an item that might help pass the time nicely.* I sat down on the bed and unzipped the backpack, which someone had repacked with far more care than I put into it originally. The item Franny had enclosed was lying on top of my folded clothes.

No one had ever given me a paper book as a present before.

The cover had the title *Why Didn't They Ask Evans?* on it, and a man stepping over cliff edge into sea-mist nothingness. An Agatha Christie, one I hadn't read in years. I seemed to recall that it was a perfect companion on a cold and rainy winter day, preferably in a comfortable armchair in front of a warm, crackling fireplace. Probably not bad for a medical quarantine either.

After a futile effort to fluff up the health center pillow, I settled back as comfortably as I could and, after sending silent thanks to innkeepers Franny and Trevor for remembering that I liked mystery classics, began reading the adventures of one Bobby Jones, fourth son of the vicar of Marchbolt, and his sleuthing partner, Lady Frankie.

[7]

A Possession Goes Missing

Sunday morning a sharp buzz woke me up. Wagner.

"Felix," he boomed, "I heard you've been quarantined, what an unusual thing to happen on your vacation. Are you all right?"

Cranky and blurry-eyed and not in the mood for answering questions, I pulled the blanket tighter around me and muttered into the omni, "I'm fine, Wagner, do you mind if I call you back?"

"Are you sick, then?"

"No. Just—not up."

"Sorry. Well, get back to me."

I let the omni fall back on the bedside table and willed myself out of bed and into the narrow shower. The hot water slowly brought me back to life and a thought entered my brain—how had Wagner found out I was quarantined? Privacy Regulation 3 prohibited the Palo Alto Health Center from releasing our names to the media, or at least I hoped so, because how uncomfortable would it be if Felix B dropped by to bring flowers or a fruit basket? Most likely, I reassured myself, Wagner had heard about the quarantine from one of his professional contacts and not read about it in the news.

There was a more sinister possibility—that Wagner was one of the out-of-uniform DIM agents peppered around San

Francisco A (and no doubt around San Francisco B as well) whose job it was to make sure DIM's rules and regulations were adhered to. They could be accountants, hot-dog sellers, sidewalk sweepers, mortuary workers, pizza delivery persons. And my boss? Being in charge of a company that designed, marketed, and sold quality culinary products, from spatulas to toaster ovens, all with user guides supplied by yours truly, was as good a cover as any. Wagner, who went around the office brimming with new ideas and infecting (though I didn't like to use that word in a health center) everyone with his enthusiasm, a DIM agent. Impossible.

I turned off the water and reached for a towel. What with Chang and other nurses coming in every few hours to check my vitals, the night had passed in strange, fragmented dreams. One particularly vivid episode had a busload of alters chasing me as I worked furiously on the first pages of my mystery novel. I was a pet in the dream, a biologically unlikely cross between a dog and the partially extinct elephant, and kept trying to type with my paws while staying ahead of the alters, until I finally woke up with a start.

Sadly, I couldn't remember the plot of the chase-worthy novel.

I put on a clean patient gown and picked up the omni off the bedside table. The neck strap was tangled up and, as I untangled it, I noticed that the little green light that was always on was not on. Now that I thought about it, I seemed to remember that the omni had been displaying increasingly urgent messages that its battery was waning; the brief call from Wagner must have drained the last few drops of power. I shook the omni in a last-ditch effort to fix it the low-tech way, failed, and left it on the bedside table.

The cafeteria was mostly empty, with sullen faces taking up one or two tables; early risers had breakfasted already and the lone health center employee staffing the cafeteria told me crabbily, "I'm clearing everything away in ten minutes. I'm not running a hotel here."

Bean and James were nowhere to be seen. I hoped they hadn't come down with the pet bug.

As I sat down with my food, Chang swooped in with a paper cup, watched me drain it, then left. I washed away the grainy feel of the pet bug medication with orange juice and hastened to finish breakfast under the ill-humored stare of the cafeteria employee. No doubt Felix B was having a more enjoyable Sunday breakfast, damn him. If only I'd been able to find out something about the guy beforehand—like where he lived and where he worked and if he had a fancy car and a house and a girlfriend...DIM regulations clamped down on information dispersal, which was a good thing when it came to keeping your own life private but a pain when you wanted to burrow into someone else's.

"Citizen Sayers?" Gabriella Love was standing next to me, hair matted, eyes puffy, but still stylish in the satiny pink robe and high-heeled slippers. She was clutching two mugs. "Did James find you? He's looking for you." She offered me one of the mugs.

"Thanks," I said, accepting the mug and wondering what I had done to merit her attention. "I haven't seen him. I just got up."

"It's tea. Peach." She made a face. "I'm planning on talking to someone about that—I *need* coffee to get me started in the morning. And also about getting a different room. I prefer to wake up to natural light, and my room doesn't have a single window. The situation is *intolerable*."

"The quarantine must be especially difficult for you."

"Well, yes—what do you mean?"

"You said that you had a project you're working on, a new movie, I assume? Everyone must be relying on you to be there."

Her face reddened from chin to forehead and nothing came out of her mouth for a moment. Then she screeched, "Are you trying to be funny?" and, turning, stormed out of the cafeteria, sloshing a beige dollop of tea onto the floor on her way out. The cafeteria employee sent a displeased look after her.

I'd heard movie stars were temperamental. For a brief moment I was glad there was only one of *her*. Just my luck to be in the same universe.

Once back in my room I saw the omni lying on the bedside table where I had left it and remembered that its battery was dead. Before heading out to find an infoterminal to contact Mrs. Noor of the Noor & Brood Investigative Services, something made me open my backpack. I had taken to studying daily the photograph which had accompanied Aunt Henrietta's porcelain dolphins, probably in an effort to convince myself that it really was real. I unvelcroed the side pocket of the backpack and reached in.

The photo was gone.

[8]

I GET
MUDDLED

Having searched the whole of my room twice, as if the photo might have jumped out on its own and landed under the no-frills health center bed, I gave up and went into the hallway. There was an infoterminal near the main door of the isolation wing, next to the guard who stood leaning against the wall staring into space. At my approach, probably worried that I was contagious, he took two hurried, big steps to the other side of the door and left me to it.

Before calling Mrs. Noor, I took a look at the news. Yesterday, on the detective's desk, I had seen large headlines spreading pet bug phobia; today the subject matter was nowhere to be found. Instead there was an inflammatory story about partially extinct animals (officials had decided that it wasn't a good idea to attempt to squeeze a pair of male and female elephants into a crossing chamber) and the headlines squawked, *Is it fair that elephants roam Universe A while Universe B zoos sit empty? Why don't A-dwellers want to share? We'd like a giraffe!* and so on. I could only assume that the pet bug was considered a managed problem or, more likely, that DIM didn't want a panicked public, given that the pet bug story had turned out to be true and not merely a rumor.

Rubbing my forehead, which had started to throb, I wondered again how Wagner had found out I was quarantined.

I really should call him back, I thought; he was my boss and a friend and was concerned about me. And wasn't there someone else I had meant to call, someone important?

I stretched my back, stiff from standing hunched over the infoterminal. It struck me that I hadn't accomplished much in Universe B other than managing to lose my Y-day photo.

Felix B had written a book. No, he hadn't written a book. Yes he had, no he hadn't.

Did it matter, really? The whole issue suddenly seemed silly, like the memory of my nightmare exposed as foolishness by the morning sun, its intangible reality receding and making room for the voice of daytime reason and light.

I was struck by the cleverness and beauty of that description.

Then another thought struck me.

Of course. It was all so simple.

I had been in a bookstore just yesterday—if the man had written any books, I would have seen them. My troubles were over. I laughed out loud, then stopped because the sound made my head hurt worse.

A face, the security guard's, appeared on the other side of the glass square situated at eye level in the door, then disappeared just as quickly. I turned to go and almost ran into Bean.

"Hello, Bean of the Passivist parents and believer that math underlies everything."

She looked at me, then shrugged off whatever was on her mind. "Do you want to go for a walk? I figured out how to get to the roof."

"Why not? Maybe it will help my headache."

"The stairs are this way and around the corner. My room doesn't have a window, does yours?" She was talking and walking rather fast, it seemed to me. "I feel like we're in a submarine, not that I've ever been in one. Well, I suppose I have, there's the one that's the naval museum—do you have the museum in Universe A?—I forget which pier it's moored at—anyway, I feel cooped up and I have a project I should be working on. No, don't ask me what it is, I can't say. It's against the *rules*."

"What isn't, these days?" I said, trying to keep up.

"Calculating pi to a ridiculously impractical number of digits. Taking belly dancing classes. Eating ice cream." She shrugged. "Heaps of fun things are not against the rules."

I stopped to retie my gown, which had started to sag in the back, allowing my undershirt to be seen, and noticed we were in front of James's room. "James is looking for me, I've heard," I whispered, "but I've decided he's the most likely of us to be infected."

"Here, let me help you. I feel sorry for him, you know. Everybody seems to dislike him."

She seemed very interested in James's problems.

"People who take pets along when traveling are just inviting trouble," I pointed out as she pulled the sash of the gown tight in the back, making me end the sentence with a gasp. "Unless he was already exhibiting abnormal behavior by bringing Murphina," I amended my statement. "You know what really worries me? If we did start acting strangely and abnormally, how would we know if it was because of the pet bug or because we lost one too many brain cells during the crossing?"

Dr. Gomez-Herrera came out of James's room studying a chart, looked up, and asked how we were doing.

"Feeling a bit cooped in," Bean said.

"I've had a breakthrough regarding *his* book. It's all well and good. Wait—I've just remembered Aunt Hen's photo is missing. That, and my head hurts." I hiccupped.

Dr. Gomez-Herrera sent a sharp look in my direction, made a quick, illegible note on her chart, then hurried along into the next room. Bean and I proceeded to the end of the hallway, through a door marked *Health Center Employees Only*, and up a narrow staircase. At the top, a heavy door opened onto a wide, flat roof, the same one where the flier had deposited me yesterday. Squinting against the bright light, I joined Bean at the railing. The air was dry and warm. Neighborhoods lay packed between us and the bay, residential areas intertwined with shops and restaurants and offices where citizens went about their usual business. With a start I realized that it was, in fact, the place of *my* usual business.

"We're in Redwood Grove," I said, surprised.

"It's Palo Alto," Bean shook her head.

"No, it's not."

"We are in the Palo Alto Health Center, Felix. This is their railing."

"I'm telling you, it's Redwood Grove." I looked around trying to spot the waterside complex that housed my small ground-floor apartment, but had trouble orienting myself. "Over there," I pointed, "yes, I'm pretty sure that's where my bicycle and I catch a people mover every morning. The people mover takes us downtown, then I bike to my office at Wagner's Kitchen. And every afternoon I bike back to the station, hop on the people mover, and come back."

"Redwood—oh, I know. Town name changes, one of the Department of Information Management's first projects. To avoid inter-universe confusion and for an additional layer of privacy. For some reason they didn't bother with large cities, only with small towns. Imagine the paperwork involved."

I draped myself over the railing. "Do you think that if we spit straight down there's any chance we might infect someone and cause all sorts of trouble?"

"Are you feeling all right, Felix?"

"Look at them," I gestured at the pedestrians in the street below us. "They're like ants in a beehive—anthill—rushing this way and that, here and there. Not interacting, just passing each other without a glance." The throbbing in my head was making it hard to think. "Can you imagine in some small town a hundred years ago, walking by another person without a word or a nod—not even robbing them, at least? Sometimes I wish I'd lived in the old days, when everything was slower and no one had to rush, when there was time to think things over."

"Isn't this what life is all about?" was her take on the bustling street below. "Moving from place to place, from activity to activity. You stop and you're dead."

That was somewhat morbid of her, I felt, especially in a health center.

"I'm a non-Passivist. I believe in getting things done," she explained. "An Activist, if you will."

"I'm a duplicate."

She turned her head to look at me.

"I have an alter," I clarified, unnecessarily.

"You know, it's not anything anyone would guess. You don't look old enough."

"Thanks, but I'll be thirty-five tomorrow, instead of six months from now. I just found that out a few weeks ago. Long story. The point is—I have an alter. And he may have already beaten me to it and written my book. No, wait," I said, grabbing hold of the sides of my head and trying to wrestle a thought out of my muddled brain. "I solved that one already. If Felix had a book I would have seen it in the Bookworm—why is it called that, do paper books have worms, like apples sometimes do?"

"A book? I thought you wrote user guides for Wagner's Kitchen."

"That's just my real-life job," I said testily.

"So that's why you came here, to see if he wrote a book. I was wondering. What kind of book?"

"A mystery novel."

"You've written one, then?"

"I'm still working out the plot," I said haughtily. "In my head."

"*There* you are."

Chang was standing behind us. "Dr. Gomez-Herrera says you're not feeling yourself this morning, Felix. I'm afraid you've come down with the pet bug. Let's go downstairs and see what we can do to make you feel better. Besides, no patients allowed on the roof."

[9]

UNIVERSE MAKER

The fog in my brain, which turned out to be not a symptom of the North American Pet Syndrome but a side effect of the medication, dissipated by morning with an adjustment of the dose and I got up my normal self and called Noor & Brood before breakfast from the hallway infoterminal.

"We found him," Mrs. Noor said after I explained where I was and that I'd be getting out of the health center today.

"Where?"

"What I can tell you for now is that he is single and resides in apartment 003 in building J at the Egret's Nest Apartment Complex in Palo Alto. That's near the bay."

"Interesting," I said.

"As to his job—"

"Yes?" I said, my heart stopping.

"He is a chef."

"He's a what?"

"A chef at the newly renovated Organic Oven Restaurant downtown."

"Huh. Anything else?"

"We'll keep digging," she promised, waved bye, and disconnected.

Some people, I suppose, might wonder why I didn't try to contact Felix B then and there and claim him as a long-lost family member—but I bet those people don't have alters. It was simple. Regulation 7 was just an excuse. I was afraid of finding out that he'd done a better job of living my life.

At least, I reflected as I turned away from the infoterminal, it seemed he had a real-world occupation and wasn't spending his days penning mysteries.

The same was true for me, of course.

I headed to the cafeteria and upon walking in saw two uniformed DIM officials at a table by the door. They seemed to be taking statements and didn't look up as I walked past. Sitting across from them was Quarantine Case 15, the father of the family with the two kids. As I walked by, I heard him say, "— we can't talk about it, is this what you are saying—"

"That is correct, Citizen Doolittle."

"—and we have to sign where?—"

I continued past to the food table and picked up a croissant, there not being anything that fell into the cheese-chocolate-or-nuts category of foods that I could taste, and a reddish tea. Bean was sitting as far away as possible from the DIM officials, which considering the size of the cafeteria, was not very far.

"What's going on over there?" I asked her, placing my tray down across from her fruit plate. My head had stopped throbbing, which was a nice change; I had spent most of yesterday, after our rooftop excursion, holed up in my room with a "Do Not Disturb" sign on the door.

"The DIMs? They are making everyone sign information-halt agreements before we leave."

"About the pet bug?"

She speared a strawberry on her plate with a fork. "Yup. We can't talk about the pet bug or the quarantine."

"To the media?"

"Or anyone else."

"Surely they don't mean *anyone?*"

"Haven't you ever had to sign a highly restrictive information-halt agreement?"

"But—I've already talked to two people about it, my boss and a private det—and someone else."

"They had me sign as soon as I came in the door and tried to give me a cover story, which was that I was admitted to the health center due to laryngitis." She picked up her tea mug and clutched it with both hands. "I told them laryngitis wouldn't work since—like you—I'd already talked to someone, a fellow graduate student, and he—Arni—would have noticed if I'd been unable to talk. That seemed to annoy them, but it's not my fault they waited 'til Monday morning to have us sign. So, it's not laryngitis, but suspected appendicitis. Of course," she took a serene sip of the tea, "there's the small matter of me already having told Arni about the pet bug when I called to tell him I'd be late coming into the Bihistory Institute today, if they let me out. I didn't feel compelled to mention that to the DIMs."

The officials had finished with quarantine cases 15 and 16 and now had their kids at the table. I heard the younger of the kids exclaim, "Ooh, a secret."

"So they want the story to die down," I said, peering into my mug and sloshing the tea around. "At least there'll be no lawsuits against James. After all, it's hardly the man's fault Murphina caught the pet bug," I added, though I was irked that the pet bug quarantine had so completely thwarted my plan to stay off the radar of local DIM officials. Hoping they wouldn't ask me too many questions, I was prepared to tell them that I was looking forward to riding the Baker Beach Ferris wheel.

Bean, who also seemed discomfited by the presence of the DIM officials, gave an almost imperceptible shrug and speared another berry. "Tell me about your childhood, Felix. What was it like?"

I sat up a bit in my chair. She wanted to know more about me. "Well," I said, blowing out my chest and deciding to begin at the beginning, "I was born in Carmel. A year or two later my parents quit their art gallery jobs, adjusted some paperwork—like I said, it's a long story, ask me about it some other time—and we moved to San Francisco. After high school—I'll tell you my high school stories another time too—I went off to the San Diego Four-Year and my parents moved back to Carmel. They opened their own art gallery but died in a boat accident shortly after. As for me, after I got out of school, I got a job putting together user manuals at Wagner's Kitchen and have been doing that ever since. That's my history in a nutshell. Speaking of history, that's your field of study, isn't it?" I added, taking a cautious sip of the tea.

"Bihistory is more related to what used to be called physics than to history."

"Oh. Because I was going to ask you my indoor plumbing question. When was it invented? I've always wondered which of my ancestors had to, er—squat in fields and who got to sit down." I noticed that the DIM officials were now interviewing Gabriella Love, their avocado uniforms presenting quite a contrast to her pink robe. She didn't look too pleased about being held up on her way to the food table.

"That's a math problem," Bean said of the plumbing question.

"Because everything is a math problem."

"Exactly. How many ancestors do you think you had in the year, let's say, one?"

"One what?" Having decided that it was either hibiscus or African rooibos, not cherry, I had more of the tea.

"Year one. You know, one BC, skip zero, *one* AD, two AD, and so on."

"Oh, year *one*, I see. How many ancestors did I have? I don't know, a few thousand or so?" I broke a piece off the croissant and began eating.

She reached for a knife and a fork and methodically attacked the crescent-shaped melon wedge on her plate. "You have two parents"—she sliced the wedge in half—"four grandparents"—cut, cut into quarters—"and eight great-grandparents"—cut, cut, cut, cut. "The number of ancestors doubles in each generation going back in time, a new generation appearing every thirty years or so." She paused to eat one of the tiny great-grandparent melon pieces. "In twenty centuries we have about sixty generations. Starting with you and doubling the number of people in each step in a geometric progression, we get two, four, eight, sixteen, and so on, all the way to two raised to the sixtieth power. That, Felix, is a *very* large number, more than a billion billion people." She went back to eating the melon.

"But wait," I protested. "How can that be? There aren't a billion billion people *now*, even with two universes, much less in the ancient world. I can't possibly have had that many ancestors."

"Duplicates. Shared branches in the family tree. Your parents might have had the same great-great-*great*-grandfather, for instance. People used to marry their cousins all the time."

"Duplicates."

"Well, er—yes. Which prunes down your family tree and intertwines its branches. Because, of course, the number of people in the world tends to get smaller as you go back in time. All the way back to that one curious toddler who was just a tad smarter than the rest of the kids in her ape family. Just think how much *she* must have vexed her parents."

"History is always interesting," I said, chewing on the croissant and thinking that it needed butter. "All those things that happened to all those people."

"I find it depressing."

"Why?"

"For one thing, there's never a happy ending. Everyone's dead."

"There is that. Can you pass the butter?"

"Anyway, to answer your question, with that many ancestors in your family tree, you are pretty much guaranteed that whatever century you pick, some of them used bushes and fields, and others got to, er—use the royal throne. One's relatives do all sorts of things."

"I've just found out my alter is a chef. Odd," I added.

"Why?"

"Exactly. Why did he become a chef? I've never wanted to be a chef. I suppose it means he has assistants." The closest I had to assistants were Eggie and Rocky, who were responsible for the day-to-day operations at Wagner's Kitchen and who had no hesitation in informing me (or even Wagner himself) what needed to be done, rather than vice versa.

"It's a myth that there is one ideal job for everyone—or one ideal mate, for that matter," she assured me. "Those who were adults when the universes diverged, well, that was different. They had identical jobs and spouses and houses. No wonder people panicked and did stupid things. But you and Felix B, that's another story. Look at our two worlds."

"They started out identical, that's true."

"Well, almost. Anyway—accumulation of differences."

"One being that we A-dwellers use omnis for reading and here you have tr—paper books."

"We do use omnis for news stories and such, but not for anything that needs more than a few minutes' worth of attention. I don't know how you do it. I like to scribble notes in textbook margins. And my shelf hosts a P. G. Wodehouse collection."

"That's like a whole tree right there, Bean."

"I know. But I started collecting them as a child—if we'd lived in Universe A, we wouldn't have been able to afford an omni anyway." She shrugged and reached for a shriveled grape, then changed her mind and left it on the plate. "Kitchen user guides here are your basic paper kind, by the way. We call them instruction manuals. Just text and a few pictures."

"Huh. The user guides I put together at Wagner's Kitchen begin with a demonstration showing how the product is used; then I add example recipes for the customer to try out, culinary hints, witty anecdotes from the history of cooking...well, you get the idea. I once put together a seven-hour user guide for a pair of kitchen tweezers."

"What on Earths does one use kitchen tweezers for?"

"Deboning fish. Did you know that only 4.2 percent of our customers bother viewing the guides?" The DIM officials, having finished with movie star Gabriella Love, were now looking in my direction, but Quarantine Case 19, whose name I'd forgotten, came in at that moment and was pounced on by the officials. I don't know what came over me. I leaned forward and whispered, "I've hired a private detective to find out all I can about Felix B."

"A detective? Did you really?" Bean said, seeming impressed. "If I were you, I wouldn't worry too much whether he's writing a book or not. As I said, accumulation of differences usually guarantees that alters' lives are unalike. In fact, alters aren't usually even the same height due to variations in childhood diet and environment. Though I do feel sorry for *her*, I have to say. It's tough having a famous alter."

"Who?" I followed her glance to the food table, where Gabriella was turning up her nose at the offerings.

"You didn't know? Her alter here in Universe B is Gabriella Love, the famous actress. She herself is Gabriella Short. Love must be a stage name."

"She's an A-dweller with an alter? Well! I assumed she was a unique. She looks too young to have been born before Y-day."

"Makeup," Bean said dismissively. "And that unnaturally white hair." She reached for the unwieldy omni resting against the neck of her gown and checked the time. "I have a meeting with Professor Max and the rest of the group coming up. Since the earliest they'll let me out is lunchtime, when my forty-eight hours is up, I'll have to do it from here." She waved around the room, indicating either the cafeteria itself or the quarantine wing. "And I'll have to say I have appendicitis, though obviously Arni will know I'm lying and everyone else will know too because Arni is not exactly reticent. I wish they'd let us change back into our clothes. These gowns are silly."

"Perhaps they are worried we'd try to escape if we had our own clothes on."

"I don't know about you, but I probably would." She paused to throw a sideways glance at the DIM officials, who were handing a pen to Quarantine Case 3, the insurance salesman, then lowered her voice. "Are you the kind of guy who keeps shelves lined with childhood mementos and photos?"

"Am I the—not really. My desk at work is so cluttered that my apartment ends up being rather sparse and tidy in comparison. When a new item adds to my desk clutter, say a set of oven mitts or a turkey baster, and I realize I have to come up with a fresh idea to describe the turkey baster—well, I wouldn't be surprised if one day I go berserk and baste everything in my office. And I know what you're going to ask—why don't I find something else to do? Because manual writing pays reasonably well and it's a secure job and I enjoy it most of the time. Still, I want a book of my own. Nothing to do with Wagner and his kitchen. Mysteries and crime in the world of cooking.

"I wonder how much free time they have," I added. "Chefs. Or are there always menus to plan, food to order, and other restaurant-related tasks, even in the evenings?"

"I suppose you and Felix B could coauthor something. There have been writer siblings before. The Bronte sisters, of course. Who else? There must be others, but I can't think of anyone else at the moment."

"Yeah, well, I don't know how they did it. The Brontes must have been bigger people—persons—English ladies—than me," I said, completely losing control of the sentence. "You know what really haunts me? What if he used a pseudonym and I've already read his book and liked it?"

"You thought you had plenty of time, then you suddenly found out he existed, and here you are." She tilted her head to one side in thought. "If it had been me, I think I would have started writing madly. It doesn't matter what. Anything, really."

"It doesn't work like that," I said, trying to spread a dab of butter onto the last triangular bit of croissant. The butter stuck to the knife. I gave the knife a firm shake and watched as the butter flew up into the air and landed on the shoe of the DIM official standing next to me.

🦆

Having signed the information-halt agreement—"...*the events of July 2020 pertaining to the spread of the North American Pet Syndrome, also known as the pet bug, from Universe A into Universe B via an infected carrier, a household pet of unknown genetic makeup, as well as all related events, including but not limited to the 48-hour quarantine deemed necessary for 22 citizens listed below, are hereby declared government property...*"—having signed the form in three places, I strode back to my room holding my gown pinched in the back with one hand, the sash having come loose again. Write a book together with Felix B or come up with something quickly, she said. Like it was that easy. What did she know about it anyway? You wouldn't catch *me* going around giving advice to people I barely knew about subjects I had no expertise in whatsoever.

The room door swung shut behind me.

The omni lay silent and unblinking on the bedside table. Great, I thought. Not only did I *not* have the option of sitting down and embarking on the first chapter of the cooking-competition-in-the-Sierras masterpiece on the tiny omni keyboard, I didn't even have the option of *reading* anything.

I noticed that the bed had been made up while I was at breakfast and that there was a small square box lying on it. I checked for an accompanying card, didn't find one, and untied the ribbon and lifted the lid off. Candy. Well, that was nice. I selected one of the soft, chocolate-dipped candies, bit into it, then quickly spit it back into my hand and dropped it into the trash bin.

Just as I had finally found where I'd left off in *Evans,* having remembered that I did have something to read after all (the process of locating the page taking unexpectedly long for someone spoiled by the omni bookmarking feature, though at least this version didn't need batteries to run) there was a knock at the door and Chang came in maneuvering a medical cart.

"Chang, do you like cherries?" I asked him as he wrapped a blood-pressure sleeve around my arm.

"Doesn't everybody?"

"I have a bad allergy. I don't think these were meant for me." I motioned with my free hand toward the candy box. "Have some if you like."

"Oh, cherry chocolates? These are from the gift shop downstairs. They're pretty good." He helped himself to one, then proceeded to pump up the blood pressure sleeve.

"No gift card on the box. It must have been misdelivered. My boss is the only person who knows I'm here, and he knows about my cherry allergy."

"They do that sometimes, if the order came through a call, forget to put the caller's name down on a card."

"Chang, if you don't mind my asking, what does your alter do?" I asked as the blood pressure sleeve deflated and he reached for a thermometer.

"Chang A? Lives in Iceland and invites me and my wife and kids for a visit every summer. The way I look at it, an alter is a good thing. If for some reason I need a blood transfusion or a donor kidney, there's an exact match available."

I hadn't thought of that. Perhaps there *were* a few incidental advantages to having an alter.

"Mmmm mmmm mm mm?" I said.

He took the thermometer out of my mouth. "Normal. How are you feeling today?"

"Better than yesterday," I said. "What does he do?"

"For a living? He's a nurse."

"And that doesn't bother you?"

"Not really. Gives us something to talk about." He gave a relaxed shrug, then seemed to think better of it. "Still, I have to admit I'm glad Professor Singh stopped after producing the one copy of the universe. Anything more would have been—too much."

He took another of the cherry chocolates and wheeled the cart out the door, and I gave my attention back to *Evans*. Having folded in a tiny corner of a page, I was able to find where I'd left off with no problem—Roger Bassington-ffrench, he of the two small *f*'s, had just entered the picture. I felt I was getting the hang of things.

Still waiting for Dr. Gomez-Herrera to sign my release paperwork, I wandered over to the cafeteria and asked Bean, "What's a mashie?"

She was sitting at a table by the door, a sheaf of papers in front of her, having just finished with her meeting, judging by the fading screen on her omni. Her patient gown had drooped on one side, revealing a patch of bare shoulder.

"Nothing in this universe, I don't think. Where did you hear the word?"

"I saw it in an Agatha Christie. Also niblick, furze, plus fours, mews—" I ticked off the words on my fingers. I had been trying to read *Evans* with an eye toward learning how the Grand

Dame of Mystery had done it but kept losing myself in the story and having to backtrack. I'd also found that I missed the instant dictionary access I was used to.

"Do you know anything about omnis, Bean?"

"You mean how they work? Sure."

"Good, maybe you can fix mine. It seems to be dead."

She took the omni from me and turned it over in her hands.

"What's wrong with it?"

"The battery. I forgot to replace it this year."

"You'll have to get a new one."

"Can't you string a wire here and there and get a little more life out of it, at least until I depart the Palo Alto Health Center?"

"I'm not the hands-on kind of scientist. I could give you a nice exposition on the theory behind event chain-tracking algorithms, if you like."

"Some other time, thanks."

I stole a glance at the papers in front of her. They were diagrams of some sort, weblike things interwoven in various colors. Bean didn't seem to mind my interest, but not wanting to disturb her work, I wandered over to the cafeteria windows. Sunlight streamed in. Below was a pleasant courtyard with wooden benches and a small pond, enclosed on all sides by medical buildings. Several milky white ducks with orange feet and bills frolicked in and around the pond.

A brief call to Mrs. Noor from the hallway infoterminal had yielded news. She had partaken in Sunday brunch at the Organic Oven, where Felix was chef. "*He wasn't there.* When I requested to talk to the chef so I could compliment his spinach soufflé, the waitress mentioned their usual chef had the week off."

"You don't think—?"

"—that he's in Universe A looking for you? No, the waitress said that something had come up and that Felix B would be going to Carmel for a few days," Mrs. Noor said from her desk.

"Carmel, did you say?" I leaned into the infoterminal.

"Yes, why?"

"I don't know anyone in Carmel. I did live there as a child for a bit, though," I added.

"Felix, I've been meaning to ask you something. Your Aunt Henrietta left you the Y-day photo and that's how you found about Felix B, but what about him? Is there an Aunt Henrietta B?"

"There isn't. Well, yes, I suppose there had to be a Henrietta in Universe B, but not an *Aunt* Henrietta, if you see what I mean. She's an aunt by marriage, my great-uncle Otto's second wife. They met and got married when I was at the four-year, long after the universes branched off."

"It's possible *your* Aunt Henrietta knew about Felix B and left him something in her will."

"I've been thinking about that. Aunt Henrietta's lawyer said that only half of her dolphin collection went to me. I assumed she left the other half to Uncle Otto, but—"

"We could peek into Felix's windows and see if we spot the dolphins on a shelf someplace. Is your half of the collection nicely displayed in your living room?"

"Er—not yet. What's the Organic Oven like, Mrs. Noor?"

"Medium-sized dining area with new cedar-wood tables and handcrafted stone on the walls. Very nice. Open for breakfast, lunch, midafternoon tea, and occasionally for a special dinner. Food is pretty good. I recommend the ice cream bombe."

"Dark chocolate ice cream topped with chunks of banana and kiwi, with orange juice drizzled on top for extra tanginess and to prevent the bananas from going brown?"

"I—well, yes."

"My mother's recipe," I said. "Was it busy?"

"Mostly, though I didn't have to wait long for a table."

We promised to reconnect after I got out of the health center, though I sensed some hesitation on her part and hoped I wasn't overstepping my client privileges by calling too often. There was nothing to be done about that, at least not until I got a new omni battery and Mrs. Noor could contact me herself.

Her words had brought back memories of my mother's cooking, an eclectic mix of dishes from all over the world, rather like my favorite lunch place, Coconut Café, now that I thought about it. Obviously Felix had been influenced by our mother's cooking as well, if anything more so, since I wasn't much of a cook and the very idea of me feeding paying customers was laughable. I sat at my desk putting together manuals for kitchen products; he wielded them.

I turned away from the window and went back to Bean's table.

"—Arni, I don't think the subtle approach is working—no, there hasn't been a chance, really, there are DIM officials all over the place. Never mind, I'll think of something before he leaves." She snapped the omni shut.

"Sorry," I said. "I didn't mean—"

"Hello, fellow quarantineers," James said from behind me. The cafeteria door he had just entered through shut softly. "Or is it quarantiners?" He was dressed in street clothing. Next to him was Gabriella Short, who was still in her pink robe and the clicking of whose heels I should have recognized. James threw a frank look at Bean's diagrams and, as if not wanting to run afoul of Regulation 10 by revealing too much information about workplace matters, she scooped up the papers and flipped them over.

"Given that we're all in a quarantine, you'd think we'd be running into each other *constantly,* Citizen Sayers—but we've hardly seen you," Gabriella said, sweeping her ice-white hair back with one hand. Wondering how much she resented being an ordinary mortal and not a celebrity, I replied, "Medication side effects. I spent most of yesterday in my room."

"You're leaving already?" Bean indicated James's street clothes.

"I'm Quarantine Case 1, not counting Murphina. Dr. Gomez-Herrera just signed my paperwork."

"I'll have to wait until Dr. Gomez-Herrera gets around to me—I'm Case 21," I said. I lowered my voice. "I've heard that Quarantine Case 3—he's in insurance sales—sneezed once too often and will have to stay the whole week."

James grimaced. "Murphina gave him a friendly lick on the face when he bent down to pick up his suitcase in the crossing chamber."

"I was the last person brought in, right after you, Felix. I'm Case 22," Bean said. "They had trouble finding me, not that I should have been that hard to find. I was merely at the Bihistory Institute, working. Which is the first place you should look for a graduate student on a Saturday morning. I use the term *morning* loosely, of course. The place doesn't begin to fill up 'til noon—"

"I'm Case 2," Gabriella said. "I'm going to see if Dr. Gomez-Herrera is in her office. She *needs* to sign my paperwork. Citizen Sayers, I hope you can join us," she called out as she clicked out the door.

I would have never dared to bother Dr. Gomez-Herrera in her office uninvited. "I wonder what Gabriella meant by that," I said, picking up my silent omni from next to Bean's upside-down papers and hanging it back around my neck.

"I'll spare you my speech, Felix," James said, "though it's quite a good one, if I do say so myself. Let's just say that DIM may hold the rights to the pet bug events, but they were still Murphina's and my fault. Gabriella had an idea—here, let me walk you back to your room and I'll tell you all about it—"

We went out, leaving Bean staring after us.

"The fact that I'm being discharged first makes me feel even more guilty," James went on as we headed down the hallway. "To make up for things, I've organized an outing to Carmel. We're taking a flier down for sightseeing and dinner, with all arrangements and costs undertaken by me. Not everyone has said yes, people have prior commitments—"

We stopped at the door to my room.

"Gorgeous weather today," James added. "No fog predicted."

"Sorry, James, I have things to attend to." I felt bad refusing the man. It sounded like he was having trouble getting others to come on his trip. But Carmel was the last place I wanted to be—according to Mrs. Noor, that's where Felix was headed. It was the perfect opportunity to snoop around his life in San Francisco B without risking running into him.

As I watched James walk past the security guard and out the quarantine wing doors, it crossed my mind that I had thought of him only as a nondescript, friendly fellow with a too-inquisitive pet. It couldn't have been easy to obtain a flier and accommodations in Carmel for a large group at short notice. Or cheap.

Dr. Gomez-Herrera dropped in exactly at noon, looked me over, and pronounced me free of pet bug symptoms and therefore not a danger to society at large. She shook my hand, said, "Enjoy the rest of your trip," and left, having signed my discharge papers.

I changed out of the patient gown into a pair of knee-length shorts and a short-sleeve shirt. Just as I had finished stuffing most of my belongings into the backpack and was looking for a place to stash *Evans*, there was a knock at the door. Bean stuck her head in. "Are you still here, Felix?"

I waved her in. "I'm packing."

"I haven't been cleared yet. Dr. Gomez-Herrera had to attend to Quarantine Case 4, who's come down with the pet bug. She's a pet psychic and rubbed noses with Murphina." Bean moved my jacket aside and plopped down on the bed. "So I have to wait some more."

"Would a cherry candy help? They are over there on the table."

"It might, thanks." She took one of the cherry candies. "I hear James is issuing invitations."

"For Carmel."

She licked cherry juice left by the candy off her finger. "I didn't get an invitation."

"Hand me that shaving kit, will you?"

She handed me the shaving kit, along with a comb I had forgotten on the bed. "James already left the health center," I said, "but maybe Gabriella will invite you. They seem pretty chummy." I opened the backpack pocket, the one that used to house the Y-day photo—it was still missing—and put in the toiletries, then slid *Evans* in next to them. I looked up. "Bean, have more candy. In fact, have them all. I have a cherry allergy.

In return you can tell me of a good place to buy chocolate. I ate all my chocolate bars."

"A good place to buy—all right, I can't take this anymore. There are some things you need to know. That it's only *fair* that you know. Only—"

I zipped up the backpack and sat on it to squash it into submission.

"—only I'm not supposed to say. What a mess," she said, thrusting her fingers into her chestnut locks and giving them a tug, a gesture I have always envied but which requires thick and plentiful hair. "Where to start...you're not an undercover DIM agent by any chance, are you?"

"Not that I know of."

"Felix, you can't go to Carmel. At least not with James and Gabriella."

"Why can't I? It sounds like a fun trip." I finished with the backpack, placed it by the door, and turned back to where she was sitting on the bed.

"James is not who he seems."

"A nondescript, friendly fellow with a too-inquisitive pet? Who is he?"

"Arni is looking into it. We're not sure yet."

I turned the room chair around to face the bed and sat down. "Go on."

"This is not a good story, Felix," she said, looking at me unhappily. "I'm embarrassed by everyone's behavior."

"It's all right. You might as well know that I wasn't planning on going to Carmel anyway."

"Remember my meeting this morning with Arni and Pak—fellow graduate students—and Professor Max? We have a new candidate for prime mover." She looked at me expectantly, as if I should have been able to understand what she meant, then jumped to her feet, knocking the candy box off the bed and spilling its contents onto the floor. "It's like this—everyone believes that Professor Singh produced a copy of the universe on Y-day—but he didn't—cause the branching between A and B, I mean—it's theoretically impossible—he was performing the same experiment in both universes, *had* to be to get them to link." She stopped and took a breath. "Let me start over. We have two universes, yours and mine, which used to be one." She lifted her hands and held them palm-to-palm in front of her, then opened her palms to form a Y. "They diverged on January 6, 1986. Midday California time—11:46:01."

"Right," I said. "From then on we went our separate ways."

"Singh didn't cause the yabput."

"I'm sorry, the what?"

"The divergence. Unofficially referred to as yet another branching point in the universal timeline. Yabput."

"Yet another...many universes, you're saying?"

"Yes."

"I thought you said you weren't a Passivist," I said, scanning the room for any belongings I might have accidentally left behind.

She clicked her tongue in annoyance. "No. Listen. A universe branches off whenever a significant chain of events is set into motion—for instance, like me coming into this room to talk to you. In the old universe I'm still in my room packing, probably the smarter thing to do. And Singh—all he did was successfully connect two budding branches. He wasn't the prime mover."

"He wasn't, you say?"

"Universe maker, if you like. Though that's a misleading term—there is no intent involved in creating a universe, not in the way the Passivists claim." Her eyes bored into mine. "We thought our database was complete, that we had everyone within the event radius centered on Professor Singh's lab, but we haven't been able to link anyone to the yabput. Then a new photo appeared on the Y-day photoboard—"

"Wait, don't tell me," I said.

She nodded. "I think James and Gabriella are searching for the prime mover as well, and that's why we've all been circling you—and Felix B."

"No, I mean, don't tell me. I don't want to hear it."

"Felix—"

I shook my head. "There's been some mistake. Check your data again. You're not laying this—this *monumental* responsibility—at my door."

"But we need your help."

"Did you take the Y-day photo from my backpack?"

"What? No. Felix—" She took a step in my direction.

"Sorry, I have to go." I grabbed my things and, before she could say anything more, was out the door.

🦆

After much paperwork—*"released from the Palo Alto Citizen Health Center with an official diagnosis of false appendicitis brought on by food poisoning"*—apparently there had been a rash of those—I was able to get past the main desk of the health center and out the front door. As I strode away oblivious to the direction I was heading in, I asked myself why Bean kept saying things that bothered me to no end, though if I were to be perfectly honest I would have had to admit that she was only doing her job, and had said more than she was supposed to in order to clue me in on what was going on. Still. Bean had said that she was ashamed of everyone's behavior—did that mean she had struck up conversations with me merely to fish for information about my past? And James too. Was Murphina even his pet or merely a borrowed prop, I asked myself as I maneuvered my backpack around pedestrians like a sidewalk slalom skier, keeping an eye out for a shop that sold omni batteries or chocolate among the stores that lined El Camino Real, the main thoroughfare of Palo Alto (or, as I knew it, Redwood Grove).

I passed a piano store, two Mexican restaurants, three tea shoppes, a movie theater advertising Gabriella Love's *Jungle Nights;* also a tourist agency offering guided tours of "buildings lost in the Universe A quake but still here in Universe B," according to the brochure thrust into my hands as I walked by and which I immediately dropped into the nearest trashcan. It occurred to me that had Aunt Henrietta done the same with the Y-day photo, right now I'd be at my desk at Wagner's Kitchen immersed in melon ballers and breadboxes instead of traversing semi-familiar sidewalks and failing to find specialty sweets stores.

Universe maker—the very idea was ludicrous.

What could my six-month-old self have done that would have been *that* noteworthy?

Wishing for some measure of normality, however small, I realized that my feet had anticipated me. I was standing in front of Coconut Café.

[10]

I BREAK A RULE

There was nothing special about the low building. Peeling paint in places, staged pictures of entrées taped inside the windows, a couple of tables out front under umbrellas. The café was showing its age, having been in business forty-some years and, at least in Universe A, having been run by the same man in all that time: Samand was old, wiry, often rude, and served the best lunch special in town, entrée and beverage for eighty dollars. His Coconut Café had weathered many things, including runaway inflation and competition from seemingly better restaurants with fancier décor and a well-heeled clientele. Samand A had outlasted them all. I was glad to see that his alter had done the same.

It struck me that Samand B, should this still be his café, would be the first familiar face I'd see in three days. Reciprocity didn't apply; he would not know my face. It didn't matter.

Noticing that the windows were maybe a tad more in need of a good cleaning than my Samand would have allowed, I went in.

It was past one, so the lunch crowd had come and gone. I headed for the counter, imagining the aroma of simmering onions and spices filling the air, but, as usual, smelling nothing.

A young woman, presumably one of Samand's daughters, stood behind the counter arranging baked goods. She was not the same person as any of Samand A's daughters, which was odd for me but nice for her. "Can I help you?" she asked without looking up.

"I'll have the Italian wedding soup."

"Sorry, today's soup is chicken noodle."

I almost dropped my identicard onto the counter. "I beg your pardon?"

"Chicken noodle."

I couldn't believe it. The name was the same, the pictures in the front window were the same, why weren't the daily specials the same? Italian wedding soup was Monday's soup, it always had been—I often picked up a bowl on the way back from work and biked home with it balanced on my handlebars. Chicken noodle was only for when you were feeling sick. It wasn't a whole meal.

"Well?" she demanded, continuing to layer coconut bars onto a plate.

"I'll have"—I glanced at the menu on the wall to make sure they had my other favorite dish—"the Persian stew."

"Certainly." She took a step to the sales register and rang up the order. "That will be eighty-five doll—why, Felix, hello!"

"Er, hello." I was fairly sure I had never seen the woman before in my life.

"Why didn't you call to tell us you were dropping by?"

"Uh—you must mean—I'm not him—that is, I *am* Felix, but—"

"How are things at the Organic Oven? Monday is your day off, isn't it? I thought you had Japanese lessons."

It was time to put an end to the misunderstanding.

"I'm not Felix B. I'm Felix A."

She gave a peal of delight. "Felix, you dog. I know you owe Lake and the other busboys money at cards, but really. What a great joke to play on everyone. Wait 'til I tell Dad. And here I was, wondering why you were dressed in those strange clothes." I felt my cheeks redden. "Listen here—"

"And we won't mention your haircut, not a word."

"Sorry, he really isn't your Felix," a voice behind me said.

"No?"

"Felix A here is just a visitor to Universe B," James added smoothly.

Samand's offspring covered her mouth with one hand, aghast at her mistake, or perhaps trying not to laugh. It was hard to tell. In any case, she clearly found James a more trustworthy source than me. "Oops. Felix never said anything to me about having a—well, I am surprised. Please accept my apology, citizen." She gasped. "Are you—"

"Am I what?" I said.

"No, her." Samand's daughter pointed behind James. "Is that—?"

"I'm not her," snapped Gabriella Short.

"Eighty-five dollars, please," said Samand's offspring, by now thoroughly abashed. She added the amount to my identicard and handed it back to me along with a paper receipt.

I studied James and Gabriella across the table as we waited for our meals to arrive.

James cleared his throat. "Is there something you'd like to ask, Felix?"

"No," I said irritably, "I merely want my lunch."

"We understand completely, Citizen Sayers," murmured Gabriella. "We're here because we hope to enter into a business arrangement, one lucrative to you as well as to Past & Future."

"Lucrative to who—to whom?" I said despite myself. I remembered that Past & Future had been the name on the business card they'd given me.

"I am glad you asked that, since it demonstrates your interest in our services and thereby provides a legal basis for continuing this conversation. I will go ahead and give you—"

"—our sales pitch," James said.

"—a few more details. Past & Future is the company that employs us. Our research and development department is particularly interested in your personal history. I would be happy to provide you with promotional materials—"

"Not interested."

"All we want," Gabriella continued as if I hadn't said anything, "is to make sure you don't enter into any arrangement that would not be advantageous to *you*, Citizen Sayers. Past & Future can offer you substantial compensation."

"Today's soup should be Italian wedding soup. It's not. Wedding soup, by the way, is more filling than it sounds. Meatballs, veggies, pasta. Good with crusty bread. Did you know it's not served at weddings? The name comes from the delectable marriage of ingredients—"

"Before I can tell you more, Citizen Sayers," Gabriella's voice rose, "we need your signature on this contract." Out of nowhere she produced a sheaf of papers about two digits thick, with *Past & Future* printed diagonally across the top page.

"It's just a formality to keep the guys in legal happy," James said.

"Who gets the Greek lamb?" Samand had appeared next to our table and was one-handedly balancing three dishes on a large round tray. James whisked the Past & Future packet out of sight and accepted the Greek kabob plate. Gabriella received her chicken noodle soup, and I my artichoke-chicken khoresh. "Be back with your salads and drinks," Samand said with a brief glance at me and left. I was grateful to him for not mentioning my alter or making jokes about my hair.

We were three A-dwellers lunching in B world. The khoresh, tender chicken pieces and artichoke hearts in a lemony sauce over jasmine rice, looked heavenly. It probably smelled heavenly too. I decided I was damned if I was going to have my lunch ruined.

"Look," I said, pushing away the Past & Future packet, which was back on the table. "I'm sorry, but I'm just not interested in doing this."

Gabriella frowned. "Your alter, the other Citizen Sayers, has already signed a contract and has been compensated. He's being interviewed at a Past & Future office as we speak. I wanted to interview him *myself*, but—"

"Yes, yes, Murphina caused a bit of a detour. I accept the blame," James said calmly. "Felix, we're close. Computer models are showing a very promising result, but there are gaps in our data. We need your help in recalling the events of Y-day."

"I was six," I said, "and that's months, not years. I doubt I could help you very much."

Gabriella made another attempt as our food sat untouched on the table. "It would be to everybody's benefit if we pooled our resources and knowledge. Especially *yours*, Citizen Sayers, if we succeeded in proving it was *you* and Felix B who started everything all those years ago—"

"Doesn't this violate Regulation 3?" I interrupted. "Citizen privacy. *Personal* privacy. I've always thought that it was redundant, calling it the personal privacy regulation. What other kind of privacy is there other than personal?"

"We aren't violating Regulation 3," she replied sharply. "Citizen Felix Sayers B gave us his permission to research his personal history, and now we're asking for permission to research yours."

"Again," I said, "my *personal* history? Do I have any other kind?"

"It's all quite legal," James said, reaching for a fork and sliding lamb chunks one by one off the kabob skewer. "Now what ideas one might generate while researching your past, that's a different question. It's a bit of a gray area, to be honest. DIM doesn't authorize new ideas easily, and the idea that people create universes—well, that's a biggie."

Gabriella sent him a cautionary look. "Your signature on this contract will permit us to freely look into your past, Citizen Sayers."

"How did you arrange it?" I asked.

She seemed taken aback by my tone.

I raised an eyebrow at James. "Did you bring a pet-bug-infected pet into this universe just to secure some time with me?"

"Of course not, Felix. Had I known Murphina was sick, I would have taken her to the vet as soon as possible, not on a trip. She's outside, in the car. We parked in the shade and left the top down." He shifted in his chair. "Look, like I said, this didn't work out the way I planned. I use Murphina in my job because she is a good icebreaker. On occasion we need to interview subjects who are less than forthcoming about their lives, downright uncooperative. Having a friendly pet around makes people more willing to talk."

I got to my feet. "The Y-day photograph. I want it back. I'll take my lunch over there," I said to Samand, who had reappeared with our drinks and salads.

Samand didn't miss a beat. "Certainly."

I carried my lunch over to a window table and ate alone, my back toward James and Gabriella. I enjoyed the khoresh more than I thought I would, and even pulled out the paper copy of *Why Didn't They Ask Evans?* After struggling a bit with the mechanics of holding the book open while wielding a knife and fork (and of avoiding greasy food spots, hand-flicking not being a page-turning option), I managed to read a couple of chapters over my meal.

[II]

THE BIHISTORY INSTITUTE

After an afternoon spent moodily wandering around town feeling sorry for myself—it being my birthday (my *real* birthday, not the false one I had been celebrating every year for the past thirty-four years; I had somehow lost six months of my life and turned thirty-five practically overnight)—I returned to the Queen Bee Inn as the ocean grew dark and a cool evening began to descend.

"Citizen Sayers, how are you feeling?" Franny greeted me from the front desk.

"Peachy. My—er, appendicitis turned out to be false. Thank you for the paper book, Franny. It did help pass the time nicely at the Palo Alto Health Center. I'm not finished reading it yet," I added, suddenly unsure whether she had meant the book as a gift or as a loan.

She gave me no hint. "We like to do what we can for our guests, Trevor and I."

As sympathetic as she was, since I had paid in advance for my room, no refund would be given for the two days I was in the health center. The news did not do much to improve my mood.

Tuesday morning found me still irritable and I was glad that the taxi driver who took me to Mrs. Noor's office, though he drove faster and even more recklessly than everyone else, was the taciturn kind and required no conversation.

"I've been trying to reach you, Felix," Mrs. Noor said and beckoned me into her office. (My omni was still dead.) I sidestepped a filing cabinet and took a chair as she added, "I have good news." She shifted a stack of papers out of the way and thus having cleared room for her elbows, leaned forward across the desk, ample chin on folded hands, her dark brown eyes on me. "You don't seem very interested."

"People are after me," I said. "It's distracting."

"You might find this interesting. Felix B was spotted entering the local office of a company called—what was it?" She flipped open the plum-coloured notebook and thumbed through. "Ham, my son, happened to be in his vicinity. Here we go. The company is called Past & Future. An unusual name. It's not a publishing concern or anything like that. They handle data for corporations and research personal histories for wealthy clients. They also have an idea incubation department—they don't bother with gadgets or trying to jump on the band-wagon with the next clothing or music fad, only with what they call first-class ideas. They are the ones who came up with that whole dinosaur-extinction-caused-by-asteroid idea last year."

"I remember reading about that. It seemed like the kind of thing that might panic the public, the possibility of an asteroid hitting one of the Earths again. I wonder how Past & Future got the idea past DIM."

"Money moves mountains," Mrs. Noor said wisely. "And they have it. Word is, they found the idea in an old science journal, claimed it as their own, and now own the rights to it. If any defense systems are put in place to guard against future asteroids hitting the Earths—well, Past & Future will get compensation for usage of the idea. I don't know why Felix B was there. Ham is on the case. You don't seem too surprised to hear about any of this," she added.

"As I said, people are after me. Don't ask me why, Mrs. Noor."

"All right. Here is one thing I bet you *don't* know. Wasn't easy to get the information either. Fortunately I have a few contacts," she said, motioning around the office as if representatives from various walks of life sat arranged on the cluttered shelves just waiting to provide inside information. "I talked to my acquaintances in the book business yesterday, one meeting over breakfast, then two meetings over tea, then a meeting for lunch and then another meeting over tea. Luckily I drink herbal and not caffeinated. I don't remember when I last spent that much time away from my center of operations here. It will be a little pricy, Felix, what with all the meals that I had to buy." She moved her large frame and the brown leather chair let out a protesting squeak. "But, to sum it up—there is no manuscript signed Felix Sayers B floating around in the book world. I had them check their records for rejected submissions, aliases, pseudonyms. Nothing. He could be actively working on something at home, of course. Finding that out will require a bit more finesse."

I caught sight of the *Hypothetically Speaking* sign on her wall. Below was a smaller sign which I hadn't noticed before. It said, *Take No Notice.* Presumably it didn't mean of the sign itself. Was it, then, an instruction to ignore other instructions—for instance, could I go ahead and tell Mrs. Noor about the pet bug even though I had been warned not to speak of the quarantine by DIM officials? Most likely, I decided, the sign merely pointed out the obvious, that detectives usually worked on the sly and therefore went unnoticed in the crowd.

"Felix?"

"Sorry, my mind is elsewhere today. I appreciate your hard work on my behalf, Mrs. Noor. It's just that there are things I must attend to." I sat up in the chair. "You could help me there, however."

"Tell me."

"I need two things. One, a place to buy an omni battery. And two, where do I find a graduate student by the name of Bean, last name unknown?"

🦆

One of the problems with finding out that you have an alter is that you suddenly feel old, like you've skipped back a generation; and you realize that all along you have been thinking of those born before Y-day—there was no other way to say it—as being *unlucky*. A unique like you knew nothing of their problems and wasn't even interested since this alter stuff would not affect you, ever; it was your parents' problem, and that of their friends, not yours.

That was before I found out I had missed the cutoff.

As I went around trying to straighten out my fake birth record, my initial reaction had been one of disbelief. (Okay, it was more like panic, but what aspiring writer wouldn't panic when faced with the prospect of his novel already having been written—by *himself*, no less?) I hadn't progressed much beyond that, but the feeling of being older had crept up on me, and I missed being young and carefree like I was only weeks ago. Strolling down the pristine campus of Presidio University, where the Institute of Bihistory was located and where Mrs. Noor had found Citizen Bean Bartholomew listed as a graduate student, did not help matters any. Youth abounded, mostly on rollerblades. I passed a group of what seemed like teenagers sitting on the grass beneath a eucalyptus tree and caught a few words of their biology lecture, given by a professor who herself looked young enough to be a student. I consoled myself that maybe they *were* teenagers, here to take summer classes.

As I neared the bihistory building, my omni buzzed briefly to signal a new message. Wagner. The fresh battery was in place and with it was gone the sensation of being disconnected from my normal life, about which I was still of two minds. There is something to be said about being unreachable, especially when you are trying to avoid being prodded by your boss to engage in regulation-breaking activities of the sourdough kind.

I muted the buzzer on the omni and went in through the front doors of the bihistory building, a three-story rectangular block with wide windows through which people hunched over desks could be seen. I stopped at the lobby infoterminal to double-check Bean's office number, which, according to Mrs. Noor, was the unlikely combination L-11-C. The infoterminal directed me to the basement.

I took the elevator down and had turned into yet another deserted hallway looking for Room 11 when I spotted Bean through a door that was ajar. She had her back to me, her feet up on her desk, and was engrossed in a thick, serious-looking textbook with notes scribbled all over the margins of its pages.

"Knock, knock," I said from the doorway.

The feet hit the floor, the textbook slammed shut. "What— Felix, hello. You startled me."

"Sorry."

"I wasn't expecting—it's just that it's very quiet here in the summer, that's all. Pak and Arni are at a seminar, won't be back until later."

"Can I come in?"

"Where are my manners? Come in, of course, sit down." She rose to her feet and beckoned me in, then looked around the room somewhat self-consciously. "Well—there's the couch, it's more comfortable than it looks. Or do you want a chair?"

The basement room was artificially lit. Three desks faced a wall each, a whiteboard stood by the door, and there was a shabby denim couch sprawled in the middle of the room. Several chairs, some plastic, some wooden, stood scattered around. A bicycle had been placed by one of the desks and an electric samovar, stainless steel and vase-shaped, hummed in the far corner next to a stack of mismatched mugs and a sink.

I took a seat on the couch, my eyes briefly resting on a poster urging, TRACE YOUR LIFE STORY. PhD–RESEARCHED REPORTS AVAILABLE. Bean started to pace around the couch. "I owe you an apology, Felix. We've been circling you like vultures, so intent on getting to the truth that we didn't consider the consequences of what we were doing."

"Wolves."

"What?" She stopped to look at me.

"I think I prefer to be circled by wolves, not vultures. I'm not dead yet."

"Wolves then," she said, resuming her pacing. "About the only defense I can offer for being a—a *wolf*—is that we're not doing it for the money. Maybe that doesn't make any difference from your point of view. Whether we do it for the money or for the sake of knowledge, I mean."

"Why the secrecy?"

"The Council for Science Safety—have you heard of it? It's a subdepartment of DIM—as it happens, we haven't, er— sought the Council's approval for this line of research yet. A bit unethical, I know, but Regulation 19 makes things very difficult sometimes. Anyway, officially we in Professor Max's group are tracking the differences in the development of our two universes." She rounded the couch and continued, "Many interesting research problems there, by the way. For instance, how did Universe B end up with a surprisingly small number of hurricanes while the nature-conscious Universe A is deluged by them? Or, more trivially but just as interesting," she said, rounding the couch again, "why is ebony the most popular color for Universe A bathtubs, but pearl for B? And why do B-dwellers have more frequent romantic liaisons? We've been running experiments with event chains, seeing where a mislabeled letter or a table with free cookies for students takes us...never mind all that." She stopped, leaned on the back of the couch, and lowered her voice. "We're also looking for the Y-day prime mover."

"Hence the sneaking around."

A pinkish tint appeared on her cheeks. "We weren't sure you were aboveboard, the way that Y-day photograph appeared out of nowhere. DIM agents sometimes lay traps to ferret out scientists engaged in unauthorized research—those not complying with Regulation 19, that is. Even for the aboveboard stuff, we have to be careful about approaching subjects—people whose histories we need—because of Regulation 3 and other information protection laws. Luckily it's been a popular thing lately." She gestured at the poster advertising the PhD–researched reports. "People come by wanting to know how they ended up where they are in their lives. We trace their storyline and in exchange they give us permission to use their life stories in our research. Earl Grey?"

She walked over to the samovar, turned the spigot, and poured dark tea into two small cups.

"And James and Gabriella?" I said, accepting one of the cups.

"Work for Past & Future, an idea incubation company. One of their products is the idea of an asteroid having hit the Earth in the past and possibly one of the Earths again in the future. Before that they cracked the Mayan number system—well, they funded some poor sap to piece things together from old sources and figure out that it's a vigesimal system, base twenty, and now"— she gritted her teeth—"they get a royalty check any-time anyone translates a date from an inscription. Your alter has signed on with them. Lemon, milk, sugar?"

"I bet Felix B wouldn't have signed on with Past & Future if they had exposed *him* to the pet bug and put him in quarantine. So they too want to prove that our universes were split apart by me and Felix B?" The rhyme echoed in my head like a melody as I watched a sugar cube slowly dissolve in the teacup.

She turned her desk chair around, an uncomfortable-look-ing wooden one, and sat down facing me, cup in hand. "*People create universes,*" she said simply. "What a discovery that would be. Up there with those made by Galileo and Newton and Darwin and Yen."

I blew on the tea to cool it down a bit and said, "Let me see if I understand this correctly. You want me as an unpaid research subject and if I sign with Past & Future, I get cash—how much, do you know? Anyway, I answer their questions, pocket the money, and leave—"

"But you'd be giving them the right to your life story."

"And really I could tell them anything or nothing, lies about my childhood if I wanted to."

"It wouldn't be unheard of. People who come in here ask-ing us to research their life stories often keep quiet about embarrassing incidents in their past, stuff they'd rather forget. It's as if they want us to prove that only the good things in their life brought them to where they are today, not the mistakes they made along the way. We even get Passivists coming by asking for proof they *didn't* accidentally cause whatever disaster happens to be topping the news at the moment."

I took a sip of the tea, which was strong, strangely satisfying, and apparently named after a British aristocrat, and I reflected that I knew how the Passivists felt. I didn't want the responsibility either.

"We'll have to make it seem like you approached us to trace your life story. It's a plausible scenario. After all, you did just find out that you have an alter and would therefore naturally be interested in influential events in your life. Uniques don't come by much."

"How likely is it that DIM will authorize your ideas?"

"It's just a matter of time," she said firmly.

"What's in it for you?"

"My PhD."

"Do you have to find the universe maker to get your PhD?"

"No, but it would guarantee a lot of people would read my dissertation, wouldn't it?" She grinned. "If you must know, the title is *Characterizing the Probability Curve of Historical Event Chain Length*—"

"Why not?

"—but I need more data to test my model. It would be nice if we could spawn off additional universes and monitor the development of events in them. Professor Singh's lab used to be in this very building, did you know? Unfortunately the Council for Science Safety won't allow any further attempts at establishing new links."

"To be perfectly honest, that's one DIM policy I'm grateful for. I feel we have one link too many as it is." I rubbed my forehead; my stay at the health center had left me with a lingering headache. "Do you really think there are multiple universes, Bean? I don't see that having only two is any less likely than a preposterously large number of them."

"It's not so much that it's less likely. It's that if there *were* only two, they would be a more particular pair, say mirror images of one another. No, A and B are not special in any way, other than that Professor Singh happened to link them. Before he did that, everyone was convinced only one universe existed and would ever exist. Singh said, 'Look around. Everything belongs to a set of similar or identical objects. People and trees and electrons.'" She looked at me bright-eyed. "No, there are more than two."

🦆

She pulled an envelope from a desk drawer. "This is how we found you."

The photograph had my father standing in front of a steel railing with thick red cables passing vertically behind it. There was a lamppost to his right and some light rain-bearing clouds in the background. Strapped to his chest was a baby carrier. With yours truly in it. All in all, a photo unremarkable to anyone but me (and Felix B, I suppose) except for one thing. I turned it over. On the back, hand-copied from the original, were two items: the photo number, 13, and the date: January 6, 1986. Y-day.

"Mine is missing," I said. "Disappeared in the health center."

"We didn't take it," she said at once. "We didn't need to. Someone posted it on the Y-day photoboard. You know, the one hobbyists scrutinize for fun to find the earliest visible differences between universes A and B."

"Aunt Henrietta must have instructed her lawyer to post it at the same time that it was sent to me. My great-aunt," I explained. "I don't think she ever dreamed it would be used in this fashion. I imagine she just felt it belonged in the collection of everyone else's memorabilia from that day. And this proves—what?" I let the photograph fall down on the desk.

"Photo 13 places you near Professor Singh's lab on Y-day. The location is the Golden Gate Bridge—within the event radius." Somewhat unexpectedly, she chuckled. "Arni was floored that a new prime mover candidate had materialized."

"Was he, Arni?"

"Sorry. I dabble in theory, Pak spends most of his time in front of computers, and Arni is the one who interviews research subjects, gathers data, that sort of thing. After we'd authenticated the photo, we pooled what information we could on you and Felix B; then Arni contacted Felix B, but it was too late. He had signed on with Past & Future. In the meantime, since I was traveling to San Francisco A for a conference anyway, I had the task of contacting you, saving Arni the trip. We have to be careful how we spend our grant money."

I took in the shabby couch and the mismatched chairs again; only the computer equipment that took up much of the desk space seemed to be up-to-date. She saw, and commented, "Don't even ask me what I earn. Anyway, I did some discreet poking around when I got to your San Francisco, figured you seemed to be on the level, and decided as good approach as any was to drop in on you at work"—here I suddenly recalled

Wagner telling me a client had come in wanting to talk to me on Friday—"but you'd already left. I caught up with you at the terminal—I was scheduled to leave late Friday evening anyway—and, well, here we are," she trailed off.

"What about my father?" I tapped the photo. "Is he a suspect too?"

"He's the wrong size."

Only the steady hum from the samovar and the computer equipment permeated the room; no outside sounds penetrated the basement office. I glanced at the whiteboard by Bean's desk and noticed a single statistic circled among the equations written on it: 24 libras. My eyes moved to her computer and the palm trees swaying in the screen saver. Behind the palm trees were probably pages and pages of personal data about me—and Felix B.

"All right," I said, "I'll do it." I couldn't say why, but I had a feeling that something about this universe-making business would turn out to matter. That is, that it would be important in a personal way, beyond any vast-cosmos and birth-of-new-worlds kind of stuff.

Bean got up off the wooden chair. "Are you sure?"

"No. Where do I sign?"

"Well," she suddenly seemed hesitant, "it's customary for research subjects to meet Professor Max first. I'm just a graduate student."

"Can I ask you something?" I said as the elevator, with us in it, ascended to the third floor. "What's the C in your office number?"

"L-11-C denotes the lower level, room 11, desk C. I know, it makes no sense to label a *desk*, especially if there are only three in the room. Official story is that it's easier for mail and students to find us that way. Personally I think it's a DIM thing, an additional way of keeping tabs on citizens." As the elevator door opened to let us out, she added, "Did you know that at one point DIM wanted to use electronic tags, like we're genetically modified pets living in the wild or something? Necessary for public security, they argued. They almost got it too because it *sounded* good: no more crime, no worry about people stealing their alters' lives or swapping them willingly without telling others...Common sense prevailed in the end."

The professor was not in, but the nameplate on his door, next to which a note was pinned with the words, *In the Lab,* made me stop in my tracks. I must have let out a sound, since I received a puzzled look from Bean.

"Something wrong?"

"Professor *Wagner* Maximilian," I pointed to the nameplate. "Your graduate advisor is not, by any chance, a rather short, stocky man in his fifties, blond hair, loves to talk? Has connections everywhere—and, I suppose, a side interest in kitchen equipment?"

"Well, yes—you didn't know, then? I guess there's no reason you would." She grinned. "We work for the same boss."

The absurdity of the situation suddenly hit me and I laughed 'til tears ran down my cheeks. Bean looked on with a slightly concerned look on her face.

I wiped my eyes. "Right. What do we do now? Wait for Wagner B so I can sign the contract?"

"Let's not waste any more time. We can get in touch with the professor on the way down."

"To the basement?"

"To Carmel. Photos 1-12 and 14 and up. We need to find them before James and Gabriella do."

[12]

MONROE'S HOUSE

The sun was high up in the sky by the time we managed to track down Bean's office mates Arni Pierpont and Mike Pak, piled into her bubble-gum pink Volkswagen Beetle, picked up everyone's overnight bags, and took Route 1 south toward the small picturesque town of Carmel. Though opposing traffic was safely contained by a road divider, I had an unobstructed view from the passenger seat of Bean's Beetle as the Pacific Coast Highway rose and fell, alternating between cliff-top vistas of the ocean waves crashing on the rocky shore below and sea-level valleys. A knee-high rail guard between road and cliff edge provided laughable protection against disaster.

"I thought you said I shouldn't go to Carmel," I said to Bean, surreptitiously wiping my copiously sweating hands on my shorts as the Beetle chugged up a particularly steep portion of the road.

"To be precise," she answered distractedly, with a glance at the mirror that hung above the dashboard and offered a back view, "I said you shouldn't go to Carmel with *James*. With Arni and Pak and me, that's a different matter."

"A different matter entirely," Arni concurred from the back seat. I'd noticed that he had a largish nose and shoulder-length curly hair. "Besides, your alter might be in Carmel already. I'm sure you want to meet him."

"Not really, no. Regulation 7 prohibits it."

"The privacy and information of alters, yes. Not if he signs a form giving you permission. And yes, there's also the Lunch-Place Rule, which probably applies to alters most of all. Even so, it seems to me that there is a curiosity that must be satisfied. I don't have an alter, so I can't speak from personal experience, but it's human nature to want to take a peek at one's alter—"

"Could we stop calling him that?" I grimaced. "Call him Felix or Citizen Sayers or something."

"Isn't it confusing to call him Felix?" Arni said, leaning forward so he could see around my seat's headrest.

"Not to me. It's not like I call myself Felix inside my head. I don't call myself anything inside my head. It's just me."

"We do assign a number to each research subject, if you'd prefer that. You and your alter are 4102A and 4102B. Culinary-manual-writer Felix and Chef Felix, if you will." While he carried on the conversation, Arni seemed to be rummaging around in the back, bumping the back of my seat occasionally. As befitting one who spent most of his time chasing down and interviewing research subjects, he was the most dapper of the three students and sported a trendy sweater and slacks in contrast to Bean's and Pak's T-shirts, shorts, and sneakers.

"Arnold, what are you doing back there?" Bean demanded, swerving to avoid a pothole.

"Picking up. Do you have a trash bag in the car?"

"Somewhere on the floor. Don't throw out anything important."

"I think I'd prefer not to refer to him by a number," I said after a moment.

"We'll call him Felix B, then. Should I call you Felix A?" Arni asked, crumpling up an old soda can.

"No. Just Felix."

"You really don't want to meet him? But he's one of your closest relatives—the closest really. Think of all you have to talk about."

I stared out the window as Bean took the Beetle down a steep grade toward a rolling sand dune portion of the road. Uniques. What did they know about it anyway?

"We're not likely to see him in any case," Bean said in a gloomy voice, recklessly taking her attention away from the road to send a resigned shrug in our direction. "Felix B is probably closeted in a Past & Future office telling them all about his childhood."

"Speaking of childhoods," Arni said, "is it true, Felix, that you had no idea you had an alter until Photo 13 surfaced? How is that possible? Your name is not nature-based, which is often a tip-off—do you need this research paper, Bean?—all right, I won't throw it out—Bean and I have nature-names since we're uniques, of course; then there's Mike Pak—"

"Wait," I said. "Arni?"

"Arni is short for Arnold."

"And—?"

"And an Arnold has the power of an eagle. There's also DIM's official list of alters, not to mention your identicard, birth certificate, health records...And how did our trusty and reliable DIM officials fail to notice that your parents shaved six months off your age?"

I sighed. "My parents paid someone to fake my birth certificate right around the time the Department of Information Management was formed. DIM just accepted the new birth date as valid. As for me—I just thought I was a tad taller than the other kids in my class. How was I supposed to know I was older than everyone else?" I was a bit defensive, because he was right. I should have realized it sooner. I had been dejected about having missed out on being unique by a hair, but when you thought about it, six months was hardly a hair.

"Do you think," asked Arni, who was unstoppable, "that your parents and his parents ever met? Maybe the four of them got together and hatched a plan to protect their offspring from the knowledge they were identical."

"I think it was sweet of your parents to try to protect you," Bean said, throwing another glance at the back-view mirror. "People certainly had much stranger reactions to the link. Were they planning to tell you when you were older, do you think, after you finished your schooling and settled into a profession and a stable life?"

"Maybe," I said. "But then there was the accident." Bean had told me that Felix's parents too had been on a Caribbean cruise celebrating their twenty-fifth wedding anniversary when a hurricane veered into the ship's path. The probability of an A storm and a B storm overlapping in time *and* place was so small, Bean said, as to be practically nil, but weather being what it is, storms did quite often anyway.

"So," I broke the silence which had suddenly descended over the car, "what do we know about Felix B?"

"This and that," answered Arni. "Much of the data is irrelevant, of course. But that's the trick, to figure out what's important and what isn't."

"Indeed," Pak said.

I had almost forgotten he was in the car. The senior of the graduate students had a deep voice, a scruffy exterior, and a worried look, like the world was about to end and he was the only one who knew about it. Bean had introduced him as "Mike Pak. Call him Pak, no one calls him Mike." Intrigued, I asked why, whereupon Pak replied, "You know at least three Mikes. Everyone does, it's a connectivity thing. I'm working on a paper on the subject. You probably don't know any Paks, however, unless you grew up in a household of them or live in Seoul." He pronounced the initial sound in his name like a cross between a *p* and a *b*. The only other thing I had found out about him was that he owned a bicycle.

I stared at the road ahead, trying to appear not overly interested in what Arni was saying—"The lab computer sifts through batches of data, compiling event chains from old newspapers, subject interviews, city records of every kind, historic footage. Your alter—Felix B—signed a contract with Past & Future and declined to talk to us. Unfortunate. What we have on him was obtained indirectly and is therefore incomplete." He continued, "It didn't help matters any that Sayers is such a common last name. We even came across a few other Felix Sayers-es that, as far we could find, were unrelated to the two of you and existed merely to confuse the issue."

"The only other Sayers I've heard of," I said, "is the Dorothy L. Sayers who penned the Lord Peter Wimsey and Harriet Vane mysteries, but she's no relation. She was British."

We slowed down briefly to pass through a DIM checkpoint. The officials scanned our identicards and waved us on.

"Yes, but what *did* you find?" I asked as the checkpoint grew smaller behind us.

"The usual stuff," Arni said, stuffing used gum wrappers into the trash bag. "You want examples?"

"Examples, yes," I said, expecting to hear the words, *He's working hard on a mystery novel...*

Arni wiped his hands on a tissue and flipped open the stylish omni hanging around his neck. "Here we go, 4102B, in no particular order: alphabet cookies in rainbow colors, honorable mention, third-grade art fair. Also from his childhood, sixth grade poetry recital, first place. Graduated high school the same year you did and also went on to the San Diego Four-Year. He was a member of the school yearbook committee in high school and of the dog-walking society at the four-year."

"No spelling bees, though," said Bean.

I had gone through a brief period in high school of entering spelling bee competitions, until an unfortunate run-in with the word *ukulele* had soured me on the whole idea.

"Jumping to adulthood," Arni went on, "there is a review of the newly renovated Organic Oven, complimenting the chef on his *pasta e fagioli* and complaining about slow service, and another calling it 'San Francisco's hidden gem.' Name of first childhood pet, Talky. Of second, Chin-Chin. Current member of Presidio kennel club. Owns a dog there—an actual dog—named Garlic." Arni stopped. "Oh, and he rents a ground-floor apartment in the Egret's Nest Complex in Palo Alto and attends Japanese for Beginners lessons on Monday afternoons, his day off from the Organic Oven."

I felt a rising irritation. Alphabet cookies and restaurant reviews. Japanese lessons and dogs. I liked dogs, who didn't, but a member of a kennel club? Was the man even related to me? "What else do you have about his private life—aggh, Bean watch out!"

A vehicle had suddenly swerved into our lane, almost cutting us off and forcing Bean to slam on the brakes.

Bean recovered and leaned forward over the steering wheel as we picked up speed again. "Is that who I think it is?"

"Who?" I asked, then realized that I already knew the answer. The last time I had seen a car this particular shade of green, its top had been down and an overweight pet had been sitting next to the driver. Today, even though it was a bright and sunny day, the top of the cucumber-green vehicle was up, obscuring the occupants of the car.

"If I had to venture an opinion," Arni said, "then I would opine that it's James and Gabriella. I guess the flier sightseeing got cancelled."

"He's been more or less behind us this whole time. I thought it was just a tailgater," Bean said, slowing down and opening additional room between us and the car ahead. "What should I do? Pass them? Take the next exit?"

"What do they want?" I said.

"You," Arni said simply.

Bean tightened her grip on the steering wheel. "I'll try to lose them."

"No," Pak said in the voice of one dealing with imbeciles. "The contract. All we have to do is show them the contract."

"Right. Felix, give me your copy."

I passed her the five-page contract with which I had chartered Professor Maximilian's group to research the storyline of my life. As if there weren't three passengers in the car whose hands were perfectly free to perform such tasks, Bean rolled down her window while controlling the steering wheel with her elbow. She stuck her head and the contract out the window and waved it in the air. "He's signed already," she yelled out at the top of her lungs, even though there was no way the occupants of the car in front of us could hear her over the road noise. The wind whipped out a single page from the contract; we lost sight of it as it disappeared behind us.

The green car in front of us sped off testily.

"There," Bean said with satisfaction as if that settled matters. She passed the somewhat thinner contract back to me and rolled up the window.

🦆

On sunny days such as the one that saw us arrive in Carmel without any further ado, tourists usually flock in large numbers to the cafés, art galleries, and quaint shops of that seaside town—or at least this had always been the case in Universe A.

Carmel B turned out to be no different. It took us a good twenty minutes to find a parking spot, during which Arni pointed out a multistory glass building squatting in the hills above town, one floor of which housed the local offices of Past & Future. I tried to picture Felix sitting inside a plush office telling Gabriella and James all about his childhood and about our parents, who had spent much of their life in this seaside town. But the image would not come. Nor could I recall a single memory from my early childhood, even though I had spent the first few years of my life here, until my parents had started a new life elsewhere with a slightly *younger* child. They had left their art gallery jobs, rented out the house, and moved the family north to San Francisco, after which we lived in an apartment, and that was home to me. After I went on to the San Diego Four-Year, they moved back to the Carmel house and opened their own gallery, but it was too late for me. I was always just a visitor.

According to Arni, 161 Cypress Lane was still standing, unlike its Universe A opposite—*my* parents' house—which had burned down in a fire last year, he said. Any answers were here in Universe B.

"Ready?" Bean said.

"Sorry, I was lost in thought." I jumped out of the Beetle, closed the car door, then slammed it with more force so that it closed all the way.

"Nice car," I said to Bean as she locked up the Beetle one door at a time.

"It does its job, but new and spiffy it's not. Don't ask me what year—well, all right, I'll tell you. It's a 1969. Original engine."

"The Beetle has its own alter," Arni snickered.

"At least I *use* my car. Arni likes to keep his two-seater garaged and pristine," Bean retorted.

"It's my baby. Lunch? Monroe isn't expecting us until later."

I perked up. My stomach had been growling for a while.

"Lunch it is," agreed Bean, swinging her bag over her shoulder. (It was the same one she'd had at the crossing, only it seemed more compact, like the bag had folded in on itself.) "Felix, you choose. It's the least we can do, treat you to lunch, after dragging you down here on a moment's notice," she said as we commenced the six-block walk that would take us to Main Street. "It's too bad Professor Maximilian was busy with lab work and wasn't able to join us," she added.

I wasn't too sure about that, since knowing one Wagner Maximilian was enough for a lifetime, but refrained from saying so.

"True, he would have picked up the lunch tab," Arni said.

Bean whacked him in the shoulder with the bag. "You know that's not what I meant. At least, not *only* that. The professor has a knack for talking to people."

"That he does," I said to her.

Shortly after three, our energy restored with a meal of seafood and lemonade, we stood knocking on the front door of a two-story Spanish-style house with an unkempt lawn and a single Monterey cypress tree out front. An old man opened the door, the grooves in his face so deep that he seemed out of place in the bright Carmel afternoon, like a wise ancient from a darker, bygone era who somehow stepped into the wrong century. Arni introduced him as Monroe. I never did find out if that was his first or last name.

"You're here," Monroe pointed out the obvious. He was wearing mustard-yellow sweatpants and a matching sweatshirt, with a loosely tied checkered robe over the whole ensemble. The four of us followed him inside as he padded in his slippers down a dimly lit hallway, under an arched doorway, and into a living room where heavy curtains blocked out any sunlight. He motioned us toward a scruffy-looking couch. Bean, Pak, and I obediently sat down. Monroe sank into the only other seating option, an easy chair. Arni took in the state of affairs, said, "Excuse me," walked out of the room, and came back a moment later with a kitchen stool.

Monroe seemed not to notice. He was staring at me. I felt the color rise in my cheeks.

"Arnold Pierpont here tells me that you just found out you have an alter." He let out a strange sound which took a few seconds to register as a cackle. "Can't you count?"

"I beg your pardon?" I said.

"The number of days on the calendar between your birthday and January 6. That's how many days you and your alter shared before going—heh, heh—your separate ways."

"It's a long story," I said, deciding that I didn't want to bare my family history in front of a perfect stranger.

"Nothing to be embarrassed about," Monroe continued mercilessly. "Look at you, all upset because you shared a few months of life with another." He let out a second unidentifiable sound, something in the neighborhood of a snort. "What would you say if I told you that I was seventy-one—that's right, *seventy-one*—when I found out that *your* sort," he pointed a bony finger toward Bean and Pak, "had gone and produced a copy of the whole world and everyone in it. Alter indeed. Well, I outlived him, heh, heh. Died in a fire, he did. Burned his own house down last year."

"We didn't make a copy of the universe," Bean rose to the defense of her sort, "we merely found it."

"Irresponsible," Monroe snapped.

"The progress of knowledge," Pak said, "never stops."

"Progress? Ask your young friend here if he considers it progress." He jerked his thumb in my direction. "Ask him if he'd be here today if it wasn't for *meddling* in nature's affairs. Luckily the government put a stop to the whole thing."

Arni sent Bean, who looked ready to explode, a warning look. "What's done is done," he said easily, "but that's not why we're here today."

"Do you have my money, Pierpont?"

Arni got up off the stool, handed Monroe a credit slip from the pocket of his sweater, and sat back down. "We appreciate your giving us the opportunity to examine the item from Felix's past."

Monroe grunted in reply, scrutinizing the credit slip.

"Is it all there?" Bean asked with an edge to her voice.

Monroe folded the credit slip and carefully put it away into the pocket of his robe. "What you are looking for is upstairs. It was here when I moved in and I kept it because you never know,

I say, and I was right because here you are. The other group, the one that got here first"—Arni swore under his breath— "they were able to start it up. They wanted to take it to their workplace, all of it, but I said no. And I told them they'd better leave it in the same condition they found it, no funny business. Same goes for you folks." He got up, quite springily for a man who claimed to have been seventy-one 35 years ago. "Top of the stairs and to the right. I'll be in the kitchen eating my dinner."

I caught sight of the clock on the wall. It was only 3:37.

Monroe noticed. "The secret to longevity—and I'm the right person to ask, heh, heh—is prunes and an early dinner every day. Don't touch any of the boxes in the attic, Pierpont, like we discussed. They are all mine. And close the door on your way out."

I hung back as the others started up the stairs.

"Er—" I stopped Monroe on his way to the kitchen. "My alter, was he here with the other group?"

"Yeah, I reckon. Unless you have a twin."

A creature slinked by, brushing against my leg with its fur. A tiny cat.

"Did he—" I wasn't sure how to formulate the question. "Did he seem *content* with his life?"

Monroe gave me a blank stare. I went upstairs.

🦆

Monroe's attic was a depository for boxes of discarded clothing, outdated appliances, and a variety of furniture, all of it old, covered with a thick layer of dust, and serving as a breeding ground for dust mites and probably larger fauna as well. A lone bulb hanging bare from the low ceiling made a feeble effort at illuminating the space. "What is that _smell?_" Arni wrinkled his nose as Pak pushed the attic door open all the way; it stuck slightly and left a clean arc on the cobwebby floor. Pak headed straight for the pile of antiquated-looking computer equipment in one corner. "Recently disturbed," he commented. He knelt down and started connecting cables, muttering softly, "Come on now."

We dusted off a few sturdy boxes and moved them around to use as seats. Bean settled down next to Pak. As they worked to start up the computer, Arni cornered me next to an upside-down refrigerator. "Just a few more questions, Felix," he urged, as if I hadn't spent most of the car ride down and all of lunch answering questions about my childhood. Any minute now, I thought, one of them will suggest hypnotizing me to get at my subconscious and retrieve long-lost details of my early life; and it wouldn't have surprised me if they did happen to know how to perform hypnosis on willing subjects. The three graduate students digging around Monroe's attic and my past seemed confident they would find answers and achieve their research goal, no matter what the skills needed or how far they took them from their own field of study, bihistory.

As I pretended to listen to Arni, who was showing me something he called an interconnectivity and propagation of events diagram, it occurred to me that I was stuck somewhere in between, with neither the blind confidence of youth that everything would turn out as imagined nor the experience that builds up as years pass that it wouldn't matter if it didn't. Did that mean I was ready to leave Wagner's Kitchen, comfortable as it was, and try my hand at something else? Perhaps it was time to burn some bridges and just _write_.

Unfortunately, there was the small matter of having to eat and pay rent. Any potential money made from a mystery novel would trickle in drop by drop as readers discovered it and gave it—one hoped—positive reviews. I felt a stab of envy for authors living in Universe B, where publishers, I'd learned, often paid a bulk sum in advance for a manuscript.

On the other hand, I consoled myself, what if publishers didn't like your novel and declined to publish it? Whatever its faults, under the omni system, everyone's work, however brilliant or mediocre or truly bad, received an equal chance. True, one usually had to wade through a bog of flashy, poorly written stuff to find something halfway decent—but it was a race for readers with a level starting line, even if there was a lot of elbowing and shoving going on.

Pak had managed to revive the computer; slowly, with much rumbling followed by a low-pitched shriek, it came to life. Arni abandoned me and went to hover over Pak's shoulder.

"Someone cleaned this keyboard," Pak pointed out as the computer monitor flickered on and off, then settled for being on. "We shouldn't have stopped for lunch."

"Monroe said to come after three." Arni shrugged. "What's done is done. Let's see if we can find photos 1 through 12 and 14 and up." Without turning around, he added, "If that's okay with you, Felix, of course. This computer has been sitting here a long time."

Monroe's pet had come up the stairs after us and was padding softly around the attic, its paws leaving tiny footprints in the dust, its whiskers peeking occasionally from behind a box. "Is that a mouse or just an awfully small cat?" I wondered out loud. Arni frowned, said, "Both, I think," and gave his attention back to the computer.

"What happened to your parents' things after they died?" Bean asked.

"I came down to collect the paintings—the ones my parents did, not the gallery artwork. Their lawyer took care of the rest and sold the house as is, with the furniture and everything. Just think, had I been more involved in the process, I would have had the pleasure of meeting Monroe earlier." I looked around the attic. While at the San Diego Four-Year, I had visited my parents once a month and had eaten their food and washed my laundry and paid no attention to the seldom-opened, narrow door that led to the second most unusual room in a California house. (The first being a basement.) Monroe's claim of ownership aside, some of the furniture did look familiar, though it was impossible to be sure, it was all in such a state of decay. A grungy rectangular thing holding up boxes in one corner might have been a Universe B copy of a white table my parents had used to plan and lay out projects for their gallery. Or it might not.

Pak tapped the keyboard. "Hmmm. This is your parents' computer, is it not, Felix?"

"No."

"It's not?"

"It's Felix's parents' computer."

"Correct, yes. Did your parents own a similar one?"

"It's been fifteen years. Plus all computers look alike to me. That one just looks squarer and older."

"It's the Bitmaster 2001. They were popular around the turn of the century," Arni said as Pak pushed back the box he was sitting on and headed wordlessly out the door, sending Monroe's catmouse scurrying behind a dresser.

"Did 161 Cypress Lane have the same history in A and B?" I asked as we waited for Pak to return. "My parents lived here, I was born, they rented out the house and moved to San Francisco. Years later, they came back, opened the Art Cave, lived happily for a while, died. Then Monroe A bought the house and burnt it down." I recalled Monroe's unpleasant cackle as he pointed out the folly of his alter dying in a house fire. "Did all that happen here in Universe B as well, except for the last part and any cracks from our earthquake?"

"Pretty much," Arni said. "Some things didn't happen on the same date and Felix's parents named their gallery Cave Art, but other than that, yes, pretty much the same."

"Art Cave is better," Bean said. "More catchy."

The exposed light bulb hanging from the ceiling suddenly went out. By the light of the open door and the bluish glow of the computer monitor, Bean felt around for an old umbrella and used its handle to tap the base of the light bulb. The light came back on. "Loose wiring," she said. I noticed that a cobweb had attached itself to her hair.

"Cobweb, Bean. I still don't understand why you think this is all necessary. There must have been a lot of people near Professor Singh's lab on Y-day."

From where she was putting the umbrella back in its place by the refrigerator, Bean replied, "Four-thousand some."

"We've ruled them all out." Pak was back from downstairs. There was no arguing with him.

"What took so long?" Arni said. Pak was carrying the thin black bag he'd kept by his side all afternoon.

"Too much lemonade. Had to use the bathroom. Don't recommend it. Now let's see what we can recover—" He pulled a sleek black device out of the bag.

"What's that?" I asked.

"Which?" They all looked at me.

"*That*," I pointed to the object in Pak's hands.

"A laptop," Arni said. "Er—it's kind of halfway between an omni and a desktop."

"Desktop?"

"Computer."

"And a laptop is a—?"

"A computer as well. They've been a bit forgotten nowadays. Lots of people used to cart them around before we had omnis."

"And an omni is—?"

"A computer too, a little one."

"Then why give them different names—never mind."

As various cables got connected and the computers started churning away, I left the students to it and, stepping over the odd box or two, headed for a skinny wooden object by the far wall. Upon examination I decided that it was a combination coatrack and umbrella stand, but it was impossible to venture a guess as to which century, much less to which owner, it belonged. I didn't recall my parents ever owning a coatrack.

What I did recall was that after we moved to San Francisco, they had worked as salespeople at art stores and occasionally as museum guides to make ends meet. They had managed to give me a happy, if not particularly abundant with things, childhood. I had never tried to put myself in their place before. A bit of a loner as a child, I had spent much of my time with my nose buried in my omni, reading away.

I wondered what Felix's childhood had been like.

My eyes rested on a solid shape about the size of a microwave oven which sat under a decomposing woven quilt next to the coatrack. I nudged the filthy blanket off with my foot, raising a cloud of dust in the process and making myself cough. The box underneath had a single word written on it in hurried, middle-of-packing kind of handwriting: BOOKS. Intrigued, I was trying to peel the tape off when I heard Bean exclaim, "Here's something—"

I abandoned the box and went over. Too fast to be read, numbers were streaming across the screen of the laptop, which wasn't on anyone's lap but propped up on top of a handy box.

"Fragments." Pak furrowed his brow. "I don't like this."

"I wonder if Gabriella and James found the Bitmaster in this state," Bean said, "or if they got what they wanted first."

"Jane, sweetie," we heard Monroe calling his catmouse from downstairs, "come get supper..."

"Let's copy what we can and analyze it later," Arni urged.

"Jane, sweetie, I have Texas cheese..."

"Hurry," Arni added. "I keep expecting Monroe to come upstairs and throw us out because we're taking too long."

"What's the matter with Felix's parents' computer?" I asked the graduate students.

"Wiped," said Pak.

[13]

4100, 4101, AND 4102

Late next morning, I took three narrow flights of stairs down to the breakfast room of the Be Mine ("the *Be* is for the universe") Inn. The bed-and-breakfast where Arni had found us lodging for the night, four closet-sized rooms with a shared bathroom, had been recommended by Franny from the Queen Bee Inn and was run by Franny's cousin, who looked nothing like her kin and whose name I hadn't found out yet. Frankly, I was afraid to ask. She seemed a bit put out by my having slept in and gave the impression of being more likely to smack me with a book than make me a present of one. "I'm afraid you've *missed* the quiche. There's cereal and fruit left. Tea and milk over there." Franny's cousin stuck her decidedly non-square chin into the air and walked out to continue her day.

Pak was still missing but Arni had already come down, followed by a hoodie-clad Bean a few minutes later. There was no one else around, the other inn guests presumably having gotten up and consumed quiche at a more acceptable hour. In silence we scrambled to pour cereal and milk before Franny's cousin returned to clear the remaining breakfast items.

I took a look at the bleary-eyed graduate students. Well into the night, huddled around the antique desk in Pak's room, we had watched him play the laptop like a maestro, typing commands and running recovery programs. Someone had made a good job of wiping Felix's parents' computer, Pak had said, but because that someone had wanted to conceal that fact, paradoxically they could not make an *excellent* job of it. Whatever the reason, it meant the recovery task on the data gathered from the memory banks of the Bitmaster 2001 in Monroe's attic was difficult but not impossible. There was a growing pile of documents on the bed by the time I had retired for the night and left them to it.

A few sips of Earl Grey, whose depth and dark hue were growing on me as a non-coffee option, cleared the grogginess in my brain. Light streamed into the breakfast room through a high window, warming the dark paneling on the walls. Outside, a warbler could be heard chirping. Across the table Bean shook her head dejectedly. "We didn't find as much as we hoped."

"I wouldn't say that exactly," Arni said and yawned.

"I know, I know. I'm not a morning optimist. Talk to me after breakfast." She pulled the hood of her sweatshirt over her head and buried her face in the cereal bowl.

"You found photos, then?" I asked Arni.

"Credit card receipts." He reached for a knife and a rather strangely shaped apple and started peeling it. "Before we had identicards, people used to carry something called credit cards to pay for things, especially once the runaway inflation took hold and coins and paper bills became impractical. You couldn't carry cash, you needed such large amounts of it, even for little things—prices were high and rose often, sometimes more than once a day. From the receipts that we found, it looks like 4100, 4101, and 4102 went on a drive—"

"Forty-one-oh-oh?"

"Sorry, I'm used to the number reference system. I meant you and your parents, the citizens Sayers, that is, Mr. and Mrs. Sayers—"

"Patrick and Klara is fine."

He finished peeling the strange apple, offered Bean and me a slice each, then wiped his hands and took his omni off his neck. "I've drafted a timeline. In 1986, January 6 fell on a Monday. It was right after the holidays, so there were few tourists around in Carmel. Your parents probably closed their gallery for the day."

I couldn't remember my parents taking a day off—even if the gallery was closed, there were always pickups or deliveries to be made, paperwork to be done, or even just regular dusting, rearranging, and cleaning of the gallery space. If they went on a vacation, it would always turn out to be a pretext for acquiring new gallery pieces.

"The first receipt dated January 6 is from a Carmel restaurant called the Big Fat Pancake—it's not there anymore—the bill was paid just before nine. After that, presumably, you all piled into your parents' car, little Felix snug in his car seat—"

"It was a brown Chevrolet," I said. "I remember riding in it." What I didn't recall was finding the experience of being driven around as a child as nerve-wracking as I found it as an adult.

"—and headed north. We know this because there is a gas station receipt on the way up and then a receipt from a parking lot within walking distance of the Golden Gate Bridge. The parking lot is part of the Presidio campus nowadays," he said as an aside. "That receipt was issued at 11:15. The yabput, as we all know, occurred at 11:46:01, and for anything beyond that point in time we have to be careful to refer to 4100B, 4101B, and 4102B, to differentiate those three persons from their Universe A counterparts 4100A, 4101A, and 4102A, the last of which is you."

"Right," I nodded.

"Photo 13, the one in your Aunt Henrietta's possession, was taken on foot near the south tower of the Golden Gate Bridge— but whether it was taken *before* the yabput or *after*, we have no way of telling. All we can say for sure is that at eleven fifteen you parked near the bridge for some photo-taking. Unless you stayed for less than half an hour, at 11:46:01 *you would have been within the event radius.*" He paused to let that sink in.

"The next and last receipt of the day was signed by Klara Sayers at a Pier 39 restaurant, a driving distance away. The Quake-n-Shake. It's still there." He checked his omni screen. "Lunch was fourteen thousand dollars—a ridiculously large amount, but that's in old dollars, before the devaluation. Paid at 1:05." He leaned back in the antique chair as far as it would go without toppling and sank his teeth into an apple slice.

I took a look at the timeline displayed on Arni's omni.

Whereabouts of 4100B, 4101B, and 4102B on Y-day:

8:59 breakfast paid at Big Fat Pancake
10:30 Route 1 gas station
11:15 Golden Gate Bridge parking lot receipt
11:46:01 yabput
13:05 lunch paid at Quake-n-Shake Restaurant

"That's it? That's all we have?" I said.

A fresh apple slice in hand, Arni shook his head. "Don't listen to Bean, it's a lot. Photo 13 coupled with the receipts puts you in the right place at the right time. Where precisely you were at 11:46:01, we don't know yet. More photos or receipts would be helpful. Pak is still running recovery programs on the data from the computer in Monroe's attic—that is, his laptop is, Pak is sleeping. There might be more there. Also, remember that this is just Felix B's timeline."

"My parents' Universe A computer no longer exists," I reminded him. "The fire."

"But Universe A gas stations and restaurants keep records. Not much from Y-day was thrown out because everything from newspapers to milk cartons to stamps is a collector's item. It'll take a day or two to get authorization from DIM for the receipt from the Universe A Quake-n-Shake Restaurant, if there is a receipt to be had. In the meantime, we should go back to Monroe's and see if we missed anything. I'd like to look through all the boxes in that attic, for one thing. Monroe claims they are his, but maybe there's a box or two left by your parents— by Felix's parents, I mean. I'll make a call and get Professor Maximilian's permission for another day here at Carmel and for some extra funds. I have a feeling Monroe is going to charge us for the privilege of searching his attic again."

"That reminds me," I said. "I need to make a call."

I went into the hallway and dialed Wagner.

"Felix," bellowed Wagner, "*there* you are. Did you get my messages?"

"Sorry, omni difficulties. I'm sending you the Golden Gate Bridge write-up." I had put something together quickly.

"The bread maker is coming along nicely. I've decided that it should be crimson, like the bridge itself, what do you think?"

"Not a bad idea, though the bridge color is international orange."

"Is it? I've found a contact for the sourdough."

"Can't do it, Wagner. I'm in Carmel."

"When you get back to the city, go to the Salt & Pepper Bakery in the Mission District. Mention my name. The rest is taken care of."

"Are we sure about this?"

"It's just a yeast culture. Besides, if I could do it the right way, I would."

"Well—all right. By the way, how did the pretzel competition go?"

"A small disaster. The pretzels were too big for the ovens and stuck to the sides."

I went back into the Be Mine Inn breakfast room. "Bean, how did you know that our Wagners were the same?"

She looked up from the cereal bowl. "I met him."

"Wagner? When?"

"When I went looking for you at your workplace. In my clumsy attempt at approaching you as a research subject."

"Oh, you did quite well," I said to her and took another slice of the weirdly shaped apple that Arni had peeled. It was very crisp.

"Did I? I didn't even have a plan. I walked into Wagner's Kitchen with the vague notion of pretending to be a prospective client with an idea for a cookie maker I wanted to market. Luckily you had already left for your vacation, so I didn't have to actually, um—lie."

"So you came into my office, Bean. What about James and Gabriella, did they engineer the pet bug scare just to secure some time with me? What is this? It's delicious."

"It's a papple. Pear-and-apple," Arni said. He thought for a moment. "I wouldn't have said that Past & Future operated that way. For one thing, they don't need to. Money opens a lot of doors and they have it. On the other hand," he added, "the way Photo 13 appeared out of nowhere made *us* proceed very carefully, and I imagine the same is true for them. Even after we'd made sure the photo was authentic, we'd planned to say nothing until we were confident you weren't working for DIM."

He glanced pointedly across the table at Bean, who was studying the empty cereal bowl in front of her. "Anyway, here we all are, so I'm guessing you're not a DIM agent and this isn't an undercover operation of some sort to ferret out unauthorized research and other Regulation 19–breaking activities."

"I'm not and it isn't." Not only was I *not* a DIM agent, I was pretty sure my name was on a list titled *Suspicious Persons* produced by a desk-bound DIM official. Having a fake birth date will do that.

🦆

Having left Pak, who had eventually shuffled downstairs, at the B&B to oversee further data recovery operations, the three of us headed back to Monroe's house, on the way encountering a group of Passivists sitting still in a circle on a somewhat dry park lawn. One of them called out to us as the sidewalk took us past them, "We are all gods, my friends. Did one of you misuse the power? Did one of you build the dam that sent our two rivers cascading down different canyons—"

"My parents were never like that," Bean said quietly as we continued out of earshot. "They merely don't like disturbing nature or making decisions."

"What do the Passivists mean, did one of us misuse the power?" I asked.

"They believe the universe maker knowingly and deliberately sent A and B on different paths."

"They are not talking about Professor Z. Z. Singh, are they?"

"No." She picked up the pace.

Monroe let us in and grudgingly allowed us access to his house again on the premise that if we found anything, *anything* at all, he would be paid accordingly. I had a feeling he had wanted to search the attic himself but was willing to let us do the job.

As Jane darted into the hallway and we followed Monroe's pet catmouse up the carpeted stairs, I said, "Felix's parents also moved the family to San Francisco, you said. What about their life there? Was it similar?"

Arni understood what I was asking. "Generally speaking. Differences between alters' lives—and universes—tend to build up slowly. You end up with many small differences, a few medium-sized ones, and one or two biggies. Oddly, alters who are *not* in contact with each other often end up living lives more similar than those who are. If I had to guess, I'd say your parents and Felix B's parents didn't keep in touch, simply because they both moved back to Carmel and opened art galleries. If Felix B's parents had told *your* parents about this great idea they had about opening a prehistoric art gallery, your parents would have found something else to do."

"By the way, I've been meaning to ask," I said as we pushed the attic door open a second time, "how did Carmel get to keep its name in both universes? I thought you said only big cities kept their names."

"Ours is now Carmel Beach and yours is Carmel-by-the-Sea. As far as I can tell, everyone mostly calls both towns Carmel."

"Where do we start?" I said, looking around.

It was a good question. Ignoring the musty furniture, the coat/umbrella rack in one corner, the upside-down refrigerator, and a couple of piles of knickknacks that were clearly more recent in origin, that left most of the room. Cardboard boxes lay stacked on top of each other, with no clues as to whether they were placed there before or after Monroe moved in.

Bean pulled out the utility knife she had bravely borrowed from Franny's cousin back at the B&B. "Let's do this systematically. We'll start by the door, each take a box, look through it, then move on around the room."

Arni pushed his long curls behind his ears and looked down ruefully at his pleated chinos. "I wish I'd worn an older pair."

"Do you even own any clothes that aren't brand new?" Bean said and handed him the knife.

The first few boxes turned out to be full of old garments, prompting more jokes about Arni's sense of style.

"I'll tell you what I wish," I said, unable to suppress a shiver as I folded a box closed. (I had always found dated, worn-out clothing to be creepy.) "That we'd thought to bring some plastic gloves. Who knows what's living in these? And what are we looking for anyway?"

"Photo albums or a boxful of receipts, if we're lucky."

We weren't. A couple of hours and twenty-some boxes later, we were still empty-handed. We had unearthed some surprising things about Monroe's past—who would have guessed that he played professional tennis abroad as a young man—but we hadn't found anything belonging to my parents that wasn't in the clothes or furniture category.

"What about that box over there?" I stood up to stretch my legs, hoping my knees wouldn't crack and asking the question so Bean wouldn't notice if they did. She was jamming a utility knife into the refrigerator door. The door opened with a *pop*, revealing rows of jars, all upside down, some broken. "Ugh. Pickled vegetables. Did you say there was a box left, Felix?"

"The microwave-sized one over there, behind the umbrella stand thingie."

"The *what* where?"

I stepped over various hazards on the floor, pretending not to hear Arni explaining in a low voice, "A microwave oven is an appliance used to heat up food. Works on the principle of exciting water molecules via radio waves. Very popular in Universe A."

"I think I remember those from when I was a child," I heard Bean say. "Whatever happened to them?"

"People thought the radiation was dangerous. Plus we have self-heating cans nowadays."

"It's marked BOOKS," I said loudly.

Bean closed the door on the refrigerator smell (which managed to permeate even my impaired nostrils) and they hurried over. Arni knelt down, wincing at the dusty stains on his chinos, and carefully slit the tape that sealed the box. He opened it to reveal, unsurprisingly, books. Bean lifted out a couple. "Hey, these are on art. They must have belonged to your—I mean, Felix's—parents."

I took out a volume. It bore the title *Stones, Tombs, and Gourds.* "Why is it so bulky, this book?"

"Looks like a museum publication," Bean explained. "A textbook perhaps."

Inside the cover page, the textbook owner had written his initials: P.S., for Patrick Sayers, my father. At that moment I didn't care that, technically, it was not *my* father's hand that had set the letters down on the page, but his alter's. I placed *Stones, Tombs, and Gourds* aside and we began carefully lifting out the rest of the box's contents and looking through the books one by one. As Bean said, "You never know." The books were all oversized, had durable covers, and spanned the range of prehistoric art, from cave paintings to megalithic monuments. It was a collection that represented both my parents' education and their interests as they went about gathering life-size reproductions of ancient art for their own gallery (though not, of course, of the megalithic monuments).

"I've always wondered about the first person who decided to make a sketch on the dank, dark wall of a cave," said Arni, who was leafing through a book with glossy pictures of the Lascaux cave drawings. "You gotta ask, what prompted him or her to do it?"

Bean put a book aside and lifted out another. "It wouldn't surprise me to find that the first cave wall sketch started a really long event chain, one that led to, say, Professor Singh discovering inter-universe vortices."

I shook *The History of Pigments: Volume I*, but no conveniently hidden receipt or photograph fell out. "And what if these people had done something more constructive with their time than defacing cave walls, like hunting or berry picking?"

"Maybe in that universe we'd still be berry picking."

"Ouch," I said. "What the—"

Bean looked over. "Paper cut. Watch out for those."

"You know," Arni mused down his large nose, "it's quite an evolutionary leap, to be able to create things that have no immediate practical use. Or to try anything new, for that matter. Who would have thought that sliding a bit of raw meat onto a stick and cooking it over a fire would yield something as delicious as steak? Just an example—I don't eat meat anymore, I'm a pescetarian now," he explained to me.

"Wagner's Kitchen markets a decent soy burger recipe," I said, staring at my finger, the sting of the paper cut far outscaling the size of it. I added, "Here's what I don't understand about this business of universe-making. I'm not sure how to phrase it, but—"

"I know what you're going to ask," Bean said without looking up from *The History of Pigments: Volume II.*

"Oh?"

"People always ask the same question. You want to ask if your dog can start an event chain, though sometimes it's about their favorite fish or hamster or whatever."

I felt a little deflated. "I was going to say duck." For no reason at all, the orange-billed ducks frolicking in the health center pond had lingered in my mind. "If people can do it, why not ducks?"

Bean looked thoughtful for a moment. "Do ducks," she said quite seriously, "create universes?—Probably."

"Just like that? All the time? With every waddle?"

"We think so, yes. With every waddle that sets off a nice long event chain, in any case."

I put the last of the books aside and peered into the now-empty box. "So how do we know that a duck didn't—?"

"We don't. As a matter of fact, a duck would be just about the right size, I suppose. From Professor Singh's old data we know that the warping of space-time that yielded A and B required a prime mover of small mass, around twenty-four libras. Anyone know what a typical duck size is?"

Arni gave *The History of Pigments: Volume III* a final shake and stood up, clearly happy to be off the floor. He dusted off his hands and pants and reached for his omni. "I'll check."

"A small-sized universe maker," I said. "So that's why you're interested in me."

"Twenty-some libras is the typical weight of a six-month-old."

"*Can* a baby set off a significant chain of events?"

"You ever been around one?" said Arni, nose deep in his omni.

Bean had picked up Monroe's catmouse and was absent-mindedly stroking it. "It *is* limiting that people are the only observers we can interview. We have yet to figure out how to ask a whale or a tortoise if they saw anything of interest thirty-five years ago."

"So far," interrupted Arni, reading from his omni, "I can tell you that your typical dinner duck is about ten libras, requiring at least two hours of roasting. Sounds appetizing for those who aren't vegetarians, but a bit on the small side for our purpose."

"Forget ducks," Bean said dejectedly, "we can't even figure out where Felix was at the moment the Y-day yabput took place. Are you sure that you don't have an old photo album sitting on a shelf somewhere at home, Felix?"

"Sorry, no. Is it all right if I secretly hope a duck did it?"

Arni flipped his omni shut. "Well, whoever it was, it certainly wasn't me. I wasn't born yet. Although I can't guarantee that a few of my molecules weren't part of the Y-day prime mover. We are all recycled, always shedding and taking in molecules, you know."

Monroe refused to let me leave with any books, insisting correctly that my A-ness prohibited me from being the rightful inheritor of any Universe B items and relented only when I pulled out my identicard and signed a chunk of my credit over to him.

Pak was in the breakfast room of the B&B and had commandeered the long wooden table for his own purposes: on it sat the laptop, a printer, an empty teacup, a discarded banana skin, a plate with only crumbs on it—and half a dozen photographs strewn about.

He looked at us inquiringly as we walked in. "Found anything at Monroe's?"

"Art books," I said, placing my newly acquired treasure, *Stones, Tombs, and Gourds*, on the edge of the table, away from the teacup and the crumbs.

"The recovery program finished running. Took the whole night and most of the morning. It found photos."

I sat down.

Arni gathered up the dirty dishes off the table and took them to the kitchen. He came back just as Pak said, rather rudely I thought, "Only a few are of interest to us. Five, to be exact. The resolution is not great—no, don't touch them, Bean, they are still wet. I just printed them."

"When you say they are of interest," I began weakly, "do you mean that they were, in fact—"

"Taken on Y-day? Indeed."

I permitted my eyes to travel over the photographs.

I don't know what I expected to see.

[14]

FIVE
PHOTOGRAPHS

t's impossible to imagine *The Hound of the Baskervilles* without the foggy and inhospitably barren English moor, or *Murder on the Orient Express* without the claustrophobic tension of the Istanbul-Calais train moving ever closer to its final station. Mood was important in a story. And in life. With Pak's words, the mood in the room had heightened from academic interest to academic fever. "Five, you say," Arni said, rubbing his hands together in anticipation.

"I've ordered them by photo number," Pak said of the items recovered from the Bitmaster.

"I suppose it's too much to hope there's a time stamp as well," Bean said, her eyes darting from one photo to another.

"It is."

The first of the photos showed my mother next to the open door of a brown Chevrolet, either in the process of strapping me into my car seat or taking me out of it; in the background a store or restaurant could be seen. "The Big Fat Pancake," Pak said. "Either right before breakfast or right after."

The setting in the next two photos I thought might be the Presidio, the area just south of the Golden Gate Bridge. One was a close-up of a peeling eucalyptus tree, groves of which ran rampant all over the Presidio; the other was a shot of my family in front of (perhaps) the same eucalyptus, clearly taken by a kind stranger. "Cute hat, Felix," Bean said. In addition to being cute in a powder blue hat, I was sucking on something and hanging on to my parents.

"One eucalyptus tree is like another. It will be hard to pinpoint where those two were taken," Arni said, sounding a bit disappointed.

And the fourth photo—

"Hey," I said, "is that—?"

Pak nodded. "It is indeed. The Universe B version of Photo 13."

The fifth and last of the photos, like the eucalyptus ones, wasn't going to be of much use to the students. California sea lions lounged in the bright sun, packed like sardines on a dozen square wooden rafts anchored in a marina and looking magnificently content. Pak tapped the photograph lightly. "The marina near Pier 39. Nearby is the restaurant where Felix B and family went to lunch, and maybe Felix A and family as well."

"Never mind that," Bean interrupted. "Did you say number 13?"

"Indeed. Thirteen B, as it were."

She bent over the photo. "It's not the same as 13A."

"No."

"So 13A and 13B were taken post-yabput."

"Indeed."

"And therefore not necessarily at the same time. That is to say, 13A could have been taken somewhat earlier than 13B, or vice versa."

"Indeed," repeated Pak as I tried to work out in my head what Bean had just said.

There was a noise in the hallway and Franny's cousin stuck her head into the breakfast room. "Tulip needs to come in here and vacuum."

"Give us ten more minutes, please," Pak requested.

From the doorway Franny's cousin surveyed the mess on her breakfast table. "I'll tell Tulip to do the kitchen first. She needs to learn how to clean a stove properly anyway," she added and left.

Quelling a sudden desire to go help Tulip, whoever she was, by telling her all about Wagner's Kitchen Cleaner—*Spray Twice, Wipe Once,* I asked the graduate students, "So—now what?"

Arni had picked up 13B and was studying it so intently that his large nose was almost touching the paper; it was a wonder none of the ink had transferred to it yet. "It's not that complicated, really," he said. "The Sayers family drove to the Golden Gate Bridge, parked, walked a bit, took a couple of photos by a eucalyptus tree—then a bit later you or Felix B did something of momentous consequences, after which you took Photos 13 and went to lunch at Pier 39."

His remark prompted me to reach into the lunch pack we had picked up on the way back from Monroe's house. "Not that complicated, you say," I commented as I unwrapped a sandwich. I took a bite. The ham-and-cheese on wheat might as well have been pink-and-yellow plastic nestled in stale cardboard. I couldn't taste a thing.

"Not complicated, perhaps, but damn difficult," said Pak and took a sandwich himself, though it looked to me like he had spent most of the morning engaged in snacking and making a big mess for Tulip to clean. "Not bad," he said of the sandwich.

"Wait—Arni, did you say it was something that Felix B *or* I did?" I raised an eyebrow at him. "You mean only one of us did something?"

Arni had moved down to where a spidery chandelier hung above the middle of the breakfast table and had placed 13A and 13B side by side under the light. "I shouldn't have phrased it that way. You and he were the same person up until the very moment the universes diverged. Whether Universe A split off and Felix's Universe B is the continuation of the original, or whether Universe B split off and your Universe A is the continuation of the original, I don't know that we can even say. It was a single moment in time. Does it even matter?"

"Oh, it matters."

"Why does the camera never capture what people's watches say?" Bean complained, moving in closer and jostling for the photos with Arni. "Pak, we're going to need more copies. And it would help if we could enlarge them a bit."

"I'll try."

"What about Patrick's navy hat?" Arni suggested to Bean as they bent their heads together over the two photos. "He's wearing it in 13B, but not in 13A. And can you make out the number on the lamppost in 13B? Is that a 41 or 71?...The baby looks happier in 13B, doesn't it?..."

By the time Tulip came in and plugged in her vacuum cleaner, darting curious looks at the jumble of photos and enlargements on the breakfast table, even Arni had to admit that we were stumped. "Let's run image analysis of the new photos and see if that tells us anything. The silver Ford in 13B was driven across the bridge several minutes after the yabput, I think. That will help pinpoint the time, at least."

As Pak packed up his laptop, I asked, "What constitutes a significant chain of events, anyway?"

Arni sent a quick glance in the direction of Tulip, who was securing an attachment to the vacuum in a dilatory manner, and repeated, "What constitutes a significant event chain? Anything that creates a universe."

"And what creates a universe?"

"Anything that constitutes a significant event chain."

"Anything that—oh, for heaven's sake," I said, and stomped up to my room.

🦆

Awhile later Bean knocked once on my door, called out, "I got it, meet us downstairs," and left just as abruptly. I took a moment to stretch my limbs, having spent the past couple of hours doing about the only thing a person *can* do while a team (two teams counting James and Gabriella) endeavors to prove said person accidentally created a universe thirty-five years ago by poring over his childhood photos with a fine-tooth comb, or is it a brush or a microscope that one pores with? Anyway—I took a nap.

Steep wooden stairs led from my Be Mine Inn tower room one flight down to where the graduate students had their rooms. (I was touched that they had given me what they clearly considered to be the best room of the four, though I found the round walls with their exceedingly narrow windows awkward to live in.) No one answered when I knocked on their doors, so I continued down two more flights of stairs to the breakfast room.

The students were bent over something at the breakfast table, their backs to me. The flower-motif posters on the walls hung a little askew, having survived Tulip's cleaning. Vacuum lines crisscrossed the carpet.

I set down Franny's paper book *Why Didn't They Ask Evans?* which I had brought down to make it look as if I had been reading for the past couple of hours, but no one noticed. (On a side note, carting a paper book around while reading it had not turned out to be as much of a bother as I'd anticipated.)

"Look closely," Bean was saying to Arni and Pak. "As I understand it, though admittedly my experience with babies amounts to zero, if you have something that succeeds in soothing the kid, you stick with it come rain or shine."

Enlargements of 13A and 13B lay side by side.

I moved closer. In the photo on the left, Aunt Henrietta's number 13, there I was, in a baby carrier hanging on my father's chest, my puny limbs dangling while I sucked on something; in the Universe B photo, 13B, Felix was in *his* baby carrier, his puny limbs dangling while he sucked on something. It was like one of those maddening games where you're supposed to find ten differences between Picture 1 and Picture 2, or in this case Picture 13A and Picture 13B. I'd never been very good at those, and the two pictures in front of me were only similar in the basics anyway: both were father-son tableaux, but 13A caught my father in a serious moment, while 13B had him doing antics for the camera, making a pretend motion as if about to toss Felix B, safely strapped in his baby carrier, up into the air; 13A was a close-up shot, while 13B had several pedestrians and a car accidentally caught on camera; light gray clouds and vertical bridge cables were visible in both, though more so in 13B. It was impossible to tell what was crucial and what was incidental.

"I know the enlargements are fuzzy," Bean said, "and the viewing angle is different, and both objects are yellow, but—"

"I see it," Arni said. "Banana. Duck."

"What?" I said and looked again.

And there, as Pak would say, indeed it was. Yellow banana in 13A, yellow duck with no feet in 13B. Cutesy pacifier attachments.

"Now *that's* interesting," Pak said.

"The duck pacifier is there in 1B and 10B as well—the morning photo taken in front of the Big Fat Pancake and the later one by the eucalyptus tree—so the day started with Felix having the duck pacifier," Bean told us, her voice rising with excitement. "But it's gone in Aunt Henrietta's Photo 13A. The change only happened in our Felix's universe."

I winced. "Don't call it that."

"Sorry. In Universe A."

"Wait," I objected, "there are a thousand tiny differences between the two photos. My father's navy hat, for one thing. He's wearing it in 13B but not in 13A. What about that? How do we know the pacifier switch is important?"

"We don't," Arni said. "But it's very suggestive. It was windy, so hats on or off, not a big deal." He produced a thick round magnifying glass and bent over the eucalyptus photo of my family like an old-fashioned detective. "Yes, I see it—the duck kind of blends in with Felix's chin—that's a magnificent eucalyptus specimen, isn't it—"

I picked up 13A and 13B. There was one additional difference. The infant in 13A (me) wore a sullen, almost peevish, expression on its round face, while the infant in 13B (him) seemed content in his baby carrier, rather like the seals lounging in the Pier 39 marina. Holding us in the two photos was my father, dressed in jeans and a striped windbreaker, having taken his family out for a Monday drive. I wondered if he was smiling and clowning around in 13B because Felix B had been better behaved—unlike Felix A, who had managed to lose his pacifier.

What had I done?

[15]

FACE-TO-FACE

"**Y**ou think the duck pacifier started an event chain?" Arni said to Bean. "How?"

"I have no idea," Bean admitted frankly, taking a chair at the Be Mine Inn breakfast table. "Maybe Felix got bored while his parents were admiring views of Alcatraz and Angel Island and chucked the pacifier at a passing bicyclist who stumbled and broke his leg—all right, it can't have been anything that big, we'd have heard about it in other Y-day interviews...er... well, there's a chance a photo taken by another tourist might have captured the moment."

"Not with our luck." Arni tapped Photo 13B with the magnifying glass. "Duck in this one, banana in the other. I don't know how we missed that. Why are they both yellow anyway? Ducks aren't yellow. Only their bills or feet, maybe."

"All bananas aren't yellow either," I said distractedly. "There are red and purple bananas too. Are you suggesting that all the grand differences between our two universes stem from these...these artificial *nipples* that my parents gave us to keep us occupied?"

"Yes and no." Arni scratched his ear. "There was a brief moment when everything in A and B remained exactly the same, except for whatever it is you and Felix B did differently at 11:46:01. Then a commuter missed her train, lightning hit a tree, a dog bit a man, sperm found an egg—some of it in A, some in B, some in both. The current state of Universe A is partly due to the original Y-day event chain, but also to independent event chains that emerged as time went on. Think of two snowballs poised at the top of a hill. Give them a nudge and they both head downhill. Where they end up at the bottom depends not just the direction they were pushed in, but on the stuff they encounter along the way, rocks and trees and snowdrifts and such."

"So some things are your fault, others aren't," Bean summarized.

"Gee, thanks," I said.

"However," said Arni, "only one event chain will lead all the way back to 11:46:01."

Bean brushed off a few crumbs that Tulip had forgotten to sweep, and started to drum on the table gently with her fingers. "The event chain...what could it have been? Felix loses his duck pacifier and doesn't like the back-up choice, the banana"—drum, drum—"maybe it didn't squeak the same way the duck did—and Felix's complaining prompts his parents to run into a toy store"—drum, drum—"but in doing so they delay an aunt buying a birthday gift and cause her to miss her bus and instead take a car to her niece's birthday party and accidentally run over the neighborhood cat"—drum, drum— "an event that *doesn't* happen in Universe B, where the cat goes on to mother a new breed of super-cat destined to achieve dominance over the human race," she ended, taking a deep breath.

Pleased with the scenario in which I save Universe A from a terrible fate, I applauded, then said, "Well, I'm still not convinced that my parents just took me out for a simple Monday drive up to the city. There had to be more to it. A reason why they closed the gallery and went to San Francisco that day."

"Unlikely feline world domination scenarios aside, Bean is right," Arni said. "We need to sit down and brainstorm and make a list of possible event chains."

"I'll run some simulations," Pak said.

"The Universe A receipts should be coming in soon," Bean said. "We'll have a better idea of how the day played out."

"We should study traffic patterns too. And check store receipts—" Arni said.

"—and accident reports—"

"—and the Y-day photoboard, in case we missed something—"

Wolves intent on their chase. I felt a sudden loathing come over me, disgust not at their prying, but at my own. Everyone is entitled to privacy. Even an alter.

"I need to make a call," I said and went out of the breakfast area into the hallway.

There was a message from Wagner. "Wanted to run an idea by you, Felix. Self-cleaning refrigerator. Remove food, push button, water shoots in from all sides and washes interior. Automatic dry. One more thing. I'm hearing some things—just be careful, that's all. Oh, and don't forget the Salt & Pepper Bakery." The omni beeped to signal the end of the message, leaving me to wonder what Wagner had meant by the warning. He had a large network of professional contacts—everyone had to eat, as he often pointed out—and on occasion those contacts operated in unlikely places.

Everyone knew that DIM's official motto was, *Information is best managed number by number.* Rumor had it, however, that the unofficial motto was, *Information is best managed by*

ELIMINATING it number by number. I suddenly realized how chilling that last verb was. The students had assumed that the computer in Monroe's attic had been wiped clean by James and Gabriella to ensure that Past & Future stayed ahead of Professor Maximilian's team. But what if DIM wanted to keep the idea that humans created universes out of the public eye? Removing key evidence from our path was certainly one way of doing it.

I shook my head and made the call I had come out into the hallway to make. Mrs. Noor answered at once.

"There's been a change of plan, Mrs. Noor," I said. "I won't require any more information about—about the party in question."

"I see. All right. I do have one morsel for you, courtesy of my daughter Daisy, but I understand if you're not interested anymore."

Wanting to cut the conversation short, I spoke a tad more abruptly than I intended. "Just send me a bill. And thanks for your help, Mrs. Noor."

"Call if you need anything else, Felix."

"Mrs. Noor, wait," I said just before she disconnected. "What do you have?"

She paused, hand midway to her omni. "You mean my morsel? Just this. Your alter is in Carmel. And he had a visitor join him. His fiancée."

🦆

"You don't have an alter, do you?"

I received a puzzled look from Bean.

"Never mind," I said.

We were on a public path that meandered along Carmel's sandy beach, our way illuminated by a full moon in a star-dotted sky, which might have been quite a romantic experience had Pak and Arni not been a few steps behind us enumerating the defects of outdated computer technology and snickering occasionally. Carmel being the kind of seaside town that shuts down not long after sunset, we had all gone out for a post-dinner beach stroll.

"Do you mind if I ask you something?" Bean said as we walked along the sand-swept path. (I kept an eye out for intertwined couples, checking each time whether the guy looked anything like me.) "You don't have to answer if you don't want to."

People always say that, but it makes you look small if you decide that, in fact, you'd rather not answer their question. "Go ahead," I said, resignedly.

"What are you stuck on?"

"Er—?"

"You *can* write, yes?"

"I can put together a decent culinary user guide, according to Wagner."

"I meant the mystery novel."

"It's not that easy. I mean, on one hand, it is. A murder early on, then another or two to thicken the plot, a sleuth on the case, a few red herrings thrown in for good measure, and finally the climax as the culprit is revealed to everyone's surprise and you flip your omni shut. I've been reading Christie's *Why Didn't They Ask Evans?*—good title, that—who could catch sight of it and not wonder who Evans was and what he or she should have been asked? Or," I said, expanding on the issue, since she had been the one to bring it up, "one could go short and to the point, like *The Hound of the Baskervilles.* Conan Doyle, by the way, bestowed sixty-some titles in all—not counting the fairies stuff—and Christie, even worse, eighty mystery novels. Eighty! Where did they find the time?" Various and sundry murder scenarios—to be brought to life in a book, of course—did often drift into my head as I sat at my desk at Wagner's Kitchen, but I'd quickly remember I needed to pay rent and give my attention back to the vegetable peelers and the rice cookers.

Bean bent down and picked up one of the pebbles lying by the side of the path. She sent it into the darkness of the ocean, narrowly missing a macar tree. "If you don't mind my saying so—*surds.*"

"I beg your pardon?"

"Irrational numbers. What I mean is, just go for it. Give it a year or two. I'm sure Wagner A will hire you back if things don't work out."

"I don't know about that. Wagner can be pretty touchy."

"Professor Maximilian too."

"It's the chicken-and-egg problem. You can't call yourself a writer until you've posted a book and it's progressed out of the Read for Free section—or, I suppose, here in Universe B, had a book published—but how do you get there without devoting the bulk of your time to writing? And what if you *do* devote the bulk of your time to writing but people don't like your book and don't want to read it? Anyway, I can't afford to take a year off. I blew all my savings buying a ticket to Universe B."

Behind us Arni's voice rose and I caught the words, "One *giga*byte," and a snicker.

"Sometimes I think I would have been better off in a job that required no writing," I mused as we continued on. "I might have been more inspired to do it in my free time, if you see what I mean."

"Like Einstein."

I raised an eyebrow. No one had ever compared me to the famous scientist before.

"How do you do that? I can't raise my eyebrows individually, only together. Einstein, early in his career, had trouble getting a job in the field of physics—imagine!—so he worked in a patent office for three years. Gave him time to think and he came up with some pretty momentous stuff. In physics, not patents. Though one imagines he was capably performing his duties at the patent office too."

We stopped to allow Arni and Pak, who were arguing loudly about the fractal degree of a particularly twisty macar tree, to catch up to us.

"You know what the problem is, don't you? It's people," I said. "If it turns out I did create Universe A, they are going to come knocking on my door, blaming everything that's wrong in their lives on me. Like I'm responsible for every lost sock or the 8.1 earthquake or spray-cheese coming back into vogue."

"We have spray-cheese here too. Besides, that's wrong."

"No, they'll blame me. I know it."

"No, I mean I suppose some people will, but they'd be wrong to do so." We continued on around a bend in the path and she reached out to touch a macar tree, its dead trunk and branches bleached white by the elements. "A universe is like a bubble. Millions of little random events and daily personal choices buffet that bubble around, pushing on it from within." She bent down and picked up another pebble and propelled it over the dark rocks into the water, which the moonlight had given an eerie sheen. It disappeared soundlessly. "Most likely the pebble harmlessly landed on the ocean floor. The universe adjusted a little, perhaps. Nothing changed but the spatial position of the pebble. But what if I kept doing it?" She bent down, scooped up a handful of pebbles off the edge of the path, and started flinging them one by one over the rocks toward the water. "Eventually...if I do this long enough...something will happen. It might be simple enough—a pebble might bop a seagull on the head and, startled, it flies in our direction and drops on our heads—er—the processed remnants of its dinner, and so we hurry back to the B&B to wash our hair, thus never having whatever life-changing conversation we are about to have. Or, less personally," she said, flinging the last pebble wildly and watching it fly in a tall arc across the rocks and disappear into the water, "a pebble could land just *so,* causing a landslide and generating a monster wave."

We paused to look around but everything seemed stable.

"An event like that would distort the universe bubble," she said, rubbing her hands lightly to get the sand off, "stretch it to its limit, spawning another universe. We'd end up with the original universe in which no monster wave occurred and another in which it did. *But—*"

The westerly breeze was blowing her chestnut locks into her eyes. She brushed them away impatiently. "But then other prime movers would set off budding event chains and new universes would spout, like a giant tree constantly growing branches, upward and outward. Like Arni said, whoever or whatever the Y-day prime mover was, they are not responsible for *all* the differences between A and B."

"Do we know that for sure?"

"The link, for one. Professor Singh linked universes A and B moments after they formed. An independent event chain that happened on the heels of yours. Think of all the stuff that we know resulted from that—the formation of DIM, the only inter-universe body. Carmel becoming Carmel Beach here. Nature names rising in popularity—"

"Oh." I tried to make sense of that. "Still."

"The idea is not new, you know. If you have the right DIM clearance, you can find it mentioned in old journals and books, all the way back to that ancient Greek, Democritus, and his idea of many worlds. All of us involved in universe-making, like a plethora of Greek gods, even the retired chemistry professor who won't let anyone park in his empty parking spot at Presidio University. Behavior which really ought to rule you out for god status. What's the matter, Felix?"

A couple had emerged from the shadows. They crossed the path and, stopping for a moment to take their shoes off, continued down the beach hand in hand.

"False alarm. I thought I saw someone familiar. What's at the bottom of the universe tree? Does it have a root?"

She gave the tiniest of shrugs. "There must be a universe that's still in the primordial state, a universe in which nothing ever occurred except other universes branching off. More like the tree trunk than the tree root, I suppose."

"Too bad I couldn't take responsibility for a really pleasant universe, like in one of those science fiction stories where money doesn't exist anymore and everyone gets to do whatever they want in life. Instead I get one where citizens have to work and warts haven't been cured yet."

"I don't know, both A and B seem pretty good to me. I like to think that we live in average universes. I'm sure there's much worse stuff elsewhere."

I stifled a yawn. "Sorry, I don't know what's the matter with me, I've slept half the day away."

She gave me a sympathetic look. "I can't imagine what it's like to suddenly find out that you have an alter. I'm sure I'd obsess constantly about which one of us would get her PhD first." She hesitated. "One more thing—to be honest, I'm not sure it's even possible to pin the universe maker label on a single person or object. Any chain of events should be traceable if you follow it backward in time, but there are those who argue that it's all guesswork, that you might as well try to figure out which flutter of which wing of which particular butterfly produced a hurricane years later. In any case, it might take decades to perfect the techniques and pool all the data, by which time we might very well be—well, dead."

Strangely enough, her words made me feel better.

"So what you're saying is the practical thing to do would have been to take Past & Future's offer of up-front money."

"Well," she laughed, picking up another pebble and aiming it toward the ocean, "all other considerations aside, yes, I suppose so."

"Hey, Bean," I heard Arni's voice behind us, "are you trying to move the whole beach into the ocean?"

🦆

Thursday dawned foggy and cold. I awoke to the first morning song of the warbler outside my window, dressed quickly and warmly, and headed out, closing the room door behind me with care so as not to wake up the other B&B guests. The landing outside the tower room was dim and in the dark I stepped on something—I rolled along with it for an instant and managed to make a last-second grab at the banister to avoid crashing down the stairs. The object responsible for making me lose my balance thumped down step by step, the sound amplified by the morning quiet, and came to a rest at the bottom. I hobbled down the creaky, narrow staircase and picked it up. It was a rubber rolling pin, toy-sized and too light to be of any use in a kitchen. The handles squeaked when squeezed.

Massaging my ankle where I had banged it on the banister, I told myself, I'm having an unusual amount of bad luck on this trip.

Unless—?

Suddenly the black car that had almost mowed me down outside the Bookworm not long after my arrival in Universe B took on a more sinister implication. I had assumed it was just an impatient commuter. And the cherry candies that someone had sent to the Palo Alto Health Center and to which I could have reacted badly—had someone wanted to extend my stay at the health center, perhaps permanently?

I checked the hallway lamp, which sat on a miniature antique table on the middle landing. The bulb was missing, the socket empty.

Only one person stood to gain from my early demise.

Even forming the thought in my mind made me seem like a mystery-writer wannabe with an overactive imagination. I was being paranoid, I decided, seeing shapes in the clouds. A child or the house pet must have left the rubber rolling pin lying around, and Tulip had probably taken out the old bulb during her cleaning routine and forgotten to put in a new one. The other things, the car and the cherry candies, were just narrow escapes from an unlucky twist of fate, like the pet bug that had sent me to the health center in the first place.

I left the toy next to the lamp on the miniature antique table and carefully (I had no desire to go back to a health center) descended two more flights of stairs. There was no one at the front desk at this early hour and the front door was unlocked, but Carmel is that kind of place. The street too was deserted. Keeping to the side of the road, there being no sidewalk, I set a course toward Main Street. There was a crisp, oceany feel to the air that bit at the nostrils and kept my pace at a brisk hobble.

I had some thinking to do.

To say that my trip to Universe B had not turned out as expected was an understatement. Life, of course, likes to throw a wrench (like a pet bug quarantine) into even the most modest of plans—and wrenches frequently landed in my plans, as if a giant celestial spotlight blazed in my direction, inviting fate to pick me, Felix A (though possibly everyone felt that way). And that spotlight seemed especially bright at the moment. For all of Bean's reassuring words, I had an unshakable feeling that the graduate students, or James and Gabriella, would pin the universe-maker label on me and somehow manage to get the idea past DIM. And I didn't want it. Didn't want the fame and the blame, the inevitable exaggerations that would follow about my role in the matter. From that point on, I would be judged by the itty-bitty, baby-sized choice I made at 11:46:01 on Y-day.

Perhaps the best thing to do, then, was to ditch the graduate students and concentrate on practical matters, like getting my hands on some sourdough starter for Wagner. I'd need to get back to San Francisco as soon as possible and make my way to the back door of the Salt & Pepper bakery.

I hobbled along, my ankle still sore where I had banged it on the banister, and made a right onto Main Street and set a course in the direction of the beach. The low-lying fog gave the gently sloping street, lined with cottages and quaint shops, a dreamy, story-like feel. A few bundled walkers getting their morning exercise were out and about, but stores were not open yet for the day, save for a teahouse whose proprietor was in a courtyard arranging tables and chairs. Had that meal not been included in my lodging rate, I would have been tempted to go into the teahouse for an early breakfast. Might grab a hot tea on the way back, I thought, if only to warm up my hands.

Farther down Main Street I paused at a bookstore, one meant for children, judging by the colorful books that sat like unwrapped presents in the store's windows next to seashells and plush toys. The sign on the door read, *Sorry, we're closed. Come back after a hearty breakfast of green eggs and ham.* I chuckled and continued on to an intersection. As I waited for a car to pass, an urge seized me, an urge to storm back to the B&B and shake everything concerning me and Felix B out of Pak's laptop. The same with Past & Future's computers—the glass building whose employees threatened to bring upheaval into my life came into view briefly as I crossed the intersection.

Was I beginning to feel sympathy for the man and was that why I had called Noor & Brood off the chase? There was a duality to the matter. On one hand, I hoped Felix B wasn't so unhappy with his everyday life as to be busily working on a novel as a way out. But if it *did* turn out that he was perfectly content with his head-chef, fiancée-boasting, member-of-kennel-club life—well, I was jealous of that too. I wasn't proud of it, but there it was.

I imagined him sleeping in a good sized hotel room paid for by Past & Future, snoring away warm and snug next to his fiancée instead of wandering Carmel's streets at this early hour. Or at least I would have, except that there he was.

He was a few steps away, striding uphill from the beach right toward me.

For a moment, he didn't recognize me. Then shock registered on his face, probably mirrored in my own. Time stopped. And then he opened his mouth to speak, but before he could get a word out, I took two steps forward, jabbed a finger at his chest, and demanded,

"Are you missing a rolling pin?"

[16]

FELIX B

He staggered back a bit. "A rolling pin? What, at my kitchen at the Organic Oven?"

"No, a rubber rolling pin."

"Don't believe I've ever owned one. Er—want a hot drink? My hands are freezing. The teahouse up the street looked open."

I pulled myself together and accompanied him back to the Las Palmas Teahouse. None of the early customers who sat inside reading printed newspapers gave us a second glance. The proprietor wiped his hands on his apron and nodded a greeting at us. "What can I get you, citizens?"

I took a quick glance at the menu on the wall and, at the very bottom, spotted what I had been sorely missing in Universe B.

"Coffee, black," I said.

"Coffee, black," said Felix B.

"Two coffees, black, it is," said the proprietor.

Wordlessly agreeing that it was too cold to sit in the courtyard, where tables waited under a shady grapevine trellis, Felix and I headed to a free table by the window. As we waited for the proprietor to fulfill our order at the lone coffee machine nestled among the many tea brewers and tea bins, my eyes went to the watercolors hanging on the teahouse walls. Eating establishments in Carmel often displayed works of budding local artists. These weren't bad.

I blew on my coffee to cool it a bit and peered at Felix over the cup. It was like looking in a mirror, only features were not reversed. Morning stubble. Pale brown freckles. Hair, thin and a nondescript brown like mine, though a good five digits longer. A hint of pudginess marked his cheeks, red from the cold morning air, and, without being able to stop myself, I put my hand to my own face to feel for any signs of cheek roundness. Our eyes met and we both looked away.

"So you drink coffee too, huh?" Felix spoke first, wiping a drop off his saucer with his finger.

"Why is it so hard to find here?"

"We overdid it—the magnus, the amplus, the double-amplus, the *triple*-amplus sizes, the vanilla, chocolate, orange, caramel, and mint flavors, the whipped cream, the frothed milk, the steamed milk, the no milk, the extra milk, the low-fat milk, the curdled milk, the decaf, the half decaf, the third decaf...It was too much. Then someone realized that tea comes in a hundred natural variations—and it's much easier to order. Parsley, hot. Oolong, cold. But I still like the occasional coffee, especially in the mornings. I tend to have a hard time getting out of bed."

The coffee was strong. I eyed the four small jars sitting in the middle of the table, wondering if any of them contained sugar.

Felix lifted the lid off one of the jars. "Sugar cube?"

"What's in the other three?"

"Lemon packets, honey, milk." He handed me a couple of the wrapped sugar cubes and took one for himself.

The man didn't *seem* like a coldblooded killer—though if he was one then it would have been child's play for him to feign indifference after planting a rubber rolling pin at the top of a badly lit staircase for me to trip on and fall down the stairs and break my neck. Nor would he be the first to do something of the sort. After crossings were first opened to the public thirty-some years ago, unscrupulous citizens had used the opportunity to switch places with their alters ("to see what it was like") or, more to the point, to dispose of their alters and take over their lives. Or so the stories went. I'd always suspected they were a bit exaggerated. That was before my run of bad luck.

If Felix B, sitting across the table from me tranquilly stirring a sugar cube into his coffee, was writing a book, murder was one sure way of getting rid of the competition. (I had not once considered knocking *him* off, but perhaps he was more in touch with our dark side.) I cleared my throat. "So, Felix—can I call you that?"

"If you don't mind if I call you Felix."

"What kind of car do you drive—one as sleekly black as the inside of a nonstick pan?"

"The inside of a—no, my car is a two-seater the color of a squishy apricot. I don't have it here in Carmel. Granola James and Gabriella Short drove me down." He took off his jacket and hung it on the chair back. He was wearing a heather T-shirt underneath. I happened to be wearing one too. Deciding to keep my jacket on, I said, "The graduate students drove me down."

"That's right, you signed on with the other camp. Seems fitting. How are they treating you?"

"They are a good bunch. I wanted to help them out. Are we violating Regulation 7?" I suddenly remembered that the DIM official at the crossing terminal had tagged the identicard I'd just used to pay for my coffee with an *Alter in the Area* tag.

"By running into each other in front of a teahouse? Surely not."

"You haven't by any chance signed a form giving me permission to contact you?"

"Er—well, I was considering it."

"So you knew I was here in Universe B."

"DIM alerts anyone whose alter crosses."

"And that's how you found out I existed."

"No, I've known about a month or so. Aunt Henrietta of your Universe A left me a Y-day photo, though I seem to have mislaid it. Did you get one too?"

"I did," I said.

"And the dolphins?"

"Forty-two of them. Some of them are quite large. To be honest, I was hoping she'd left me some money," I said in a sudden outburst of honesty.

"I could have used some extra cash too. I've been paying for Japanese lessons. My fiancée's parents are visiting soon and I want to make a good impression when I meet them. Melody—my fiancée—she and I met at a kennel club—here, do you want to see a picture? She's back at the hotel. I woke up early for some reason." He went on, "Melody says a honeymoon to Universe A is not in our budget. But you have seen both. What do you think of mine?" he asked, suddenly seeming quite human.

For a moment my mind was blank. Traffic, laptops, suitcases with wheels, they all seemed too ordinary to mention.

"Uh—I met a girl," I said.

"Well, well. Good for you. What's her name?"

"Bean."

"She's a unique?"

I nodded. Felix was seated nearer to the door and, as the bell chimed and we turned to look at an early morning walker coming in for a beverage, I caught sight of the back of Felix's head. The experience was like being in front of one of those 360-degree mirrors in a clothing store, only stranger.

Turning back, Felix repeated, "Well, well. An inter-universe romance. That could get tricky. Though since she's a unique, at least she can live wherever she likes. I wish they'd leave us alone."

"DIM?"

"Well, yes, though I meant James and Gabriella and your student researchers and their Professor Maximilian who keeps sending me requests for interviews even though I've told him I've already signed a contract with Past & Future." He scratched his nose. "Regulation 7 aside, is it even legal for us to be talking about this? As I said, I did sign a contract."

"I signed a contract too, with the graduate students, but I dare anyone to inform me that we're not allowed to talk about universes. I mean, that's—everything."

"James said that reality is essentially a pie."

"I beg your pardon?"

"I asked him for a kitchen analogy."

"I wish I'd thought of asking for a kitchen analogy. I've been told universes are like bubbles. Also like tree branches."

"The pie crust, James said to me, is sturdy and dependable, like gravity. The apple always falls to the ground, never veers off into the clouds. Next, he said, is the pie filling—soft, fluid, comes in many flavors. It's what life brings to reality. We build parking lots and wear ties and compete for survival. And then there is the random stuff, like lightning strikes. The raisins strewn throughout the pie."

"I've never eaten a pie with raisins in it," I said. "Ugh."

"I've never *made* a pie with raisins in it. But ultimately it's just a pie, James said—different universes, different pie flavors. And different pie flavors is where our choices and actions are landing us."

"Bean—the girl—said that they're looking for a small universe maker. I'm hoping they'll find a universe-making duck."

"I know what you mean. Really, what weighty choice could a six-month-old drooler possibly have made? And who needs the spotlight that will shine on us if it turns out to be true?"

"Then you don't want to be the universe maker any more than I do? I just assumed, since you signed on so quickly with Past & Future—"

"I was merely going along with it. Got a trip to Carmel out of it and some spending money for Japanese lessons. They didn't tell me about this universe-making business until we got down here, anyway. Besides, you signed on too," he pointed out, raising an eyebrow at me.

"I did, didn't I."

"Thirty-five years ago we happened to be in the vicinity of Professor Singh's lab and a photo snapped on the Golden Gate Bridge proves it. So what?" He took an irritated sip of his coffee. "How do we know that a seal or a fish swimming by—or as you say, Felix, a duck on a nearby pond—didn't do it? *Can* wildlife create a universe?" he said, frowning (and making me wonder if I had that many lines on my forehead.)

An omni buzzed and we both reached around our necks.

"Mine," Felix said.

"Good morning, Chef Felix," said a familiar voice, accompanied by faint barking in the background. "Ready for a new day of research?"

"Morning, Granola James."

"Great day, isn't it? Murphina and I just got back from a jog. Breezy out there. You having a solitary cup of tea?"

"Something like that. Listen, what time do you need me?"

Woof, *woof.*

"Murph, I'll get you a second helping in a minute. As soon as you can, Felix. Gabriella has more questions for you."

"All right, I'll be there in a jiffy. By the way, can Murphina create universes?"

"You bet."

Felix flipped his omni, a classy one that looked like it might have been a recent birthday present, shut. "Sorry, have to go. At least I get to be interviewed by Gabriella Love's alter. Have you met her?"

I nodded. How terrible to be known as the alter, not the person. Finishing off what remained of my coffee in a single gulp, I asked, "Felix, do you have your sense of smell?"

"Yes, why do you ask? One can't be a chef without a sense of smell."

"You'd probably be making a lot of things in your kitchen with cheese, chocolate, and nuts in them. Cherry allergy?"

"Ah, that I have. No cherries in my kitchen."

He swung his jacket over his shoulder and I followed him out the teahouse door and through the courtyard, taking the opportunity to study his form. His body shape was just like mine. A convex middle. The hazard of working in a kitchen, no doubt.

"What is *that?*" I said once we were back on Main Street. The fog had started to lift, leaving tenuous wisps hovering over sand dunes at the beach end of the still-deserted street. Nearby stood an abominable structure, three stories of stained, dingy cement. I had not noticed it before.

"That? Just a parking structure for beachgoers."

I thought of Carmel's orange grove in Universe A, the white blossoms on the trees making their appearance in spring while last year's blood oranges still hung ripe; the fragrance of the blossoms (I'd been told) outdid the best the Pacific Ocean could produce. A favorite spot for kids during the day and for lovers after dark. The Lunch-Place Rule had promised that things in Universe B would be superior, inferior, or the same. It had been hard to see the old Golden Gate Bridge in its rightful place, an improvement over what was there in Universe A now. Coconut Café had been the same. Worse was the hardest of the three.

"I should call Gabriella and let her know I'm on my way," said Felix, turning to go and reaching for his omni.

"Wait," I said. "How's the book coming along?"

His mouth dropped open and his hand froze midway to his neck. "What did you say?"

"Never mind, it's not important."

"How do you know about the book? I haven't even mentioned it to anyone at work yet. Melody is the only one who's seen it—unless someone has been checking my computer logs or rifling through my trash for discarded edits. Boy, they're really digging into our lives, aren't they?"

"How *is* it coming along, then?"

"Not too bad, I suppose."

"Oh. Is it cooking-themed, by any chance?"

"Of course. And mystery-themed. Wait—" He paused and looked straight into my eyes. "You're not writing one yourself, are you?"

"Writing? No."

"Good. That would have been awkward. *Really* awkward."

[17]

PROFESSOR MAXIMILIAN

A couple of hours and one meal later, the graduate students and I had left Carmel behind us and were back at the Bihistory Institute. Felix was already writing a mystery novel, I kept repeating to myself, already writing. Longing for the good old days when I only thought he was trying to kill me, I slumped onto the denim couch in the middle of the graduate students' office. "Am I going to be able to take my father's textbook along when I cross back to Universe A?" I held up *Stones, Tombs, and Gourds* limply. It was a heavy book.

Arni picked some lint off his desk chair, a plastic one with a seat cushion, and sat down facing the couch and stretched out his legs. Bean's Beetle made for a cramped ride. "Nobody expects your information content to be exactly the same on the way back. Not you, not your luggage. It's theoretically impossible. An extra book is well within the allowable limits."

"Even though it's a textbook full of learning and knowledge?"

From the whiteboard where she was busy taping enlargements of 13A and 13B side by side, Bean answered, "It's nothing compared to the complexity and information content of your brain."

I took that, at least, as a compliment.

Pak came in, making me realize he'd left the room and sporting a spandex outfit so skintight he could have been earning good money at any bar as an exotic dancer. "I'm off for a bike ride," he announced. "Keep me posted." He fetched his bicycle, which stood leaning against the side of his desk, and steered it out of the room as Arni said, "Professor Maximilian should be down shortly."

In my newly foul mood, I didn't care if I met a hundred copies of Wagner. Failing to make myself comfortable against the lumpy back of the denim couch, I opened *Stones, Tombs, and Gourds* to a random page, balancing the textbook on my knees. Something inside caught my finger immediately. It was only a little postcard, blank and long forgotten. I moved it to the back of the book, then examined the book's contents. It was no secret that I had failed to inherit the art gene, but many of the glossy images spread across the pages were familiar from reproductions I'd seen in my parents' gallery—the much debated Venus of Tan-Tan from Morocco, or the Danube River piscine sculptures, their bulging fish eyes as disconcerting in the originals as I had found them in the clay reproductions in the gallery—and the aurochs and felines from Lascaux cave walls, which made for great posters, were there too. I spent a few minutes fully engrossed in the textbook, having forgotten where I was and why I was there, the highest compliment one can pay a book, I suppose.

My reverie was interrupted by Professor Maximilian swooping in, his personality immediately filling the room the same way that Wagner's does. He bounded over to where I was sitting on the couch and shook my hand vigorously. "Visualize a sphere centered on Professor Singh's old lab right here in this building. The sphere includes all classroom and department buildings on campus and extends north about halfway across the Golden Gate Bridge"—he gestured in what was presumably the right direction, though I found it impossible to orient myself in the windowless office—"and juts out west into the ocean and east into the bay. South it encompasses the Presidio Golf Course. And, of course, stretches an equal distance into the air and an equal distance down. Are you following?"

I gaped at him. Listening to Wagner's double do what Wagner did best—talk—about a subject unfamiliar to me and *my* Wagner was a strange experience, to say the least. I closed my mouth and the textbook and looked the professor over with undisguised interest. He had the same slightly tanned look and untidy blond hair as my boss; instead of Wagner's well-pressed Peruvian shirts and slacks he sported a cinnamon cardigan and beige chinos, an outfit just as stylish, I suppose, in its surroundings. Professor Maximilian was no taller than Wagner.

Now perched on the arm of the couch facing me, the professor continued, "On this particular Monday morning, inside the sphere we had many potential prime movers: students and professors, research and administrative staff, librarians, campus visitors, maintenance crews, food vendors. It was, however, winter break, so quite a few of the students and staff were absent. Farther away from campus, we had residents of houses that fell within the sphere, also Golden Gate Bridge tourists and tour guides, bicyclists, surfers, Baker Beach nudists, Presidio golf course golfers—"

"Nudists at Baker Beach?" I raised an eyebrow.

"That was before they built the Ferris wheel," Arni explained.

"—and also cars, buses, trucks, sailboats, and tour boats with their operators and passengers. Who and what else can we add to the list?"

For a second I thought the professor's question was directed at me, but Bean answered. "Pets and wildlife—dogs and cats, almost-dogs and almost-cats, birds, squirrels normal and giant. Fish and seals, and, though no one reported seeing any, perhaps a great white shark or a whale. Also redwoods, cypress trees, eucalypti, macar trees. Insects. An unstable boulder or two. And other prime movers of the biological and geological kind. More wildly, a meteorite might have fallen into the sphere," Bean added. She had pulled her wooden chair away from her desk and was straddling it, her arms folded across the chair back. "And I've always wondered what lies buried in the Presidio. The land used to be an Ohlone village site, then a Spanish garrison, then a military base before becoming part of the university campus. A lost piece of ammunition buried somewhere could explode one day and cause one heck of an event chain. Other than that, about all that's left from Presidio's past are the old gun batteries and the cemetery."

"We can probably ignore the cemetery occupants," Arni said dryly, "but they do get occasional visitors."

"Also rain," Bean added, "a rogue wave, a particularly dense patch of fog, a hailstorm, and other meteorological occurrences that might have found their way into the sphere. None were reported. Just some benign clouds bringing light rain later that afternoon."

"Clouds? A rogue wave? Meteorites? This is crazy," I said. "What could a eucalyptus tree possibly have done? Shed bark? Grown a micro-digit taller?"

Arni got up to stretch his back and headed to the sink, where he commenced rinsing the vase-shaped samovar. "On occasion a little bit of craziness is helpful. As to eucalypti— they are not native to California. They were brought over during the Gold Rush from Australia as a fast-growing source of timber, but the wood cracked and split and didn't turn out to be suitable for construction or railroad building at all. Today their roots cause all sorts of trouble to foundations of buildings and to underground pipes and also suck up great amounts of water and outcompete other plants. They peel a lot too. I'm sure we could think of plenty of event chains that a wayward eucalyptus peel could cause."

"So then," I asked of the room, "anything—furry, bald, alive, dead, liquid, mineral—could have split A and B? No one told me this."

"Sorry, I thought you understood," Bean was the first to answer, with a glance at the professor. "Where universe-making is concerned, the important thing is *what*, not who. You or me, a lightning strike, the apple falling off a tree, it doesn't matter. Most things are part of an existing event chain or are insignificant—a raindrop falls, a bird chirps, you hiccup or have a conversation with an omnimarketer. But every so often it happens—another thread is added to the weave of history, *a new event chain is set in motion*. It might last a second. A few minutes. Millennia. That idea put forth by Past & Future, about an asteroid striking the Earth sixty-five million years ago, well, if it did—*crack!*—a universe split off in which dinosaurs are gone and mammals rule, while in the old one, for all we know, dinopeople are having this conversation. What kind of tea are you making, Arni?"

"Darjeeling."

"If Hurricane Swilda hadn't hit Washington, DC, would three-quarter pants have come back into vogue?" she went on. "Had peas not grown well in Gregor Mendel's monastery garden, would we have the science of genetics and almost-dogs and giant squirrels today? If the great potato chip craze of the nineties hadn't happened—"

I was sitting up straight on the edge of the couch. This was excellent news. If anything could create a universe, it made it so much less likely that it was me. "What happens after an event chain peters out?" I asked.

"The universe seamlessly merges with similar ones," Bean said.

"And how do we know the Y-day event chain hasn't petered out and we haven't already merged seamlessly? Maybe whatever Felix B or I did—if it *was* one of us—caused a tiny nothingness of an event chain with uninteresting, blink-twice-and-you-miss-them consequences?"

She hesitated. "The length of an event chain is a tricky number to come by. The interaction between our universes has further complicated matters. Having said that, the computer projections for the Y-day event chain are showing an expected length of—this is just a rough estimate, you understand—"

Professor Maximilian, having caught sight of photos 13A and 13B on the whiteboard, leapt off the couch arm and took two quick strides over to them.

"—of nine hundred years."

[18]

PRIME MOVERS

"**N**ine hundred?" My hands found *Stones, Tombs, and Gourds* and I tried to iron out a page corner that had folded on itself. The aurochs on the front cover, lyre-shaped horns jutting forward, mineral pigment on stone proof of the power of endurance of even the most delicate of man's creations, met my eye. "Aurochs is singular *and* plural," I said. "Nine hundred years—so few things survive that long—even buildings— just a handful of books—the *Epic of Gilgamesh*, the Egyptian *Book of the Dead*, the *Iliad* and the *Odyssey*...the *Poems of the Traveling Soldier*—"

"Euclid's *Elements*," Arni threw in.

"Nine hundred years is mind-boggling, I know," Bean said comfortably. "But really, it's mediumish. Halfway between what the pyramid builders in Egypt achieved—four millennia and still going strong—and the forty-six seconds of the average event chain produced by a human sneeze."

"That last figure has always seemed a bit on the short side to me." Arni, having left the samovar humming gently, was back at his desk. "It takes that long just to reach for a tissue and blow your nose and look, then you have to dispose of the tissue and wash your hands, all the while worried that you're coming down with something. Then there are the residual droplets the sneeze leaves on surfaces, which may infect the next person to come along and occupy the space, then that person infects someone else, and so on. A sneeze can generate some pretty long event chains, it seems to me."

"You wash your hands after sneezing?" Bean said from her desk.

"Doesn't everyone?"

Professor Maximilian had been studying the two photos Bean had taped side by side on the whiteboard. Without turning around, he said, "On the day Professor Singh was conducting his experiment, counting you and your parents, there were 4102 persons within the event radius—in our sphere of interest, that is. This was the Institute of Physics back then. No better way," he added wistfully, "to spend a school break, when there are no classes to teach, than to run experiments with universes." His head moved between the two photos like a woodpecker's bobbing for worms. "Pacifiers...banana...duck...I see."

Arni had typed a password into his desk computer to access a database. He tapped the screen with a fingernail as text and images began streaming. "The Y-day database. Scans of the Physics Institute visitor logs. Ocean level and temperature data. License plates of cars that passed through the bridge tollbooths and also a pedestrian count from the tollbooths. Interviews with 4102 persons times two minus anyone deceased. A picture of an English Department printer that went haywire and spewed out endless copies of a Rabindranath Tagore poem that morning..."

"A prime mover disturbs the universe," the professor explained to the whiteboard, "like Mother Nature giving birth. A new universe is spawned—"

"Please," I said, "please, no more analogies. I'm having trouble keeping track of them."

Professor Maximilian turned to face the couch. "Perhaps a demonstration is in order." In a single fluid motion he lunged forward and punched my shoulder, making me instinctively shrink into the couch. "I do believe I just created a universe by lightly tapping you on the shoulder. In the universes where I gave you a different example, you think nothing of it. Here, on the other hand, you refuse to have anything to do with me until I apologize for violating your personal space." He chuckled. "I think we can conclude that even after I apologize there'll still be subtle and long-term consequences in our future interactions, eh?"

It was probably a safe conclusion. As was that there were definite differences between the Wagner standing by the denim couch and my boss, who never threatened to punch me, even if I missed an important deadline at work. "Where did Punch and No-Punch—sounds like an ad for fruit juice—split off *to*?" I asked.

"Where? Punch and No-Punch are both here. They share this room. They share that samovar in the corner. The white-board. This couch."

🦆

"None of this makes sense," I complained.

"Makes sense?" Professor Maximilian said sharply. "Of course it makes no sense. Doesn't mean it's not true. If anything it's less strange than the old view, that one person's choices irrevocably and forever turn the course of human history, like the assassin's bullet." He glared at me with scientific zeal. "Say you go around shooting all kangaroos in sight. Is it more likely that *you* get to decide that kangaroos should be extinct, everywhere and for all time—or that you merely achieved your goal in *this* universe, but there are plenty of kangaroos hopping about in plenty of other universes in which you were never born or in which you were a model citizen?"

Arni, who had gotten up to pour tea into four mismatched mugs, offered one to the professor.

"If you did go around shooting all kangaroos in sight," the professor said thoughtfully, accepting the mug, "who would be the prime mover, I wonder? I, who gave you the idea, you and I both because we participated in this conversation, or the person who invented the laserinne that you would use to shoot the kangaroos? Or are we an inseparable complex system that constitutes a prime mover as a whole? Never mind that. My predecessor Professor Singh assumed he made a copy of the universe with his experiment. He was wrong."

The professor put the mug down on Bean's desk and took two strides back to the whiteboard. With a red marker he drew a thin twig, like a sideways Y. "Singh linked two universes as they branched off. A and B immediately began to sprout new branches because of other, independent event chains." He deftly drew more branches, spreading and multiplying the Y like a growing crack in a shattered glass window. "This is an important point. What we call Universe A is merely a subbranch of the original A. Because a universe carries with it all of its past history, including the link, each subbranch of A has stayed linked to each subbranch of B—"

"Why is that an important point?" I asked.

"It's an important scientific point."

The professor went silent, rubbing his chin in thought like Wagner did when pondering knotty issues such as the right number of speeds in a blender or the optimal capacity of a saltshaker.

Bean broke the silence after a moment. "Professor Maximilian's research showed that the Y-day prime mover had to be small, around twenty-four libras."

"My thesis fell through," Arni said cheerfully. "I was convinced that one Olivia May Novak Irving was the prime mover. I had to start over because of the twenty-four libras. The woman is petite, but not that petite."

"Why her?" I asked.

"It was a nice strong event chain that started with a boat tour and ended with a missed interview for a lucrative job. That reminds me." He checked his stylish omni. "Three new messages. Olivia May's staff making sure I'm on my way over. I'm expected after her yoga class. She's interested in tracing the pivotal events in her life and I didn't think I should stop helping her merely because she didn't fit into our research anymore."

"Good for you," I felt compelled to say.

"Plus she makes a generous donation yearly to our research fund." He drained his tea and grabbed his jacket. "I'll see you later. Bean, let me know how it goes with the Gretchens."

Arni's exit seemed to shake Professor Maximilian out of his trance. He turned toward the door. "Keep things under your hats, kids. It's hard enough getting any research published these days, much less something as groundbreaking as this. Let's find the Y-day event chain first so we can show how A and B came to be. You are our best research lead there, Felix—"

"Oh, okay."

"We'll deal with the necessary authorizations later. There are universes beyond A and B. I intend to prove it."

The door swung shut behind him. I was left rubbing my shoulder and noting that the professor had not, technically, ever gotten around to apologizing.

🦆

As Bean and I exited the building, encountering a sweaty Pak wheeling his bike back through the front door and into the elevator, I asked, "Where did you say you were going, Bean?"

"To interview a witness to the events of thirty-five years ago."

"I think I'll come with you, if you don't mind," I said, my shoulder still smarting. This was *my* vacation, after all, and if I wanted to spend it finding out what my parents had been doing in San Francisco on a particular Monday thirty-five years ago, that was my business. Wagner A would have to wait. Besides, engaging in underhanded bread dealing wasn't part of my job description.

As the Beetle sputtered to life and Bean pulled out of the parking spot and with alarming speed headed away from the Bihistory Institute, I said, "Bean, do you think there is one right job for everyone?"

"Twenty-seven."

"I beg your pardon?"

"It's been shown that there are on average twenty-seven occupational niches in which a person could happily work. Hundreds more in which a person could *un*happily work, of course. I don't think anyone has researched those," she said, speeding up further to make a changing traffic light.

"I was thinking of Wagner and the professor."

"I know what you mean. Culinary companies and bihistory research seem to be about as far apart as you can get, occupational-niche-wise. I don't know what skills and interests one needs to run Wagner's Kitchen, but they can't be substantially different from those needed to run a research group. Both Professor Maximilian and your Citizen Maximilian seem first-rate at their jobs."

"Strange the choices people make. Agatha Christie started her career as a nurse, Dorothy Sayers worked in an advertising agency, Conan Doyle ran a medical practice, Edgar Allen Poe gave up a military career to write."

"I suppose we could ask the professor what made him choose bihistory. He was a teenager when the universes diverged."

"I know."

"You agree we should ask him?"

"No, I mean, I *know*," I said, making sure my seatbelt was tight around my chest as she sped up to beat a second traffic light. "I've figured out why Felix B ended up a chef and I didn't. It happened one December."

"What did?"

"I came down with a sinus infection and lost my sense of smell. And taste, to some extent. Before that—well, one of my friends in the neighborhood, Julia, had a play kitchen. It was fun. She went on to become a financial consultant. But here's the weird thing. Even if I got my sense of smell back, I don't think I could be a chef. It seems so stressful. All those hungry people waiting with their forks and knives. Not to mention having to spend all day on your feet. And yet that could be me—*is me*—working at the Organic Oven." I shook my head.

Bean finally having been defeated by a firmly red traffic light, we had stopped at an intersection; it abutted a small neighborhood park complete with a fountain and a handful of ducks waddling about. I caught Bean's eye.

She shrugged. "The fountain is within the event radius, but the ducks look too small. Unless they had large ancestors—how long do ducks live? Anyway, I don't think the fountain was here thirty-five years ago. We're better off sticking to the fake duck on your pacifier."

As the light changed and we left the fountain behind us, she said, "What can you taste?"

"Sorry? Oh, taste. There is no rhyme or reason to it. Cheese, chocolate, nuts, yes. Also soup. Any kind of berry, no. Chicken, sometimes. Coffee, always, but bread—I used to love the smell of freshly baked bread. Now it tastes like a clean sponge. Don't even get me started on pizza. Or crackers."

"I can see why you ended up writing about food and kitchen stuff. Kind of like doing theory instead of practice."

"I suppose. If I couldn't experience it, I could at least spend my time writing and thinking about it."

"But you want to write mysteries also," she said, her eyes on the road, sounding puzzled.

"Why not?"

"It seems, with all due respect, a completely different thing."

"You said," I raised an eyebrow, "that there are twenty-seven occupational niches in which a person could be happily employed. Maybe Wagner's Kitchen was the first and novel-writing would be the second."

"Touché."

"Besides, I have a feeling that food and cooking will creep into it one way or another. Not recipes, I don't like it when novels contain gimmicks like songs or video every other page. Perhaps a culinary competition as the setting and a broiling pan or nutcracker as a murder weapon."

There was a sudden loud noise.

"Relax, Felix. It's just the Beetle backfiring."

I let go of the dashboard. I had briefly forgotten about Felix B—and *his* book. Shading my eyes from the bright sun, I dug out my sunglasses. "Honestly, this San Francisco weather, it's either wet and too cold, or it's dry and too hot. There's never a happy mean."

"You seem different," Bean commented, glancing over at me. She changed lanes, taking us out of the Presidio toward Pier 39.

🦆

The Quake-n-Shake Restaurant occupied a coveted spot near the water end of Pier 39 and had an entrance flanked by two tourist shops, one selling sweets and the other T-shirts saying, "I've been to the ORIGINAL Golden Gate Bridge." A familiar creature sat outside the windows of the sweet shop, breathing heavily and drooling down one side of her jaw. At the other end of a taut leash was Gabriella Short. Murphina saw us first and, temporarily forgetting about forbidden delicacies, pulled Gabriella in our direction, making her stagger.

"Where's James, sweetie?" Bean bent down to rub Murphina's pale head and I edged away just in case Murph was still carrying remnants of the pet bug.

Gabriella, having recovered, tugged on the leash without much luck, the hefty creature outweighing her by a significant amount. She answered coldly, "James is inside getting her a treat."

Murphina wagged her fluffy stump at the word.

"Not chocolate, I hope," I said pleasantly. Gabriella's ice-white hair, arranged in a gravity-defying knot on one side of her head, was the exact shade of Murphina's coat. It was uncanny.

"They sell pet-safe treats, I'm sure."

"Have you been inside?" Bean gestured toward the Shake-n-Quake.

"Why James and I are here, and whom we may or may not be interviewing, is confidential information. By the way"—this was addressed to me—"I should mention that *we* don't make our clients do legwork."

"Never?" Bean said evenly, still stroking Murphina's head.

"I don't mind being here," I said hurriedly. "I'm on vacation. I'm getting to see the city—"

"Occasionally," Gabriella went on, continuing to tug on Murphina's leash, but the almost-dog would not budge, "*very* occasionally, a client's help is needed—to get into Monroe's house, for example—Monroe insisted—"

There was a sudden shriek, making us all start.

"I'm not her," Gabriella snapped. "Go away."

Murphina growled and a disappointed movie fan slinked away.

James came out of the sweet shop carrying a small lumpy bag. He acknowledged us with a friendly nod. "Fancy meeting you here," he said as Murphina, tail wagging, received her bone-shaped treat.

"Great minds think alike, or at least follow the same research leads," Bean said. She went on with barely a pause for breath, "What happens if Past & Future finds the universe maker first?"

James gave Murph another treat, which she wolfed down in a single gulp. "Chew, Murph, don't forget to chew. That's the question, isn't it? Patent the idea, if we can get permission from DIM. Make the Felixes famous. After that, it's up to the marketing department. I'm sure they'll think of ways to make myriads of money off the whole thing."

Bean snickered at the candid statement.

"They are good at making money," James confided.

"And we're not," Bean said. "We merely want to figure things out and write up the results, then move on to the next problem."

"But why is that?" said James. "Nothing wrong with making money. Comes in handy."

"I suppose it does. And we do like fame. The science team that found the universe maker. Sounds nice—Nobel Prize nice—doesn't it? Sadly, not even in the old days, before DIM's Council of Science Safety dispensed with them, did students get Nobel Prizes. Take astronomer Jocelyn Bell and her discovery of pulsars, or geneticist Fabrizio Minnelli and his invention of giant squirrels while in graduate school—"

"Are we going into the restaurant, Bean?" I said, feeling left out of the conversation.

"Of course," Bean recollected herself. "Interviews to be done."

"We'll wait out here until you're finished inside," James said graciously. He stumbled back a bit as Murphina pressed in on him, mooching for another of the bone-shaped treats.

"Citizen Sayers," Gabriella sent a final remark in my direction, relinquishing the leash to James, "don't forget that Past & Future would be happy to take you on as a client if you decide to nullify your contract with the graduate students. Feel free to contact James or me at any—"

Bean pulled me into the restaurant.

[19]

THE GRETCHENS

"**N**ow if only you'd asked me thirty-five years ago, I might have been able to help you. You're a little late," said Gretchen A, a sturdy, forthright, broad-shouldered woman who gave me a friendly nod acknowledging my A-ness. "Why didn't you people come by earlier?"

"We didn't know then," Bean said, raising her voice to make herself heard above the din of the dining area.

Gretchen A indicated the kitchen with her head. "Gretchen is in the back, if you want to talk to her, but to be honest with you, I don't think she'll remember your Y-day customers any more than I do—even if we were allowed to give out customer information. Who are you people anyway?"

"I'm Bean Bartholomew, a graduate student at the Bihistory Institute." Bean pulled out her identicard and showed it to Gretchen A. "Citizen Felix Sayers here has asked us to research his life story. He wants to know why his alter became a chef and he didn't." She paused, then moved closer to the hostess station and lowered her voice. "Gretchen—may I call you that?—if you don't mind, take your memory back to Y-day. It was a Monday in early January, a chilly day under a partly cloudy sky. Back then, like now, the Quake-n-Shake was a popular tourist spot and operated at full capacity throughout much of the day. On that particular Monday the electricity flickered just before noon and went off for a moment. Some time later Felix's family came in for lunch. This couple with a baby."

Gretchen A shook her head at the photo Bean was holding out. "Dears, I wish I could help you. Look around."

It was just after two o'clock and the Quake-n-Shake, as Bean said, was operating at full capacity. The restaurant clearly catered to families; many of the tables included small humans of assorted lung capacity and throwing ability. Harried waitresses balanced large trays between closely placed tables on their way to and from the kitchen. I wondered what kind of behavior might have made me a memorable customer.

"So that's you in the photo," Gretchen A said to me and gave her head another lively shake. "I'll tell you what I remember most about Y-day—not a thing! It was just an ordinary day. We didn't know that Professor Singh had made a copy of the universe, not until months later. Then they said it was the day we had the blackout, but we used to have them so often. Never lasted long, a couple of minutes maybe—but they always came at the most inconvenient time, like right in the middle of the lunch hour rush! And the inflation, let me tell you, was something fierce. We gave up on having printed menus and put up a board with prices in chalk. Every day, just before we opened, I'd erase yesterday's prices and write in new ones. Those were strange times." She sighed and handed the photo, the eucalyptus one of my parents and me, back to Bean.

Bean put the photo back in her bag, seeming at a loss for a moment.

"What about the time difference?" I nudged her. The Universe A receipts having started to come in, we'd found out that the Quake-n-Shake bill signed by my mother— lunch buffet for two adults, applesauce for one child—had an earlier time on it than the one signed by Felix's mother. Twenty minutes.

"Time difference, right," Bean pulled herself together. "Gretchen, what would have caused a discrepancy between a Universe A bill and a Universe B bill? Remember, this would have been shortly after the yabput—"

"The what, dear?"

"Shortly after Professor Singh made a copy of the universe," Bean said, wincing at the inaccurate description. "A twenty-minute difference in the lunch bills paid by Klara Sayers A and Klara Sayers B."

"Back than customers paid in advance, when they came in. Seems kind of embarrassing now, but times were hard. So, twenty-minute difference in lunch bills—one party arrived earlier than the other." Gretchen A picked up several menus and crayon boxes and left her post to seat a family that had just walked in. As we waited for her to return, Bean leaned over to me and whispered, "I wish Arni were here, he's better at this. He told me to start with 'Take your memory back to Y-day...' and to remember to be polite."

Gretchen came back and said, "Anything else you wanted to know, dears?"

"So people paid when they came in," said Bean, who seemed to have perked up a bit. "That's interesting. One final question, Gretchen. A young woman with a stain on her blouse came in, also around lunchtime—"

"Was that Y-day? Oh, I've always wondered what happened to her." Gretchen A clasped a hand to her chest. "Almost in tears, poor thing, on her way to a job interview. She wanted to use the bathroom to wash off the stain on her blouse. Wasn't success-ful, for as I could have told her, you can't just dab pomegranate juice off. I've always wondered what happened to her and if she got the job."

"She didn't. Not in Universe A," Bean said.

It was an example of how unalike personal outcomes could be. Olivia May Novak Irving of Universe B, the research benefactress to whose house Arni had gone, had led a life of success, retiring well off after a career of working as an idea developer. Olivia May of Universe A, on the other hand, had not only *not* gotten wealthy working as an idea developer, she'd never even been heard of in the idea development industry. No one knew why. Bean had said that Olivia May A was last seen by an acquaintance walking into the Quake-n-Shake on Y-day with spilled juice on her shirt.

"You *do* remember her?" Bean said. "Would you mind not mentioning that to anyone else unless specifically asked? Others will be coming in to ask questions about Y-day. In fact, we'd appreciate it if you denied remembering anything about Felix here at all."

"I *don't* remember anything about him. So the pomegranate lady didn't get the job and her alter did?" Gretchen sighed in sympathy. "I never like to hear that. That was Y-day, you say? It wasn't right, you know, for Professor Singh to make a copy of the universe like that without asking anyone. The government put a stop to all that, but look what a mess it's left! Luckily Gretchen and I get along like two chestnuts in a roaster." (Instead of retiring, Bean had said, Gretchen A and Gretchen B had tossed a coin, sold one of the Quake-n-Shakes, and joined forces in running the Universe B restaurant. Seemed fair.)

A sudden low rumble quieted all conversation in the dining room. The rumble lingered, then rolled out and dissipated to the tinkling sound of glasses and dinnerware.

Gretchen A sent a calm look over her dining room. "A four-pointer, maybe five?" She bent down to pick up the boxes of crayons that had slipped off the hostess table and I disentangled myself from where I had been crouching under a bar stool. Bean, lending Gretchen a hand with the crayon boxes, asked, "The young woman with the pomegranate juice stain, did she stay for lunch?"

"I don't think so, dears, just went into the bathroom for a few minutes. Last I saw, she was heading out the door, her shirt wet and stained purple."

Gretchen B didn't remember anything of import either. She mentioned the blackout, denied ever seeing me before in her life, and reminisced fondly of the old days as she stood next to Gretchen A, the identical hostess dresses making them seem like giggly twin girls dressed alike by an indulgent mother.

"Good luck, dears," the Gretchens called out as we headed out of their restaurant.

🦆

The doors of the Quake-n-Shake swung shut behind us, Gabriella, James, and Murphina having gone in to talk to the Gretchens. "Maybe Arni will have more luck," I said to Bean. "There's a chance Olivia what's-her-name remembers seeing me when she came in the restaurant."

"Olivia May Novak Irving," Bean supplied. "Wrong universe. Arni is at the house of Olivia May B, who *didn't* spill her pomegranate juice, never went into the Quake-n-Shake, and got to her job interview just fine and became rich."

"I don't know how you keep this stuff straight in your head, A-this, B-that."

"We could suggest a change from A and B to the Lost Duck Universe and the Happy Baby Universe. Think it'd catch on?" I pointed to the specialty store whose doors neighbored those of the Quake-n-Shake. "I've been looking for one of these." We found a bench free of tourists and bird droppings. "You know," I confided to Bean, offering her a seal-shaped chocolate and unwrapping one myself, "Pier 39 is exactly the same here as it is in Universe A. The tourists, the street performers, the ice cream parlors, the big-bellied sea lions yapping and barking at each other in the marina, the white-and-blue boats, the shops selling factory-made seashells...I'm having trouble processing it all. Being here and not *there*, it being so similar, if you see what I mean. I keep forgetting where I am." I broke the head off the chocolate seal. It was hollow.

"I feel we're getting somewhere," Bean said, mouth full. "Your family arrived at the Quake-n-Shake early. By a full twenty minutes—in time to interact with Olivia May A."

"Maybe there was a reason my parents left the bridge early, only we haven't discovered it yet." The chocolate was tourist-quality, more sugar than cocoa. I could barely taste it.

"Perhaps they simply cut the walk short because you were crabby."

"Or maybe Felix B got carsick on the way from the bridge to Pier 39 and *his* parents had to stop the car to clean him up and it took twenty minutes."

"That would read well in a research paper." She took my chocolate wrapper and crinkled it with hers, then leaned across the bench and dropped them into a trashcan. "Let's give Arni a call and see if he has any news."

We reached Arni outside the Nob Hill residence of the benefactress and bihistory aficionado, Olivia May B. Arni listened to what we had to say, told us he was heading back to the Bihistory Institute to tackle the task of analyzing incoming Universe A receipts with Pak, watched me hand Bean another chocolate-shaped seal, and then disconnected after commenting, "You two *do* realize that universes with no chocolate in them must exist?"

Bean and I spent the afternoon timing driving routes from the Golden Gate Bridge parking lot to the Quake-n-Shake Restaurant, which yielded little useful information as far as I could tell, only more wear and tear on Bean's Volkswagen Beetle and an unusual experience for me called filling up the tank. A few of the routes took us through the main part of the Presidio campus, within viewing distance of the Bihistory Institute, others by the winding and scenic seaside roads. They all took about the same amount of driving time, mainly because the direct routes were more congested. No matter how narrow the street or heavy the traffic, Bean drove as fast as possible, carrying on a conversation all the while. She wasn't alone. Cars zipped along all around us like unusually fast and focused sheep determined on getting back to their meadow a microsecond early.

"Bean," I whispered urgently at one point.

"What's the matter?"

"I think someone is following us. Look how close that car is." I had been following it in the little mirror on my side of the car.

She glanced up at the back-view mirror above the dashboard. "It's just a tailgater. Why are you so jumpy?"

"No reason."

"Not to make you more nervous or anything, but objects viewed in the right side mirror are actually closer than they appear to be. Like the back of a spoon, the mirror gives a wider view, but cars look smaller and farther back then they really are. Don't worry. The car behind us will stop if there is a red light."

I turned my neck to look at the car behind us as the Beetle shook bravely as we navigated an uneven street. The driver was a little old lady whose head barely reached over the steering wheel. She honked to get us moving faster.

Bean put her foot on the gas, saw me grip the dashboard, and commented, "Cars are handy. How would we perform our timing experiment in a people mover?"

"With difficulty," I admitted as Bean pulled into the Golden Gate Bridge parking lot and jolted to a stop. "This one will require walking." She got out and fetched a ticket from the self-service machine and a straw hat from the car trunk. She stuck the ticket inside the front window and the hat on her head. "According to the parking receipt we got off the Bitmaster, your parents parked here at eleven fifteen on Y-day."

"Which way?" I asked. Walking paths led from the mostly full parking lot in two directions.

"Good question. The paths were here thirty-five years ago, though they've been widened recently. One of them— that one—gets you to the bridge quickly, via the elevator. The one over there kind of winds its way uphill through the Presidio, by the old gun battery, and eventually gets you to the bridge."

"I think I've been on it," I said, frowning at the geography, "though it's hard to say." Where I was used to seeing a people mover station, there was a pretty eucalyptus grove—was this where a kind stranger had taken Photo 10, the one of my family?

"At eleven fifteen, you and your parents headed toward the bridge via the elevator or the longer Presidio path. Binary decision. A literal fork in the road."

"I see. If we took the shorter path, we were on the bridge when Professor Singh made a copy of the universe—when the yabput occurred, I mean—and if we took the longer path, we were in the Presidio somewhere."

"Correct."

"And you and I?"

"Split up and time the paths."

"Great," I said, pulling in my stomach. "I've been feeling a bit sedentary. A walk would be just the thing. I'll take the longer one," I added chivalrously.

"Well—all right. See if there's anything interesting thirty-one minutes into your walk."

"Thirty-one minutes—?"

"Eleven fifteen plus thirty-one yields yabput time."

She adjusted the wide-brimmed hat and we split up.

I set a moderate pace. The path started out narrow, zig-zagged up a hill, then rolled over an exposed ledge and became wide and flat. On this portion of it there were summer students jogging, rollerblading, and scootering instead of attending whatever classes they were nominally here for. More than a few were recumbent on the well-watered campus lawns working on tans instead of algebra. As I walked along, I alternated between being quite sure that the path still existed in Universe A and that I had been on it at some point and being quite sure that it didn't and that I hadn't. Not that it mattered in the least. It's just that it was a nice path. In my own Universe A, the Presidio was not a university campus but an agglomeration of museums—there was the popular fashion museum, also a nature museum with a pond and an arboretum, a soccer museum, next to it a museum of Universe A accomplishments, and in the middle of it all the tiny but well-known surfing museum. People mover line 66 circled the whole thing.

Occasionally I caught sight of the bridge as the path took me past student dormitories, classroom buildings, an auditorium, and a long row of tennis courts. Beyond the tennis courts I puffed up a steep portion of the path and entered a eucalyptus grove, a large one where the grass was sparse and yellowish. I exited the grove to the sight of an abandoned gun battery with cliff-top views of Baker Beach and its Ferris wheel. The battery was a nineteenth-century remnant of the need to defend the city from attack from the sea; the Ferris wheel, slowly turning basketfuls of tourists, was a record-setting eyesore that must have been difficult to keep stable and upright on windy days. There were plenty of places (like the gun battery) that seemed just right for throwing a duck pacifier at.

That reminded me to check my watch, and I discovered that the thirty-one-minute mark—the one Bean had requested I take note of—had already passed.

"Great," I said, tried to figure out how long I had overshot the mark by, got muddled in the math, and decided to press on instead of trying to go back.

It was all very complicated, I thought as I began to descend the long wooden staircase that would take me to the bridge, but complicated wasn't necessarily a bad thing. I was keeping my fingers crossed that the professor's calculation would turn out to be wrong and that Olivia May or a lively egret or sea lion would emerge as the culprit. If that failed, then my only hope was that Felix B would turn out to be the guilty party of the two of us, that is, that *his* universe was the one that had branched off.

As to the other thing—as the great detective Sherlock Holmes put it so well, it's a capital mistake to theorize before one has data. I needed to know more, to sneak a peek at Felix's novel to see if it had that *something* that makes a book a must-read, high-publicity product that bursts on the scene—or a slow-emerging-but-steady-selling classic that endures for years on reading lists. It occurred to me that Mrs. Noor could probably think of a clever way of obtaining a copy of Felix's book. "Leave it to me," she'd say, and that would be that. I felt foolish for calling her off the case but too embarrassed to call back and say I'd changed my mind.

It was time to take matters into my own hands.

As I moved out of the way of a young rollerblading couple on their wobbly way down the staircase, it struck me that it might be nice to invite Bean out for a meal. The Organic Oven, perhaps. I could get her opinion on the dishes I couldn't taste.

She was at the bridge vista point, lost in thought under her hat.

"There you are." She checked her omni. "Forty-seven minutes exactly."

"How long did it take you?"

"Ten. That's including a five-minute wait for the elevator." She handed me one of a couple of bottles of water she seemed to have purchased while waiting.

"I didn't rush," I defended myself, twisting the bottle open and taking a grateful drink. "I went at what I imagined the pace of a couple carrying an infant—for almost fifty minutes!—might have been. By the way, I completely missed the thirty-one-minute mark, sorry. Do you want me to go back?"

"We can get Arni and Pak down here and repeat the timing experiment. Wouldn't that be something, to find the pacifier you lost all those years ago somewhere on a Presidio path?"

"Not really, no."

"Well, it wouldn't be here anyway. We'd have to look in Universe A. Only the bridge is no longer there and the Presidio has been bulldozed into a museum complex. What we *can* do is at least pinpoint the two potential yabput spots."

"I have to say, if it was me—well, I *was* there, but you know what I mean—I'd have taken the shorter path."

"Probably," she agreed. "And your family likely would have made a stop here before continuing on to the bridge."

Here was the vista point we were standing on, a circular patch of cement level with the bridge deck and protected by a wooden railing from the drop below. Tourists milled around reading information panels and taking photos. Who could blame them? The sky was wide; the sailboats, lively; and Alcatraz and the larger Angel Island, squatting in the middle of the bay, picturesque. The bridge, with its brick towers, was more like a whimsical work of art than a bit of connecting road.

"Not a bad view," said Bean. "If you were going to create a universe, this would be the place to do it." I noticed she was checking the time again. She saw me watching and, taking her hat off and twirling it on her finger, said awkwardly, "Er—we'll have to leave finding the two yabput spots for tomorrow. I have to go."

"Was it something I said?"

"I have a class. It helps me think better if I take an occasional course that has nothing to do with bihistory. Soap Making. Maltese Poetry. Pet Sequencing. That kind of thing." A pinkish tint spread across her cheeks. "This summer it's, well—it's Belly Dancing for Beginners."

Once we were back in the parking lot, she said, "Don't let me keep you from finishing your walk. If you go that way," she pointed to a third path, which I hadn't noticed before and which led into the pretty grove of eucalypti, "you'll end up back at the Bihistory Institute. Arni can give you a ride back."

"I think I'll ask Pak where I can rent a bike."

I took a swig of the water and watched as she sped out of the parking lot. So she liked belly dancing. Who'd have guessed?

[20]

I PEEK INTO A WINDOW

Pak looked blank when I asked him where I could rent a bike, so I purchased a baseball cap from a street vendor, hailed a taxi, and gave the driver a Palo Alto address. After a long, jolting ride, the taxi deposited me near a set of stucco rental housing buildings by the bay. The Egret's Nest Apartment Complex.

I paid the driver, tugged the price tag off the baseball cap, tut-tutted at the logo along its rim—*Best and Brightest Start with B*—and stuck the cap low on my head. I didn't want any of the complex residents mistaking me for Felix B as I followed a stone path through the center of the complex, by a community pool where kids splashed in the still-strong late afternoon sun, and on toward building J. I noted in passing that the combination playground/outdoor gym that existed in my reality was here a large parking lot with numbered spots.

Just before I reached the patio of building J, from which stairs led to various upper-floor apartments, it struck me that a little more stealth might be in order. What if Felix B had returned from Carmel and happened to look out of his window and immediately saw right through my baseball-cap disguise?

I could always say I was here to pay him a visit, but I wasn't.

I pulled the baseball cap as far down as it could go around my ears, moved to the shady perimeter of the building, and cautiously continued on. A delivery person carrying packages was nearing from the direction of the parking lot. He gave me a tip of his hat and took the stairs two at a time to the top floor of building J. The three elderly residents playing bocce ball on the building green did not notice me.

The Egret's Nest Apartment Complex. Built next to the San Francisco wetlands, where the bay met solid land in a marshy hodgepodge of water, grass, and wildlife, it was affordable, basic, and had great views from the coveted top-floor apartments. Moving stealthily along the shaded side of the building, I turned a corner into the sunny back area where windows and porches faced the bay, hurried past several porches of no interest, and finally stopped next to my own ground-floor one, still keeping to the wall out of sight of anyone inside. A pet-walker who happened to be on the wetland walkway sent a puzzled look in my direction. I gave her a reassuring smile to show that I wasn't here to rob the place and waited until the walker and her pet, a shuffling long-necked ostrich with the manner of a placid lamb, moved out of view, then took a quick look over the porch railing. The sliding-glass doors were closed, the shades drawn. There were no signs of life within.

I'd overheard the students discussing that it was unusual for alters to choose identical living spaces, especially in a large, populated area like San Francisco and all its assorted neighborhoods. Our shared appreciation of apartments with views of marshy water had led both Felix B and me to apartment 003. What if my future mystery novel and his already-in-the-works (nearly completed?) one turned out to be alike to the tune of plagiarism? Since his book would be the first to make its appearance into the public eye, mine would be relegated to second-rate status, to be always known as a cheap imitation. Maybe if I sat down and wrote something *really* quickly, I thought, I could turn the tables on him.

I slid from the porch to the study window, having remembered that I rarely bothered pulling its shade down—the sun did not do much more than illuminate a bit of carpet through the small window in the stucco wall. The shade was indeed rolled up. After a final glance around to make sure there were no other path walkers nearing, I brought my eyes close to the glass, screening out the bright sunlight with both hands.

The first thing I saw was a pendulum clock halfway up the wall, which, as pendulum clocks always do (and pits too, I suppose, though one doesn't run into too many of those) brought to mind Edgar Allen Poe's famous tale. Next to the clock was a watercolor of the Carmel house, one done by our mother way back. Just out of sight was an oil painting showing a shapely alabaster foot with a bit of cloth draped over it. Nearer, just below the window, an easy chair with an ottoman looked comfortable for reading. Within reach was a tiered bookcase, and on the ottoman sat a large opened mailing box. The other half of Aunt Hen's collection of dolphin figurines. Shipping to Universe B must have set her estate back a pretty penny, I thought.

Below the pendulum clock and the paintings, a desk hosted a computer, its screen dark. By the keyboard lay a loose stack of papers. The top page had text printed on it and edited with a red pen. My eyes went to the trashcan under the desk, which was overflowing with crumpled paper. Universe B writers went through sheaves and sheaves of paper when they needed to proofread, apparently. I moved my head and hands along the window trying to find an angle that would afford a better view of the pages on the desk and in the trashcan—at least a page number—when I spotted out of the corner of my eye a discarded page, one that had fallen on the floor. I turned my attention to it, trying to decipher the upside-down content. About a dozen short phrases covered the page, some crossed out, others underlined or circled, like a used grocery store shopping list. I glued my face to the window in an effort to read the list—was one of the circled phrases *Killer Cocktail* or was I misreading that?— and an underlined one, *Butcher's Beef*—and another, crossed out, *Murderous Beets*—and next to it *Bleeding Beets,* circled— and another, *Devil's Dish*...Suddenly I knew what the phrases were—it was a list of titles for a mystery series, that's what it was, with an amateur sleuth who was a chef or a caterer—how many had Felix written already?—I began counting the circled ones—

A tap on my shoulder almost made me shriek.

"Citizen, kindly explain your actions." The DIM official, perspiring heavily, pulled at the turtleneck of his avocado uniform, clearly unhappy to have been called out in the heavy late-afternoon heat. (The bird-walker, no doubt.)

"I was—I was just checking whether a friend was at home," I said, my heart in my throat.

"A friend? Your identicard, citizen."

I surrendered the identicard into his sweating hands and continued babbling. "I thought my friend might be back from Carmel, but he wasn't answering his doorbell, so I thought I'd walk around to the back here and peek into his windows just in case he was asleep. But all I could see was his study, just some dolphin figurines and a computer and a list of book titles..." I trailed off.

"Visitor from Universe A, huh? Your actions violate Regulation 3 concerning personal privacy, citizen. I don't know how things are done *over there,* but here we expect *all* citizens to mind *all* regulations to the letter." He unfolded the familiar list of regulations from a pocket and held it up for me to see.

"Of course, sorry. I don't know what I was thinking. As I said, I was just checking to see if my friend was at home, I know he wouldn't mind—"

"You could try calling your friend and leaving him a message," the DIM official pointed out, giving the now slightly moist identicard back to me.

"Yes," I said, "yes, I'll go ahead and do that. Good idea."

"I'll let you off with a warning this time."

Fanning himself with the regulation list, he headed for the shade. I slunk away.

[21]

OLIVIA MAY
NOVAK IRVING
OF UNIVERSE A

In the morning I called Wagner via inter-universe communications and left a message asking for a favor, then took the stairs down two at a time to the main parlor of the Queen Bee Inn. Trevor, whom I hadn't seen since my first morning in Universe B, was behind the front desk, reading a printed newspaper. He looked up as I said, "You probably don't remember me, I've been in and out all week. Just got back from Carmel, before that I was at the Palo Alto Health Center—"

"You don't look sick, Citizen Sayers."

"No, the stay at the health center was a false alarm. Food poisoning."

"Not from our breakfast, I hope."

"No, no, not at all. It wasn't even food poisoning really. More like a mild stomachache. Not even that. Nothing to worry about." I added, "Here's the book which your wife kindly sent to me at the health center." I had finished reading *Evans* the previous night after getting back from a nearby movie house (where I'd spent two absorbing hours in the popcorn-enhanced experience of watching *Jungle Nights* starring Gabriella Love, movie star and alter of the woman determined to make me a client of Past & Future and prove me universe maker.) As to the paper book, I had decided that Franny had no doubt only meant to lend it, not make a present of it. She was probably expecting it back.

"Keep it," Trevor said of the book and pushed it back toward me across the front desk. He turned a page of the printed newspaper and a headline jumped out at me—an arrest had just been made by the Council for Science Safety.

"Who is it?" I said.

"Who is what?"

"Who got arrested?"

He spun the newspaper around so I could read the article. An archeologist had, apparently without authorization, stumbled on the ruins of Atlantis at the bottom of the Mediterranean and was trying to raise a serendipity defense. It didn't look good for him.

I wordlessly headed into the Nautical Nook, taking *Evans* with me.

🦆

Body doubles. Even before alters had come into the picture, body doubles had made useful (if somewhat of a cop-out) mystery suspects: a doppelganger, the look-alike of a living person, would be seen getting into a train or on a foggy street, like in Christie's *At Bertram's Hotel*, but would invariably turn out to be someone wearing a wig. As I sat below a mounted fake shark spreading cheese onto a bagel in the nautically themed breakfast room of the Queen Bee Inn, my thoughts were on my own doppelganger. If Bean was right, then not only were there two of us, but a whole menagerie: Felix 1, Felix 2, Felix 3, Felix 4…, all living slightly or wildly different lives, like a set of distorted mirror reflections in a haunted house at a fair. I dabbed more camel cheese onto the bagel and tried to picture a universe in which there were no rainbows or summer rain showers, or where books had never been invented, or where people liked to eat cheese made from goat's milk or even cow's milk. There was something oddly comfortable about the idea. It seemed easier in a way—aim for the middle of the pack, maybe somewhere around fifty or so, live happily.

It struck me that one of these other Felixes might entertain the idea of running down people in crosswalks or planting rubber rolling pins on top of steep staircases. It was just that, having met him, Felix B didn't seem *that* different from me. That was almost the whole problem.

On the other hand, what did I know about him, really? I'd only had one conversation with the man and a quick peek into his study.

I washed down the rest of the bagel with papple juice and went outside to find that Bean had maneuvered her Beetle into a parking spot under a sign that said, *Fire Department only. No stopping or parking.* I got in and she zipped back into traffic.

"Bean," I asked after quickly securing my seatbelt, "what methods does DIM use to enforce Regulation 19?"

"Methods? What you might expect. They perform unannounced lab inspections, bring scientists in for questioning about their own research or a colleague's, plant listening devices, confiscate research notebooks and equipment...that kind of thing. They do arrest people on occasion—did you hear about the Atlantis archeologist?—and send them to work camps for a spell. I want to thank you, Felix," she added, her eyes on the road, not seeming very concerned that she might end up at a work camp for a spell. "This is your vacation and here you are spending it helping us." She hit the brakes at a red light and turned toward me with a smile. "Though I know you're hoping we'll find a universe-making duck."

It was a nice smile. Luckily my omni buzzed and I was saved from having to be struck speechless any further.

"Felix," Wagner said from behind a stack of electric salad spinners, "I got the number you wanted."

"Already? Wagner, it's barely been half an hour."

"It took only a couple of calls. Egg and Rocky helped me—they are climbing Folger Peak today—a nice hike, they say." Wagner emptied a bag of lettuce into one of the salad spinners, doused the lettuce with water from a pitcher, put the lid on, and set the spinner spinning. "I talked to the woman, introduced myself. She didn't seem—where are you?"

Bean had jolted to a sudden stop to avoid driving through a cable car.

"In a Volkswagen Beetle. Go ahead."

"She didn't seem eager to be interviewed but relented after I told her that you'd just found out that you have an alter. She's agreed to talk to you. You only," he repeated, taking the basket out of the spinner and checking the amount of water underneath. "I'll send you her number."

"Wagner, I never know how you pull these things off. By the way, you haven't used that Golden Gate Bridge write-up yet, have you? I don't think I'm happy with it." It was true, I wasn't. I winced inwardly at the clichéd phrases I had used, seeming to recall writing, *To make golden loaves of bread, turn to the Golden Gate Bread Maker.* I must have been really distracted.

"We'll wait to package the bread maker until you obtain the item from the Salt & Pepper Bakery," he said in what he probably imagined was a reassuring reply, and reached for the next salad spinner.

"Are you picking something up for Wagner at a bakery?" Bean, who had been pretending not to listen, asked as we rumbled over the cable car tracks.

"Sourdough bread starter."

"I'm not the only one breaking regulations left and right, then?"

"Wagner found Olivia May of Universe A."

"He did? Where? How?"

"Wagner has connections everywhere. Where he found her, he didn't say."

"Arnold will be pleased. After all the time he spent talking to Olivia May B, he's been frothing at the mouth to interview Olivia May A. I have to admit, I too am dying to know where she's been all this time. Regulation 3 makes it hard to find people, but we never got even close. We figured she'd moved abroad or died or something. We'd better contact her before she changes her mind about talking to you," she added, making a dashboard-clutching U-turn, prompting a couple of angry honks. "I'll call Arni to let him know. We can go to the two potential yabput spots later."

"Also to lunch. There's a restaurant I want to try." I gripped the dashboard as she dialed with one hand, steering with the other. "That is, if I make it out of this alive."

🦆

The 4102 citizens caught within the event radius on Y-day accounted for 8204 storylines—half of them in A, half in B— all of them catalogued painstakingly by the graduate students.

One of the storylines (number 221B) belonged to Olivia May B, who had gotten rich developing ideas; another (221A) to Olivia May A, who hadn't. We were about to hear the A-dweller's story via inter-universe communications.

Olivia May sat cross-legged on a yoga mat in the middle of a wooden floor in a room with no furniture in it. She was petite and lean in a mango-colored bodysuit, just as Arni had described her alter.

"I teach yoga," she informed me of the obvious. "This is my school. Mango Yoga."

"Mango is a wonderful fruit," I agreed from where I was sitting at Arni's desk, "though hard on the hands. Wagner's Kitchen makes a nifty hands-free fruit peeler—"

"I have a new name too."

I heard Arni shift—he was standing by the wall, just out of the visual range of the omni, along with Bean and Pak. Unethical, perhaps, but as Pak had pointed out, Olivia May A had specified that she wanted to talk only to me, not that there be no one else in the room. Professor Maximilian was elbow-deep in a lab-experiment of some kind and had told us to go ahead without him.

"What is your new name, then?" I asked.

"Meriwether Mango."

"Very natural," I complimented her.

"I strongly recommend a closeness to nature. It's good for the body and the mind." She inhaled deeply and let her breath out slowly through pursed lips. "Have you ever done yoga?"

"I've been meaning to get more exercise," I admitted. "All the free samples at Wagner's Kitchen, where I work, well, a lot of them are desserts, and even my diminished taste buds spring to life when chocolate is invol—" I thought I heard a light cough and switched mid-word to what Arni had instructed me to say, though the question came out more abruptly than I intended. "Where have you been since Y-day?"

"Why do you wish to know?"

"I believe that it bears in some way on the storyline of my own life."

"And why are you interested in tracing the story of your own life? You know what happened."

"But I don't know *why*."

This was the real answer, I realized. I didn't want to be the universe maker, but I was curious. There was also a certain addictiveness to the possibility of it being true, like being told I might be of royal blood or have secret superpowers.

She sighed. "I don't see how my story matters, but since you seem to think it's important, I'll tell you what happened. I was on an hour-long bay cruise," she began her tale. "To calm my nerves before a job interview. For a position in the research and development department of Many New Ideas, Inc. Have you heard of them?"

I nodded. It was a well-known Chinese company. So that's where Olivia May B had gotten her start.

"I was young, I wanted the job, and," she shifted her position on the mat and began to stretch her neck from side to side, "I'm told I would have done quite well in it...but that turned out to be my alter's life, not mine. The morning began well enough. The tour boat left Pier 39 and made a wide arc around Alcatraz Island—and what a lovely but cold day it was. I got a cup of warm pomegranate juice from the refreshment stand and went above deck and found a seat. The water was a bit choppy, but I was soaking it all in, the vitality of the ocean, the seagulls, the fresh air...I still enjoy sailing." She seemed to recollect herself.

"But you wanted to know what happened. It wasn't anything much, just a moment of inattention. Pomegranate juice down my suit and the front of a cream silk blouse, can you imagine?

"Someone brought me napkins and I soaked up the juice as much as I could, but there was not a lot to be done about it on the boat. I had to wait until we docked back at Pier 39. I was the first one off the boat and hurried into a nearby restaurant to clean myself up. The hostess tried to help me, but it was a lost cause. By then it was too late to go home for a new outfit or into a store to buy one—it's not a quick process buying women's clothes, you know—and still make it across town to the offices of Many New Ideas in time. So I decided there was no point in going to the interview, not looking like that."

"Sorry," I said.

"I was young. I thought it mattered how I was dressed. But really, it was the best thing that could have happened. Two days later, I boarded an ocean liner, spent a year travelling the seas, then got off and made my way on foot to Jodhpur. I spent my working life there, first learning yoga and massage techniques, then teaching them. When I finally returned home, I had a different name and enough money to open a small yoga studio. I am semiretired now. I keep an eye on things and teach an occasional class. I may not be wealthy, but I'm quite content with how my life turned out."

The way she spoke, quickly and without thinking, left me with the impression that it was a practiced statement, one she used to convince herself as much as others. As with Gabriella Short, it had to be tough having a rich and famous alter. On the other hand, people are sometimes happy but don't realize they are.

"What I really wanted to know," I said, "is whether you remember anything about the restaurant. The Quake-n-Shake."

Meriwether Mango would have been walking off her cruise and into the Quake-n-Shake shortly after twelve thirty, potentially allowing her storyline to intersect with my family's as we arrived early at the restaurant. Her alter, Olivia May B, had walked off her cruise at the same time, strolled past the Quake-n-Shake, and headed to her interview.

"I was there with my parents," I added.

Meriwether gave me a blank look.

"The Quake is where you went to clean your blouse," I explained.

"What kind of thing do you mean?"

"Anything unusual. A family you noticed in the dining area, a couple with an unhappy baby—"

She shook her head. "Not that I can remember. But keep in mind that I was distraught. I think I was actually crying," she added composedly. "I don't recall any of the customers from the restaurant. Is that all you wanted to know?"

I remembered something. "Your alter—Olivia May—she's taking yoga classes now."

"Is she?" Meriwether said, seeming uninterested, but I knew better.

🦆

"That's that," Arni said as the students returned to their desks and I headed to my usual spot on the couch. "She's been in Jodhpur," he said to Professor Maximilian, who had just burst in through the door. "Came back as Meriwether Mango, which is why we had trouble finding her. Looks like an independent chain that started with spilled pomegranate juice. I had wondered if your mother, Felix, happened to walk into the restaurant restroom as Meriwether was cleaning her shirt and offered a sympathetic ear or help getting the pomegranate juice off and inadvertently contributed to Meriwether deciding to skip the job interview at Many New Ideas. But nothing like that seems to have taken place—"

Bean clarified, "The event chain being you lose duck pacifier—the Sayers family leaves bridge early—you cross paths with Olivia May—she doesn't apply for a position at Many New Ideas—omni not invented in Universe A. An easy nine hundred years of consequences."

"Say what?" I said. "Omni not invented?"

Pak spoke up from his desk. "Olivia May Novak Irving."

"Didn't you know?" Bean said. "Olivia May B invented the omni while working at Many New Ideas. It's named after her."

"Huh," I said. "I thought omni stood for, you know, everywhere and everything. After all, everyone does use them and they are everywhere around people's necks."

"They weren't in the beginning," Arni said, always ready with the history. He was typing as he talked. It looked like he was updating a file. I saw him key in the words *Meriwether Mango. Warm pomegranate juice. Yoga. "I decided there was no point in going to the interview, not looking like that."* He went on, "Omnis were first designed and marketed for postal carriers. Because of the runaway inflation, prices of stamps changed daily, more than once a day even. New DIM laws were popping up too about which information could be sent through the mail and which couldn't. Constant updates were needed. That's where omnis came in. Light, cheap, portable. Good for communication, for updates, and so on. They hung around postmen's necks.

"Incidentally," he added, "early models were tried out in the marketplace as substitutes for paper books, but the screens were hard on the eyes and the page turning feature too slow. They never caught on as book readers here in Universe B. By the time the omni made it to Universe A, the technology had advanced." "And so paper books disappeared from Universe A," Bean said.

"But Olivia May Novak Irving with her spilled pomegranate juice is not the universe maker because—?" I asked.

"She's too massive. Too much matter in Olivia May." Arni shrugged off the loss of his favorite research lead. "Pity. It's a nice strong event chain."

"Is the event chain we're looking for the strongest one we'll find?" I asked.

Arni put his hands up and made the universal too-complicated-to-explain gesture. "Well—"

Professor Maximilian, who had been standing at Bean's desk perusing the textbooks on it (*Bihistory's Histories, Mathematics through the Ages, Bubbles: Soap Making Techniques, The Maltese Poet*), looked up. "Say Bean here comes in one morning with a runny nose, sneezes, and spreads her cold to Pak." He pointed across the room to Pak, who was leaning back in his plastic, cushionless and wheeled chair, feet up on his desk, listening to the discussion. "The next day, Pak feels like he's coming down with something and orders soup at lunch instead of his usual salad. This saves him—the salad greens weren't washed properly and he would have otherwise gotten food poisoning and died a week later."

"Not if he used Wagner's New and Improved Lettuce Purifier," I said, a little disturbed by the professor's choice of example.

"From outside of our thought experiment, we know that Bean's sneeze initiated the fateful chain of events—she sneezes,

Pak is saved." The professor picked up another of Bean's text-books (*Shimmy, Gyrate, Undulate—Belly Dancing Exercises*) and peeked into it. "But within the soup and salad universes, this would not be obvious. Consequences are often unexpected and hidden, and decisions that seem current can be part of event chains already set in motion. Are you following?"

"Yes," I lied.

Pak folded his arms behind his head and said, "Historians in the soup and salad universes, not knowing about Bean's sneeze, would probably debate whether their two universes diverged the moment I placed my order—or later, when I took the first forkful of salad or spoonful of soup. Or perhaps," he added, "they would decide that it happened even later, when I either die or don't."

"To answer your question, Felix," Professor Maximilian concluded, "we can't go by what seems important—the stuff that makes it into the newspaper or the big decisions we make in our lives. The smallest moment may matter."

"Alexander Fleming discovered penicillin," said Arni, who had moved to the sink where he was rinsing used tea mugs, "when mold spores landed on a petri dish he hadn't gotten around to washing. One could argue that a mold spore initiated that event chain by landing on the petri dish, or that Alexander Fleming did by leaving used petri dishes lying around his lab. Probably his parents get the credit by failing to teach him to be neater in his daily life. In order to figure out the real answer, we'd need access to a universe in which Fleming *didn't* discover penicillin so that we could compare it with ours, see where their histories start to diverge." Arni tossed the paper napkin he'd used to dry the mugs into a trash bin, making me wince at the casual waste of paper, and returned to his desk. "The first week after Y-day, there was a new speed dancing record set in Hong Kong, a fire on a luxury ship in the Caribbean, an upsurge in bottlenose dolphins migrating past the California coast, and a lightning storm in Caracas—some of those happened in A, some in B. And all over the world different babies were being conceived in A and B. Uniques."

"Except for Pak," said Bean.

"Wait, Pak, I though you were like twenty-something," I said.

"I am."

"Pak's a rare breed, an incidental alter," said Arni. "A post Y-day one. The same two people getting together, on the same day, one couple in A and the other in B, with a particular spermatozoon finding its way to the same ovum, yielding genetically identical persons—well, that's an occurrence that verges on zero probability."

"What does your alter do?" I asked Pak.

"Fishes."

"If not Olivia May's, what chain did you start, Felix?" Arni thumped his desk lightly.

"Couldn't Felix B have run into the *other* Olivia May?" I suggested.

"And done what? The other Olivia May did nothing out of the ordinary. She got off the tour boat and went to her interview as planned. Besides, by the time Klara, Patrick, and Felix B came into the Quake-n-Shake for lunch, five minutes past one o'clock, Olivia May B was well on her way to her interview downtown."

"Part of the problem in pinpointing event chains," Bean said, wrinkling her brow, "is that no one ever looks at their watch. People are vague observers. They tend to remember if something happened around the moment the electricity went off because of the power sucked up by Professor Singh's apparatus—but can't tell you if it was ten minutes before or ten minutes after. We didn't get a chance to ask Olivia May what time she spilled her pomegranate juice, but I bet she wouldn't have remembered anyway."

Professor Maximilian had been frowning at something at Bean's desk.

"What," he asked very deliberately, "is this?"

[22]

TIME STAMP

Thus far during my stay in Universe B, I had acquired two paper books. One was the Agatha Christie which Trevor had insisted I keep and which at the moment was in my jacket in Bean's car. The other was *Stones, Tombs, and Gourds.* Professor Maximilian had picked up the art book from where I had forgotten it yesterday next to *Shimmy, Gyrate, Undulate* and had been absentmindedly turning its pages. He'd taken something out of the chapter on Japanese pottery and was holding it by the edges.

"Yes, what *is* that?" I repeated the professor's question. "I found it in the middle of the book. It's like a narrow postcard."

"It's a bookmark," Arni said, rising to his feet and staring at the object in question.

"They kept it," Bean exclaimed. "The souvenir bookmark— they were giving them out that day—I don't believe it—"

Pak coasted in his chair over to Bean's desk.

"You see, Felix," Arni said, speaking quite calmly, "there used to be a toll for pedestrians crossing the Golden Gate Bridge, along with the usual car toll. The city needed extra revenue to deal with the runaway inflation. To make up for the unpopular toll, they occasionally gave out cheap souvenirs—balloons one month, key chains the next, and so on. And bookmarks in January of 1986. Most people threw them out in protest of the unpopular tax. Patrick and Klara Sayers, it seems, didn't. On the back," Arni added, still very calmly, "there should be a stamp."

I got up off the couch to join everyone at Bean's desk. The bookmark was just about the size and color of an uncooked lasagna noodle. One side held a printed sketch of a San Francisco cable car. The professor turned the bookmark over. Along the bottom edge of the otherwise blank flipside there was a row of text. The faded ink, clearly the result of a human hand crookedly feeding paper into a machine, read:

SE 1-6-1986 11:39 $20.00

"Huh," I said. "I didn't notice that before."

The samovar in the corner beeped to announce the readiness of a new batch of tea. Pak coasted over to the appliance in his chair, turned it off, and coasted back.

"That settles it," Arni said. "At 11:39 the Sayers family was at the south end tollbooth, just crossing onto the bridge. Seven minutes later the yabput happens—"

"We were right, Felix!" This from Bean. "Your parents did take the shorter path to the bridge."

"How do we know the stamp doesn't stand for 11:39 p.m.?" I asked, just to be contrary. "Maybe my parents got the bookmark from a friend who went for a midnight walk and who kept it as a souvenir of Y-day. Or maybe my parents were on the bridge at that hour for some reason. We still don't know why they drove to San Francisco that day."

Arni shook his head briefly. "The stamping mechanism used twenty-four-hour time. In that case the bookmark would read 23:39."

"Fine." I went back to the couch.

"You're right, though," Arni added, gingerly taking the bookmark, "about it being a keepsake. This would be worth a lot to a collector."

"I wish I had a counterpart in Universe A," the professor said rather randomly as Arni passed the bookmark to Pak, who took it carefully by the edges. "Another bihistorian, I mean. The institute isn't even there in Universe A, not anymore. The mob—well, you know the story. My alter devotes his time to cooking products."

I felt an unreasonable desire to defend my boss and his mission of creating and marketing quality kitchen appliances, gadgets, and cutlery. "Have you met Wagner?" I said to the professor from the couch.

"Once. We tried to figure out what chain of events led him to found Wagner's Kitchen—for instance had the institute *not* been destroyed in A, would he have ended up a bihistorian? I credit a high school class trip to what was then the Physics Institute with inspiring much of my interest in the subject." Hands folded behind his back, the professor commenced walking in a slow circle around the couch, just like Bean had that first day when I came into her office. "The timestamp on this bookmark places Felix within the event radius a mere seven minutes before the yabput. We can probably confirm that the bookmark belonged to Felix's parents via fingerprint identification—handle it only by the edges, Bean—"

"Sorry."

"The bottom line is that this is historical and scientific evidence, which, if destroyed, would be irrecoverable. It is therefore imperative that we preserve the bookmark for posterity and not allow it to fall into the wrong hands."

"The hands of Past & Future, you mean? Of James and Gabriella?" I asked.

The professor waved Past & Future aside. "They do not concern me. Only one side here has an interest in burying the bookmark. Only one side frowns upon research into the existence of multiple universes and the idea that ordinary citizens create them. It was they who, I believe, tried to wipe blank your parents' computer in Carmel."

"DIM, you mean? You want to prevent the bookmark from falling into the hands of DIM's Council for Science Safety?" I asked. "How do we do that?"

"We might need help on this one. Let me think."

He proceeded to think, circling.

🦆

"No one likes to bring this up," Professor Maximilian stopped and spoke into the hushed room, "but Professor Singh didn't tell anyone about the link between A and B for several months, while he—*they* really, the two Singhs—worked on stabilizing the information exchange system. They sent notes back and forth. When the world finally learned the truth—I was fifteen years old and let me tell you, it was an exciting time. The first few attempts at sending an egg across, failure, failure, failure, and then success—and soon enough people were crossing too. It wasn't long before things started to go downhill, alters disrupting each other's lives, and everyone turned against Singh and his ideas. The end result, as you know, was that crossings, scientific research, privacy matters, and all information-handling entities became strictly regulated. It's also why we have DIM agents dropping in for surprise inspections a few times per year." He rubbed his hands together. "As luck would have it, they are coming by tomorrow."

I gaped at him from the couch. "As *luck* would have it, did you say?"

"How do we know they're coming?" Arni asked.

"I have my connections," Professor Maximilian echoed one of Wagner's favorite statements. "Tomorrow is Saturday—DIM assumes any unauthorized research would be done on weekends, which is why I always perform my unauthorized research with an open office door, in the middle of the day, during the work-week. It's a very conveniently timed visit for us. I am going to give the bookmark to the DIM agents."

"What?" Arni and Bean said in unison. Pak seemed more silent than usual, if such a thing is possible.

"Kids—" It was the first time I had seen Professor Maximilian (or *either* Wagner Maximilian, for that matter) hesi-tate about what he was going to say. The professor studied the linoleum that marred the floor of the graduate students' office and rubbed his chin. Finally he raised his head. "This can go no further than this room."

We all nodded in agreement. Has anyone ever done other-wise upon hearing those words?

"I wish I'd had the chance to meet him. Professor Singh, I mean. By the time I started graduate school the physics depart-ment was gone, replaced by the bihistory department, and Singh was at the work camp where he would stay until the day he died. But Singh's laboratory is still here, undisturbed, boarded up since the day of his arrest. It's downstairs," he added, point-ing at the linoleum, which struck me as odd since we were in a basement office.

"More importantly," he added, "it still works."

"What does?" I said.

"Singh's equipment."

"You've opened a new, unofficial link between A and B?"

He shook his head. "No, see."

"See what?" I asked.

"Universe C, not A or B. This way."

[23]

THE LACE HEDGEHOG

"It's a universe very much like this one," whispered the professor, seeming quite pleased with himself now that the cat was out of the bag. "Very much like this one," he repeated, rubbing his hands together like a mad scientist in a cartoon, except that he seemed sane enough. We had stopped at the end of the basement corridor. There was a steel door. "All right, I should tell you that you enter Singh's lab at your own risk," the professor said, his voice still low. "Not from the apparatus, of course, but there's a chance the DIM agents might show up a day early. Unlikely, and in any case, I'm merely showing you around the building, which hardly constitutes unauthorized research. Still—"

Before I had a chance to reflect on whether this was a good idea, he unlocked the steel door with a surprisingly ordinary key and let us in.

A set of concrete stairs led down to the subbasement lab. The open door had triggered a switch, causing a row of ceiling lights to come on. Several modern-looking computer stations dominated the large space; next to one wall lay a mound of haphazardly deposited electronic equipment and, on the opposite side, shelves held lab supplies. At the far end of the room, there was an iron railing I couldn't see over. In the very center of the lab, a small cylinder waited on a circular platform, like a kitchen water boiler someone had placed on a tall stool and forgotten. Several cables of various colors and thickness led from the cylinder to the computers and elsewhere.

Pak took the stairs down two at a time like he was used to the place and started flicking on the computer monitors one by one. We followed him down, Professor Maximilian going last and locking the door behind him.

The professor slipped the key into his shirt pocket. "I found the lab key in the back of a desk drawer the day I moved into my office—Professor Z. Z. Singh's old office. Couldn't figure out what it opened. Then one morning while walking around the building trying to figure out a particularly knotty research problem, I found myself in the basement and remembered the key." He headed straight for the cylinder, lifted up the lid, and checked inside. "No notes from Max C. The research problem I was grappling with at the time was how to estimate the mass of the prime mover whose actions had warped space-time enough to bifurcate the universe. Being able to run lab experiments with Singh's equipment resulted in a breakthrough and we were able to come up with the twenty-four-libra figure."

"We?" Bean asked, her voice even.

"Pak and I," the professor admitted, replacing the lid. "I didn't want—well—I didn't want to involve too many students in this."

"It doesn't work like a modern crossing," Pak said from a computer station, perhaps to distract Bean. "Only small objects can be transferred to Universe C and back."

"Pak and I snuck in new, faster computers during lunchtime one day, and also a power source independent of the main grid. It used to take Zachary Zafar Singh three hours to transfer a note—a simple piece of paper—from one universe to the other.

It takes us less than a minute. The equipment still loses a few bits here and there in the transfer because of link skips and interference. I wouldn't try it on anything animate." Seeing my expression, Professor Maximilian clarified, "Scrambled eggs. The Singhs discovered that it's very hard to put an egg back together once you've taken it apart."

"There was a race between the A and B teams of physicists to see who would be the first to accomplish transfer of animate matter," Arni said. "The problems were many—stabilizing the link, speeding up processing time, eliminating interference from visible light and other electromagnetic waves straying into the field."

"Which side won?" I asked.

"Neither. The scientists discovered they needed each other's cooperation."

"In any case, we have what we need, a stable connection kept open by the continual exchange of air molecules. To send an object to Universe C, you place it inside the cylinder. Any notes *from* Universe C arrive there as well. The cylinder is both the Inbox and the Outbox." The professor beamed at the Inbox/Outbox like a proud parent.

I wandered over to the railing and peered down. Below, a thin, corkscrew-shaped tube burrowed in both directions into a tunnel, like a giant, never-ending apple (or papple) peel. I turned back to face the room and asked the most obvious question first. "But what *is* Universe C?"

"It's a budding universe," said the professor. "Just branched off yesterday."

"Seventeen hours, eleven minutes, and fifty-three seconds ago, to be precise," Pak said from his computer. "Fifty-four seconds...fifty-five..."

"And this?" I pointed down at the apple peel.

The professor cleared his throat. "That's an old Singh vortex generator. Luckily Singh and his students could never get it to work."

"Why?"

"They didn't have enough power to generate so powerful a vortex."

"No, I mean why luckily?"

"An unconstrained vortex of that size would have converted all nearby matter, including this lab and probably the whole side of the building, to information and exchanged it with whatever was in its place in a neighboring universe."

I took a step away from the railing. "It's not going to accidentally beam us somewhere, is it?"

"No danger of that."

I stepped over some cables and went to the Inbox/Outbox and, like the professor had, lifted up the lid and looked inside. It was empty, save for some newspaper shreddings layered on the bottom, ready to be exchanged with whatever arrived from Universe C, presumably. With a start I realized what I was standing in front of—a miniature version of the crossing chamber in which I'd been turned into a number and back. "The link to Universe C is in *here*?"

"A link is a two-sided information-swapping mini-vortex that can be enlarged as needed," said the professor, who clearly thought he was speaking lucidly. He was by the wall shelves, standing on a stool to reach a container with office supplies. He took the container off the shelf and started rummaging in it. "I think we have some notepaper left...Think of it as a puff of air vibrating as it's continuously being converted to information and exchanged. As a matter of fact, links between universes occur naturally, though mostly in microscopic form, which is why we don't notice them. I've always wondered if that's how the odd sock disappears from laundry on occasion," he chuckled without looking up from the container of office supplies.

"I don't see anything other than newspaper shreddings."

"It drifts around," Pak said from where he was watching the clock tick off the seconds that moved ours and Universe C apart.

Just for a moment I thought I saw a shimmer of something in the cylinder, like a bit of warm summer air dancing above hot pavement, but I lost it. I put the lid back on and turned to where Pak was sitting. On the worktable next to his computer sat a plant, a multi-limbed cactus with delicately intertwined white spikes all over it, like dangerous cake frosting; on the top of each limb, barely open purple buds were beginning to droop. Immediately above the cactus a watering can sat on a platform. Attached to it was a small black box, a counter, a switch, and a pulley that looked like it could change the angle of the platform.

Pak noticed my interest.

"The lace hedgehog? My mother's birthday present," he explained. "I'm planning on giving it to her next week. One can only link to a fresh universe. The professor and I set up the radioactive decay apparatus and turned it on seventeen-some hours ago after making sure the event radius encompassed this room only. There was an even chance that the hedgehog would get watered."

"You linked a watered-cactus-happy-mother-universe to a dead-cactus-irate-mother-universe. Interesting," Arni said.

"Did we get the dry one or the watered one?" Bean asked. She reached over and poked the dirt at the base of the lace hedgehog with her finger. One of the wilting flower buds fell off the plant. "Dry."

"Wait," I said. "You're holding a universe open on the assumption that your mother will get mad at you if she gets a wilted birthday plant? Maybe she'll just be happy to get a present, Pak, same as if you gave her the watered one."

"She won't."

Professor Maximilian, still rummaging around on the supply shelves, waved his student's parental issues aside. "If Max C and Pak C haven't found their bookmark yet we can tell them about it. Tomorrow we turn one of the bookmarks over to the DIM officials, who'll leave happy and won't bother us for a while. We really need to get more notepaper. We don't keep research notebooks for obvious reasons, but that has its inconveniences."

"Back up a bit," I said. "One of the Professors Maximilian will have a bookmark and the other nothing?"

"Correct."

"How will you decide which Maximilian gets the bookmark?"

"It doesn't matter. Maybe we'll toss a coin."

"And the universes will reconnect once the cactus is watered?"

They all gave me a strange look.

"Perhaps I didn't explain it well." The professor got off the stool and came over to where I was standing. "Our radioactive decay yabput yielded two universes, watered and dry. We—all of us—exist in both. And whatever universe we're in, watered or dry, will seem to us to be a continuation of Universe B. The other will seem like C." He chuckled. "My counterpart is probably at this very moment explaining the plan to *his* graduate students. Either he or I will get to keep the bookmark, continue the work, and report back to the other. Simple enough."

I looked down at the professor. "Won't you mind if you're the one unable to continue your research?"

He folded his arms across his chest. "Mind? Of course I would mind. I'm open to suggestions if anyone has a better idea."

"Perhaps the group that ends up without the bookmark can create two new universes," Bean said after a moment, "and get a bookmark from each—one to keep, one to give to DIM officials—and then each of those universes could create two new ones, and each of those two more, creating a kind of a cosmic geometric progression."

"I get it. It's like the number of ancestors doubling in each generation as you go backward in time," I said as the professor picked up a taller chair, took it over to the shelves, and climbed on it to check the top shelf. I heard him mumble, "There's got to be paper somewhere. Max C and I will need to exchange a few notes on this..."

I was going to say, "Let's forget the whole thing before it's too late." Instead, looking around the disordered room with its computer cables leading everyplace, shelves overflowing with supplies, and old equipment piled in a heap in the corner, I said, "It's interesting to see where it all began. Singh's laboratory is so, er—untidy. I was picturing something more sinister, a sterile lab with men in white coats."

It had to have taken spunk, I thought, to descend daily into the subbasement to tinker with universes.

"Professor Singh had graduate students helping him," Bean said, as if reading my mind.

"Glad you like it, Felix," Professor Maximilian chuckled from the shelf without turning around. "Nothing wrong with showing a visitor or two around the building. You"—his remark was addressed to me—"could hardly be accused of performing unauthorized research. I, on the other hand, have waited a long time to be able to get my hands on some experimental equipment...a long time...

"But you're right," he added briskly and got off the chair. "Everyone best leave this room. We have a coin to toss. Sorry, kids."

"What?" Bean exclaimed.

"Except for Pak. I need an assistant. We'll do it this afternoon. That should give us plenty of time to obtain the extra bookmark and be ready for tomorrow's surprise visit by the DIM agents. In the worst case"—he shooed us toward the stairs— "if things go badly and DIM finds out about Universe C and revokes my research authorization, well, maybe I'll try my hand at doing something else after I get out of the work camp." He unlocked the door and opened it for us.

"Culinary products?" I asked from the doorway.

"I was thinking along the lines of a self-cleaning kitchen. Modular, with seven components for a typical household and eighteen for a restaurant. The book, Felix?"

I handed him *Stones, Tombs, and Gourds,* which I had been clutching the whole time, the bookmark peeking out of it. Next to me Bean took out a small notepad, similar to Mrs. Noor's, out of the back pocket of her jeans and ripped off the top few pages and handed the rest to the professor. "You'll need this. I've been using it for note-taking in my belly dancing class. Ask Bean C if she's figured out what event chain the duck pacifier started."

"Ask Professor Maximilian C if he's figured out why my parents were in San Francisco that day," I said. "Wait, there should be a Felix C around, shouldn't there? Ask him instead."

Arni chimed in. "Ask Arnold C if he's finished working with Olivia May and if I can have his notes—"

Professor Maximilian locked the door behind us.

[24]

THE ORGANIC OVEN

My routine at home each workday morning was to jump from a bicycle to a people mover to a bicycle and again in the reverse direction from my office each afternoon. Missing that daily exercise and feeling my midsection ballooning by the minute, I picked up the pace and so was the first to step into the only intersection we had to cross on our way from the Bihistory Institute to its parking lot. The moment of inattention almost cost me my life, or at least a broken bone or two. A car suddenly appeared out of nowhere and would have splattered me if a hand belonging to Arni hadn't pulled me out of harm's way.

"Universe B," I gasped, watching the car speed away and noticing that it was as sleekly black as not a thing in a kitchen except perhaps the inside of a nonstick pan, "doesn't seem to like me very much. That's the second time that's happened. Pedestrians have the right of way, don't they?"

"One can't be too careful," Arni said, releasing my arm.

After that I pretty much had to invite him to lunch too.

🦆

The Organic Oven was just as Mrs. Noor had described it—the newly renovated dining room held square tables fashioned from rustic, roughly finished red cedar with a touch of elegance provided by the silverware, wine glasses, and the basket of breadsticks which sat waiting on each table. Handcrafted natural stone decorated the walls. A lingering lunch clientele occupied maybe a third of the available tables.

Whether the head chef was (a) still in Carmel, or (b) back at work in the kitchen, concealed from customers' eyes by a set of swinging doors, or (c) in his study in the Egret's Nest Apartment Complex feverishly working on the next novel in his mystery series—or *(d) driving around town in a black car with its windows darkened*—there was no way of telling.

Neither Bean nor Arni commented on the fact that I had chosen the Organic Oven as our lunch destination, though I thought I heard Arni murmur, "Doesn't this *really* violate the Lunch-Place Rule?" as we sat down at our table.

Expecting a reception similar to the one I had received at the Coconut Café—mistaken recognition—I cringed when the waiter appeared, but he simply placed menus into our hands and left.

Bean cleared her throat and opened her menu. "Let's see, what looks good?"

I took my time reading the menu. It was printed on rough—organic?—paper and consisted of a single page with a dozen lunch entrées listed on the front and a dessert and drinks list on the back. A well-known rule of thumb is that it's the cheapest, not the priciest, item on a menu that reveals how good a restaurant is. My eye stopped midway down the list. There it was. The humble chicken breast sandwich, the first item I usually order at a new restaurant in a quest to find one reminiscent of the crusty-bread-tender-chicken-tangy-pickles combinations

I remembered from my early teen years before I lost my sense of smell.

All the strategy had gotten me so far was a list of ways to ruin a chicken sandwich: overcooking the chicken to a dense slab, slicing it too thick or too thin, smothering it in huge dollops of sauce, under-seasoning it to tofu-ness, wrapping it in bread that was mushy or rock hard, pairing it with a pile of boring, salty potato chips...Let's see what *your* staff can do, Felix, I thought.

"I think I'll have the duck l'orange," Arni said. "Just kidding. Enough of ducks and duck pacifiers. Caesar salad with wild caught salmon and natural camel cheese it is," he said to the waiter.

"The handmade fettuccini with spinach pesto," Bean ordered.

"The free-range chicken breast sandwich," I said to the waiter, then added after he left, "No, it doesn't."

"What?" Arni said.

"Violate the Lunch-Place Rule, my being here. I've never had lunch at the Organic Oven before. I don't even know if there *is* an Organic Oven A."

"And what if Felix B is in the kitchen?" Arni asked.

I recalled him saying that people sooner or later invariably faced their alters to satisfy their own curiosity. He didn't know, of course, that I had already met Felix. I felt reluctant to mention it.

"I don't plan on going into the kitchen."

The waiter reappeared with a large pitcher, poured water into our glasses with a flourish, and said, "Transported here weekly from hidden springs in the Sierras."

A strange mood had come over me. Recklessly for my identicard balance, I decided to order wine for the table. "We'd like some wine with our lunch. Do you have Napa Valley Zinfandel—?"

"Of course." He wrote the order down. "Our wine is made from pesticide-free grapes misted with spring water and when ripe picked by hand at sunset, then crushed the old-fashioned way and aged in oak casks. The wine is subject to the inter-universe import tax," he added.

"Inter-universe import tax?" I said. "What about the local wines?"

"Scratch that," interrupted Bean before the waiter could answer. "Water is fine."

As the waiter, looking miffed at the loss of the extra tip, stalked off, Bean explained. "Our Napa Valley isn't producing any more. Too much precipitation. It rots the grapes. California B imports its wine from California A. It's become somewhat of a luxury item."

"A consequence of the global warm-up," muttered Arni. "On the plus side, all the rain means we haven't had a drought in years."

"Why did you let the global warm-up get out of hand?" I asked sharply.

They stared at me.

"Never mind. I don't know what made me ask that."

"Universes are like people," Bean said. "It's easier to see the solutions to other people's problems. It's the loop."

"Did you say the loop?"

She reached over and selected a breadstick from the basket in the middle of the table. "Suppose you never made a single choice, like Passivists do. Don't. Whatever. Just sat in a park under a tree all day avoiding trouble. It wouldn't work. Eventually something would happen. Maybe not the first day, or the next—but wait long enough and *something* would. What, no one can tell you. You might be stung by a bee or bopped on the head by a falling branch or catch pneumonia from spending soggy nights in the park." She poised the untouched breadstick over the table. "I'm going to let the breadstick fall in a moment. About all I can tell you in advance is that it's going to roll about a bit on the table and then stop. I have no idea in which direction it will roll and I have no idea where it will come to a stop." She let the breadstick fall. It immediately came to a wobbly rest on her silverware and did not roll. "Humph. You see? Arni here and I, we *think* that proving you and Felix B are the universe makers will bring us our PhDs, lead to good jobs, make you two famous—but who knows what will really happen? We'll probably end up in a work camp for violating Regulation 19." She shrugged, retrieved the breadstick, and took a crunchy bite.

I reached across the table to take one of the breadsticks myself.

"Life's unpredictability is a good thing, in my opinion," she went on after a moment. "The first adventurous marine creature that decided that it might be a good idea to crawl out of the seas onto that interesting, warm, dry stuff we call sand had no idea what it was getting into, I'm sure...I am getting off track. What was I saying?"

"Why it's hard to see the solutions to your own problems. What's in these?" I asked, suddenly distracted from the topic at hand.

"They're just sourdough breadsticks," Bean said.

"I can taste them."

"Never liked sourdough myself," said Arni. "Too sour. In my opinion, bread should be neutral."

"Anyway, as to the loop," Bean went on, "we all know that we have the power to change our lives. But in the back of our mind is a tally of all the times that things didn't turn out as expected because of random chance, other people's behavior, false assumptions we'd made, or the disconnect between how we see ourselves and who we really are. We therefore know that most likely things will not turn out as we expect them to, so we try to take *that* into account but end up going in circles and doing nothing. It's like that old bit of advice, how do you dress well?"

"How?" I asked, reaching for a second breadstick. Just like that, Regulation 10 be damned, I found myself on board with Wagner's plan to obtain the sourdough starter for Universe A.

"By doing it with confidence. And how do you gain confidence?"

"I get it. By dressing well," I said through a full mouth.

"The loop is one of the tenets of Passivist philosophy," Arni threw in.

"Yes," Bean replied a trifle testily, "but that doesn't make it wrong."

Arni shrugged. "Don't try to change things. It's a safe creed to live by."

"How many are there?" I said, having finished with the second breadstick and looking over the chicken sandwich the waiter had just brought.

"Which?"

"Tenets of Passivist philosophy."

"Seven." She ticked them off one by one. "Disturb nothing. Be still. Stand aside. Do only what you must. Embrace the loop. Give everything. Keep nothing."

"Did you go to many Passivist meetings as a child?" I said. There was an inviting beet salad accompanying the chicken sandwich. I speared a helping onto my fork.

"Every seven days."

"What did you do at them?" I asked, the sweetness of the beets awakening my palate further.

"Not much."

A busboy had finished clearing the dishes off the neighboring table; he swept up the crumbs, then wheeled a cart stacked with dirty dishes through the swinging doors, permitting a brief glance of hanging pots and pans. "If Aunt Hen hadn't left instructions in her will that a photo be mailed to me along with half of her porcelain dolphin collection, I wouldn't be here today eating this delic—this sandwich," I said. "I keep wondering if the pet bug quarantine was an unexpected outcome, as you say, or whether James and Gabriella did it on purpose."

"Does it matter?" Arni replied. "Maybe Granola James took his pet for a walk in the woods, Murphina partook of infected droppings, and, unaware, James brought her to Universe B where you petted her head—"

"She licked my hand," I corrected him.

"Or he realized she'd gotten infected and took advantage of that fact to position himself in your vicinity. If he did plan it, he probably didn't expect to see Bean there."

"Or that I'd be grounded by the pet bug medication in my room at the health center for much of my stay."

"Irrelevant in any case," Arni said. "The law differentiates between premeditated murder and involuntary manslaughter, between deliberate pursuit of unauthorized research and a serendipitous discovery. Event chains don't care."

I cared. Inconveniences were best left to fate, in my opinion.

"Tell me more about your Passivist childhood, Bean," I said, wrapping my fingers around the second half of the chicken sandwich. "Did you live on a farm?"

"I had a veggie garden and made my own clothes. The clothes were not very good."

"What about your parents? Does it bother them that you're not a Passivist nowadays?"

"They neither approve nor disapprove. If you like we can take a drive down to the farm tomorrow—Saturday—so you can see what it's like. Everyone sits around and talks and does nothing much after the day's work is done. It's quite pleasant, actually, now that I think about it."

"I have to go back to Universe A tomorrow. My entry permit expires midafternoon. I survived being turned into a number once, can't say I'm looking forward to doing it again."

"Tomorrow? That doesn't give us much time," Arni said. "Anyone know hypnosis? Perhaps there is a chance your subconscious self remembers what you did with the duck pacifier. Did you say something, Felix?" He accepted a refill of spring water, then added in a low tone after the waiter left, "I've been sneaking looks into the kitchen whenever the waiters go in and out. Can't see much from this angle, though."

"I wonder what kind of car he drives," I said.

"Felix B? Why, do you need a ride somewhere?" Bean asked.

I shook my head. The Organic Oven and an adjacent grocery store shared a parking lot, whose attendant had requested sixty dollars for an hour's worth of parking. I had taken my time paying him, but didn't spot a black car with darkened windows anywhere in the parking lot. I thought I *might* have caught a glimpse of a two-seater the color of a squishy apricot parked by the back entrance of the restaurant, however.

"You ate that sandwich quickly, Felix," Arni said.

I balled my napkin onto the empty plate. "I guess I was hungry."

"Why don't we ask our waiter if the head chef is here? I could say I want to compliment him on his Caesar salad with the wild caught salmon and the natural camel cheese. It was quite good. Just a hint of anchovies and lemon...scrumptious." Arni scraped the last bit of salad from his plate and finished it off.

Bean glanced over at me and pushed the leftover fettuccini strands around her plate with her fork. "My pasta is a little soggy."

"Or one of us could pretend to be looking for the bathroom and accidentally walk into the kitchen—"

"Let it rest, Arni," Bean said.

"Really? Why? I'm curious. Isn't anyone else curious?"

"Compliments of the chef."

The waiter was back. He was brandishing a large dessert plate with cheese balls, chocolate chunks, and a medley of nuts on it.

We split it three ways.

[25]

THE OLD GOLDEN GATE BRIDGE

The sidewalk along the length of the bridge had, on one side, a shoulder-high railing preventing a fall into the cold and hostile water below; on the other side, a single step led down to (equally dangerous) noisy and speeding traffic. Tourists moved along, not staying in any one spot too long. The increasing wind was bringing in low-lying fog, chilling intrepid walkers and threatening to obscure the sun and the two bridge towers.

If Arni and Bean were to be believed, the old Golden Gate Bridge was the scene of the crime.

Nor were they the only ones who thought so. We had overtaken Gabriella and James at the elevator which carried pedestrians from the parking lot to the bridge deck. The representatives of Past & Future were trying to get the almost-dog Murphina, who had her considerably large backside firmly planted on the ground, to consent to an elevator ride. As we passed them, we heard James say, "Murph, come on, I know it's not the woods, but it'll be fun...we can climb the stairs to the top of one of the towers if you like—and look for lampposts number 30 and 41 on the way—"

I zipped up my jacket, conscious of being in a state of ambivalence. The signals my stomach was emitting—*excellent meal*—struggled against those from my brain—*damn him, he's good in the kitchen, what if he's equally good at writing mystery novels?* I couldn't decide if it was worth swallowing my pride and calling Felix to find out which sauce he'd flavored the chicken sandwich with or to ask for the beet salad recipe. Subduing a digestive aftereffect, I joined Arni and Bean, who were counting off lampposts, many of which had their numbers worn off by age. "Eleven...twelve." Bean raised her voice above the din of the traffic. "I wonder what the professor and Pak are doing." She took a slurp through a straw of the drink she'd gotten to go at the Organic Oven while I took care of the check.

"What is that, anyway?" I asked equally loudly and pointed to the oversized cardboard cup in her hands.

"A smoothie."

I shrugged in ignorance.

"You know, fruit blended with juice, yogurt, and ice?"

I shrugged again.

"You mean you've never had one? This one is orange-banana-raspberry. Want a sip?"

The smoothie was like a melted fruit sorbet, only less sweet, and was quite refreshing, even more so on a hot day, I imagined. "I wonder if it's a copyrighted Universe B idea," I said, passing the large cup back to Bean via Arni who was walking between us. "Wagner might want to look into it."

"Fifteen..." Arni counted off.

As we continued on, an odd thought crossed my mind— what if the pacifier episode, as I had started calling it, had initiated a chain of events whose consequences had *yet* to occur, like the assumed anger of Pak's mother at her wilted birthday cactus? Bean had said that the Y-day event chain would last nine hundred years. Nine centuries. A millennium, almost. The time scale was so large I couldn't wrap my head around it. Had

I set in motion a slow cooker of an event chain, one that would simmer and bubble away quietly for years before finally blowing off its lid and spewing stew everywhere? Unlike the cement structure firmly under our feet, the Universe A bridge was no longer there; but could the duck pacifier, after thirty-five years, still be hidden in a crevice in one of the bricks or stones reused in building the *new* Universe A bridge, poised to—do what? Catch the attention of a curious seagull who'd try to make a meal of it, then, disappointed by the rubbery consistency of the item in question, lurch into the path of one of the traffic control fliers that occasionally buzzed the bridges, making the flier crash and causing an untold number of casualties that would all be my fault?

"You don't get a sense of just how long the Golden Gate Bridge is until you try to walk it," Bean said. She was limping slightly. ("Belly dancing injury," she'd said.) "From afar, the turreted towers and the terra cotta color, like that of a flower pot, make it look fanciful, smaller than it really is."

"Terra cotta? It's always seemed more of a faded mahogany red to me," Arni said, glancing up at the thick suspension cables, where a recently cleaned section revealed the original color undulled by car exhaust fumes and salt corrosion. At the far end, fifteen stadia from where we'd started, the bridge met the yellow-brown cliffs of the Marin Headlands.

"It's international orange," I said, striding on.

"Really? I didn't know that," Arni said with interest. "Twenty six...But do you know where the strait gets its name?"

"Because of the yellow-brown Marin cliffs that it abuts?"

"No."

"Because of the gold rush of 1855?"

"No."

"What, then?"

"Lamppost twenty-eight...I'm glad we don't have to walk all the way across, it's too cold today. The strait was given its name by one John Fremont, explorer, politician, military officer. Apparently it reminded him of a historic harbor in Istanbul called the Golden Horn. Twenty-nine...thirty. That's it." Arni stopped. He pulled out Aunt Henrietta's Photo 13A. "Why don't you stand by the lamppost, Felix, and take the place of your father holding you. It will help us visualize the moment in time."

We had already paused at the seven-minutes-from-the-toll-booth spot and found nothing remarkable there.

I obliged, aware that the last time I was here—on this very bridge? On a bridge identical to this one, brick by brick and cement slab by cement slab?—I hadn't even known how to operate my own two feet. Arni commanded something as I took a position between lamppost number 30 and the bridge railing, but it was impossible to hear what over the din of the cars crossing the bridge and the wind whipping my hair back.

"What? I can't hear you," I cupped my ear.

"Take a step back," he bellowed and gestured toward the bridge railing.

I took a step back.

"One more half step," he bellowed again.

I took a half step to the railing, feeling the cold metal through the back of my jacket. Below, the ocean water churned about, its tint deepening to gray-blue as the sun went behind the low clouds again. It seemed a long way down.

Arni handed Bean the photo and framed the tableau in front of him between his hands. "What do you think?" he spoke into a sudden brief drop in traffic.

"That's the spot," she concurred. "Lamppost 30 on the left, vertical bridge cables in the background. Move toward us a little, Felix, maybe a quarter of a step, and imagine yourself holding your six-month-old self. I wonder," she added, "if your mother took the photo on your way *to* the first of the bridge towers—everyone climbs at least one of them for the view—or on the way back."

I edged forward, my eyes still on the water. "What if a school of seals—smallish ones—made Meriwether's tour boat swerve and thus initiated the Y-day event chain?"

"Meriwether didn't mention seeing any seals. Why, do you see any down there?" Arni asked. I shook my head. It was impossible to see anything in the choppy, white-capped water. A minute or two later, they joined me at the railing as Arni explained, "A group of seals is called a pod or herd or rookery, not a school. Or—pretty oddly, considering their flopping skills on land—a harem."

"I think I'm a seal when it comes to belly dancing," said Bean. "I don't seem to be able to do much other than flop around." She limped aside to let a bicyclist pass.

"No seals today, but we do have an occasional bicycle." Arni nodded toward the retreating back of the brightly and tightly clad cyclist. "And pedestrians, strollers, buses, cars. Also seagulls and other birds," he added, echoing my earlier thoughts. "Moments before this photo was taken on this very spot, Felix interacted with *someone or something* from his baby carrier, thereby setting off a nine-hundred-year lasting event chain, unless we're completely wrong about the whole thing. Could the pacifier have landed on a car and been driven away? How far can a six-month-old throw anyway?"

We looked at each other blankly.

"I'll add it to my research list," Arni said. "Come, people, think. Professor Maximilian needs us to figure this out. The bookmark placing Felix on the bridge is not enough—even two of them, when and if the professor gets the other one. We need a solid event chain."

"Maybe a couple driving by saw Felix B happily sucking on his duck pacifier and thought, what a cute baby, and went on to have a dozen children of their own," Bean said.

"What if I took the damn thing—" I began.

"And those children will beget their own children, and those their own children, and so on for nine hundred years."

"—and pitched it over the railing—"

"Or the couple driving by saw our Felix A here raising a ruckus about losing his duck pacifier and they thought, what a cranky baby, and went on *not* to have a dozen children of their own."

"—and a seagull caught it midair and swallowed it and then, startled by the experience, flew over to Fort Point and caused a surfer to fall off his surfboard and forever eschew surfing from that point on and take up politics instead?"

"No one reported anything like that," said Arni.

We recreated the Photo 13B tableau near lamppost 41 a bit farther on, then went into the first of the two castle-like towers. Spiral stairs in the center of the tower offered alternating views through slit-like windows, first of the bay, then the Marin Headlands, then the ocean, then the city, and finally the bay again just before we reached the mesh-enclosed top of the tower where a 360-degree view unfolded. The fog was making quick strides and had already engulfed the south end of the bridge. The level of humidity in the air had risen, and Arni's long curls were beginning to frizz up. I eyed the various nooks and crannies in the aging bricks, which, like the trash-filled bottom under the spiral stairs, offered plenty of places in which a pacifier could have hidden (and been carted away or ended up at the bottom of the bay as the result of the 8.1).

We continued past the first tower onto the drawbridge segment between the towers—the bascule, as I had learned it was called. As we neared the halfway point, I expected to see a gap where the two sections met. None existed. A flap extended from one bridge section onto the other.

Suddenly there were signs of action all around us. A cargo ship had cleared the seawall and was getting bigger by the minute. We were about to have the ultimate bridge-walker's experience—the raising of the drawbridge. Traffic quickly ground to a halt, leaving the bascule section empty; harried city employees ushered citizens behind safety gates. We found ourselves herded onto the Marin side, giving us a view of the city as a backdrop to the passing of the ship. With an eerie grating noise and the clanging of chains, the two halves of the drawbridge commenced lifting, rattling the section we were on and sending several seagulls away. The ship sounded its horn. Tourists were snapping photos all around.

"Franny and Trevor, the innkeepers of the inn where I'm staying, grew up on a ship this size," I said as we watched the cargo vessel, loaded with immense shipping containers piled neatly like kids' multicolored building blocks, glide through. "Had to have been quite an experience. What kind, whether insular or worldly, depends on how often they pulled into port, I guess."

No one was interested in talking about innkeepers. I couldn't blame them. There's always something mesmerizing about the working of heavy machinery, partly an expectation that things might go wrong, causing the whole thing to come crashing down on your head, but also a sense of accomplishment that the human race had built something so grand. (Along with which comes the realization that *you*, an individual member of that same human race, would have no idea where to begin, bridge-building wise, even if you had a large pile of bricks and the several million years or so it took to get from apes to this point.)

"You know what puzzles me?" Bean said as the drawbridge descended to the level position and we turned to the railing to watch the cargo ship churn toward the port of Oakland. She moved closer to Arni and me so we could hear her as vehicle traffic resumed in the four bridge lanes, two in each direction. "How did DIM agents know to wipe Monroe's computer? Was it just routine destruction of old information or something more, like Professor Maximilian said? In which case, how did they find out that we're looking for the universe maker in the first place? We're pretty careful."

"You think DIM has been spying on you?" I said.

"Of course," Bean said.

"Undoubtedly," Arni said.

"We even thought that you might be a mole."

"A what, Bean?" I said.

"A mole—you know, an operative, a DIM agent trying to catch scientists breaking Regulation 19."

"Oh, a spider. No, I'm not a DIM spider or mole. But come to think of it, when I asked my boss to help us locate Olivia May Novak Irving A, otherwise known as Mango Meriwether, he called back with her number awfully fast—perhaps they knew that it would be a dead end and that we would learn nothing of consequence. *And* Wagner knew about me being in quarantine even though our names were never released to the public." Put that way, my boss and his network of acquaintances sounded positively sinister.

Bean frowned. "Has anyone given you anything since you got to Universe B?"

"Not really," I said. "Well, just a book."

[26]

THE END OF A BOOK

"Who gave you a book?" Bean demanded in a loud whisper that could barely be heard over the din of the buses and cars thundering by and occasionally rattling the sidewalk we were on.

"What book?" Arni demanded in an equally low tone from my other side.

Puzzled by their manner, I lowered my voice accordingly. *"Why Didn't They Ask Evans?"*

"Evans who?" said Arni. "I don't have an Evans in my database."

"No, *Why Didn't They Ask Evans?* is the title of the paper book. An Agatha Christie," I explained. "You've seen me reading it, Bean. The innkeepers at the Queen Bee Inn sent it while I was quarantined at the Palo Alto Health Center. Franny and Trevor. This morning I tried to return the book, but Trevor said to keep it. I've never gotten a paper book as a present. I think— yes, I have it here—" I unzipped my jacket and pulled out the book from an inside pocket.

"Toss it," Bean hissed.

"What? Into the water? But it's a book!" I protested, keeping a firm grip on the item in question. "Besides, won't that draw attention to us?"

"It might," Arni agreed. "Did the innkeepers give you anything else?"

I shook my head. "Not really. They recommended the Bed & Breakfast where we stayed in Carmel—you don't think—Franny said the Be Mine Inn was run by her cousin—"

"Cousin, hmm," said Bean. "More like coworker. Well, we knew they were keeping tabs on us."

"Wait," I protested, "this doesn't make sense. Even if the Department of Information Management was paying special attention to me because of my fake birth date, what are the chances that I would happen to stay at an inn run by DIM agents? Franny and Trevor seemed perfectly nice—"

"Humph," said Bean, taking a disbelieving sip of her smoothie.

Arni shrugged. "Franny and Trevor probably send regular reports to the Department of Information Management on their inn guests, especially visiting A-dwellers. Maybe this time they were asked to perform a special service."

Bean sent a mean look in the direction of the Agatha Christie, which I had wrapped in my jacket in an effort to render the presumed microphone embedded in it worthless. "We could fling it into the bay when no one's looking," she said, giving the railing another appraising glance.

"Never mind," I said. "With my luck it would probably land on an unsuspecting surfer or a yacht—"

I stopped.

Bean sucked in her breath. "Land on an unsuspecting—*of course.*"

"Back then the tour boats made a U-turn under the bridge, in a wide arc around the first tower usually, before heading back into the bay," Arni said slowly, like he was working something out in his head. "Tourists loved it. The ocean level was low, so they didn't need to raise the drawbridge. It could have gone right over the bridge railing, or through it—the slats are certainly far enough apart."

Bean finished his thought. "We'd assumed that your paths crossed at the Quake-n-Shake Restaurant, but you didn't need to come in direct contact with Olivia May to—"

"To ruin her life?"

"—to make her part of your event chain. Duck pacifier lands on tour boat, passenger spills pomegranate juice, misses interview, and so the omni is never invented—and then advanced Universe B models arrive with a bang." She gasped. "Felix, you're responsible for paper books being gone from Universe A.

"So it *was* you," she added, eyes wide. "I'm not sure I ever really believed it."

"I *knew* a duck had something to do with it," I said, feeling a sudden urge to make duck soup and twisting my jacket tighter around the Agatha Christie.

"We have to hurry back," Arni took charge of the situation. "If there is a microphone in the spine of the book, then DIM agents overheard all our conversations. What if they know about Professor Maximilian's," he lowered his voice again, "Universe C experiment?"

"I don't think that I had the book with me," I said, "when we were in Professor Singh's old lab—"

Unable to reach either Professor Maximilian or Pak on their omnis, we hurried back in the direction of the parking lot, with Bean hobbling along trying to keep up on a bridge now wholly shrouded in fog. We passed James and Gabriella arranging Murphina in the Photo 13A tableau at lamppost 30 on the way and made it to the Bihistory Institute just in time to see two uniformed DIM agents escorting Professor Maximilian out of the building and into a marked car.

It was a mean thing to do to a book, but I doused *Why Didn't They Ask Evans?* with a melted orange-banana-raspberry smoothie and dropped it into the nearest trashcan.

[27]

THE BEGINNING
OF A BOOK

Alone in the Lilac Room of the Queen Bee Inn, I found myself at the tiny hotel desk staring at the floral wallpaper as the sun dropped below the horizon. The chair was uncomfortable, my hand unused to writing anything longer than a grocery list, and the hotel notepad awkwardly shaped, like a bee.

I threw caution to the wind, damned all alters, and began the story.

🐤

The ice storm had coated everything with a thin, slippery veneer. R. Smith took a step out the front door of his lodge and immediately grabbed at the wooden handrail to avoid falling. He carefully continued down the stairs, making a mental note that the decaying autumn leaves needed to be swept. At the bottom of the stairs he paused. The air was crisp and the sky had that feeling of being freshly washed, with a wispy cloud or two hanging around for effect. Bluer still was the lake, views of which were to be had through the Douglas firs fronting the lodge, their branches laden with icicles like early New Year's decorations.

It was too early to be thinking of winter holidays, R. Smith reminded himself. Right now his job was to get the lodge ready for the annual Autumn Cookery Competition. Keeping to the grass rather than the slippery path, he continued down to the lodge parking lot. The grass crunched under his feet with every step and around him tree branches, heavy with ice, creaked and groaned. He thought of all the work that needed to be done: leaves swept into compost bins, gutters cleared of debris, lodge rooms cleaned after a long summer, the kitchen equipment needed for the competition cleaned and disinfected. He hoped the ice storm hadn't damaged the gondola lift at the neighboring Gold Peak ski resort. Lodge visitors and the competition attendees liked to take the twenty-minute ride up the mountain to enjoy views of Lake Tahoe.

In the parking lot a lone car sat in the closest spot, right where he had left it last night after a harrowing drive up the mountain through the storm. He hadn't bothered to carry in all of his luggage, only a small bag with toiletries. Now he needed a change of clothes.

He started to chip at the ice on the trunk lock with his keys, devising and rejecting possible themes for this year's competition as he did so. As always, the theme would be a surprise for the attendees, revealed on the opening night. Last year's Flour Arrangements from Around the World *(the competitors had forgone the ubiquitous wheat flour for the less familiar rice, soy, and the South American quinoa) had been a success, a quinoa chocolate cake taking the top prize.*

He managed to get the key into the trunk lock, then stopped. Something was different. At this time of the morning on most days, delivery trucks and cars would be rumbling past as they followed the curve of the lake toward competing motels and cabins of yearlong residents, all the way to where the road ended in a large circle at the ski rental place at the base of the mountain. Everyone must be getting a late start because of the storm, R. Smith thought.

Out of the corner of his eye he noticed sunlight gleaming off metal somewhere on the lake beach. Without knowing why, he abandoned the car trunk and crossed the road, twice slipping on the slick surface but managing to just avoid falling, to examine what lay on the sand.

R. Smith had never seen a dead body before. The first thought to enter his mind was, she must have been killed just before the ice storm hit.

There was no other explanation for the glistening layer of ice that coated the body as if it were a natural part of the landscape. It coated the woman's face, on which shock registered, like she had just gotten some unexpected news, and glistened off her long hair, which was as white as the ice itself.

It coated the knife.

🐥

I put the pen down and looked up from the bee-shaped note-pad—right at eye level, there was a small tear in one of the pale purple wallpaper lilacs. For a wild moment I wondered if Franny and Trevor had cameras installed in walls to spy on their guests and report on any regulation-breaking activities to DIM. Shaking my head at my increasing paranoia, I leaned back in the chair to read what I had written, adjusting a word here and there.

It wasn't a bad start. I wrote down the first sentence of the next chapter:

R. Smith didn't recognize her.

I scratched that out and instead wrote,

The woman seemed familiar, like R. Smith had seen her before.

I gathered the pages and put them away in my backpack, then went to bed.

[28]

I DEPART THE QUEEN BEE INN WITH A JAR

Waking up with a start, I opened my eyes and saw pale purple flowers all around. It was morning, I was still at Franny and Trevor's inn, and it was Saturday, my last day in Universe B. I got up, showered, donned my last clean shirt and pair of shorts, then set upon the task of gathering my belongings. As I wrestled a plastic bag containing dirty laundry into the backpack, I was reminded of the call I'd received in the midst of packing for my trip to Universe B. My presence had been requested at the local DIM branch. The fake birth date arranged by my parents hadn't been my fault or even my preference, but an unsmiling person had introduced himself as Agent Dune, led me to a windowless office, and asked an hour's worth of questions. I was worried that I'd be charged with falsifying personal data, but in the end Agent Dune had issued a new identicard for me and told me that I was free to go after paying the data correction fine. I've never gotten out of a place so fast.

I scanned the hotel room for a missing sock (hoping it hadn't been vortexed somewhere through a micro-link). So Franny and Trevor, innkeepers and welcoming hosts, had been spying on me. Via a book, no less. Rather obviously in retrospect, it was Franny who had taken Aunt Hen's photo while repacking my bag and sending it on to the quarantine wing of the Palo Alto

Health Center. According to Bean, the photo was gone from the Y-day photoboard as well, as if it had never existed.

Yesterday, after watching the marked car take the professor away, we had checked the subbasement lab and found it locked. Pak was nowhere to be seen, his bicycle gone. As there didn't seem to be anything else to be done, the three of us had parted to go our separate ways, Bean looking so gloomy that I felt it would be bad form to invite her to a romantic dinner. I returned to the Queen Bee Inn instead—with a glass jar in my pocket.

I bent down to look under the desk for the wayward sock. Professor Maximilian had been arrested, presumably for breaking Regulation 19 and perhaps also for additional crimes. Regulation 4, for one, governed the exchange of people and objects between universes A and B, but no doubt could be applied to unexpected transgressions if necessary—like the creation a new Universe C by watering (or not) a lace hedgehog cactus and then transferring bookmarks back and forth.

The sock was under the bed. I rolled it up with its partner, found a place for the pair in my backpack, then glanced around the room to make sure I had everything. Last night, on a writing high, I'd been sure that my Chapter One was the best beginning to a novel anyone had penned since the Sumerians invented writing and would blow out of the water any mystery series cobbled together by Felix B.

This morning I had folded five thin pages of scribbled bee-shaped hotel stationary into my backpack. It wasn't much.

For one thing, I had absolutely no idea who had killed the mysterious woman found lifeless on the beach by R. Smith, lodge owner.

On a smaller note, there was the commonplace name I'd given him (the R to be revealed to me and the reader at some future point in the novel). I had chosen Smith because I'd read somewhere that Agatha Christie, though she had an interesting character in her Belgian detective Hercule Poirot, had become irritated after a book or two with all the "foreign" mannerisms and French phrases that had to be inserted into the dialogue. But what if Felix B had chosen the name Smith for *his* detective? Jones, Wang, Garcia, Brown, they all carried the same problem. Maybe Wojciechowski or Lindroos-Rangarajan was the way to go.

I'd think about it later, I decided, zipping up my backpack. For now, R. Smith owned a ski lodge and hosted an annual cooking competition during which odd things, like murders, occurred; a new case for him to solve each year meant a potential mystery series of my own. Given that he drove a car, Smith lived in Universe B and was also, I had a feeling, recently divorced. His wife—Maria? Jane? Sally?—same problem as with Smith— had in previous years helped get the lodge ready each fall and had even suggested last year's theme of International Flours, but a dislike of winter boots and slushy roads had taken her on a different life path. After filing for divorce, she had moved off the mountain to work in Las Vegas as a—what? Well, I'd think of something; maybe a dentist. It didn't matter. I liked it. It provided a nice, handy reason why R. Smith was alone at the lodge, as well as opening the door for a potential love interest later in the book.

And perhaps R. Smith's alter could make an appearance too. Maybe he could be the sidekick, like Holmes and Watson, or Poirot and Hastings. Smith and Smith.

I was oddly pleased that I had managed to write the whole of Chapter One in words only. There had not been any other choice with pen and paper, of course, but I had not once gotten stuck and needed a stock image of a lakefront lodge or a quick shot of light reflecting off a bloody knife.

Before leaving the room, I carefully lifted the glass jar out of the side pocket of the backpack and checked it. The yellowish, frothy mixture looked the same as it had last night when I'd procured it at the back door of the Salt & Pepper Bakery. I unscrewed the lid and took a whiff; I thought I detected a hint of the aroma of bread and beer, but it might have just been my smell-impaired nose playing tricks on me. (It wasn't unusual for me to detect phantom smells, only to hear from other people that there was nothing actually there.) I gently tilted the jar left and right, watching the pancake-batter-like dough slide and stick against the glass. For 170-some years this little yeast-bacteria civilization had been propagated from one generation to the next—use half for today's bread, save half for tomorrow's batch. Bakeries going out of business, changing weather patterns affecting the local environment, the earthquake demolishing storage areas—no one was quite sure what had contributed most to the sourdough starter being lost in Universe A. I put the lid back on and tightened it. Until I could safely get the jar to a refrigerator at Wagner's Kitchen, the centuries-old method called for a daily stirring and a flour-and-water feeding of the dough, something I'd have to take care of as soon as I got home.

At the Nautical Nook breakfast buffet I ran into Franny. Head held high, she said, "We all must do our part to help protect society. Trying to prove the Passivists right. Not very nice."

I checked out, thanked Franny and Trevor for their (somewhat strange) hospitality, and took a cable car through the morning fog to Presidio University. Except for a crew of energetic and scantily dressed sand-volleyball players engaged in a morning game, the campus was mostly deserted, the bulk of the summer students still asleep at the Saturday nine a.m. hour. The bihistory building itself was unlocked, though most doors leading to offices and labs were closed and I passed not a soul in the hallway. I took the waiting elevator one floor down to the basement.

The hallway in front of the students' office was dark, but the light inside the office was on and visible as a thin strip under the door. As I approached to knock in the morning silence, something stayed my hand. A silhouette had disturbed the thin line of light under the door. For no explicable reason, I put my ear to the door. At first nothing could be heard; then there was a sharp, silence-piercing moan and a hissing sound, followed by a crash. Somebody swore. The silhouette by the door moved— and a dark stain, visible even in the poor light, spread under the door and onto the hallway linoleum.

[29]

WE WAIT, BUT NOT LONG

I burst through the door. Arni was standing on the other side, nursing a finger. The bright red stain by his feet was slowly spreading in all directions away from the upturned can on the floor. There were dark green specks in the red.

"Damn it," Arni repeated. "I burnt my finger on the can. Hi, Felix."

"What," I said, "is that?"

"Tomato soup. I should know better. I pulled the top off and the can heated too quickly. I didn't have time to put it down."

"Why are you having—tomato soup, did you say? With basil, it looks like, and fire-roasted tomatoes?—why are you having soup for breakfast?"

"We don't keep breakfast food on hand, only late-night snacks." A drawer on his desk was open and I could see rows of cans and what looked like popcorn bags.

"How can you think about food at a time like this, Arni, when we don't know what's happened to Professor Maximilian?" Bean was hunkered down on the denim couch with her legs drawn against her chin.

"Hey, I came straight in without eating breakfast. I'm hungry."

The door opened behind me and bumped me in the back. I moved out of the way to let Pak in. He was carrying his bike, careful to avoid the steaming red patch on the linoleum. The bike's front tire was flat.

"Pak, what happened?" Bean and Arni asked in unison.

Pak set the bike against his desk. "A shard of glass on the road." He bent down to secure the bike to the leg of the desk, as if someone might take it even in its damaged state.

"No, last night, with the professor," said Arni, who was at the sink wrapping a wet tissue around his finger.

"Was Professor Maximilian taken away to give a statement about the bookmark? Or was he"—Bean's voice wavered—"was the professor arrested and sent to a work camp?"

Pak shook his head.

The office door bumped me again and this time I moved all the way over to the couch and sat down next to Bean, who slid over to make room for me.

Professor Maximilian waited until the office door had swung shut behind him, then announced, "Hello, kids."

His blond hair and eyebrows seemed a little wild, as if he hadn't slept all night.

[30]

THE PROFESSOR'S SNEEZE

"**D**o you kids have any tea? I need something to refresh me."

The professor stepped over the steaming tomato-soup patch and perched on one corner of Arni's desk, his legs not quite touching the floor. Arni looked down at the tomato-soup mess, thought better of it, and instead went to the samovar and filled a mug. He handed it to Professor Maximilian. "It's cold, sorry. Yesterday's. We haven't had a chance to make a fresh batch."

"Ah, thank you, Arnold. That should do fine." Despite his demeanor, telltale bags were visible under the professor's eyes and he sat hunched forward, like it was an effort to keep his shoulders up.

"What happened?" I asked as Arni threw a handful of napkins down onto the spilled soup. I watched them turn red.

"As you know—strong tea, this, Arni—as you know, the plan had been for either Max C or me to give up the Y-day bookmark. Unfortunately the DIM agents showed up before Max C and I had a chance to decide which one of us would get the two bookmarks. I am not sure why they came a day early—"

"They probably overheard our conversations," Arni interjected. "Via a book in Felix's possession."

I sent him a displeased look. It wasn't my fault that I was too trusting of literary presents.

"—a book, you say, interesting—anyway, the DIM agents knocked sharply on the door of my—of Professor Singh's lab. Immediately I knew who it was, even before I saw their green uniforms. It was the kind of knock that startles you any time of the day, even in the middle of the afternoon. I turned off the equipment and let the agents in. They introduced themselves as Agent Sky and Agent Filbert.

"Max C and I had been about to toss a coin, so to speak. We had agreed to write down 'heads' or 'tails' and exchange the notes. Matching results—both notes reading H or T—he'd get the two bookmarks. Mismatched results, I'd get them. Turning off the equipment suddenly and irrevocably severed the link to Universe C."

"A bit must be exchanged," Pak explained from his desk behind the couch, "every 1.2 picoseconds to keep the link open. Communication traffic between A and B takes care of that usually."

"Wait a minute," I interrupted the professor's story as the reality of what Pak was saying sank in. "The connection between A and B can be lost without a way to get it back? I didn't know that." Realizing that I'd sat down with my backpack still on my back, I took it off, careful to keep it upright because of the sourdough starter jar inside. I wasn't sure how much sloshing around was permitted.

"All thirty-three crossing points would have to fail at once. Highly unlikely," Pak dismissed the issue.

"So there we were," the professor raised his voice slightly. "Two unfriendly DIM agents, one bookmark, a forlorn cactus near Pak's computer, and a note with nothing written on it yet."

"I happened to be in the bathroom during all this," Pak explained, as if that was somehow a failing of his biological self.

"Agent Sky wanted to know if there was any unauthorized research going on. Regulation 19 was mentioned. The best course of action, I decided, was bold-faced denial." The professor straightened his back. "No, I said to her, no unauthorized research. We can debate the ethics of that later."

I tried to imagine what it would be like if kitchen user guides, whose creation was already governed by Regulation 10 (workplace information), were suddenly deemed illegal or if I needed permission every time I began a new one, and felt a rising indignation. (And I didn't even *like* making kitchen user guides all that much really.)

"Good for you," I said. The students nodded in agreement.

"I claimed I was servicing the apparatus," the professor went on. "That if the Singh vortex generator wasn't attended to every thirty years, it would spontaneously turn on and start to twitch and shake and shoot out miniature Singh vortices that would float around the room and out the window and waft through the campus and the rest of San Francisco, along the way changing everything they encountered to information and swapping it with strange and unknown objects from faraway universes."

"But that's not true?" I asked, somewhat concerned.

"The spontaneously turning on part isn't. I further assured them that the servicing procedure was simple and would be over in an hour or two, if they cared to come back. Unfortunately the DIMs elected to stay and watch the servicing of the equipment. They told me they were going to inventory the lab, my office upstairs, and the offices of my graduate students afterward. They did not ask about the bookmark."

"Maybe they didn't overhear us talking about it, then," Arni said.

"I told you," I said, "I told you that I didn't have *that* book, the spy book, with me when we found the bookmark in the middle of the *other* book, the art book—"

"What *did* they overhear, then?" Bean frowned.

"Well," I admitted, "I had Franny's book with me on Monday when you came into my health center room, Bean, and told me I was the prime candidate for universe maker. Sorry.

"It was also in my possession," I added as Bean opened her mouth to speak, "in Carmel—Wednesday, was it?—when you pointed out the banana and duck pacifiers in photos 13A and 13B."

She was looking a little worried. "You don't think I'll get in trouble, do you?"

"So they know we are looking for the prime mover," the professor shrugged. "It's not a new idea—Passivists have been saying for years that people create universes. DIM's objective is that the idea stays just that, a mocked assertion by a fringe group. Arresting us would legitimize it. Much better to simply remove evidence from our path—take Photo 13 off the photoboard, wipe Monroe's computer, that kind of thing. The DIM agents watching me in the lab did not seem to know about any of that, however. I got the feeling they were sent to rattle me a bit, serve as a warning. The clamp on the flow of information extends to their own organization. It's one of the reasons it takes them so long to do anything."

The professor finished off his tea in one big gulp, shuddered, then went on. "So there we were, Agents Sky and Filbert leaning against the lab wall silently watching and I with a note in my hand with nothing written on it yet. I decided to go ahead with the original plan—though there was the small problem of needing a new universe to put the plan into action.

What I did was this. I wrote 'H' down with my right hand and simultaneously turned the vortex generator back on with my left. The event radius was small, barely surrounding the generator, but one never knows with these things. All sorts of weird things could have happened, like Agent Sky or Filbert walking over and saying something of importance—I know, not likely with DIM agents—and thus managing to *be* the event the device picked up on. In any case, I got lucky—the bifurcation was achieved and my H universe and the corresponding one in which I had written 'T' linked. I had a new Universe C, or better yet, Universe D.

"I was confident that the person at the other end of the link now knew exactly what to do." The professor paused, Wagner-like, for effect. "I placed my bookmark in the Inbox/Outbox to be sent to Max D. After two minutes, I looked inside the cylinder, expecting to see the bookmark gone. It wasn't. For a moment I thought that the equipment had malfunctioned, then I realized what had happened." The professor pursed his lips. "It was *his* bookmark that was sitting in the cylinder. We had exchanged them. Apparently he too thought he was giving up the bookmark. I sent his bookmark back, he sent mine back. I gave up and placed newspaper shreddings in the cylinder and waited for him to send me his bookmark. There was nothing. He too was waiting.

"At this point Pak tried to come back into the room but was prevented from doing so by the DIM agents."

"It was a bit startling, to say the least," Pak said. "They asked my name, told me that a calibration was in progress and that no students were allowed due to the sensitive nature of the material. I figured the smart thing to do would be to get on my bike and leave."

"It was," Professor Maximilian said. "As for me—it was clear Max D and I needed to have a detailed exchange of notes to clarify matters. However, it's one thing to write 'H' or 'T' and claim you needed it to test the device, and another thing entirely to exchange wordy notes. As I stood there deciding what to do, one of the purple flower buds detached itself from Pak's mother's cactus. It landed in the thick layer of dust on the table. I picked up the flower, and the disturbed dust—thirty-some years of dust accumulation is a lot of dust—made me sneeze. And that's what gave me the idea."

The professor jumped to his feet from where he was perched on the corner of Arni's desk and crossed the room to the white-board. He picked up a marker and sketched an outsized human nose and what looked like rain bursting forth from it. "When you sneeze, you see, droplets spread away from your face in a short-lived burst. The sneeze clears the sneezer's air passages and serves to spread infectious droplets and help the virus find a new host." He turned around to face us. "So I thought—that's the problem, I've been thinking too small. What I needed was more droplets, a critical mass."

"I'll take some tea," I whispered to Arni, thinking, only a lunatic or an experimentalist in the grips of a promising experiment would refer to creating a completely new Universe D as thinking small.

Arni passed a mug to Bean, who passed it on to me.

"I also realized," Professor Maximilian continued, "that Max D may or may not have just sneezed himself. I quickly penned a short note and placed it in the Inbox/Outbox. Then I waited, periodically giving the DIM agents more details about the disastrous consequences of not servicing the vortex generator properly. Finally I received a note back from Max D, discreetly read it, and disposed of it. We were in agreement. Think, kids. How would you prove there are universes beyond our two?"

"Er—bring in viewers to watch the process of linking to a new one?" Bean said.

"Think bigger."

I croaked, "Sugar, please," having tasted the tea, or, more precisely, the dregs of yesterday's tea.

Arni passed a handful of sugar cubes down. "Get three alters in the same room," he said.

"Not bad, Arnold," Professor Maximilian said from the whiteboard. "No one would blink at seeing a person and his alter walking down the street, but three identical persons—now that would surprise quite a few people. Triplets aside, three alters prove three universes exist. Ten alters prove ten universes exist. A hundred alters—well, you get the idea. I'd like to see what DIM would do if a hundred copies of *me*"—he thumped his chest lightly with one hand—"marched down Market Street. It's a pity we can't attempt a human crossing in Professor Singh's lab. Because the idea only works with people, not things, of course. What would you kids say if I showed up with a dozen Rosetta stones or a hundred Mona Lisas?"

"That you have a very good forger working for you," Bean said.

"Exactly. With a little effort and ingenuity you can copy a document, fake a painting, paint another Beetle pink to match Bean's car. To be convincing it has to be either people—or *information.*"

Pak sat up in his chair.

Professor Maximilian twinkled at him. "Each of us has secrets, little or big. No one but Pak here knows the combination to his bike lock. If I walked over to your desk, Pak, and entered the sequence 31-4-15 into your lock, you'd be—"

"Quite surprised," Pak finished the sentence for him.

"Pak D, who came into work earlier this morning than our Pak did, kindly supplied me with the lock combination so I could demonstrate the point."

"I had a flat tire," our Pak said.

The professor accepted a refill of his mug from Arni. "Thank you. I decided to test my idea on the DIM agents. I turned to them and said, 'Agents Sky and Filbert, would you assist me by thinking up a question relating to an event from the recent past, just before you came in, perhaps? I require this to test the logic feature on the device.' There is no such thing as a logic feature in Singh's equipment," the professor added for my benefit.

"After a minute or two of deliberation, Agent Filbert cautiously approached and handed me a note. He had written: *Where did I dispose of my piece of gum just before I entered this lab?*

What idea did I get watching this? his partner Sky had added below.

The professor partook of more tea. "I sent through the note with the agents' questions and soon received a reply from Max D and *his* agents:

"Nowhere—you swallowed it.

"Microphone embedded in food—good for up to sixteen hours of listening time before being flushed away.

"'Ah, the logic feature seems to be working fine,' I said to the two DIM agents.

"I now knew that the idea would work," the professor continued his story. "Agents Filbert and Sky, somewhat puzzled, were beginning to show signs of impatience, so I volunteered that I had a newly discovered historical document to turn in.

They consulted briefly whether a bookmark, even a Y-day one, constituted a document, before deciding that indeed it did and perhaps took precedence over finishing the inventory. The end result was that they drove me to their bureau where I filled out the necessary paperwork and left the bookmark, along with an art textbook belonging to Felix's parents."

"You left my art book? But I wanted to take it back with me," I complained, trying to sit up on the denim couch but merely managing to sink into a different spot on it. I had poured smoothie on *Why Didn't They Ask Evans?* and now I had lost *Stones, Tombs, and Gourds.* Except for the glass jar in my backpack, I would be leaving Universe B empty-handed.

"Sorry. While at the DIM bureau I took the opportunity to point out that similarly abandoned and forgotten books may harbor bookmarks or other Y-day items that an unscrupulous researcher could use for his own ends, say to try to legitimize the ideas of the Passivists. Highly unlikely that DIM officials would find anything of the sort, but it will serve as a distraction. They were typing up a report as I left.

"Luckily," the professor added, "if we can count on anything it's that the Department of Information Management moves slowly. They'll be back, but by then—"

"It'll have started," Arni said.

[31]

NETWORKING

"*What* will have started?" I asked from the couch.

"Max D and I have been up all night setting in motion an omni campaign," explained Professor Maximilian. On the whiteboard behind him the disembodied sneezing nose hung like the cat-less grin of the Cheshire cat. "Messages are spreading as we speak. My mailbox is already flooded with replies." Seeing my expression, he continued, "It's quite simple. I send everyone I know—and I know a lot of people—an epistle, an *Ask Me* proposition. They forward *Ask Me* to everyone *they* know, leading to an exponential growth of recipients. We'll reach almost everyone in the city by the end of today, I expect, and much of California in less than two days, and farther out by the fourth day—"

"But what does the proposition *say?*" I interrupted.

"Ask me a question, something that no one but you knows the answer to."

"And?"

"I obtain the answer from your Universe D alter."

"I think I see," I said.

"Your Universe D alter knows everything about your life, every little, insignificant detail—up to late yesterday afternoon, when I bifurcated B and D. I place the questions in the Inbox/Outbox and send them to Max D; he contacts the corresponding alters, gets the answers, and sends them back. Meanwhile,

I'm doing the same here, gathering answers to questions from Universe D to send back. Unless people decide we're mind readers, they'll have to accept the idea that they have alters out there, alters they don't know about. Imagine knocking on a stranger's door already knowing that he dropped a slice of toast butter-side-down on the floor yesterday morning, then ate it anyway."

"To be honest, my first thought would be that there's a DIM agent spying on me," I said, "not that another version of me happened to know that."

"And if I also knew that the reason you didn't bother re-toasting and re-buttering was not because you were in a hurry to get to work but because you wanted to catch a glimpse of your favorite neighbor on your way out, even though she's twenty years your senior and happily married?"

"I don't have any neighbors like that," I said for Bean's benefit. "So that's it? Omni messages."

"All we need to do is to convince enough people. As long as I can, I'll generate a fresh universe every few hours so I can give up-to-date answers. Universe E, Universe F, Universe G... however many I can get away with."

"Where do the building materials for these extra universes come from?" I asked. "The molecules and electrons and whatnot."

"Ah," said the professor, "but where do the molecules and electrons and whatnots in our own universe come from?"

The graduate students joined him in front of the whiteboard. The nose was erased. Equations were written, diagrams sketched. "Let's see," Bean said, "if we compare the expected rate of spread of Professor Maximilian's *Ask Me* proposition with the usual DIM response time to these things, we can expect two or three days at the most—how many people can we reach in that time?—"

"A secret way to pass things between universes. You could do a lot with that," I commented as they marked and erased and argued back and forth.

"*No,*" said four voices at once.

"I was just speculating on the possibilities," I attempted to explain.

"No," Professor Maximilian repeated. "Professor Singh's apparatus is not to be used again, not after we are done. This is—an emergency. It would be too tempting, too easy to go down that path. Crossings must be regulated. At some point in the future, when the human race is ready, I believe we will have a whole alphabet of universes to travel to and visit, like we have countries now."

"Are we sure people want to know about all this?" I asked the professor.

"They have a right to know. And they want to know. And do you want to know how I know that they want to know? Because for all the havoc and hysteria Singh's link has caused, no one has ever suggested simply severing it and disconnecting A and B. What have we done instead? Stabilized the link and opened multiple crossing points. Thirty-three of them.

"Just think," he added, "how surprised young people are going to be when they find out they aren't uniques after all."

"I certainly was." I got up off the couch and walked over to the whiteboard and stared at the equations. "Does this let me off the hook? You don't need me now, do you?"

The professor capped the marker in his hand. "It's not that simple. *Ask Me* only proves that universes beyond A and B exist, not how they are formed. We need you and your story, Felix, in order to show how A and B came to be. That it's a natural process."

"You need a universe maker," I said dully.

Professor Maximilian dropped the marker onto Bean's desk. "If only we had a clear-cut event chain—"

"We do," Bean said, beating Arni to it.

[32]

WHAT MADE OLIVIA MAY SPILL POMEGRANATE JUICE?

"**S**o we never asked the right question," I said, dialing the number of Meriwether Mango, formerly Olivia May Novak Irving A. "Like in the professor's *Ask Me* proposition, the question is as important as the answer. In *Why Didn't They Ask Evans?* that is the key question, why *did* no one ask Evans—"

"Evans who?" Pak asked.

"It's an Agatha Christie book—I doused it with strawberry-banana smoothie."

"*The* strawberry-banana smoothie," Bean corrected me. She was standing just out of sight of the omni, keeping her hands busy by straightening the stack of textbooks on her desk.

"*Evans* is about the adventures of one Bobby Jones, fourth son of the village vicar, and Lady Frankie," I explained to Pak, redialing. "A man goes over a cliff, all sorts of things happen, but it's not until Bobby and Lady Frankie ask the key question—"

"Yes?" Arni said. "Why didn't this Evans get asked? And what was the question that didn't get asked?"

"I don't want to ruin the ending for you. I admit I rather wish paper books had not vanished from Universe A," I added as the faint ringing of the omni began anew. "Interesting things seem to happen around them—the spying by Franny and Trevor, the bookmark placing me on the Golden Gate Bridge on Y-day... Interesting things seem to happen around paper books."

"I suppose they do," Arni said dryly. "One could also say that despite your best efforts to thwart its invention by making Meriwether Mango miss her interview at Many New Ideas, the omni still ended up rendering paper books extinct in Universe A."

"I gave it my best shot."

"Yes?" Meriwether Mango finally answered from her yoga studio, clearly irritated at being disturbed. "I have a class to teach in a few minutes. I'm doing my pre-stretches."

One of Bean's textbooks toppled over.

"Are there others in the room?" Meriwether demanded, leaning into the viewframe of the omni. "I specifically requested—"

"A potpourri of universes—what?" Professor Maximilian, having briefly dozed off on the couch, was jolted awake by Meriwether's voice.

"May I?" Arni said to the professor and hunched down next to my chair at Bean's desk. "Just a single question, please, Citizen Mango." Before she could refuse, he went on, "What made you spill pomegranate juice that day on the tour boat?"

Meriwether sighed. "This is really important, then?"

"Yes."

"You won't believe me," she warned.

"Try us," Arni said.

"Very well, then. I was above deck—you know how the tour boats have several rows of seats up there—the water was choppy, like I said, but that wasn't why...we were turning under the bridge and this thing—an object—came flying at me. Landed at my feet and startled me, and I jerked the cup in my hands and spilled pomegranate juice all over my cream blouse."

I opened my mouth to speak but Arni nudged me silent with his elbow.

Meriwether adjusted her position on the mat and moved her omni accordingly, giving us a different view of the yoga studio. She closed her eyes and went into a stretch that seemed to defy the limits of human flexibility. "If you must know, it was a silly little yellow duck. It had a patch on the bottom, like it had been part of a child's toy. Just came flying out of nowhere. I was convinced someone on the boat was playing a joke on me. I was so angry. But there was no way of telling who it had been. There weren't any kids near me on the boat."

"Did you happen to look at your watch at the moment the duck dropped down on the boat deck?" Arni asked.

She opened her eyes. "No, why would I? You know, I've never told anyone what happened, because it was so humiliating. But that's the whole story." She pulled herself up to her feet, picked up the omni, and moved to the studio window, brightening the image and making the fine lines on her face visible.

"I did it," I said to the woman whose life had intersected with mine three and a half decades ago.

"I beg your pardon?"

"It was me," I said more loudly. "Sorry. So sorry."

She frowned. "You were on the boat?"

"On the bridge above."

"You—you must have been very young at the time."

"Six months. Duck fell off my pacifier."

"I see."

She spent a long minute staring out the window.

"Thank you," Meriwether finally said. "It means a lot knowing that it wasn't done on purpose."

"You've helped us immensely," Arni said, rubbing his hands together.

"Have I? Six months old—you have an alter, then—Felix?" It was the first time she'd addressed me by name.

"He's a chef at the newly renovated Organic Oven and has a fiancée and two dogs. Also"—I winced—"he's writing a mystery series."

"Did you keep it, by any chance?" Professor Maximilian demanded, leaning closely into the omni viewframe. "The duck. Did you keep it?"

She sighed. "I'm embarrassed to say I did. It was such a life-changing moment."

"Mango Meriwether," the professor proclaimed, "how would you like to be more famous than Olivia May, the creator of the omni, ever will be?"

🦆

Leaving behind Arni to mop up the now-cooled tomato soup and Pak to help Professor Maximilian with his *Ask Me* campaign, Bean walked me out of the bihistory building. She seemed distracted, like it hadn't sunk in yet that a lot of people were going to read her dissertation after all.

"Bean, er—you have work to do, I know, but do you want to have a bite of lunch before I go?"

"How much time do we have?"

"I need to be at the crossing terminal by two thirty."

"Why two thirty?"

"My tourist stamp expires eight days exactly from when I crossed from A to B."

"The Beetle is parked this way."

The fog having cleared, the bright sunshine had compelled Bean to warp down the rim of her wide-brimmed straw hat as she drove. I wiped a smudge off my sunglasses and slipped them on, pondering the fact that I had elected to set my mystery novel in a cold, snowy setting, but maybe that was the whole point. You get to write about places removed from your own reality, the act of writing transporting the author, as much as the reader, elsewhere. And what about that old bit of advice, write about what you know? I had gone skiing at Lake Tahoe a few times in my life and knew a fair bit about culinary competitions, but what did I know about murders? Zip. Zero. Absolutely nothing, other than that someone had spent the last week trying to kill me.

As we left the Presidio behind us, I thought of Professor Maximilian and the stack of questions piling up on his desk. He had promised to keep my name out of the spotlight as much as possible, though I sensed that he did not want to compromise his scientific integrity by completely ignoring my role in the matter. I hoped that Meriwether Mango's life story, when heard along that of the omni inventor Olivia May Novak Irving, would carry the day and I wouldn't have to hide out in some backwater Universe Z to escape all the attention.

Before I could suggest a Baker Beach picnic or a return to Pier 39 for a bite to eat, Bean made a rolling right turn at a stop sign, taking us onto a wide lane with a row of palm trees down the center. She slowed down the Beetle and started looking at house numbers.

"Who lives here?" I asked, gaping at the elegant villas.

"Fourteen ten...fourteen twelve...Your Aunt Henrietta wants to meet you."

"Don't be silly, Bean," I said sharply. "Aunt Hen is dead."

[33]

AN AGED RELATIVE

A garden path lined with ornamental cactuses and sculpted shrubbery led to a large, well-kept villa. Posted on the front was a doorbell list with the abbreviated names (as per Regulation 3) of the occupants of six condominiums, two condos on each floor. *H. S., 1ˢᵗ floor, left.* The stained glass, impeccably clean front door was unlocked.

"She called us this morning—wanted to get in touch with you," Bean said as we stood knocking on the door of *1ˢᵗ floor, left.*

"Felix B might have thought to mention that Aunt Henrietta B existed."

"You've met him?"

"Ran into him in Carmel."

"Perhaps he assumed you knew about her. After all, one doesn't generally say, 'By the way, so-and-so is still with us.' Rather the reverse."

The condo door opened by itself, allowing us access into a narrow hallway. I followed Bean past a coatrack, an ornate mirror, a cabinet displaying sea-life-themed knickknacks, and into an equally densely furnished living room.

"Well, sit down," an old lady commanded from the sofa, putting her door remote away. Henrietta Sayers.

I sat down into the first chair I saw.

"No, over HERE, Felix, dear," Aunt Henrietta patted the cushion next to her. I moved over to the sofa, sliding my legs under a wicker table; on it waited a large leather box and a tray holding three small cups.

"And take those things off your necks, please," Aunt Henrietta added. "I don't like to be interrupted."

Bean took our two omnis into the hallway and hung them on the coatrack and I took the opportunity to glance around the room. Numerous sea-motif figurines occupied shelf space and dreamlike photographs of jellyfish covered the walls. I was reminded that Aunt Henrietta had spent a long career as a marine biologist.

Aunt Hen had been my *great*-aunt Henrietta, a relation through marriage on my father's side, my great-uncle Otto's second wife. Uncle Otto had once sent me a remote-controlled, three-speed airplane with retractable wheels as a birthday present, forever cementing the good will of a ten-year-old. He had met Aunt Hen late in life. They had gotten married in their eighties. A framed formal photograph of Uncle Otto sat among the sea-horse figurines.

This Henrietta, strictly speaking, was not related to me at all, but I could not think of her in any other way than as Aunt Henrietta. She was just as I remembered her, a small, frail, withered dynamo with more than nine decades of life experience behind her.

As Bean took the stiff armchair I had vacated, Aunt Henrietta reached up and gave me a pat on the head like I was still a ten-year-old and not someone who, even sitting, towered over her. Like my Aunt Hen had, she seemed to have gone a bit deaf over the years and occasionally shrieked a word or two in each sentence.

"So you are my other GREAT-NEPHEW, are you?"

"MORE OR LESS," I said.

"There is no need to shout, Felix, dear. And I know that we're not related on PAPER," she added with a bony-handed dismissive wave of the practicalities of linked universes, "but I've always felt we're family. And this is your GIRLFRIEND?"

"This is Bean," I said, moderating my voice. "I'm helping her with her bihistory research."

"Are you, now?"

"Pleased to meet you," Bean said.

Aunt Henrietta looked me over. "You're thinner than HE is."

"Thanks," I said.

"You should try to EAT MORE."

There was a shrill whistle, making me jump.

"Just in TIME. Child, can you bring in the hot water from the stove?"

Bean got up and went into the kitchen. She came back with a silver kettle and proceeded to pour steaming water into the three cups waiting on the wicker table.

"None for me, thanks," I said. "I've had too much tea this week."

"Nonsense, Felix, dear. It's chamomile. Aids the digestion."

Bean met my eye and passed me a teacup. Delicate white-and-yellow flowers floated in the steaming water.

"So you figured it out, DID YOU?" Aunt Hen shrieked suddenly. "I told Patrick and Klara it wasn't a good idea to change Felix's birth date, but they DIDN'T LISTEN. Patrick and Klara," she shook her head, "always had VERY progressive ideas. ARTISTS."

"You sent me—that is, Aunt Hen left me a photograph. That's how I found out."

"Left you a photo in her will, did she?"

"If you happen to have any old photographs—" Bean said.

Aunt Henrietta wrinkled her nose, deepening its natural furrows. "IF I had any photographs—I'm not saying I do—well, I never said a word to my Felix about his TRUE age, not until he came to me and told me that he'd met YOU, Felix, dear. He's embroiled in some scheme to prove he's the universe MAKER, my Felix is. The idea sounds like it has some SCIENTIFIC merit, I'd say. What did she DIE OF?"

I hesitated. Aunt Hen, to the best of my knowledge, had died of extreme old age, but I felt it would be tactless to say so.

"Er—she tripped in front of a people mover."

"Speak up, dear."

"People mover," I repeated more loudly, immediately regretting the lie.

"Good way to go. That's how I'd like to die—out and about, not lying in BED."

"So Felix's parents never gave you any baby photos of him?" Bean tried again. "A photo taken on Y-day?"

"Y-day, you say? Well, there was a POSTCARD."

"Why didn't you say so, Aunt Hen?" I said. "A postcard—"

"You didn't ASK about a postcard," she pointed out. "Here, hand me that box."

I moved the round leather box, which was heavier than it looked, from the wicker table to the middle of the sofa between us. Aunt Hen took the lid off and proceeded to finger through the jumble of old photographs, letters, and documents. After only a couple of minutes she pronounced, "There." A youthful smile crossed her face. "I was still onboard in the Mediterranean then, my last project before I retired to teaching. Letters often took more than TWO months to REACH us."

In the postcard, the Golden Gate Bridge looked much the same as it had yesterday when I'd traversed its sidewalks, except that the cars driving across were antique-looking, in silver, beige, and other subdued colors. The space on the back was filled in my mother's handwriting (or rather, Felix's mother's handwriting, since the stamp on the Universe B postcard trailed Y-day by a week.) I read the card, then passed it to Bean, who read it aloud, pausing here and there to decipher a word:

Dear Henrietta,

Hope your expedition is going well. We had a lovely day today, drove up to San Francisco for an afternoon pickup of a new acquisition, and had time for a walk on the Golden Gate Bridge first. Little Felix almost lost his duck pacifier—you know how fond he is of that thing—it bounced off the bridge railing but luckily landed on the sidewalk. I don't know what we would have done if it had gone overboard!

My love to you and Otto,

Klara

"Wait a minute," I said as the meaning of my mother's words sank in. "You knew my parents *before* the universes diverged?"

"Yes, of course. I knew your father when he was a child."

"That's impossible. Aunt Hen and Uncle Otto met and got married during my first year at San Diego. I'm sure of that. I had to go to the wedding and wear a tuxedo."

"Then why did *she* have a baby photo of you, the Aunt Henrietta of your Universe A, Felix?" said Bean.

"I have no idea."

Henrietta B gave a ladylike chortle. "She always was a bit WILD, Henrietta was. Otto and I got married at eighteen, dear Felix. We were working together in the Mediterranean when this postcard came." She tapped the postcard with a long, arched, yellowish nail. "Not long after that we found out we now had two universes and there were COPIES of everybody! Quite a scientific discovery. You won't get many people to say this, but I LIKE that we have two universes. The more, the MERRIER, I say. But things did get out of hand for a while. Klara and Patrick wanted to shield you from all that."

I took a sip of the tea, felt something grainy in my mouth, and returned one of the chamomile flowers back into the teacup.

"It was decided that the two branches of the family would not keep in touch. PITY. I've always felt you and Felix were my great-nephews equally. As for Henrietta A," Aunt Hen sniffed, "she and her Otto got a DIVORCE a couple of years after Y-day—some silly spat over money. MY Otto and I never let MONEY stand in our way. But they remarried later, you say?" She shook her head and dug something else out of the leather box. "There is no harm in letting you see the photograph now, I suppose. It came with the postcard. Klara and Patrick later asked me never to show it to anyone and I haven't, not until today."

It was a faded and yellowing version of the photo Bean and I knew as 13B.

"So my parents did drive to the city for a new gallery piece," I said, picking up the postcard again. "I assumed that there would be more to it than that. I wonder what the acquisition was. It doesn't matter in the least, but it just seems right to know, somehow."

"I can tell you the answer to that, Felix, dear. It was an oil painting—a Venus, a NUDE," said Aunt Henrietta.

I remembered it. Not from the gallery. The shapely alabaster figure had hung on my parents' living room wall and captivated the interest of a teenage boy. Later, as I was gathering my mother's watercolors and other keepsakes from the Carmel house, I'd packed the Venus into the protective boxes with the watercolors. I'd been meaning to unpack the paintings and put them on my walls for a long time.

Aunt Henrietta took a sip of her tea. "I am looking forward to the mystery DINNER, I have to say."

"I beg your pardon, Aunt Hen?" I thought she had gotten confused about who we were and why we were there.

"My Felix is hosting a mystery dinner party tonight at his Organic Oven. Last month the theme was Imperial Russia and I played the part of a duchess. This time we're a party of snowbound Alaska explorers. Sometime during the evening someone will get KILLED—I hope it's not me, it's deathly BORING being the victim—and the rest of us will get clues and try to figure out who did it and why. Dear Felix will be stopping by later to bring my instruction packet."

"Mystery dinner party? Huh." I got up. "We should be going, Bean. I don't want to overstay my tourist entry permit. Besides, er—I have work to do."

Without moving from sofa, Aunt Henrietta asked, "What are you planning on doing with your LIFE, young man?"

"I work for a kitchen company."

She didn't seem to hear me.

"I'm writing a book," I pronounced more loudly.

"Are you, now?" said Aunt Henrietta. "About WHAT?"

"It's a mystery."

"You don't SAY. It must run in the family, the taste for mysteries. Not as useful as a COOKBOOK, perhaps, but often a satisfying read. Here, HELP me up."

Bean and I took an arm each and gently helped Aunt Henrietta to her feet. Leaning on a cane, she made her way across the room to a door I hadn't noticed before.

"In here." She pushed the door open with her cane. The cramped space, probably meant as a large closet, held floor-to-ceiling glass-fronted bookcases.

"Most of it is academic materials. Marine biology textbooks and periodicals. Of no interest to you, of course. But down there—yes, that might be just the thing." She shuffled over to the far bookcase, opened the glass door, and tapped the row of books on the bottom with her cane. "THAT one, dear Felix. At the end."

I knelt down and retrieved the book she had indicated.

"It's the 1934 printing of *The Nine Tailors*. The first edition," Aunt Hen said. "My favorite of the Dorothy Sayers books. The dust jacket is ORIGINAL. The nine tailors are BELLS, not suit-makers, and Dorothy herself is NO relation, of course. The book is out of print, though YOU have access to it, no doubt, on that endless shelf that hangs around your neck. Still, I'd like you to have it, Felix, dear. I don't know how anyone can read on those little screens."

"The font size is adjustable. Or you can have it read to you," I said. "First edition? Dust jacket?"

"The very first—the original—printing of a book. Dust jacket—well, self-explanatory," Bean said from the doorway.

"It can read a book to you? In that case I might have to give it a try," Aunt Hen said. "After all, when Socrates faced the brand-new technology of the written word, he DID NOT LIKE

IT at all. It takes time to get used to things. Though if you are going to use a machine for reading it should at least be shaped like a book. Why does it open up to a CIRCLE?"

"I suppose Olivia May Novak Irving would know," I said. The Dorothy Sayers had clearly passed through many hands. The dust jacket was a faded brown, whether by the hand of time or because of poor printing quality, I couldn't tell, nothing like the glossy colors I had seen on the covers of the volumes in the Bookworm. The edges were worn and there was a grease stain on the spine. The paper looked a tad moldy.

"And what about ROMANCES?" Aunt Henrietta said. "Don't look so surprised. Did I say I ONLY liked academic periodicals and mysteries? A romance is a good POOL-side read. Are omnis WATERPROOF?"

"Not usually," Bean said.

"Thanks for the paper book, Aunt Hen," I said. "Do you collect dolphin porcelain figurines? I have half of—that is, do you want—"

"THOSE things," she guffawed. "A waste of time AND money. I collect SEA HORSES, much more sensible. Good resale value."

As we stood on the apartment doorstep on our way out, Aunt Henrietta nudged my leg with her cane and asked, "Is HER Otto still alive?"

"I—yes, he is. Last I heard he was doing a world tour of marine sanctuaries in—well, in Aunt Hen's honor."

"My Otto has been in greener pastures these twenty years. I wonder..."

Quite inexplicably, Bean bent down and gave Aunt Henrietta a quick hug and a peck on the cheek. Women do strange things sometimes.

"Thank you for everything, Aunt Henrietta," she said.

Aunt Henrietta waved us off. I could hear her yelling, "SEND ME YOUR BOOK," as Bean and I went out the front door of the villa and proceeded down the garden path.

A cactus flowering by the side of the path caught my attention.

"Hey, that looks like Pak's mother's cactus, only bigger. He said it was called a lace hedgehog, didn't he? I wonder how sharp those spikes are." I knelt down to examine the multi-limbed plant. Without warning, I saw a flash of something rush at me and connect. Slowly I straightened up and looked down at the Dorothy Sayers I was hugging to my chest, away from cactus spikes and dirt. There was a small and round hole in it. It hadn't been there a second ago.

"What is that?" Bean said. "It almost looks like a—"

She didn't finish her sentence.

In the sculpted shrubbery behind the cactus the increasingly loud sounds of a scuffle could be heard. Then someone said, "I've got her."

[34]

I HAVE AN
ARCH-NEMESIS

Mrs. Noor, accompanied by a younger, male version of herself, stepped out from behind a camel-shaped shrub and onto the path. "She's over there," the detective said, gesturing behind her and panting. She was clutching a hardcover book much bigger than the smoldering *The Nine Tailors* in my hands.

"Bean," I said, "this is Miss Mar—Mrs. Noor from the investigative agency Noor & Brood."

"And my son Ham," Mrs. Noor said.

"And her son Ham."

"And—well, this is Felix B," I said. He was standing behind Mrs. Noor and Ham.

Bean said hello.

We followed Mrs. Noor, Ham, and Felix B back through the gap between the camel shrub and a peacock-shaped one and into the heart of the garden. Pink and white roses in bloom encircled two wooden benches. One bench was empty and on the other sat Gabriella Short. Her chic summer dress clashed horribly with the laserinne lying on the ground just out of her reach. I noticed that she was holding her hands rather stiffly behind her back.

"I will not say one word without my lawyer," Gabriella informed us and looked away.

Mrs. Noor sat down heavily on the bench opposite Gabriella. "Gabriella," she said, struggling to catch her breath, "has been scheming to dispose of you, Felix."

"Are you reading something, Mrs. Noor?" I pointed to the book in her hands.

"This? It's *The Chicago Manual of Detecting.* I keep it in my car for reference and such."

Bean was looking at me. "Felix, did you hear what she said?"

"Yes. I knew someone was trying to kill me."

"Why didn't you say anything?"

"It sounded crazy. Also—well, I thought I knew who it was," I said, avoiding meeting Felix B's eye.

"I'll let Ham tell the story," said Mrs. Noor. "I had my suspicions, but he did the legwork. Go ahead, Ham, dear."

Ham pulled out a notepad identical to the one carried by his mother, though his was blue, and flipped it open. "Item one. Tuesday. Subject trails client on Route 1 from San Francisco to Carmel Beach in car driven by male companion of subject. Also present in vehicle, one almost-dog and client's alter."

I remembered that Mrs. Noor had said one of her children didn't seem to be cut out for a detective. Ham seemed very detectivish to me.

"Granola James and Gabriella Short, employees of Past & Future, drove Felix B down to Carmel," elaborated Mrs. Noor. "They were right behind you for a while. A light green convertible with its top up. Ham was right behind *them* trying to figure out what was going on."

"We showed them the contract I signed. Out of the window of Bean's Beetle," I said.

"Showed her the contract?" Mrs. Noor said. "She can't have been happy about that. I imagine she felt you escaping her grip, going out of her sight. Perhaps with slightly more detail, Ham, please," she added.

"Item two. Wednesday. Subject observed going into premises of Carmel B&B where client staying. Time: around midnight. Reason: unknown. Unable to ascertain."

I recalled the item that had almost sent me crashing down the stairs at the Be Mine Inn. Had Gabriella snuck into the B&B after everyone had retired, unscrewed a light bulb, and arranged the rolling pin where I, the only occupant of the upper floor with its one tower room, would be bound to step on it in the dark and lose my balance and take a tumble down the stairs? It was such a classic mystery story scenario that I couldn't believe someone had done it for real.

"Item three. Friday. Subject back in her own car. Black Speedster. Lost track of whereabouts in city traffic—"

"Wait," I interrupted. "That's Gabriella's car? The car as sleekly black as the inside of a nonstick pan? The car that keeps trying to run me over?"

"I'm afraid so," Mrs. Noor said. "It's a rental," she added as if that was somehow relevant.

"Later regained eyes on subject," Ham continued. "Item four. Six minutes ago. Subject attempts to laser client. Thwarted by Mother and self." He snapped his notebook shut.

Mrs. Noor smiled at Felix B. "*This* Felix contacted me not long after you did. Had a problem. Wanted to know more about his Universe A alter, had been informed by DIM that he was in town. Client confidentiality prohibited me from telling either of you that I had met the other one, but I gave you what information I could about each other. And when Felix B called me, concerned about Gabriella's behavior—he found some of her questions about you, Felix, quite *odd*—I had Ham look into it."

"She wanted to know if I thought you liked swimming alone or if you ever took walks unaccompanied late at night," my alter ego said.

"Very perceptive of you, Felix. And so I had Ham keep an eye on Gabriella," Mrs. Noor went on. "Ham followed her here, watched as she waited in her car until you went inside, and then concealed herself in the shrubbery. Highly concerned, he called me for backup. I came as fast as I could. I ran into Felix B at the garden gate."

"I'm bringing Aunt Henrietta her character kit for tonight's mystery dinner," Felix said, explaining the sizable rectangular box he was carrying.

"Unfortunately," said Mrs. Noor, "Gabriella was able to get a single blast off before I could knock the laserinne out of her hands with this." She held up *The Chicago Manual of Detecting*. "As I said, I like to keep it around for emergencies."

The *Manual* was twice the width and height of *The Nine Tailors* and looked like it could take the first edition Aunt Henrietta had given me, even before it had gotten perforated while saving my life, easily in a fair fight. Eying the still-smoldering Dorothy Sayers in my hands and reflecting that Professor Maximilian was right and that little things—like what reading material you happened to have around—mattered, I asked, "But why? Why did she do it?"

"The old story," sighed Mrs. Noor. "Revenge."

[35]

THE MOTIVE

I had almost forgotten she was there, as impossible as that seemed. Gabriella Short fixed her gray eyes on me and said only one word, then looked away.

"*You.*"

"But what did I do?" I asked quite stupidly.

"You ruined her chance of being an actress," Mrs. Noor said. "There can only be one Gabriella Love."

There can only be one Gabriella Love. A child's pacifier had bounced off a bridge railing—and landed on the right side for Felix B, who was standing silently next to Bean, and on the wrong side for me. In my Universe A, the rubber duck had detached and fallen and Gabriella Short had not needed to change her name to something more marketable. It's difficult to be famous when your alter has gotten there first. More to the point, she never stood a chance. In Universe A, movie theaters had faded away over the past two decades, replaced by other forms of entertainment. It's particularly difficult to be a movie star where there are no movies.

"Gabriella—" I opened my mouth to speak.

"You ruined my life," she spat out. "We are not on a first-name basis."

"Citizen Short, then. It was a single moment in time—"

"Can you imagine what's it's like to see your own face everywhere—on billboards, T-shirts, ads? At the crossing terminal *she* was on the cover of a Universe B fashion magazine that I wanted to buy. I could barely face the humiliation at the checkout stand. To be constantly mistaken for a celebrity, the disappointment when they realize you're not *her*—"

She seemed to be saying quite a bit for someone who wasn't going to say one word without a lawyer.

"—and it's even worse back home in Universe A, because there no one looks at me at all, like I'm invisible. I never pretend I am her when I come here, you know. Never." She spit the word out.

"*Doppelganger*," I said.

The unfamiliarity of the word took her by surprise. She caught her breath for a moment.

"German word, coined when there was only one universe and it was a bad omen to see yourself," I said. "Literally means body double, usually a sinister, ghostly apparition. If you glimpsed your doppelganger it meant something bad was about to happen."

"Not the case nowadays, of course," Felix B said tactfully.

Bean was standing next to him with her hands on her hips, glaring at Gabriella. "You could have stayed home in Universe A. You could have avoided coming here where your alter is so popular."

"But why should I have to? I *knew* you had done it," she said, not taking her eyes off me, "from the minute I saw you in the crossing chamber, looking at suitcases and idly browsing on your omni without a care in the world."

"Hey! I had plenty of my own concerns," I said sharply.

Before more could be said, DIM officials descended on the scene and took statements from everyone, then left after declaring the day's events to be government property, thereby prohibiting us from discussing said events with third parties. "She wanted me to be her understudy. Her understudy!" yelled Gabriella as they led her away. I sat down heavily next to Mrs. Noor. "I *knew* people would blame me." Bean was still looking stunned.

"It took me awhile to believe it too," said Felix, giving Bean a reassuring squeeze around the shoulders. (There were only the four of us left, Ham having gone on a mission for another client.) "It was clever of you to notice there was something going on, Felix," Bean said. "You probably saved Felix's life."

"Yes, murder," I said loudly. "She had it in for me." I proceeded to recount my other narrow escapes—the attempted hit-and-runs, the rubber rolling pin in Carmel—and also mentioned the cherry chocolates sent to the Palo Alto Health Center. "Luckily I didn't swallow any. She must have found out about my allergy somehow."

"She was foolish to attempt murder at a health center," Bean said.

"Why?" Mrs. Noor said. "It seems an excellent place to do it. People are always dying in health centers. It must have been aggravating for her that her attempts kept failing."

I thought of something. "Was she responsible for the pet bug quarantine? Did Gabriella think exposing me to the pet bug would get rid of me?"

"No one was responsible, as far as we could tell," Mrs. Noor said. "It was just one of those things that happens by chance."

For some reason I believed her.

"I'm just glad we were able to stop her in time," Mrs. Noor added, putting down the *Manual* on the bench next to her and leaning over to inhale the scent of a particularly eye-catching rose.

Or did we? I could almost hear Professor Maximilian saying, *Did we stop her in time?* "Five murder attempts," he'd have said. "There is a universe in which the first attempt succeeded and Gabriella ran Felix over shortly after his arrival in Universe B. And another in which the hit-and-run failed, but Felix succumbed to cherry chocolates in the Palo Alto Health Center. And another in which the first two attempts failed but Felix broke his neck in Carmel tripping over a rolling pin. And another in which the first three attempts failed, but Gabriella ran over Felix in her car yesterday, having tried that method again. And also one in which the first four attempts failed, but Felix died a few minutes ago because he wasn't holding *The Nine Tailors* in front of his chest or because Mrs. Noor didn't have *The Chicago Manual of Detecting* with her and was therefore unable to stop Gabriella in time. Isn't that interesting?" the professor would have said, and I would have killed *him* in all possible universes.

"Do we think," Bean said as if talking to herself, "that Gabriella got a job at Past & Future with the idea of figuring out who ruined her life, or did the idea slowly dawn on her as she researched the Felixes' life stories?"

Someone barked.

Bean shook the thought off and greeted a heavily breathing Murphina. "Hello there." She bent down to rub the creature's pale, furry head. We heard a voice say, "Murphina, where are you?" and the bushes parted to allow James to join our group.

"Hello, Felix. And Felix." He looked around. "Has anyone seen Gabriella?"

Yes, I thought. Government agents just took her away after she tried to kill me for the fifth time. It seemed socially awkward to say so, however. There was also the small matter of the edict the DIM officials had given us before they left; the events of the past twenty minutes—Gabriella's final attempt to get rid of me because I was the universe maker—were not to be divulged to third parties.

"Gabriella tried to kill Felix," Bean said to James. Murphina had rolled over on the white pebbles bordering the rose beds and was letting Mrs. Noor rub her belly. "Felix A, that is, not Felix B."

"No, that can't be right," James said. "Gabriella called me and asked me to get here as fast as I could to assist her in an interview." He slicked his black hair back with one hand and kept looking around as if expecting Gabriella to jump out from behind a rose bush or a giant-squirrel-shaped shrub at any moment.

"To interview someone?" Felix B said. "My Aunt Hen, you mean?"

"Ah," Mrs. Noor said. "That must have been her alibi. Gabriella needed a legitimate reason for being here. No one would have suspected her."

James heard all the facts, wordlessly attached a leash to Murphina, and started to pull her through the shrubbery toward Aunt Henrietta's apartment.

"James, wait," Bean said.

She took him aside and I heard her begin to whisper about Professor Maximilian's omni campaign and James's exclamation of surprise; then his frown disappeared and even from afar I could see the wheels beginning to turn as he nodded in under-standing, probably already brainstorming about possible ways of turning the newest developments into a monetary advantage for Past & Future.

"It's only fair that he knows," Bean said defensively when she came back.

Felix B had been leafing through the *Chicago Manual*. He closed it abruptly and raised a high eyebrow at me. "I'm happy everything turned out all right, but did I hear Aunt Hen call out something about a book as I opened the garden gate? I thought you said you weren't writing one, Felix."

"It was the truth when I said it."

"And now?"

"And now," I blurted out, "I've started a novel about a murder that takes place in the Sierras just as a cooking competition is about to get underway. The detective's name is R. Smith." I winced. "Don't tell me if you're writing the same thing. No, tell me, I want to know."

Felix B said nothing for a moment, then a slow smile spread across his face. "Mine is a cookbook."

"Is it? *It is?*"

"I'm calling it *Cooking Up a Fiendishly Good Mystery Dinner Party*. Lots of recipes, of course—like for the Baked Alaska that we're having at tonight's Alaska mystery dinner—and Bleeding Beets—beets are a must at a mystery-themed dinner party, that ominous dark red—Killer Cocktail—Butcher's Beef—Devil's Dish—Chocolate Guillotine—" He counted off the recipes on his fingers. "And there'll also be suggested plots, characters, costumes, historical settings, tricks of the trade, that sort of thing." He gave a sheepish grin. "It's more work than I expected. The recipes have to be simplified—seven ingredients maximum is what the publishers want, because more than seven and people get discouraged and won't buy the cookbook. Not too many exotic spices either, as if turmeric is exotic..." He shrugged. "Being a chef pays reasonably well and I do like doing it—but

I want more, a book of my own, maybe make enough money to open my own restaurant. I am thinking of calling it Bistro Mystery and having weekly mystery dinners, not the once-a-month that the owners of the Organic Oven consent to."

I stared at the man. I had been wrong about him on all accounts. Like dough braided into challah bread or one of Wagner's giant pretzels, our shared interests—mysteries and food—had intertwined, but in a different way in his life than in mine. The user guides I put together at Wagner's Kitchen included recipes and anecdotes from the history of cooking, but the former were provided by our Creative Cooking department, not by me. I had never been tempted to incorporate my own food preferences, much less recipe ideas. My whole body felt lighter and I almost did a little jig. "Did you get an advance for it, your cookbook?" I asked.

"Not for someone like me, an unknown. And I have to find someone to stage the food and take photographs."

"I can hook you up with some people," I heard myself saying. "Wagner's Kitchen, where I work, needs that type of stuff done all the time."

🦆

Felix B having gone up into the villa to take the Alaska mystery dinner kit to Aunt Henrietta, the garden gate closed behind Mrs. Noor, Bean, and me. "Mrs. Noor, how did you know I was the universe maker and that that's why Gabriella kept trying to kill me?"

"Everyone was swarming around you and Felix B like flies, if you'll excuse my inelegant comparison," Mrs. Noor said, making Bean wince at the unflattering description of her research group. "Also there was the fact that Gabriella reminded me of a past client. A young man, adopted as a child, came into my agency wanting to find his biological parents. He was certain they could help him realize his financial dream of opening a casino, something his adoptive parents could not. We found his biological parents, but they couldn't help him either and so he ended up becoming bitter and committing a crime to get the money. A sad story. He forgot, you see, that he was in charge of his own life. As did Gabriella Short."

"Are you familiar with the works of Agatha Christie, Mrs. Noor? I believe you'll find that you and Miss Marple have a lot in common." I added as we walked the detective to her car, "I suppose it *was* my fault, movie theaters disappearing. Universe A was set on its path by me."

"Nonsense," said Mrs. Noor. She raised a stern hand and a passing car stopped to allow us to cross the street. "If you are going to argue that, then it follows you're responsible for *everything* in Universe A. The pristine national parks. The clean air. And I've heard the public transit system is quite nice. Plenty of good things in A—"

"Microwave ovens," I contributed. "Coffee."

"There you go," Mrs. Noor said, twisting herself into her two-seater and depositing *The Chicago Manual of Detecting* onto the passenger seat. "I don't think we're prepared to give you credit for any of those, are we? So you don't get the blame for the bad or the inconvenient things either."

"Mrs. Noor, thank you for everything," I said, realizing that I had neglected to thank Felix B for saving my life.

"As I said, I'm only sorry she was able to get off a shot."

"I can't help but wonder what would have happened had I *not* spotted your detective agency across the street from the bus depot or if there had been a tour bus leaving immediately. And what if Aunt Hen's gardener had planted clover instead of cacti—or if Gabriella had been a better shot—or if Dorothy Sayers had written a thinner book than the 331 pages that make up *The Nine Tailors*—"

"Never mind all that. Thinking like that only leads to a state of inaction."

"The loop," said Bean. "What does your alter do, Detective Noor? You seem like a good person to have on our side."

"She started out as a detective and ended up as a DIM agent. What can you do. I'll send you a bill, Felix," she added and roared away.

[36]

THE CROSSING
TERMINAL

"**S**o you've started it, then," Bean said, unwrapping a burrito from its tinfoil package. She had driven to the crossing terminal so speedily that we had time for a quick stop at the Crossing Cantina.

"I've written Chapter One." I felt strangely calm and confident saying it. I hoped the confidence would linger a day or two. "I'm going to try to write the whole thing in words only," I said, unwrapping a burrito myself.

"Can I read Chapter One?"

"It's not done. I mean, it's done, but it's not ready for reading, not yet."

"You'd think you'd have gone off mysteries after being—"

"—the victim of repeated murder attempts by a vengeful would-be actress who considers me responsible for her life *not* taking the path it otherwise might have?"

"Well, yes."

"Luckily I started writing before I found out I was being stalked by a vengeful would-be actress, et cetera. The whole business with Gabriella simply doesn't seem real. I think I prefer to treat it as if it never happened. Unhealthy, perhaps, but so what?" I popped a corn chip into my mouth and started crunching away. "Besides, in a proper mystery there's *always* a murder. Attempts—even five of them—do not count."

"I'm glad Gabriella's murder attempts were unsuccessful."

"Me too. Quite relieved actually."

"When a close call like that happens and everything turns out all right, I end up feeling bad anyway and thinking of the Beans in all the other universes where the outcomes weren't so good. Can you pass me a napkin?"

"You feel bad for *you* in the universes where Gabriella succeeded?"

"You know what I mean." She hesitated, napkin in hand. "Er—Felix, I've been meaning to apologize for saying you were responsible for paper books being gone from Universe A. It was the link that allowed the omni to be imported from Universe B, so it's Professor Singh's responsibility as much as anybody's. Like Arni said, had events been allowed to run their course, the omni wouldn't have been invented in Universe A, or at least not for who knows how long."

"I'll forget all about it if you come up with a good pseudonym for me. I'm going to need one. To avoid any potential confusion with Felix's cookbook, should it hit bi-universe status and become a runaway bestseller that everyone buys for their partner on Valentine's Day." Also, my recent experience had caused me to become acutely aware of the advantages of anonymity.

"Like Mark Twain?"

"Or Mary Westmacott," I offered.

"Who's she?"

"Agatha Christie writing romance novels."

"Mark Twain chose a pen name from his steamboat days—a call of river depth on the Mississippi—so maybe you can find a phrase from the culinary world."

"Red Saffron? Serrano Pepper?" I caught sight of the saltshaker sitting next to the bowl of guacamole. "Sal Del Mar?"

"All of those sound like you're the child of Passivist parents who picked the name by sticking a pin into a list. I can see that the issue will require some thought." She was watching a group of Passivists shuffle by us on their steady trek through the terminal. I wondered how soon Professor Maximilian's network of questions and answers would reach people going about their lives, and how long it would take to prove that Passivists weren't, in fact, nuts but correct in their basic idea. Something occurred to me. "I'm thankful that I got to see Aunt Henrietta again—come back from the dead, so to speak. And if she dies here anytime soon, there's always the possibility that I could visit her in some third universe, isn't there?"

"Visit your favorite relatives in universes where they haven't died yet, that sort of thing? It might catch on. There might even be a universe in which people have figured out how to live forever."

I offered her more of the guacamole, then scooped up the last bit with a chip. "This whole alphabet soup business, lives A to Z in universes A to Z—does it matter what we do, if our most carefully thought-out actions are on par with the rolling rock and all outcomes occur *somewhere* anyway?"

"Wouldn't you rather live in a world where you did the right thing," she said, efficiently crumpling up her burrito wrapper, "than in one where you were a jerk and didn't stop for pedestrians?"

Even a bicycle rider like me knew what she meant. I took quick stock of my trip to Universe B. I was leaving with a jar and a measly couple of pages of a novel in my backpack, owing my life to my alter, lacking a wheeled suitcase, and Bean—well, Bean did not like crossings.

"Listen," I began, "I might have misled everyone when I said I don't have anything from my parents. There are a couple of boxes at the bottom of my hallway closet, one box with paintings and another that their lawyer gave to me after their deaths. Letters, photos, stuff like that. I've been meaning to look through it ever since I found out about my real age. I don't know if there's anything of interest there or if you even need anything more now that you have Olivia May's and Meriwether's story, but I thought you should know."

She looked down as if wondering whether she should throw her plate in my face, but ended up only thoughtfully rubbing a guacamole smudge off her finger. "Better not risk shipping the box. One of us can cross to Universe A to go through it. Seeing if there's anything of research value there will take a few days, I suspect."

My omni beeped. Wagner. Inquiring about the sourdough starter, no doubt. I got to my feet and picked up the backpack, careful not to disturb the glass jar inside. "I better go. My crossing stamp is expiring any minute. Don't want DIM officials taking any more notice of me than they already have. Er, Bean— one more thing," I added.

"What?"

"For heaven's sake, don't send Arni or Pak for the box. One talks too much—"

"—and the other too little, yeah."

🦆

The three books that I'd briefly had in my possession were on my mind as I waited to be turned into a number again.

Stones, Tombs, and Gourds, the prehistoric-art book whose pages had harbored a bookmark from a more recent past, was now in the hands of DIM officials. The Christie mystery *Why Didn't They Ask Evans?*, with its concealed eavesdropping device, I had destroyed via a smooshed-up fruit drink. The first edition of *The Nine Tailors,* irreplaceable as it was, was beyond repair.

Revenge, that was Gabriella's motive. I'd found a different one for the story I'd begun on bee-shaped hotel stationary. The woman with the ice-white hair found lifeless by R. Smith after the mountain storm was, I'd decided, an artist. She had been hired by R. Smith to make decorative food sculptures for the upcoming cooking competition. The artist—Griselda? Selene? Nadia?—has an alter, also a sculptor but a shade less talented. And it's the alter who decides to kill, not to take Griselda's place—too obvious and overdone as a motive—but because she knew her chances for fame would be greatly improved by having an alter who was the victim of a violent and notorious crime.

Pushing aside the thought that perhaps Felix had gotten it right and I was meant to write a cookbook but had messed everything up by getting a sinus infection years ago, I imagined the final scene of the novel…in the lodge library, a cozy room stocked with comfortable armchairs, with snow gently falling outside and a fire crackling in the fireplace as R. Smith reveals that one Griselda killed the other Griselda to an audience of gathered suspects, after which the remaining Griselda tries to bean him with the fireplace poker and is taken away.

A thought struck me. I had given my victim/murderess Griselda ice-white hair, almost like I'd subconsciously realized all along that the similarly named Gabriella, with her flowing ice-white hair, was somehow involved in the repeated attempts to get rid of me.

Now there was only one question left, I told myself as the crossing chamber door slid shut and the lid started to glide into place across the skylight. Was the idea good enough—for me to quit my job at Wagner's Kitchen and apply myself to writing full-time, that is? There was no way of telling without sitting down and finishing the damn thing, but the best way to go about doing that *was* to quit. I suddenly felt like a Passivist, trapped in a loop, unable to act.

One decision after another, that's what life was.

Soup or salad. Elevator or stairs. Shower or bath.

Give Bean a call as soon as I got back, or wait a few days.

You never knew *what* might set off a significant chain of events.

THE END

AUTHOR'S NOTE

The Golden Gate Bridge in our own universe is a 1.7-mile (15 stadia long) suspension bridge, not the combination suspension/drawbridge reminiscent of London's Tower Bridge that it is in Universe B. San Francisco summers are foggy and on the cool side here as well, making for a brisk walk or bike ride across.

The California Gold Rush took place in 1849.

Macar trees do not grow here.

Caesar salads are made with cow's milk Parmesan.

And there is no Ferris wheel at Baker Beach.

ACKNOWLEDGMENTS

Thanks go out to Alex Carr, my editor at AmazonEncore, for being intrigued by the title and pulling out a manuscript languishing on last year's contest shelf and liking it; to Jill Marsal, for graciously agreeing to represent me; to Sarah Burningham and Sarah Tomashek, for helping get the word out; to the art and editing team at CreateSpace for turning a manuscript into a book; to Mary Alterman and Jo Cravens for many writers' group meetings, even when the snow was knee-deep; to the teachers at Woodpark Montessori for imparting many bits of preschool wisdom to my son Dennis as I wrote and edited and wrote and edited; to my friends and family for all their encouragement, even when they didn't quite understand why it was taking so long; to the light of my life, Dennis, for keeping me grounded and for introducing me to many imagined worlds of his own; and, most of all, to my husband, John, for coming along for the ride and for being steadfastly certain it would all work out in the end.

ABOUT THE AUTHOR

Photograph by John Baron, 2010

Neve Maslakovic spent her early years speaking Serbian in Belgrade, in former communist Yugoslavia. After stops along the way in London, New York, and California, she has settled in Minneapolis-St. Paul, where she lives with her husband and son. She earned her PhD in electrical engineering at Stanford University's STARLab (Space, Telecommunications, and Radioscience Laboratory) and is a member of the Loft Literary Center. *Regarding Ducks and Universes* is her first novel, and she is hard at work on her second. Visit her at www.nevemaslakovic.com.